To Claire

I hope you enjoy!

JM

J N Lowther

DARKER MATTER –
BOOK 1
DAKOR'S DARKNESS

Limited Special Edition. No. 15 of 25 Paperbacks

In his debut novel, the first in the *Darker Matter* trilogy, J N Lowther draws upon his extensive martial arts experience for the fight scenes.

Jim is a Financial Planner and lives with his wife in the leafy county of Cornwall in the UK.

For those who dream.

J N Lowther

DARKER MATTER –
BOOK 1
DAKOR'S DARKNESS

AUSTIN MACAULEY PUBLISHERS™
LONDON • CAMBRIDGE • NEW YORK • SHARJAH

A CIP catalogue record for this title is available from the British Library.

This is a work of fiction. Names, characters, businesses, places, events, locales and incidents are either the products of the author's imagination or used in a fictitious manner. Any resemblance to actual persons, living or dead, or actual events is purely coincidental.

ISBN 9781528902410 (Paperback)
ISBN 9781528902427 (Hardback)
ISBN 9781528957250 (ePub e-book)

www.austinmacauley.com

First Published (2019)
Austin Macauley Publishers Ltd
25 Canada Square
Canary Wharf
London
E14 5LQ

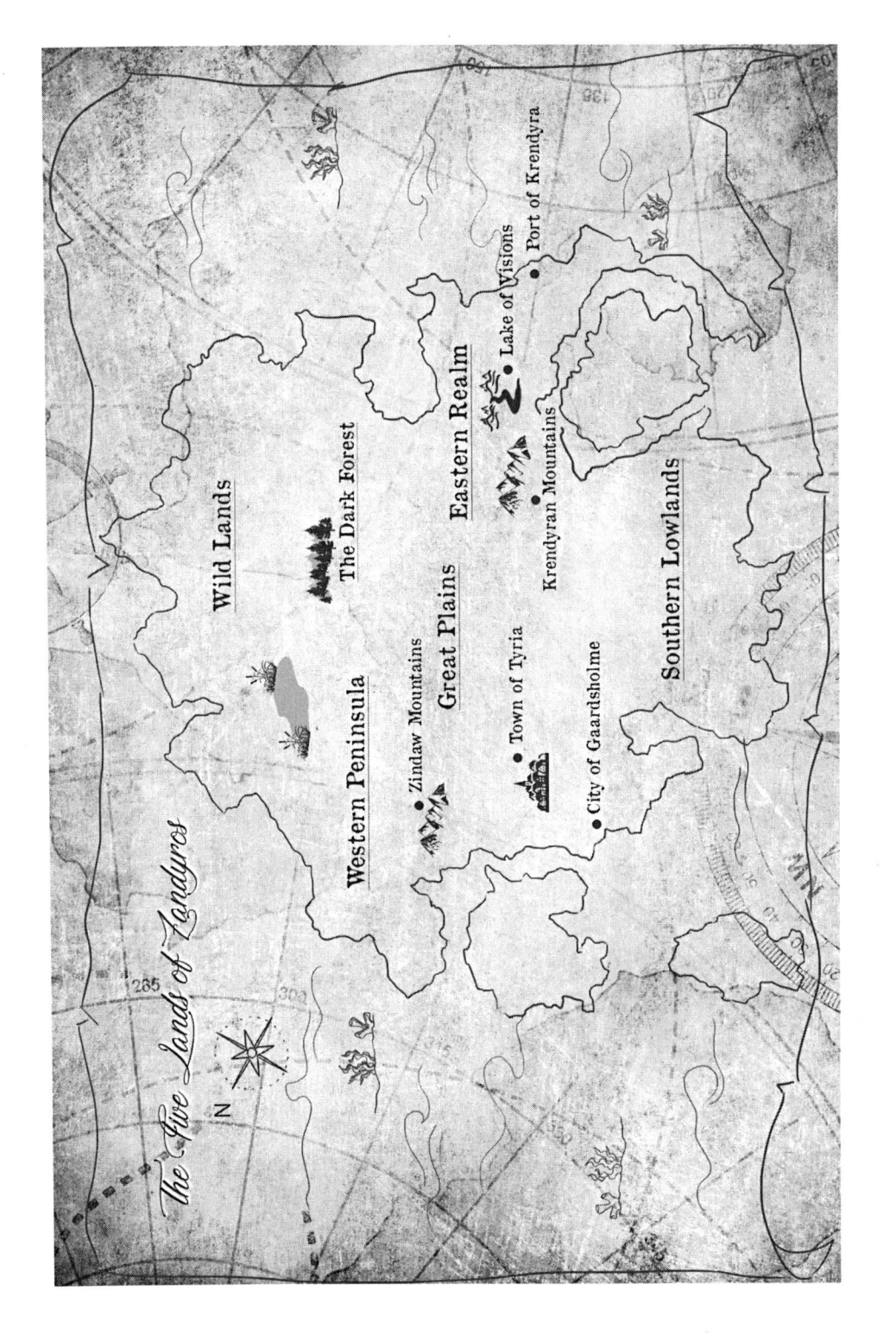

Part I
Awakening

Chapter 1
The Chemist

Bradley White pulled off the motorway and followed the signs to Greenhaven. He was hungry and had plenty of time before his next appointment which was less than ten miles away and besides, he had never been here before. It was a short but very pleasant drive through a winding country road before he entered the sleepy village of Greenhaven.

Bradley White worked for a large pharmaceutical company as a drugs representative, spending his working day on the road selling to retailers and through doctors and other prescribing health professionals. He had been doing the job for the last ten years and was making a reasonable living from it, earning significantly more than the national average wage. But that was the problem. The company he worked for had been taken over a year ago by a much larger American drugs company and they didn't do *reasonable*. They expected outstanding results from their reps and Brad was struggling to keep up with his ever-increasing sales targets. He used to enjoy his job and actually looked forward to going on the road at the start of each week, but now he was dreading the sound of his alarm clock every morning. At forty-five years of age, Brad felt trapped. He had drifted from one job to another after leaving school and this was the first job that he had ever really felt was right for him. The only jobs that he had ever had were in sales. He wasn't a particularly good salesman but took the jobs because these were all that were offered to him.

Brad drove around Greenhaven in the vain hope of finding a fast food outlet, or even a café, but without any luck. In fact, there was not much of anything in Greenhaven, except for a small corner shop. With a bottle of cheap warm cola and a lukewarm pasty in his hand, Brad headed back to his car. It was then that he saw a small chemist shop that he hadn't noticed earlier.

As a drug company representative, *he hated the abbreviation of rep*, he knew all the chemists on his patch, but this one was new to him. He got out of his car and crossed the street to the shop. From the outside it looked antiquated, with its oversized bottles of brightly coloured water in the window which were commonly used fifty or more years ago to identify such places. He opened the door and a bell clanged as the door shut firmly behind him.

How quaint, he thought.

There were no customers in the shop and it looked even older on the inside. As he had always been fascinated with pills and potions, Brad scanned the shelves while he awaited the arrival of a shop assistant. He had heard stories of old shops that had been boarded up and forgotten about for years, and this place looked like it had been stuck in a time warp. There were pills and potions for all manner of ills, all of which were contained in very old-style packaging. It was more like a museum than a shop, odd and yet fascinating at the same time. Brad was still picking up bottles and packets when the

Chemist, standing behind him, cleared his throat. The sound startled Brad who hadn't heard his approach.

The Chemist was of indeterminate age. At first sight, his unkempt grey hair and stoop gave the impression of great age. But there was something about him that told another story, one that Brad couldn't quite figure out. For a moment, Brad was transfixed by the man and felt like the Chemist could see right into his very being. There was something about his eyes. Brad had never seen eyes quite like these, the edges of his irises looked like they were tinged with a thin zig-zagged, orangey-red corona. Brad felt uneasy, something about the man and the shop was very wrong and he wanted to leave but then the Chemist spoke.

"How precisely can I help you, young man?" the Chemist asked in a heavily accented tongue that Brad couldn't place.

"I don't really know if you can help me."

"I wouldn't be so sure of that," came the swift reply. "Tell me what ails you, young man?"

Brad hesitated for a moment then said, "I've not been feeling good for some months now. I get tired quickly and find it difficult to get motivated. My marriage is suffering because I just don't want to do anything when I get home and my libido has all but vanished. My GP says I'm depressed and has prescribed anti-depressants, but I haven't taken any yet. I'm a pharmaceutical sales representative and know only too well about their side-effects." Brad, who was normally reserved, couldn't believe that he had just blurted all this out, without even pausing for breath.

The Chemist looked at him appraisingly. "Yours is a common enough malady in this day and age. You feel that you were put here for a purpose, but you don't know what that purpose is. You work hard and strive for success, but achieve little. You know that things should be better than this, easier for you, you deserve better, but you know that will never happen. You feel that the answer to all your problems is close, but you just can't reach it. Does this sound like you, young man?"

Brad was stunned by the old man's response. In just a few short statements, he had summed up Brad's entire life. Some of these things Brad had consciously thought about, others he hadn't, but everything the Chemist said made perfect sense to him. It felt like an epiphany. In this instant, the old man knew Brad better than anyone else did, better perhaps than he did himself.

"Y…yes that pretty well sums up my life right now," was Brad's hesitant reply. "Which is why I feel so shit," he added.

"Tell me young man, do you really want to get better? Or are you just another one of those mealy–mouthed, gutless whiners who prefers to stay the way they are so that they can continue to moan about their lot?" The zig-zagged, orangey-red corona around the Chemist's irises pulsated menacingly.

Brad knew that he should turn around and leave this strange place right now. The Chemist was arrogant and rude and something about all of this was very, very wrong. But he couldn't leave. He felt disconnected and detached, as though he was not really there at all and was watching events on a cinema screen. The words of the Chemist cut through Brad's defences with the precision of a surgeon's knife. He wanted to leave but was rooted to the spot, transfixed by the presence of the man who stood before him and the power in his words. If he had had any control over his body, he would have felt fear, but even that was denied him. He literally couldn't move.

"I want to get better." The words were Brad's, but he was unaware that he had spoken them aloud.

"Well chosen, young man," came the response. "Come with me."

The Chemist led Brad to a small treatment room to the left of an archaic looking till and sat him down inside.

"This is a new treatment, but I need to check a few things first," said the Chemist as he took Brad's pulse followed by his blood pressure. "Okay, you seem fit enough for the treatment."

The Chemist opened a drawer under the desk and pulled out an old looking wooden box that was plain looking apart from some strange symbols that marked the top and sides of it. The symbols looked ancient and almost hieroglyphic in nature. Whatever their meaning it was indecipherable to Brad.

"The treatment consists of a short course of tablets that must be taken before you go to bed each night. You will also need to wear these bands."

The Chemist produced two bands that were impossibly black and appeared to absorb all light that ventured close to them. They were so black that they were difficult to see clearly, their edges indistinct and blurred. Brad had never seen such a substance before and he sat there mesmerised. Without warning, the Chemist leaned across the table with incredible speed and grabbed his wrists. Brad recoiled from the other's touch which was icy cold and tried to escape his grasp, but it was like a steel vice and he was held fast. The Chemist released his grip for the briefest of moments, not long enough for Brad to escape and snapped the black bands around his wrists.

Brad felt nothing where the bands touched his skin. Where once they were impossibly black, now the bands glowed an intense crimson colour. Without warning, the glow intensified and then exploded into a massive conflagration that burned with the intensity of a supernova for the briefest of moments before it vanished. Phosphenes clouded Brad's vision. And yet, as bizarre as it seemed, he felt no pain. Brad looked at his wrists as the Chemist released his grip. There were no burns or markings of any kind, neither was there any evidence of the bands. They had completely disappeared.

"Don't be concerned about the bands young man, they are made from a new material that attaches itself and becomes one with the host. You cannot see them, but I can assure you that they are there. The light you saw was the bands activating," said the Chemist.

"What do they do?" Brad said in shock from what had just happened.

"They will change your life. I promise you that," came the reply. "But don't be concerned, you won't experience any ill effects, and the bands can be removed at a later date if you are not completely satisfied. But that won't happen."

Brad knew that all of this was wrong, that he should demand that the bands be removed immediately, that this technology couldn't possibly exist, but for some reason, he didn't argue with the Chemist. "What happens now?"

"The course of tablets is for three days but you won't notice much for a couple of weeks. Then the changes will happen quickly. Here take the tablets," said the Chemist.

The packaging was odd in that there were no markings or instructions.

"How much do I owe you for this?" asked Brad.

"This is a new treatment and the manufacturer is offering it free of charge to the first users. All that I ask is that you do not discuss this with anyone. I will contact you again soon," the Chemist said as he walked Brad to the door. Brad couldn't wait to get outside. The shock that he had felt earlier was threatening to turn into panic. As Brad turned the door handle with a shaking hand, the Chemist grabbed his shoulder and squeezed sending a shockwave like electricity through his entire body. Brad's fear disappeared in an instant and a strange numbness took its place.

"Until we meet again," the Chemist said as he ushered Brad out of the door. "Don't forget to take the tablets, remember they are good for you."

The numbness he had felt moments earlier intensified, clouding his thoughts as he walked the short distance to his car. By the time he got there, he had forgotten about the strange old-fashioned shop, the Chemist and the impossibly black metal bands that had been absorbed into his body. He put his hand into his jacket pocket to get his car key and felt the package that contained the tablets.

I mustn't forget to start taking these tablets when I get home. The voice in his mind was his own but the words were not. *They will do me good.*

Bradley White started his car and drove off.

Chapter 2
Zoryn Dakor

Zoryn Dakor sat in an old disused storeroom high up in the West Wing of the Royal Keep and looked at the two metallic strips on the table before him. They were each a little less than a centimetre or so wide and no more than three millimetres in thickness. They were just long enough to wrap around each of his heavily muscled wrists. The substance was impossibly black and absorbed light so completely and so utterly, that it couldn't escape the Black Metal's invisible grasp. The substance appeared to be at once both real and insubstantial, a paradox, a contradiction, a meeting of what was and what could never be. It was unlike anything that Zoryn had seen before and he was impatient to put its fabled magic to the test. He had waited a very long time for this moment.

Some months earlier, Draxan Longseer had offered Zoryn an amulet that he said would give him magical powers unequalled in any of the Five Lands. He said that it was made from Black Metal. In exchange, he demanded Zoryn's word that he would make him the leader of the Eastern Realm and destroy any that stood in his way when he came into his power. The lands of the Eastern Realm would be set free from all ties with the Five Lands, other than any trade and commerce treaties that they decided to keep. It was an easy promise for Zoryn to make. If he gained control of the Five Lands, agreeing to Draxan's terms was a small price to pay. It would, of course, make Draxan very rich in the process, but also an ally, an ally that Zoryn could manipulate and control. The Eastern Realm was renowned for its spices and fine textiles and of course the prowess of its Fighting Mages who were the finest magical fighters in any of the Five Lands. A strong and grateful ally was exactly what Zoryn needed.

Draxan said that the amulet had once belonged to Jal Chindo, the legendary ruler who, centuries earlier through conquest, brought about the beginning of what later became known as the Five Lands. The amulet, Draxan declared, had been fashioned from Black Metal which many believed to be a myth. But even if the legend was true, it had been lost in antiquity and no mention had been made of it in any of the histories since the reign of Jal Chindo. Zoryn was not convinced that this part of Draxan's story was true, but if the amulet was indeed made of Black Metal and if the substance was only half as powerful as legend had it to be, then its might was incalculable.

Zoryn was naturally distrustful of everyone and doubly so of Draxan's offer to give him the most powerful magic that had possibly ever existed. Everything and more, which Draxan wanted he could achieve himself with the Black Metal, so why give it to him? Draxan's argument centred around Zoryn's legitimacy to the throne as he believed that Zoryn would face much less opposition than he would if he simply usurped the position. There wasn't a power that could stand against the might of Black Metal in open warfare, but a conquered people would find other, less obvious, ways to deal with their vanquisher. Whether by accident or design, Draxan's words sowed the seed in Zoryn's mind of how he could seize power from his brother, Sanjin Dakor, King of the Five Lands. Zoryn accepted Draxan's offer.

Before Zoryn had had his vision, shortly after meeting Draxan Longseer, he didn't believe that there was such a thing as Black Metal even though he had heard countless stories about its power. He dismissed those that set out to find it as fools. But now it consumed his every waking thought and it had become his obsession. Legend had it that Black Metal was immeasurably more powerful than White Metal. It worked in a totally different way and he knew that if he could gain mastery over its powerful magic, nothing could stand in his way. With the might of Black Metal, he would defeat his brother and claim the throne. He was born to lead and it was just an accident of birth that had made his older brother the King of the Five Lands instead of him. Zoryn could sense his destiny drawing closer. What once had just been a dream, now was within his reach.

The amulet consisted of a large heavy-linked, but well-crafted chain, made from the finest quality gold that Zoryn had ever seen. The centre setting was a filigree of fine golden threads, intricately interwoven and holding in place what appeared to be a large black gemstone. The stone was blacker than Zoryn would have believed was possible and its unreflective surface gave it an otherworldly quality. On closer inspection, Zoryn could tell that it wasn't a gem at all. It was made of some kind of metallic substance, but it was unlike anything that he had seen before. It was oddly warm to his touch and he had the strangest feeling that there was intelligence in its unfathomable and unreflective depths.

The substance was so black and so difficult to focus on, that it was only after he had the amulet in his possession for several days, that Zoryn could see the damage that Draxan had told him about. A large sliver of the substance was missing. Its light absorbing qualities prevented him from clearly making out the extent of the imperfection, but he could feel rough edges where a piece had been taken away. Draxan told Zoryn that he had kept some of the substance back to fashion a weapon that would take him some time to make. Zoryn had plans for the weapon and it was agreed that Draxan would let him have it.

The Black Metal could be cut and hammered into shape, but it was impossible to break or damage in other ways. It could be moulded when hot but even the heaviest hammer couldn't mark it when it was cold. Zoryn suspected that the missing sliver would yield more than enough Black Metal to make the weapon, and he suspected that Draxan was withholding some for himself.

Zoryn used a dozen or more smiths to remove the Black Metal from the amulet and to fashion it into the bands that now lay on the table before him. It had taken most of the substance to do this. The smiths were never left alone with the material and were paid handsomely and threatened, in equal measure, to ensure that all knowledge of its existence was kept secret. Every scrap of Black Metal was weighed each day and even the tiniest piece had to be accounted for. The smiths didn't know what they were dealing with as Zoryn ensured that only those without innate magical ability were selected. The wiser amongst them didn't ask any questions; the few that did paid a very high price for their curiosity and were not seen or heard of again.

Zoryn had a high amount of innate empathic magic. Whilst others with empathic magic used their skills to help treat sick and injured people, Zoryn used his abilities against others, either by anticipating their responses in combat situations, or by manipulating them to do his bidding. Empathic magical ability also made the individual sensitive to other magic and Zoryn could sense the powerful magic radiating in waves from the bands in front of him. Its magic was keen to his senses. He could feel it and was hungry to wield the power that the bands contained.

Zoryn placed the strips around each of his wrists, not knowing what to expect. The Black Metal felt warm and alive and receptive to his touch. As soon as the ends of each band touched, they instantly fused together so completely that it was impossible to detect the join. It looked as if the bands had always been complete. Zoryn felt a wave of exhilaration sweep through his body. He knew from the moment that he had first seen the Black Metal that it contained power, but he had had some doubts about whether it was as powerful as legend claimed it to be. But now, he was convinced.

The warmth that he initially felt when the bands touched his skin, started to increase, getting warmer and warmer and then hotter and hotter. A dull crimson glow appeared at the edges of the bands becoming brighter and brighter and instinctively Zoryn knew that the Black Metal was accessing his own magic. As First Warlord, he was a highly trained general and able to think clearly in even the most trying circumstances and it was his military training that helped him to stay calm as the heat generated by the bands and the incandescent crimson fire, threatened to engulf him utterly. Then, just at the point when he was convinced he would not survive, the heat and all the pain that went with it, disappeared in an instant. The crimson fire faded to a dull glow and as Zoryn looked at his wrists, he saw that the Black Metal of the bands was also fading. Within a few short moments, the bands had disappeared completely. Zoryn rubbed his wrists in disbelief. The Black Metal had gone, not a trace of it could be seen. *But how could that be?* It was then that he noticed that the powerful magic he had sensed from the bands earlier had not disappeared; it was still keen to his senses. The magic was no longer outside of his body, it was within him and he could sense that it was starting to change him already.

Chapter 3
Dakor's Darkness

The moment the Black Metal bands touched his skin, he was changed forever. Its magic was both new and yet strangely familiar, like meeting someone for the first time who you instantly felt you had known forever. And so, it was with Zoryn Dakor and the Black Metal. Although there was no visible sign remaining, the bands had become a part of him. Zoryn could sense its presence inside his body, but it wasn't in his wrists where he felt it; it was everywhere. His senses were heightened beyond anything he could imagine, and his every sensation was more intense, more vivid, than he had experienced before. He could feel the strength of his body, his own innate magic and knew that it had been amplified far beyond any level that should be possible. With his new-found strength came a feeling of euphoria and in that moment, he believed himself to be invincible.

The one thing that scholars of magic agreed upon was that if Black Metal existed at all, it was a paradox. There had been much debate over the centuries since Jal Chindo, and the debate still raged on. But whatever the scholars' position, they all felt the same way about the nature of the so-called Black Metal and that was that it shouldn't exist. Some went even further, arguing that it couldn't exist in this world and it must have come from someplace else, another world even. Very little was known about it and even less about its discovery. All that was known had been gleaned from stories and songs that had been retold over the generations.

It is said that Jal Chindo discovered Black Metal but never revealed how, or where, he had found it. He was a secretive and fearsome warlord who cared little for academics and scribes. A man that couldn't bear arms and fight struggled to find a place in his court. He distrusted everyone and forbade, the few scribes he agreed to keep, from recording any mention of Black Metal in the court histories. What little had been recorded stopped abruptly when Jal Chindo died in the last of the Great Battles. And so it was, that centuries later, Black Metal remained a mystery.

Zoryn had chosen a little known abandoned storeroom high up in the West Tower of the Royal Keep to begin his experimentation with Black Metal. It was a part of the keep that was never used and was barely visited by anyone, but even so, he took extra care making certain that no one had followed him. Only Draxan Longseer knew that he had the substance in his possession and as far as Zoryn was concerned, that was one person too many.

***

Black Metal wasn't banned in the Five Lands because most thought it probably didn't exist. However, any newly found magic had to be reported to the state immediately. The penalty for non-disclosure was severe and in extreme cases could result in the death sentence. Zoryn Dakor cared nothing for the rules and laws of the kingdom, seeing them as an extension of his brother's dominance over him. His reason for keeping the Black Metal a secret far outweighed the risk of getting caught with an unlicensed magic. This was what he had been waiting for all his life; an advantage that only he possessed and that no one could stand up against.

Zoryn had also kept it secret from Kaiya, his lover and the one person that was the closest thing to a friend that Zoryn would permit in his life. He had no time or need for the companionship of others and never fully let his guard down, even with her. She was, after all, his accursed brother's wife, the King's wife, and the risk of Sanjin finding out that he had Black Metal was too big a risk. So, he kept it a secret.

As much as it was possible for Zoryn to trust anyone, he trusted Kaiya, but not with knowledge of Black Metal. He was certain that if Sanjin discovered its existence he would seize it and lock it away beyond the reach of anyone. That was one of the things that he despised about his brother the most: his refusal to take risks and use his military strength to expand the domain of the Five Lands. He was weak and didn't deserve to be king, but his reign wouldn't last for very much longer. Of that, Zoryn was certain.

Sanjin Dakor had no magical ability of his own and was distrustful of those that did. However, he understood the value of magic and employed the services of some of the more talented magicians to serve the crown in various capacities. Zoryn was certain that Sanjin had magicians amongst his ranks that, aided by White Metal, could mind-skim and thereby read an individual's dominant thoughts and feelings. Zoryn could detect the probing magic of others and could easily shield his own thoughts. Kaiya, however, could not. She had no innate magical abilities. He smiled to himself as he thought that one or more of his brother's mind-skimmers must have skimmed Kaiya's thoughts and knew that he had been fucking her since before she had wed Sanjin. He doubted that any of them would have the temerity to tell their King out of fear of what Zoryn would do to them if he found out. That was the way Zoryn liked it. His empathic magical ability meant that he knew how to intimidate and threaten others by sensing what they feared most. He rarely had to lose his temper or resort to violence to achieve dominance over others; his malign presence and reputation were menace enough.

***

It was late in the afternoon by the time Zoryn left the storeroom. He made his way to the old training platform that had been built centuries earlier at the top of the West Wing of the Royal Keep. An interminable flight of rough-cut stone stairs, that were crumbling with age, led to a heavy, iron-bound oak door. Zoryn tried the handle and was surprised that it turned as easily as it did. There was no lock on the door as there had never been a need for one. The ancient hinges submitted to his great strength, admitting entrance to the flattened rooftop as he pushed his way through the doorway. The former training ground was a courtyard that was completely circular in shape with a diameter much larger than would seem possible judging by the narrow stairs that lead up to it. However, by a remarkable feat of construction and considerable use of magic, the builders of this place had built an almost gravity defying saucer-shaped courtyard that sat on top of the tower. A wall of flawless obsidian black granite circled the courtyard to a height of six feet. The rock formed an impenetrable barrier and had been designed to prevent any rogue magic blasts, unleashed during training, from damaging other structures nearby, or the inhabitants of the keep.

The black granite had been infused with magic, centuries earlier, to enable it to absorb magical blasts and contain the magic within its crystalline structure. The

19

practice ground had been used by the students and masters of the Royal Keep, to perfect their skills should they ever be called upon to defend the Five Lands against attackers. Before it had been built, training accidents had killed both students, masters and any person unlucky enough to have strayed too close when the accident happened. Property had also been damaged or laid to ruins; such was the power of the magic that was unleashed during training. The masters had tried training students using only limited power but all that came from this were poorly trained magicians who were easily beaten in battle. The training ground was so well built that the only risks were to those that trained within its protective wall. Those without were safe and the masters were able to go back to using full power in their training exercises.

The wall had been constructed in such a way that every time it was hit by a magical blast, it absorbed the magic and became stronger and better able to absorb even stronger blasts. It also had a tendency to absorb light which made it appear so black. What the architects of this place had not considered was what would happen to all the magic that the wall had stored up over the centuries that were to follow. It had been assumed that training would always be required and would always be performed in this courtyard. But training methods changed and adapted over time and different places were deemed more suitable for these changing requirements. The training ground high atop the tower in the West Wing of the Royal Keep was no longer needed and was abandoned and consigned to history. Over time, it had been forgotten about and the accumulated magic of centuries of use, that was contained within the obsidian black of its perfect granite wall, had lain dormant. Waiting until it was required again, waiting until this moment.

Zoryn had been here many times before although not for a number of years. But unlike his previous visits to this place, this time he could sense the magic in the granite wall, it was keen to his senses. He could feel the magic it contained gently pulsate in anticipation, in expectation of what was to come. His own magic seemed to respond as if it was reaching out to join with the magic that surrounded him. For a moment, he was distracted and was unaware that he had walked into the centre of the courtyard. It was then that he realised that the magic within him was not in fact reaching out, it was drawing in.

It was both the strangest and most exhilarating experience of his life. Zoryn could feel his strength increase as he drew more and more magic into his body. He was not consciously doing it, it was just happening, a by-product of the Black Metal. Zoryn was aware of every inch of his body; his senses heightened way beyond anything he could imagine and in particular, he became aware of his wrists. As he looked down at them, he saw a band of the deepest crimson circling each wrist where he had placed the bands of Black Metal earlier. The Black Metal itself wasn't visible, but the crimson glow burned with increasing intensity until he could barely look at it. This time there was no heat, no pain. Zoryn dragged his eyes away.

It was now fully dark and the brightness from his wrists left phosphenes in his vision, making it even harder for him to see anything clearly for a moment or two as his eyes adjusted. The sun set quickly in this world, and he had lost track of time and didn't know how long he had been standing in the middle of the courtyard. As his vision started to clear, he realised that something wasn't right. It should be much darker than this. It was a clear night and the stars were visible above him, but their meagre light was not sufficient to light up the courtyard in this way. Zoryn looked around and saw that a glow was coming from the black granite wall that surrounded him. It was an eerie light, a phosphorescent glow that gave everything around him an other-worldly look.

In an ironic twist of fate, the wall that had been designed to contain magic, to absorb magic, was releasing its pent-up magic to him. The phosphorescent glow increased in intensity, and the crimson light emanating from his wrists also increased until both were almost blinding in their intensity. How long this continued Zoryn didn't know nor did he care; the power that he was absorbing was intoxicating, and he didn't want it to stop. He felt more and more magic entering his body with every passing second. A dazzling light display twisted and swirled around his body with the force of a thousand maelstroms from the magic that was rushing towards him from the wall. Fierce vortices howled and eddied in their frenetic haste to find their new home, their new master. Then without warning, the magic flared once in a catatonic blast, briefly transforming the night into day and then the courtyard once more succumbed to the darkness of the night.

For long moments, there was nothing but darkness and silence. And then, the rumbling began. At first, it was more of a feeling than a sound. And then it increased in intensity, slowly at first and then faster and faster until Zoryn could feel the tower beneath him tremble as if it were alive. The rumbling picked up speed and increased quickly in pitch and intensity. The rock beneath him was now shaking so violently that it was all Zoryn could do to stay upright. With a deafening scream of stone being rent apart, the granite wall shattered into millions of tiny fragments that exploded outwards with volcanic force.

Zoryn Dakor stood where he was, stunned, in the centre of the training ground, high atop the West Tower of the Royal Keep in Gaardsholme. His motionless form a statue carved in exquisite detail with every feature of his handsome face and muscular frame set against the desolation of the courtyard and its shattered wall. The contrast was striking. Time around Zoryn Dakor stood still, or at least that was how it appeared to him, as his mind raced to make sense of what had just happened. He had heard the stories of Black Metal's ability to absorb magic from others, from people like him that had innate magical powers. But he had never considered that it may also be able to draw on the magic in inanimate objects that were themselves a source of magic.

The conflagration on top of the tower must have been witnessed by everyone within the Royal Keep and probably everyone in Gaardsholme, and Zoryn knew that even now armed guards would be on their way to see what had happened. "Let the bastards come. I will kill them all," he declared as he shook his fist at the night sky. It was then that he noticed his hands, they were glowing, no not glowing, they were pulsing with light. Zoryn looked at his hands in disbelief and at his wrists which burned with a crimson fire that left him unharmed. As he watched, he noticed that the interval between each pulse was getting shorter and with each pulse, he felt the power within him scream ever louder for release. He tried to force the pulses to slow down by sheer strength of will and just for a moment thought he had succeeded as there was a noticeable delay between pulsations. But he didn't have the strength to resist them for long and the gap between the pulses increased again and soon became barely measurable.

The five guards who stormed through the heavily iron-bound door to the old training ground had no way of knowing that their presence would be the catalyst for the greatest blast of the most powerful magic that had ever been unleashed in the Five Lands. Zoryn was a powder keg waiting to explode. He had absorbed more magic than he could possibly contain, than anyone or anything could contain, and their abrupt arrival was the trigger. Two of the guards instinctively fell to the ground as Zoryn wheeled on them and punched the air in front of him screaming something incoherent as a blast of blinding crimson instantly erupted from his fist. Without conscious thought, Zoryn unleashed all of the magic that he had absorbed in a single blast of devastating force. The three other guards didn't stand a chance and were killed instantly as the blast ripped through them as if they weren't there as it hurtled on its way towards the far horizon.

The angle of Zoryn's blast had saved the two fallen guards. Any lower and they would have died with their comrades. Even though it had happened so quickly, when they reported to Sanjin Dakor afterwards, both men told how the blast itself appeared to be narrow and like no magical blast either had seen before. Both men had distinguished careers in the Elite Guard and had seen magical blasts used in combat situations, but they had never witnessed anything with the power and concentration of that unleashed by Zoryn Dakor that evening. They had also never witnessed, or heard of a blast that was such a brilliant crimson in colour. But the strangest thing of all was that it took a tremendous amount of power to launch a magical blast and because of this they never lasted for more than a fraction of a second before they ran out of power. Even the most powerful magicians could not maintain a blast for more than the briefest of moments. The guards both agreed that the blast that erupted from Zoryn's fist lasted considerably longer. How much longer they were unable to say with any accuracy, but each testified that the blast lasted for at least five or even ten times any they had ever witnessed.

The blast should have run out of power after it killed the guards, like every other magical blast would have done. But Zoryn's crimson blast illuminated the night sky with preternatural light as it blazed away from the old courtyard. Its speed and angle had now taken it high up into the night sky on an unknown trajectory. Those that witnessed the sight likened it to a thousand or more fire-crackers that had been fired off at once. But even this comparison fell short of describing the spectacle that had turned the night over the city of Gaardsholme into day.

Zoryn's blast picked up speed as it raced higher and higher into the night sky, reaching an impossible height as it roared its way into the firmament. It was now many miles from the old courtyard, so far away that the distance would have been impossible to measure. To the inhabitants of Gaardsholme, the blast looked like a massive star of the purest and deepest crimson burning in the sky above them, overshadowing all others and drowning out their feeble light. But then, without warning it detonated.

For a long moment, there was no sound, just an explosion of blinding crimson light that burned the night sky as if it were tinder. And then, the shockwave hit. The tower of the West Wing of the Royal Keep was rocked by the blast, shaking it to its very foundations. Other buildings in Gaardsholme did not fare so well and many were shaken apart or flattened completely. Those that witnessed the explosion high above them were thrown to the ground and momentarily blinded by the supernova magnitude of the detonation. All that witnessed the phenomenon were left with phosphenes that danced in front of their eyes, obscuring their vision for long moments. When their sight eventually cleared, they knew instinctively that something was very wrong. At the epicentre of the blast, an area of indeterminate size, there were no stars. The stars in that part of the sky had simply vanished. It wasn't that they were obscured by clouds: it was a clear night and there wasn't a single cloud in the sky. There were simply no stars at all in an area of inky blackness that stood out all the more so by their absence. It was an eerie sight and struck fear into all that witnessed it.

The convulsive force of unleashing the blast had brought Zoryn to his knees. The release of magical power had happened without any conscious effort on his part and had been automatic, an instinctive reaction. He couldn't have prevented it if he had tried. Had he been in control, he would have attacked the guards anyway and so maybe the magic had reacted to his thoughts. If so, that made Black Metal even more formidable as a weapon. All magic required some action, or direct contact, to make it work, but it would appear that the magic of the Black Metal worked on a deeper, more instinctive level.

Zoryn had felt incredible as his body absorbed the magic from the training ground, more alive than he had imagined was possible and powerful beyond any meaning of the word. But when the magic left him, in the pent-up fury of the blast, it had taken something of him with it, leaving him bereft of not just his new magic, but his own strength and innate magic. His breathing was shallow and laboured, and his heart was barely beating as he fell to the ground unconscious.

Chapter 4
Council of Lords

"Will my brother live?" Sanjin Dakor demanded as he addressed the coterie of Royal Physicians and healers that stood before him. The assembled members of the Council of Lords were silent in deference to their King as he addressed the court.

"We don't know for certain Sire," responded his personal physician Myri as she stepped forward to reply to her king. "By rights, he should be dead. Nobody has ever survived using a fraction of the magic that Lord Zoryn wielded and yet somehow he lives."

"What can you do for him?"

"Little, Sire. We tried to help his body repair itself by giving him some of our own magic, but it became too dangerous and we had to stop. All we can do now is wait and hope," Myri replied.

"Dangerous, how do you mean dangerous?"

"We tried on three occasions to transfuse some of our magic into Lord Zoryn. The first time the physician lost too much magic too quickly and collapsed. We didn't understand why this happened until the second physician repeated the attempt and nearly died in the process."

"And the third occasion?" Sanjin asked.

"We put safeguards in place to protect the physician, to break the link with Lord Zoryn if anything went wrong. We didn't take any chances, or so we thought. We did everything that we could to protect him, Sire. But the speed with which his magic was drained from him was much faster than we could have possibly predicted. He died immediately the healing link was established. It was clear that a very potent magic was at play, but it was unlike any magic I have ever come across. It cut through our wards as if they weren't there at all." Myri hesitated for a moment, the normally dispassionate physician struggling to control her emotions as they threatened to overwhelm her. "I believe that it was my error that lead to the death of the physician. If only I'd made the wards stronger or attempted the link myself, he would still be alive."

"Who was it that died, Myri?" the King's tone was softer now, in response to Myri's palpable hurt.

"It was my beloved husband, Rhynn," she replied, her voice barely a whisper but heard by all in the silence of the court.

Sanjin turned his attention to Derryn, the leader of the Council of Magic Users. "And what does the Council believe happened to my brother, Derryn?"

Sanjin could feel the bile rising in his throat. His brother, Zoryn Dakor, had caused the death of Rhynn, a good physician and a good man. He doubted that Zoryn intentionally drew magic from Rhynn, killing him in the process, but Sanjin had no doubt that Zoryn was to blame and must answer to the court.

"There are no doubts in the minds of the Council my liege. We believe that Lord Zoryn has used Black Metal," Derryn replied.

"But that's ridiculous, Derryn. Nobody knows for certain that Black Metal even exists, and where the fuck would Zoryn have got it from? It hasn't been heard of since Jal Chindo. How does the Council answer that?" Sanjin Dakor demanded, barely controlling his rage.

"It pains me to admit that we don't have any answers yet my King, nobody does, but I can assure you that we are doing everything we can to find out."

"So, what makes you so sure my brother used Black Metal? Did you find any of it on him?"

"No Sire, nothing was found," Derryn replied.

"So, my question stands Derryn: what makes you and the rest of the Council so sure he used Black Metal?"

"It's the nature of what your brother did, Sire; he literally blew the top off the disused keep, and you've seen for yourself what he's done to the sky. What he did should not have been possible. Before the events of a fortnight ago, I would have laughed at anyone who said that a man could punch a hole in the sky and destroy, or whatever it is he's done, to the stars that lay beyond it."

Sanjin ignored Derryn's momentary lapse of good judgement in the way he answered his King, dismissing it as the same stress that they all were feeling since the dramatic events of the last two weeks. In a less aggressive tone, he continued, "What does the Council make of this darkness that Zoryn has created; should we be concerned about its appearance in our skies?"

"I don't believe that what Lord Zoryn has created or destroyed was a deliberate act on his part, but I think that we should be very concerned my lord. The council agree that Lord Zoryn somehow managed to accumulate more magic than he could possibly contain and when he attempted to use this pent-up power, he lost control of it, resulting in a blast of unimaginable magnitude. This is why we are convinced that he used Black Metal. If the legend of Black Metal is true, then it is the only substance that could possibly have contained that amount of magical power."

"Do we know what this darkness in the sky is, and does it pose a threat to us?" Sanjin Dakor repeated.

"I cannot say with any certainty at this time my lord, but whatever it is, it shouldn't be there and until we know for certain, if indeed we ever will, it should be regarded as potentially dangerous. We have never seen or heard of such a thing before, and in truth we don't know what it is, or at least the Council can't agree on what it is. But I have my suspicions," Derryn replied.

"And what do you suspect?" the King of the Five Lands asked.

"I disagree with the other members of your Council my liege. They are convinced that Lord Zoryn has blasted to oblivion everything that got in the way of the magic he unleashed, even the very stars that shone in that part of the night sky. The sheer amount of magic needed to do such a thing is incalculable and must surely be beyond even an army of Black Metal wielders."

"So, what do you think Zoryn has done?" Impatience returning to Sanjin's voice. The Council and, not least, its leader had a knack of annoying Sanjin Dakor with their endless talk and debate and their steadfast refusal to come to the point quickly. He was a warrior king, a pragmatic man who found resolution to most problems with the hard steel edge of his sword. He was not one to tolerate endless debate and conjecture. Derryn, however, was no fool and sensing his king's annoyance continued. "I think that Lord Zoryn has punched a hole through the fabric of what lies between our world and the stars, rather than having destroyed the stars. I believe that Lord Zoryn may have created a portal between the stars and that this portal is distorting our view of the sky."

"And what do the other council members make of your theory?"

"They think that I've taken leave of my senses, my King," Sanjin laughed.

"And have you, Derryn?" he asked, his tone once again softening. Sanjin respected Derryn's humility. The man might irritate him but Sanjin had made him the leader of the Council of Magic Users for his assiduousness and his determination to stand up for what he believed in, whatever the cost to him personally.

"In truth my lord, I am beginning to wonder that myself. But one thing that the Council has always agreed on is the possibility that other worlds may exist out there among the stars. If I am correct my lord, we may not be the only world witnessing this new phenomenon and that is what really concerns me."

Sanjin Dakor brought the session to a close and dismissed the members of his court. As they filed out, he caught the arm of his trusted General.

"Not you, Zanshin," he said. "I require your counsel."

"Yes, my lord," General Zanshin replied.

"I want you to detail a continuous watch of this darkness in the sky from several different vantage points. If Derryn's fears turn out to be founded, we need to make sure that we are ready to meet anything that should venture through this *portal* of his."

"I will arrange this as soon as you dismiss me, my lord."

Sanjin smiled. He doubted that Zanshin bought into Derryn's theory. He was too practical a man for that, and he also left conjecture to the academics. But he knew the importance of military intelligence, and Sanjin suspected that Zanshin had already put the watches in place and that he was humouring his king.

"So Zanshin, what other news do you have for me?"

"Sire, my report will not be what you want to hear. We have been fighting this war of attrition for many years and history shows us that there have been numerous times when we have both taken and lost ground to our enemy. But things seem to have changed recently."

"Changed in what way, Zanshin?"

"I'm going to struggle with this because I know that you are a man of hard facts and not given to less tangible matters, but it seems to me that our enemy is growing in confidence. It's almost as if their cause has been strengthened in some way."

Sanjin Dakor frowned as he regarded his General.

"You are my most trusted military adviser, Zanshin and a man I have fought alongside in battle. You are right, I do not like what I'm hearing, but for you of all people to bring it to my attention means that you believe this to be serious."

"I'm afraid that it may well be, Sire. A man without a cause is easily defeated by a superior force, but give a man a cause, a reason to fight and give his life if need be, then you have a serious problem and you had better be prepared."

"I think it's time we increased our surveillance measures and deployed additional resources to the Western Peninsula. I want you to increase flyer activity and arm them. The time for covert surveillance is over. If our flyers can get information and attack our enemy, then they are to do so. I want them to pay particular attention to weakening our enemy's logistics; a hungry army will find their motivation hard to keep up, no matter what drives them." Sanjin was pacing the room as he delivered the General's orders to him.

"At once, Sire."

"Well not quite at once Zanshin, have my squire fetch us some Krendyran wine, and you can tell me all about the trouble your sons are getting into at the military academy!"

26

Chapter 5
Zoryn Awakens

Zoryn Dakor's sleep was dark and dreamless. His strength so completely drained that he didn't even have the energy to dream. But slowly, as his strength started to return, he did begin to dream. At first, his dreams were random and unconnected and made little sense. But over time, his dreams began to coalesce, as swirling fragments of memories smashed into creations from the darkest reaches of his subconscious mind, creating a seething maelstrom of sounds and images that denied him of the rest his body desperately needed. To those physicians and others that tended him, he appeared to have a raging fever as his body convulsed and his sheets were soaked in sweat. But whatever was afflicting him, it was like no fever his healers had ever encountered before as his skin was cool to their highly trained touch.

Zoryn had no real sense of self and no way of tracking time, so the point at which the dreams took on meaning was impossible to identify. The transition was gradual at first, or so it later seemed to him, but time had no meaning to him as he lay in bed in his suite in the Great Citadel. He was being tended to by the court's most trusted and brilliant physician Myri, but Zoryn knew nothing of this as he was unaware of anything outside of the dream world that held him captive.

As the days passed, he dreamt of places that he knew well and others that he had never been to, places of great beauty and some where untold dangers lurked. The contrast between these places was so great that even in his torpor he knew that they had to be vast distances apart, or maybe even on different worlds. Zoryn had little interest in science, but he had heard the debates between his brother's advisers who argued endlessly that other worlds may exist and could even pose a threat to the safety of their own world. He was a warrior and knew nothing of this and cared even less for such talk. But the places he had seen in his dreams were vivid to his senses, so much so that he increasingly felt as if he was actually there.

Zoryn quickly discovered that by exerting his will he could control the dreams, because unlike normal dreams, he was capable of rational thought as he lay asleep. By thinking of a beach lapped by waves from an azure ocean, he found himself there, feeling the soft warm sand between his toes. Changing his thoughts to more rugged surroundings, he was instantly transported to a bleak and craggy moorland where even the toughest of bracken fought hard to survive the inhospitable environment. The exhilaration that Zoryn felt each time he 'transported' himself to another location was intoxicating, and he travelled to more and more places in his quest to satisfy this new hunger.

It was quite by chance that Zoryn found himself on a world inhabited by people that seemed like those from his own world. But this place was strange, something about it was different and it took him several long minutes to work out what it was that made it stand out so much. And then, he knew what it was; this world had no magic. He could sense magic in all of the other places he had visited. On some worlds, the magic was palpable and in others delicate, like the finest gossamer on a summer's breeze. But on this world, he couldn't detect any magic at all. The concept of a world without magic was so alien to him that he decided to stay longer and find out more about this strange place.

It was difficult to judge the passage of time, because Zoryn was still weak from his use of the Black Metal high atop the tower that housed the old training ground. His weakness was slowly passing but he still kept slipping in and out of consciousness without warning. The inhabitants of what had now become his favoured world seemed oblivious to his presence, even as he walked among them. Looking down, he could clearly see his own body, but those around him could not. As he explored his surroundings, he observed that machines, of all descriptions, had taken the place that magic commanded in his world, performing all manner of tasks. Zoryn liked this place, he liked the machines, he could see the extra power and might they would give him, but most of all he liked the fact that the people were weak. They had no natural magic of their own and there appeared to be no magic in the world itself that they could draw upon. *Conquering these people will be child's play!* He thought to himself.

Zoryn started to become aware of his surroundings, but he was still too weak to surface from his dream world entirely. He was, however, able to tell the two worlds apart now. On a couple of occasions, he felt an increase in his energy. It was the suddenness of these inflows of energy, that meant that it could only have come from magic. He knew that he was still critically weak, but on the second occasion, he felt something inside him trying to attach itself to the source of the magic, as if to draw it into him without any conscious effort on his part. The third time was different.

***

The magic from the Black Metal bands, that had become part of Zoryn Dakor when the substance had fused with his flesh and sinew, absorbed the magic of others, draining their magic in the process. Myri did not know and had no way of knowing, that Zoryn Dakor possessed the mythical Black Metal. How could she? It hadn't been heard of for centuries, and most scholars doubted its existence. Besides, she was a physician and left matters of magic to those healers that had innate magic of their own. Their gifts were amplified using White Metal, a substance whose use was carefully controlled by the state. It was her lack of innate magical ability that saved her life. The same could not be said for her husband, Rhynn.

In almost every other respect, the day of Rhynn's death was unremarkable. Myri's day had started much like all the others over the last two weeks since Zoryn Dakor had fallen into a coma-like state, except that today she felt confident and was certain that she was getting closer to bringing him back to consciousness. Rhynn, however, had woken in an amorous mood and despite his obviously aroused condition, Myri was not in the mood for lovemaking and wanted to get to the royal suite to get on with her work. Grabbing an apple for her breakfast, she kissed Rhynn on the cheek and promised to make it up to him later as she hurried from their room in the servant's quarter of the palace. She had no way of knowing that she would never be able to make good on her promise to her beloved husband.

A well-trained healer could give enough magical energy to start the process of recovery in another, but not so much that it would weaken themself unduly in the process, or put them at any real risk. Rhynn was unsurpassed in his ability to use his innate magic for the healing of others and had given of his energy in this way hundreds of times before. This time, however, his magic would be further strengthened by the piece of White Metal that he held in his fist. Rhynn had used White Metal many times before but each time the thrill of using it, of feeling its magic mingling with his, was like it had been the very first time. The way it joined its magic to his innate magic was so complete – it was almost sensual. White Metal was used in many ways throughout the Five Lands, but Rhynn was convinced that it was at its most potent when it was channelled through a healer to treat the sick and injured. He was confident that he would succeed where the other physicians treating Zoryn had failed.

Myri, however, did not share her husband's confidence and was not prepared to take any chances this time, not after the other two healers had lost so much of their magical power and so quickly when they had attempted the procedure before. She made sure that Rhynn put protective magical wards in place to sever the connection with Zoryn should the same thing happen to him. Similar wards were used by the Mages of the Eastern Realm in times of combat to ensure that if captured, their enemies could not drain their own magic to use against them. Rhynn was confident that he could sever the connection anyway and that the wards were not needed, but he went along with his wife's wishes, knowing that he wouldn't win the argument anyway. He was more experienced than the other healers that had tried before him, and he was prepared and knew what to expect, whereas they were taken unawares. There wasn't a magic in the Five Lands that could penetrate the magical wards that had been put in place.

It was as if the Black Metal had its own consciousness, as if it knew what was going to happen, that an opportunity to draw another's magic would present itself. Zoryn was in a dreamless phase of his coma, which cycled between such periods and other periods of intensely vivid dreams, when Rhynn approached his bedside. Zoryn was unaware of his surroundings, let alone the presence of Rhynn, until the moment that Rhynn pressed his outstretched palm against Zoryn's forehead. This was the age-old way that magical healers transferred energy into their patients. It was the most direct way to send their healing magic.

Rhynn touched Zoryn and willed his magic into him and in that instant, the magic of the Black Metal flared into life. It had been greatly diminished by Zoryn's cataclysmic release of magic atop the abandoned tower, but it had steadily and stealthily drawn tiny amounts of magic to itself, to Zoryn, from the magic expended by those nearby in their efforts to revive him. A blinding fire of the deepest crimson surrounded Rhynn's body, enveloping him in its deadly embrace. Those in the room had no time to react to save their fellow physician. In a moment that could only be measured in a heartbeat, the crimson fire flared and then went out and as it did so Rhynn's lifeless body fell to the ground. Myri and the two other medical attendants ran to Rhynn's aid, but they were too late: he was beyond their care. His body was badly burned, and even if he had survived the initial explosion of magic, there was little doubt that he would have died an agonising death from his injuries. The worst of his burns were to his left hand where he still held the piece of White Metal. But it wasn't white anymore. It had turned grey and porous and crumbled to the touch. Its magic had been drained utterly, something that should not be possible. Everything had happened so quickly and the attention of Myri and the other physicians was so focused on Rhynn that they didn't notice that Zoryn's eyes were open.

Chapter 6
Kaiya

Kaiya had to be careful. She was after all, the King's wife and her every move was followed. It was stifling and she was always on her guard, never able to truly relax. And yet, despite the restrictions that had been placed on her life, she had been having an affair with the King's brother Zoryn for the past year. Sanjin Dakor had the power and she had always been attracted to power, but Zoryn had qualities that his brother did not. He was dangerous, unpredictable and feared by everyone. Everyone that was apart from Sanjin and this, Kaiya believed, would be the undoing of the mighty King of the Five Lands.

Sanjin Dakor was a warrior king and was quick-witted and intelligent. He had had the finest of educations and was groomed for the role of king from birth. He ascended to the throne when he was barely in his twenties, when his father, the old king, died. Sanjin's rule was just. He was a hard man to please and expected much from those around him, but he was fair, and it was these qualities that earned him the respect of his subjects. But he had a weakness. He knew that his brother was flawed emotionally and that growing up in his shadow, it was only to be expected. But Zoryn had taken it harder than any could possibly have imagined. He had grown from being a spoilt and spiteful younger brother, into a dangerous and scheming adversary.

Sanjin could see it long before his council of advisers had the temerity to approach him with their concerns. He knew that Zoryn could never be allowed to rule, but so far there had been no issue from his marriage to Kaiya. In the absence of an heir apparent, Zoryn was next in line for the throne, and Sanjin had little doubt that he would take any opportunity that came his way to claim the throne. But despite everything, Sanjin loved his brother.

Sanjin blamed himself for how Zoryn had turned out, for not recognising the signs along the way, for not acting before it had become too late. Kaiya believed that his love for his brother was the fatal flaw in her husband's armour and the one that would allow her and her lover to seize control of the Five Lands. Zoryn cared nothing for Sanjin and neither did Kaiya.

Kaiya was strikingly beautiful. At five-feet-three-inches, she wasn't the tallest woman in the court, but she was powerful. She had the most perfect skin and her limbs were slender and had the burnished colour more associated with those from the Eastern Realm. Her eyes were of such a dark brown as to appear almost black and her shoulder-length hair was soft and lustrous brown. Men found her steady gaze hypnotic and it made them feel like they were the only person in the room when she spoke to them. Women found her unwavering eye contact intimidating and her thoughts unreadable.

Kaiya didn't have any magic of her own, but she didn't need it; her power came from within. She was ruthlessly ambitious and had an unshakable belief in herself. She came from a humble background where people aspired to a life in service to a wealthy landowner or tradesperson. People like her were not expected to succeed. But Kaiya believed from an early age that her destiny was to become a great ruler. She never discussed this with anyone. It wasn't because she feared ridicule: there had never been a female ruler in the Five Lands; it was because talking about it with others who couldn't help her achieve her goal was a waste of her time. Time that could be spent on more worthwhile pursuits.

Men fought for her attention, but she barely noticed them, particularly those that had nothing she wanted, which was the case with most men. But Kaiya was not like the courtesans who would use their bodies unashamedly to get what they wanted. She had only taken a small number of lovers and these she selected to satisfy her desires and when she grew bored of them, as she always did, they were discarded without a second thought.

Kaiya wound her way through the great citadel to the royal suite, her bodyguard tailing her, until she arrived at the room where her lover was being tended. "Wait for me outside," she said as she turned to face the Elite Guard who had been appointed to accompany her by her husband.

Spy more like, she thought to herself.

Although detailed to follow and protect her, the guard could not disobey a direct order from Kaiya unless her life was in danger. He nodded silently and waited for her to enter the room before taking his position to guard the door.

Kaiya waved her hand dismissively at the physicians attending the comatose body of Zoryn Dakor as she entered the room. "Leave us," she ordered.

"But your highness, Lord Zoryn is gravely ill and we must stay with him," the oldest-looking physician replied.

"Lord Zoryn has been like this for the last two weeks, and your potions and magic have done nothing. Now leave us." Kaiya's tone hinted at reprisals if she wasn't obeyed. No further resistance came, and the physicians filed out of the room.

"My love, what has become of you, why do you not awaken?" Kaiya sat in a chair by Zoryn's bedside as she brushed his handsome face with her delicate, highly manicured fingers as she had done so many times over the last two weeks. Zoryn's eyes flashed open instantly, his powerful gaze burning into her very being. Kaiya flinched instinctively. But something wasn't right, something was very wrong with Zoryn's eyes. The shock of his awakening momentarily stunned Kaiya, making her initially blind to what she could now clearly see. The edges of his irises looked like they were tinged with a thin zig-zagged, orangey-red corona that seemed to burn as if on fire. Kaiya flinched again and tried to pull away but Zoryn grabbed her in a steel grip.

"My love, I am returned to you." His familiar voice deep and rumbling with the menace of distant thunder.

"Returned?" Kaiya replied, still in shock.

"Yes, I have been to other worlds and have seen many things, and I now know how I will rid the Five Lands of my accursed brother's rule."

"But my love, how can this be? You have been in a coma for the last two weeks and have not left your bed. I will call the physicians back; I fear that the effects of the coma are still upon you." Zoryn sprang from the bed and was on his feet in an instant lifting Kaiya from her chair. *How can this be possible,* she thought. *How can he have so much strength?*

"Come, my love," he laughed as he spoke, "it is time to show you what Black Metal is capable of."

"Black Metal, you have Black Metal? But I thought it was a myth, a legend. Are you still ill, my love?"

"Ha." Zoryn laughed. "Let's see, shall we my love and future queen?" Zoryn held her in a lover's embrace and the room started to fade as it spun around her. For a long time they fell, tumbling and spinning. There was light and colour, but they were moving so fast that the colours melted into each other. It felt like they were inside a never-ending kaleidoscope. And it was cold, numbingly cold in fact. Kaiya could breathe but there was no mist from her breath and no wind or breeze despite the apparent speed of their movement. She lost all sense of time and space and could have been tumbling for a minute or a year, and then without warning they fell hard onto solid ground. Kaiya tried to prize herself up, but vertigo consumed her and she once more fell to the ground. Black spots crowded her vision and consumed her.

"Wake up, Kaiya," Zoryn said as he gently shook her awake. Kaiya's eyes opened.

"Where are we?"

"I don't know what this place is called, or indeed where it is, but I have been here before."

"But how can that be, Zoryn? You've been in a coma for the last two weeks and haven't left your bed!" Kaiya responded as she shook her head in an effort to clear the last vestiges of the vertigo.

"Truly I don't know, nor do I particularly care." His tone was as imperious as ever, as if even this seemingly impossible translocation were somehow an everyday occurrence and somehow beneath him.

"What do you know about this place?" she asked.

"Little. I have been here in my dreams and know that it is in some ways similar to Zendyros, except that the inhabitants of this place are weak and there is no magic here."

"What sort of place doesn't have magic?" Kaiya exclaimed. "And what do you mean *similar to Zendyros?* Where are we, Zoryn?"

"Ha, so many questions, my sweet! Of one thing I am certain: we have left our home far, far away. I do not share my brother's interests in star gazing, but I am sure that wherever this place may be, it is not on our world."

"But if we have truly left our world, how are we to return? Can we return Zoryn?" she asked anxiously.

"I don't know Kaiya, I've only ever travelled here in my mind, but I'm pretty sure that we can go back whenever we want to, assuming that we ever want to go back."

"If this place doesn't have its own magic Zoryn, can you still use yours?"

"I haven't tried yet, but I believe that I can; although the magic I now wield is not just my own."

"I don't understand, if the magic isn't yours, then whose is it and how can you use it?"

"I formed an alliance with Draxan Longseer. He too wants to see the end of my accursed brother's reign. In exchange for making him ruler of the Eastern Realm, he has given me the gift of Black Metal."

"Black Metal, Zoryn." Kaiya still couldn't believe what she was hearing. "I thought that it was just the stuff of legend and didn't exist."

"As did I," he replied. "But Longseer found the lost amulet of Jal Chindo."

"So, this accident that put you into the coma…"

"Yes Kaiya," Zoryn interrupted, "it was my first experiment with Black Metal. I think I may have underestimated its might somewhat."

"Somewhat, Zoryn!" It was now Kaiya's turn to laugh. "You blasted a hole in the sky! Why didn't you tell me about it?" Her tone now sombre as she realised that he had kept this from her.

"How could I tell you? Your husband has spies everywhere Kaiya, and I am certain that your thoughts are read by his magicians."

Kaiya's cheeks reddened at the thought of what her private thoughts may have revealed, not only about her, but about her trysts with the King's brother. "But that would mean that they know about us?"

"That is beyond doubt. But they are hardly going to go running to the King of the Five Lands to tell him that his brother is fucking his queen right under his nose now, are they?" Zoryn roared with laughter.

"I think that you are enjoying my discomfort Lord Zoryn," she said coquettishly. "So, now that you have brought me to this place, what next?"

"Now my Queen, we have work to do. I have plans for my brother and this place will help me to achieve them."

Chapter 7
White Van Man

"What the fuck do you think you're playing at?" Brad shouted out his car window as he blared his horn at the guy in the white van. He was on his way to his office, driving largely on autopilot as he had taken this route more times than he cared to remember. The van had pulled out of a junction, seemingly oblivious to the existence of Brad's car. It cut him up so badly that he had to swerve violently to avoid hitting it and then he narrowly missed a head-on collision with an oncoming vehicle.

Like most men of his age, Brad had testosterone issues when he was behind the steering wheel of his car, and it took little provocation to piss him off and today was no exception!

Why do they always fucking drive white vans? he cursed to himself.

Without warning, the van driver screeched his vehicle to a dead stop, so suddenly that smoke billowed from his tyres and the air was instantly filled with the suffocating acrid stench of burnt rubber. Brad barely managed to stop his car without hitting the van.

Brad was no stranger to road-rage incidents and knew from experience that these types of confrontations generally played out in one of two ways: Either there would be an exchange of insults at a safe distance accompanied by posturing and the inevitable *next time I'll kick your fucking head in.* Or some pushing and shoving and maybe an exchange of blows, or worse. He wasn't a brave man and despite his hot-headed reaction, the last thing he wanted was a confrontation. Unfortunately his options appeared to be reducing rapidly as the driver's door of the van started to open. Even if he wanted to drive off, he was blocked by the proximity of the van in front of him and the closeness of another motorist behind him. He was trapped.

Realising that an aggressive confrontation was now inevitable, Brad remembered his Krav Maga instructor's advice from the evening course he took a few years ago. The instructor, who Brad thought had probably never been in a real fight in his life, said that in a confrontation you need as much space as possible, whilst limiting the room available to your opponent. He knew that if he stayed in the car, he was a sitting duck. Brad shoulder barged his door open with such ferocity and speed that he was already out of the car and closing in on the other man before he had chance to think any more about it.

The van driver hadn't expected this and seeing Brad standing less than a couple of metres away, experienced a brief moment of doubt. *How did he get there so fast?* he thought.

The feeling soon passed, however, as he appraised Brad with the same calculating look that a hunting animal eyes its prey and any remaining doubt was quickly gone. *This twat is going to get the hiding of his fucking life.*

Van man looked every inch the thug and stood at least six-foot-tall with sinewy arms and legs that only get that way after years of heavy manual labour. His skin was brown and weathered and his hands looked like clubs. He wasn't a nice person and was from the wrong side of town with all the clichéd baggage that came with it. Violence was second nature to him, and he had many convictions for assault. Only yesterday, a restraining order had been served on him that had been instigated by his *fucking bitch of an ex-wife*. It wasn't that he had particularly wanted to see her, after all he had been fucking her younger sister for the last six months. It was being ordered by some *prick of a judge* that he couldn't go near her house again, or even get within twenty feet of her; that had really pissed him off. Some bastard was going to pay for the way he felt today and providence would appear to have handed the solution to him on a plate in the form of the *twat in the BMW* who now stood in front of him. Van man would have smiled if only the contorted muscles of his face remembered how. "I hate wankers like you," he spat with vitriol as he advanced towards Brad.

Bradley White was not the tallest or biggest of men and hardly cut much of an imposing figure. He stood a little under five foot ten inches tall, had greying dark-brown hair, a soft belly, wore glasses for short sightedness and his face had become rounded over the years. Brad didn't exercise and was finding it increasingly hard to keep the pounds from adding to his expanding waist. He didn't look tough at all, and he certainly wasn't a hard man. In fact, he looked just like the typical victim of crime you see every day in the tabloid press. He knew that reasoning with the guy would only make him look weak and make an attack inevitable. His only hope was that the man that stood in front of him may just be a bully that enjoyed intimidating his adversary rather than attacking him.

"Get back in your van and fuck off. I don't want any trouble." The words were out of Brad's mouth before he had given any thought to what he would say.

Van man laughed a hollow and humourless laugh as he responded, "You office wankers are all the same; gutless twats, the fucking lot of you. Sure, you don't want any trouble; you make me sick."

Brad felt oddly detached as he stood facing this man. Where was the fear, the adrenaline rush? He had been in similar positions before and every time it had been the same; his heart would feel as if it would break out of his chest at any moment, his legs would feel leaden and his vision would become tunnelled. The effects of adrenaline would make him hyperventilate, and the twin feelings of fear and anger would battle for supremacy inside him, and amost inevitably fear would win out. But not today. Today, he felt nothing; there wasn't even a hint of adrenaline. Brad felt disconnected, detached, as though he was not really there at all and was watching events on a cinema screen. He had had similar feelings in the past, particularly if he was overstressed or anxious and a similar dream-like, unreal feeling, would always precipitate a panic attack. But not this time. This time, although he felt detached, it was not a dream-like state. No, this time everything felt real, in fact, more real than he had ever felt before. He was aware of everything around him; from the hard ground that he could feel through the soles of his shoes, to the faint breeze as it brushed against his skin, as if flirting gently for his attention. He was calm and relaxed, despite the fact that he stood facing the hardest and most aggressive looking man he had ever encountered in his life.

Van man, on the contrary, was a seething mass of anger. The threat of imminent violence was palpable and growing by the second. Brad could feel the tension building and the reasoning part of his mind warned him that this was not going to end well.

"I told you I don't want trouble," Brad hissed as he looked the guy square in the eyes.

"Well, trouble is what you've fucking well got," van man snarled as he closed the distance between them. "I'm going to kick your fucking head in." Without pause, van man thrust his left hand forward and grabbed Brad by the throat with a vice-like grip and pushed him toward the grassy verge by the side of the road without releasing his grip. His right hand pulled back making ready to punch him in the face. Brad managed to regain his footing and held his ground despite his attacker trying to push forward again to gain more of an advantage. Van man tightened his grip and Brad could almost feel the guy's fingerprints imprinting into his skin. Despite the obvious threat to his life, Brad remained completely calm and even now, there wasn't the merest hint of adrenaline. He was detached, an onlooker watching this unfolding scene without emotion or involvement. And then, without warning, he struck.

Brad brought his hands up, and in a move he had learnt from Krav Maga, cupped his fingers and pulled down hard and fast against his attacker's hands. Van man's grip broke instantly, despite his considerable strength and the force of the plucking motion pulled the man forward violently. Instinctively, Brad tucked his head down and to one side, just in time, so that the top of his head made contact with his assailant's nose, stunning him. Brad took a half step back and struck van man with both hands in the centre of his chest. "Back off," he shouted as he struck him. The force of his attack knocked this hulk of a man back a clear three or four feet and nearly knocked him to the ground. But for a moment, Brad was as stunned as his opponent. In the instant he struck the man, he saw, or at least he thought he saw, what he could only describe as an explosion of crimson light. It lasted only a moment and was gone.

Van man struggled to his feet and without hesitation, Brad leapt at him and punched him in the face twice with astonishing speed and power, hitting him so hard that he felt something go in his hand. *That's going to hurt later,* he thought.

Van man fell to one knee and looked up as Brad pulled his head back by grabbing his hair at the back of his head and hammered a blow with the underside of his fist on the man's nose which erupted in a fountain of deep red blood. For the briefest of moments, both men's eyes locked and Brad could see the fear in the other's face.

"Your eyes, your fucking eyes." Van man's face contorted in fear and disgust as he tried to look away. "What the fuck are you?"

Brad didn't answer and grabbed the man's hair a second time and this time smashed his knee into the side of his head. Van man fell hard and was unconscious before he hit the ground. Blood was flowing freely from his nose which was clearly badly broken. Brad stood over him poised and ready to strike again, looking for the slightest movement to warn him that his opponent may yet be able to mount an attack. But there was no movement from the man who lay where he fell. Only his ragged breathing broke the silence. Brad turned and walked over to the guy's van and got inside. Turning the engine on, he drove the van a few feet forward, moving it out of the way of his car so that he could drive away. After closing the door and locking the van, he threw the keys over a nearby hedge. He knew the man was in no condition to pursue him, but he wasn't prepared to take any chances. There was a queue of cars behind Brad's car with the occupant's rubber necking, but not one met his gaze, or said a word as he got into his car and drove off.

Five miles down the road, Brad felt compelled to pull over. He stopped the car and the full realisation of what had just happened hit him with the force of a freight train. He got out of his car just in time as a wave of nausea crashed over him and he threw his McMuffin and hash brown up all over the double yellow lines he had parked on. He reasoned that it must have been delayed shock because he had felt nothing at the time. But strangely, he felt nothing at all even now, no remorse for the violence of his actions only a few minutes earlier, or any concern that there may be repercussions. This was not like Brad, who was by nature anxious and worried about practically everything. His body seemed to be reacting to what had just happened, but his mind was not, or if it was, it was on a subconscious level. He got back into his car and glanced in his rear-view mirror and saw that he was a mess. His hair looked like it did when he first got out of bed in the morning and his tie was pulled down into a small tight knot and a button was missing from his collar.

Brad drove for about five miles to the nearest service station and looked at himself in the cracked mirror of a toilet that clearly hadn't been cleaned in weeks. He straightened his tie and tidied himself up as best as he could. Washing his hands, he was a little disturbed by the amount of dried blood that was coming away as he scrubbed at them. It was then that he noticed an angry looking dark purple swelling on the back of his right hand and he could tell that something was broken. But there was something else that looked wrong about his hands, or to be more precise, his wrists. Around each one was a circle of the deepest crimson that seemed to be glowing slightly. At first sight, he thought they may be burns but they didn't look much like burns and there was no pain.

He must have had something on his hands when he grabbed my wrists. Brad reasoned with himself, but he couldn't recall being grabbed in such a way during the confrontation.

He regarded his reflection in the mirror and for the briefest of moments was convinced that something about his eyes looked wrong. He caught a glimpse of what looked like zig-zagged, orangey-red coronas around his irises and then they were gone and his eyes looked normal again. *Shit! Looks like I'm going to get a fucking migraine now!* He cussed inwardly. *It would have to be today of all days.*

It was the last Wednesday of the month which meant only one thing; today the entire morning would be wasted in a sales meeting at his office. *Sales meeting, that's a laugh,* Brad thought. He loathed and detested sales meetings which were just an excuse for his fat lazy slob of a sales manager to throw his, not inconsiderable, weight around and boast about his successes when he was a sales rep. *That asshole couldn't sell if his fucking life depended on it,* Brad got back into his car and headed for the office.

Chapter 8
Sanjin Dakor

Sanjin Dakor was troubled. As if the sudden and unexpected disappearance of his brother wasn't bad enough, his forces were experiencing much greater than usual trouble in the Western Peninsula. They were taking losses, more so than they had at any other time. This was war and he understood only too well that losses were inevitable in times of conflict, but this just didn't make any sense to him. Unlike a conventional war, his enemy didn't organise themselves into identifiable groups. He believed that his enemy was fighting for control of the Western Peninsula. Their strategy was to use small groups of men rather than a larger force and it was proving to be very effective. This was guerrilla warfare. They would launch hit-and-run strikes before Sanjin's forces could mobilise any retaliatory action of their own. This had not been too much of a problem in the past, as Sanjin's army was well prepared and had crushed each attempt with hardly any losses, but his enemy was learning from their encounters, as each strike became more and more effective.

The Western Peninsula had three main ports that, if in the hands of the enemy, would give them a staging point to mass an army that could arrive by sea. Sanjin had concentrated his forces around these ports and they were well defended. The problem lay in the large stretches of lowland that formed vast beaches that backed onto unusually deep water. These were perfect landing sites for a small enemy force to launch raids and disappear as quickly as they had arrived, which was precisely what they did. The enemy knew that to defend the entire shoreline would be beyond even the reach of the army of the Five Lands so the attacks continued.

Sanjin had no doubt that the skirmishes were just that and that sooner or later, larger forces would follow. But up until now, his enemy had seemed content to test the defences and resolve of the defenders without committing all of their resources. The attacks had been going on for the last twelve months and from the nature of the skirmishes, Sanjin originally thought that this would be a very drawn-out affair. But recently, the frequency and severity of the attacks signalled a shift in the enemy's tactics. He believed that General Zanshin's report, which he had delivered a few days earlier, had been credible and that the enemy was more organised and more confident. Sanjin was certain that a major attack was imminent.

Strangely enough, it was unclear to Sanjin exactly who they were at war with as no group had been clearly identified. He had his suspicions and felt that the attacks were coordinated by one or more foreign power, but without proof he couldn't send an expeditionary force, and besides there were a number of countries that could be behind this. There wasn't a single foreign power that had the might and could possibly stand up against the armies of the Five Lands, but an alliance of disgruntled neighbours, well that was another matter altogether. Sanjin was of the opinion that whoever may be behind the attacks was using mercenaries, as those that they had captured or killed were from a number of different races.

The central land of the Western Peninsula was a scarcely populated area consisting largely of a mountain range and a huge lowland marsh area. Around the perimeter of the marsh, the land was rich and fertile and supported a ring of farms. These farms produced food for the entire region which was sold by merchants from the nearby capital city of Gaardsholme. However, there was one reason and one reason alone that the Western Peninsula was so important, and that was that deep within an almost impenetrable wooded area, surrounding a section of the mountains, was the mine of Renshaw. It was the only White Metal mine and as far as anyone could tell, it was the only source of the substance in any of the lands. The exact location of the mine was widely known as it used to be a major source of iron ore. That was until the vein ran out and a prospector stumbled across a strange white metallic ore that greatly enhanced the magical abilities of those that came into contact with it. And so it was that White Metal was discovered, and the mine was renamed after the prospector's family name.

White Metal was a substance that had been coveted ever since and was now firmly under state control. Security around the mine was tighter than in any other part of the kingdom. As with any object of value, there was a black market in White Metal, but it had been infiltrated by so many of Sanjin's covert agents that illegal trading in it was dangerous. Such was the risk of the substance falling into the wrong hands that lethal force was sanctioned against illegal traders. A few such traders were spared just long enough that they could be tried in court and made an example to others foolish enough to try it for themselves.

Sanjin Dakor's forces had built a fearsome reputation over many years and were the best trained, best motivated and most effective fighting force the Five Lands had ever seen. They had proven themselves in battle many times, both in defence of the Five Lands and in campaigns overseas. They were known for their near ruthless efficiency, and they never left a battlefield until their enemy had been utterly defeated. To start a war with the Five Lands was folly, and for more than twenty years there had been relative peace between the Five Lands and its neighbours.

At the core of the Five Lands Army was the Elite Guard which was made up from the very finest soldiers. They were sworn to protect the mine of Renshaw and to keep it under the control of the crown. The selection process was tough and the fall out and injury rate during the training, was higher than in any other military corp. Only soldiers with five years or more service could apply and fewer than ten percent of applicants completed the training. Even then, there was no guarantee of a place in the Elite Guard. Answering only to Sanjin Dakor, the Elite Guard was unlike any other military unit. Keeping the mine under the control of the Five Lands was so crucial that the Elite Guard were empowered to take command of all forces in the area if they were under attack.

Three garrisons had been constructed in close proximity to the mine. One was a training camp to keep the soldiers fit, sharp and battle ready. The second was a barracks containing a minimum of thirty men that could be deployed anywhere within twenty leagues of the mine in less than half a day. The third garrison's purpose was a mystery to all but a select few and it was heavily guarded. Its gates were rarely open and when they were, little could be seen from the outside, other than an empty courtyard. It was rumoured that the Great Mages from the Eastern Provinces came there to teach Sanjin's Elite Guard their unique way of fighting. They used the magical powers of the ore to enhance the soldier's innate strengths and abilities.

A knock on the door to his private quarters heralded the approach of a messenger.

"Enter," barked Dakor.

"Sire, General Zanshin is here to see you."

"Show him in and fetch some wine."

General Zanshin entered the room and thumped his fist to his chest whilst bowing his head and kneeling to the ground on one knee, showing the correct level of respect to the mighty warlord. "Get up Zanshin, I want to hear your report and don't tell me what I want to hear; tell me what the fuck is going in the Western Peninsula."

"I increased our surveillance as you ordered, and it is clear that our enemy is changing its tactics. The attacks are more organised and more confident than before. I'm convinced that they are probing our defences with these hit-and-run tactics. I don't believe that they are really trying to hurt us, although I'm sure they would if they could, but they are definitely using the attacks to gather intelligence. There's organisation and method to these attacks. They are not as random as we once thought they were."

"If you're right Zanshin, this is completely out of character with their strategy up to this point. It sounds to me like they are building up to a major offensive," Sanjin Dakor asserted.

"I believe that you are correct my liege, but it still doesn't really make any sense. For a start, they don't have the numbers to cause us any real concern and up until now, they didn't seem to have any organisation."

"But now..." Sanjin started the sentence for his general.

"But now my lord, I have my doubts. I don't believe that our intelligence is wrong about their number, which we know has never been that great. But I am convinced that someone is organising and motivating them. Our enemy, it would appear, has found a purpose other than to be just a minor irritation."

"How seriously do you take this new threat?" Sanjin asked.

"Very, my lord. Any change in the behaviour of an enemy should be taken seriously especially when that enemy is growing in confidence for no obvious reason. There is something else that we should consider, my lord."

"That it could be a decoy for an attack on another front?" Sanjin Dakor was pacing as he spoke, the motion adding energy to his thought process.

"It wouldn't be the first time that an enemy of the Five Lands has used such a tactic against us. I have taken the precaution of fortifying our defences on the eastern flank, just in case that's what they are up to, but our enemy's ruse seems a little too obvious for my liking."

"Yes I agree, Zanshin. It sounds like we are being offered a fool's choice."

"My thoughts exactly. With your permission, I will send reinforcements to our training garrison in the foothills of the Zindaw Mountains."

"Good thinking, Zanshin. If we base foot and horse there, our cavalry can reach the western front within a day's ride and our soldiers can be sent as reinforcements, following a day or so after, if called upon."

"Precisely!" Enthused the normally reserved Zanshin. "I recommend that we split the detachment into three. We send the horse under cover of night by the most direct route to the garrison, and a battalion of five hundred soldiers can leave at the same time heading east across the great plains my liege. It is imperative that our enemy believes that we have taken their bait, and I think that five hundred soldiers should attract that sort of attention."

"And what do you recommend for the third group?"

"I propose to split the battalion once they are a day's march from Gaardsholme. My plan is to send fifty men at a time, over successive evenings, to head back west towards Druckers Pass. It should take each group about a week or so travelling at night to make the journey. They can then join the cavalry on the other side of the mountains.

It will delay the full deployment by about two weeks in all, but it gives us the best chance to build our forces close to the western front without making it obvious to our enemy's spies."

"Good. If your plan works, it will give the impression that we have taken the bait and perceive a tangible threat from the east. My concern Zanshin, is that two hundred and fifty men won't be enough to stop an army if we are attacked from the east."

"I have prepared a small detachment of Elite Guard to skirt the Great Plains to see if there is any evidence that our enemy is massing to the east. They will leave tonight. I also want to call up the reserves immediately. We should garrison five thousand here at Gaardsholme and send two and a half thousand east and then wait until we gather more intelligence. It will take a week or two to mobilise that many, but we should be able to crush any attack from the east without committing too large a force and leaving us vulnerable to a major attack from the west."

"We need to send word to Draxan Longseer and see what support he can muster from his people. If we are attacked from the east, his men could cut-off their retreat, and then just maybe we can finish this once and for all."

"Yes, my lord. We have horse and men, but we could do with more warrior magicians, a cohort of Draxan's finest based at Gaardsholme should do it. This would greatly strengthen our defences and counter any magical attack in case our enemy has managed to recruit any magic users. I don't believe that we should take any chances."

"As always Zanshin, this is a well-considered plan, and you have my agreement. I take it that the foot soldiers are ready to go?" Sanjin stopped pacing as he smiled and considered the grizzled features of the old general.

"Now that I have your approval my lord, the soldiers will leave this evening. Our enemy's spies should believe that we take the threat seriously, and a night deployment will suggest that we expect an imminent attack. It should also distract them so that they don't notice the small numbers of Elite Guard slipping out in civilian clothes much later," Zanshin replied.

"Good. Just one more thing, Zanshin."

"Yes, Sire."

"You are not to go with the cavalry."

"But my lord…" Zanshin started to protest.

"No, you are too valuable to risk at this stage, the time may come Zanshin, but it isn't now. You are to stay at Gaardsholme. I need you by my side so that we can stay one-step ahead of our enemy. I have no doubt there will be plenty of fighting left for you when our enemy finally decides to reveal their hand, and when they do, Zanshin…" A murderous glint appeared in the eyes of the King of the Five Lands. "You will ride out with me, and we will crush those bastards together like we have so many other enemies of the state."

"Yes, my lord!" The bloodlust bringing a flush of excitement to the old general's face as the years fell from his visage. "It will be like it was before this accursed peace!"

Sanjin Dakor roared with laughter as he slapped his trusted general on the back.

"That it will Zanshin, that it will."

***

It was some hours later that Sanjin Dakor retired to his sleeping chambers. The walls and ceiling of this room were suffused with an extract of the White Metal which meant that when someone entered the room the ambient temperature and light were at just the right level. On opening the door, he noticed that the magic had already been activated which meant that someone was already in his chamber. Sanjin pushed the door hard with his left hand as his right hand grabbed the pommel of his short close quarters sword that was always strapped to his side.

"Sire, you scared me," came a feminine voice as soft as silk and as warm as a summer's breeze. "You're not going to draw that fearsome weapon on me, are you?" Her tone was both mocking and seductive. Sanjin took in the sight in front of him: Katzin leader of the House of Secrets lay on his bed in her favourite outfit which consisted of a thin translucent black veil to the lower half of her face and nothing else. Katzin had the body of a temptress and the sexual appetite of a predatory beast. Sanjin released his grip on the sword and undid the buckle, letting the sword and scabbard fall to the floor.

Some time later, they dragged themselves out of bed as servants brought in Sanjin's evening meal. Their conversation was relaxed as they ate. "Katzin, how's business in the Western Peninsular?" Sanjin asked before taking a sip from his wine glass.

"As you know my liege, it's not the safest of areas for us, so only the bravest and most desperate of my order work that region. The people there are less than trusting, but they do pay well," came the reply.

"Who are your customers there?"

"Mostly lower-ranking officers from your army and the occasional enemy combatant who hasn't spent all their money on grog." Grog was the term used to describe any of the multitude of cheap watered-down beers that were popular with the lower paid.

"The information that your people have gleaned for me in the past from this region has been of little use tactically, but I want you to step up your operations there, Katzin." Sanjin Dakor was looking into the distance pensively as he spoke. "Send in some of your higher-class operatives. There have to be some in our enemy's rank that know something of value to us."

"I will do as my lord commands of me." The seductive mocking tone had returned to Katzin's tone.

Later that evening, Sanjin lay alone in his bed. He was too wired to sleep despite the late hour and the bottle or two of wine he had consumed. It was not uncommon for him to stay up all night, and this looked like it might be another one of those nights. Katzin was his closest friend and confidant, and he sought her counsel and company above all others, even above that of his wife, Kaiya.

Katzin was beautiful and had the most amazing body a man could ever desire. Physically, there was little difference between Katzin and his wife; they were both extremely attractive, confident, independent women with keen intellects and sharp wits. In many ways, it was their similarity that attracted Sanjin to both women. What separated them was not immediately clear and had only become so to Sanjin through the course of recent events. Katzin, although streetwise and capable of extreme acts when necessary, was inherently a good person. She did her duty when called on by the state, but never took any pleasure in it if that duty involved harming another. On more than one occasion, Katzin had come to Sanjin for solace when the burden of her duties had threatened to overwhelm her.

Kaiya on the other hand had proven herself to be hard and cruel. It was the discovery of her real nature and her feelings, or lack of feelings and the callous disdain in which she clearly held him and all those around her, that shocked Sanjin the most. His discovery of this only coming a few days ago when he was approached by the magicians he had tasked to read her thoughts.

Sanjin had his suspicions that all was not right, and was becoming increasingly suspicious of his wife's behaviour but had nothing more than his suspicions as evidence. That was until she disappeared at the same time as Zoryn. It was then that the magicians revealed the true extent of her treachery to him. Sanjin was certain that they had known for longer than they revealed to him and that they had not come forward in fear that Zoryn would exact retribution on them for informing against him. Sanjin was furious at both the betrayal of his wife and brother and also at the weakness of those who served him. Kaiya clearly had a soul as black as obsidian and as hard as tempered steel. It was clear to him now that she had used him and his position ever since she had first met him. Their whole relationship had been a sham, a part of her plan all along. It was these thoughts that teemed and multiplied in his mind when he retired to his bed and were the cause of his recent restless nights.

Sanjin no longer loved Kaiya; that had ended the day he found out that she was sleeping with his brother. He would never have believed it possible that the strong love that he had for each of them, could turn to bitter hatred. And it wasn't just because of their betrayal of him personally. It was the way they had betrayed his people, their people, the people of the Five Lands, that was what angered him the most.

Zoryn and Sanjin were brothers, born to the mighty Dakor House and destined to be leaders. Their childhood was different to others. From an early age, both brothers showed exceptional promise and were intelligent and sharp-witted. However, seemingly subtle differences in their personalities started to show early on and marked them apart. Zoryn was the stronger of the two brothers and took naturally to the fighting arts. So much so that the combat masters of the Military Academy would pair him with older, stronger and more experienced sparring partners. He was never beaten and only Sanjin was his equal; although the two were rarely paired together by the combat masters.

Those that trained with Zoryn rarely escaped injury, and there was a certain reluctance from his fellow students at the academy to train with him. Even some of the lesser masters only trained and sparred with Zoryn because that was their job, and a combat master with a reputation for avoiding conflict would not stay in his employment for very long. On more than one occasion, Zoryn had lost his temper during training and had to be dragged off an opponent, who by then was either unconscious or severely beaten.

Zoryn's mood could be best described as mercurial. He may be perfectly calm one moment and then become highly aggressive, with little or no provocation the next. Zoryn did not have an 'off-switch' and never showed compassion for a weaker or less-able opponent, even during training. Some said that this demonstrated Zoryn's passion for training. Others, who preferred not to voice their views too loudly, saw Zoryn for the danger he clearly represented to everyone around him. There was even some unrest amongst the Guild of Masters, but many saw Zoryn as the younger brother who was trying a little too hard at times to emulate the achievements of his older sibling. Whatever the reason, Zoryn Dakor was a dangerous man.

Sanjin was also a talented fighter, but his main strengths lay in the tactics and strategies of war and these were areas in which he excelled. What separated him from his brother was his compassion. He was without doubt the finest student the Academy had trained in its long history, and his calmness and ability to make key decisions under fire, marked him out to be the great King that he was clearly destined to be.

Chapter 9
Lauren

There was a minor injuries unit not too far off his normal route to the office, near the city centre of Sanderswick, so Brad headed there to get his hand looked at. He reasoned that at this time of day, the wait would be relatively short and he would not be too late for the sales meeting. *Oh, what joy!* he thought. Brad's day was not improving.

"Your X-ray results confirm it Mr White; you have a simple fracture of your index finger. It will need to be immobilised and will take about six weeks to heal. The strange thing though is that the break is consistent with the injuries we treat boxers for, or those involved in street fights. You must have fallen badly when you tripped over your cat." The doctor was clearly not convinced by Brad's poor cover story, but it was the best he could manage off the cuff. He didn't want to draw any unwanted attention from the police. Unfortunately, he had aroused the suspicion of the doctor. *Are doctors compelled to inform the authorities in these cases?* he thought to himself. Brad had no idea, but he suspected the worst. "Yeah, bloody animals," Brad replied. "If it wasn't for my wife, those mangy cats would be up for adoption!"

The doctor looked unconvinced, but unless he were to call Brad a liar, there was little he could do. "Go to the waiting room and I will arrange for a nurse to bandage your hand. We will need to see you again when the swelling goes down to fit a plaster cast. Make an appointment to come back in three days."

Brad waited for what seemed like an eternity in the waiting room until a nurse appeared. *Well, worth the wait!* He thought, as he was greeted by a very attractive, slim nurse in her early twenties.

"Come with me," she said as she led him to a treatment room. The nurse gently bandaged his hand and made polite conversation as she did so. Brad, however, found it difficult to concentrate as the closeness of the nurse, with her slim but perfectly proportioned body, made his cock respond in an inappropriate way! In fact, in recent months he had had difficulty getting and maintaining an erection with his wife Gina, and had all but given up trying. So to get a spontaneous erection here, at the minor injuries unit, was totally unexpected. *This could be a little embarrassing if I have to stand up!* he thought. Fortunately, the final stage of applying the bandage was quite painful and his uncomfortableness soon subsided.

"Thanks for this," Brad said to the nurse. "When will I see you again, I mean when should I come back here?" *Shit!* he thought. *How did that slip out?*

The nurse smiled. "Book an appointment at reception on your way out to come back in three days. If the swelling has subsided, we'll put a plaster cast on your hand." Brad couldn't help but think that maybe she had noticed his earlier erection, because the way she said *swelling* and the way she looked at him left little doubt in his mind.

"Here's a prescription for some pain relief; you have a nasty fracture Mr White, and you will need this. Make sure you follow the instructions to the letter." With that, she handed him the prescription and a leaflet about fractures and their care and recovery. Brad left the clinic and as he put the leaflet on the passenger seat of his car, he saw some writing that he hadn't noticed earlier. There was a heading on the leaflet that read '24-hour Helpline' and beside it in very neat ballpoint pen handwriting it simply said, 'Lauren' by her telephone number.

Brad arrived at his office at 11.30 am; the sales meeting was planned for 12.00 pm and the other reps were starting to arrive. *It's funny,* he thought. *I fucking hate sales people with their false charm, sunbed tan and bling. So why on Earth did I choose to fucking be one?* He had been a reasonable achiever at school, and although he had been in top sets, school never really inspired him and he did as little as possible to get through, often less. Brad left school with passable grades leaving a trail of disappointed teachers in his wake. His parents grew up in the sixties and their attitude towards his schooling had been, *as long as he's happy and not getting into trouble, that's fine by us.* Seeing schools as part of the 'establishment' by his parents, Brad's lack of commitment and any real involvement with the education system was hardly a surprise to anyone who knew him. So here he was, mixing with people he didn't like and doing a job that he had drifted into more by apathy than design. Sales meetings were an anathema to him; the air would be choking with the twin stenches of bullshit and over-inflated ego. To make matters worse, the meeting would be presided over by his obnoxious sales manager. He could hardly wait to go in!

The sales manager's door opened just wide enough for him to poke his ferret like face out and call Brad inside. Brad entered the room and noticed that Bill's ruddy faced complexion seemed even redder than normal. This was a man who sought solace in a bottle of Jack Daniels every night. Bill met his impossibly attractive young wife on a dodgy internet dating site and after a quick marriage, he became her personal cash machine. He knew that she didn't love him and would never bear him children, but at least she would suck his cock, or bribe him with other sexual favours, whenever she wanted money! Brad laughed to himself ironically, *I may not suck cock for a living, but it sure feels like this company is fucking me in the ass.*

In Brad's mind, the only reason Bill wasn't the oldest virgin in town was down to the fact he had money. *Oh yes, he has money alright,* thought Brad. *And every fucking penny of it has come off the sales of me and the rest of his team, and none of it by his own efforts.* Not that Brad particularly cared for the sales team anyway.

Bill was liked by management due to the one skill that he possessed in abundance; he was probably the best *brown noser* that Brad had ever met and in this line of work he had met many over the years.

Brad had not been happy in his job for some time now. It was made worse by the company moving the goalposts and changing the remuneration package often and without warning. Just when he was earning good money from a new drug, the company would lower the commission on that drug in favour of some other drug they decided to promote.

"You wanted to talk with me, Bill?" Brad said as he entered Bill's office.

"Yes, come inside," Bill replied as he circled Brad to close the door. Brad felt as if he was prey. "You know what this is about." Bill pointed his index finger at Brad as he spat the words.

"I haven't a clue," was Brad's honest response, "but I've no doubt that you will tell me."

"I've had personnel on the phone; the police want to speak with the driver of your car about an incident that happened earlier today. Perhaps you would care to enlighten me."

"Not really, in fact not at all. If the police want to talk with me, that's my business and has nothing to do with you."

Bill was fuming. "If it involves company property, like your car, it is very much my business."

"Inspect the car, here take the keys; it's parked on the fifth floor of the guildhall car park, be my guest." Brad half threw the keys at Bill. *Although I hate the twat, I have never been this rude to him before* Brad thought. *It's like my words are coming out by themselves.*

"Your hand is bandaged as well. What have you been doing?"

Brad ignored Bill's question. "Now, if you don't mind, I have a sales meeting to go to."

"Well smart-ass, your attendance may be cut short. The police are on their way here as we speak. I will overlook the way you just spoke to me as you are obviously in the middle of, I don't know what, but if you…"

"Watch what you say." Brad cut Bill off in mid-sentence. "I won't be threatened by you or anybody else." He could feel his pulse quicken, as again his words seemed to have a mind of their own. *Where are these words coming from?* he thought. Something in Brad's face, in the way he stared him down, shook Bill to the core and just for a moment, he saw something that looked like orangey-red fire in Brad's eyes. It was there and then it was gone.

Brad had never really answered Bill back before and in the three years or so he had known him, Bill had never known Brad to lose his temper. But something had changed; the Bradley White that stood in front of him, threatening him was different, dangerous even, and Bill was afraid. He did not respond as he lowered his gaze submissively, hoping that the moment would pass. Brad walked out of his office and closed the door behind him. Bill's pulse was pounding so loud in his temples that he could hear it. He was no stranger to conflict; in fact, he was a bully and had hit many people over the years who pissed him off. The confrontations rarely escalated into full fights, but when they had, Bill had usually ended up on top, largely due to his aggression and the amateur boxing experience from his youth. Many times, he had faced a bigger, stronger or better opponent and had felt the adrenaline rush, but he had rarely, if ever, been afraid. Today, Bill felt real fear and didn't know why.

The sales meeting started a little later than usual that day. Everyone was there, and the usual banter eased off a little as Bill made his entrance. Not really wanting to be in the spotlight just yet, Bill started the meeting with the usual *round robin* where each rep took in turns telling the group about their successes during the last week. "This is going to be fun," Brad muttered under his breath, as Stuart, the area's star salesman, stood up and unashamedly boasted about his recent successes. Stuart was a good salesman, but in Brad's estimation the guy was a complete jerk. He was the sort of person who had everything, appreciated nothing, and deserved fuck all. After a seeming eternity, Stuart sat down. Brad, however, would not have been surprised if Stuart had got up again to give an encore!

"Bradley White, let's hear about your week." Brad was brought back to reality by Bill's introduction. *I really hate it when people I care nothing about call me Bradley,* he thought. Only his wife, mother and brother called him Bradley. His real name was William Bradley White, but the William had been dropped in childhood as his mother soon decided that he was more of a Bradley than a William, besides he had found it easier to say Brad when he was young. *Thank goodness for that,* he thought as he cringed at how life would have been had he been known as Willie White. *Mother must have taken way too many magic mushrooms when she chose my name!* Brad's mother, despite being in her seventies, was still very much a hippy.

Brad stood up when it was his turn. He was used to public speaking and whilst not being the most captivating speaker, he did this stuff for a living and was professional. However, speaking at sales meetings was not something he enjoyed and his delivery today was just enough to get by.

The sales meeting wore on interminably, and Brad's attention started to wander. He replayed the events of the morning over and over in his mind. Something was bothering him. It wasn't the confrontation, or even the violence; it was more to do with how he felt during the whole thing. Something wasn't right about it. The only way he could describe it was that he had felt detached, pretty much throughout. It had certainly been real, but it felt as if he was an onlooker rather than a protagonist. He felt neither fear nor rage during the confrontation, which was bizarre and not at all like him. When Brad had been involved in previous altercations, his memory of exactly who said what, where and when was generally hazy afterwards. He would put this down to the adrenaline and the *heat of the moment.* But as far as today was concerned, he could recall every detail with crystal clarity and even now he felt strangely disconnected from the events of the morning. It was like he had simply been an observer.

Shifting a little in his seat to relieve the numbness in his ass from sitting down so long, Brad felt something digging into his leg. Reaching into his pocket, he pulled out the fractures leaflet that had been given to him at the minor injuries unit. He was sat at a conference table and was able to take his mobile phone out of his pocket, and keeping it below the level of the table, so as not to be seen, he composed a text message. 'Hey Lauren, any tips for relieving the pain? Bradley White.' He pressed send and sent the text to Lauren. *Pretty crap text,* he thought. It was only then that he gave any thought to the injury to his hand, which despite his message to Lauren, wasn't causing him any pain at all. *Oh well, I guess the pain will catch up with me later!* he thought.

'Shiatsu works for me,' was the almost instant reply. 'It's all about applying pressure to certain areas of your body which in turn provide pain relief to other areas.'

Brad could feel a stirring as he imagined what it would feel like to have Lauren's hands applying pressure to his body.

'Would you be able to show me how to do this?'

'Sure, we can't have you suffering!'

Brad knew how to close a deal. He was, after all, a seasoned salesman with many years of experience. 'Are you free tonight Lauren? I can get away between 7.00 pm and 11.00 pm x'

'Wifey out then? x' Lauren's response was a little too close to the mark for comfort. *Fuck it,* thought Brad. *What's the point in bullshitting her!*

'Yes she is, so I'm all yours! x'

'Good,' was Lauren's reply, 'don't worry I won't wear perfume so you won't need to worry about Mrs White finding out! x' Brad was in no doubt now that they both wanted the same thing.

'What would you like me to wear for you Brad? x'

Fuck me, thought Brad. *I must be dreaming.*

'Something tight and short, bordering on the slutty side works for me!'

'That shouldn't be a problem! I'll see what I can do. You really are a bad boy! Pick me up outside the clinic at 7.00 pm and don't be late, we don't have much time! x'

Brad was not sure he could wait until 7.00 pm; it was going to be a very long day!

His reverie, however, was cut short by the unexpected entrance of Lynda into the sales meeting. She went up to Bill and whispered something to him and they both looked up at Brad. Lynda was fifty-eight and was the driving force behind Bill. She was probably the most capable and formidable person that Brad had ever met. Everyone was afraid of her, not least of whom was Bill. Lynda could kill at fifteen paces with sarcasm sharper than the finest steel blade. Brad had never known anyone get the better of her in a dispute or confrontation and only the foolhardy challenged her authority. Lynda ran the office with military precision and was the only reason that Bill remained in his position. Brad had often wondered why she had not been the instrument of Bill's corporate destruction and came to the realisation that having a weak boss, who she could manipulate, was how Lynda wanted it to be. It was almost a symbiotic relationship if that was at all possible between a predator and its prey! Classically elegant and immaculate in her appearance, Lynda radiated *don't fuck with me* out of every pore. Brad got on better than anyone with Lynda, but their relationship could hardly be called close. The look she gave Brad made it pretty clear that something bad had happened and when Bill made an excuse to leave the meeting and asked Brad to join him, his suspicions appeared to be confirmed. Once outside the room, Bill informed Brad that two police officers were waiting in his office to interview him.

It had been a shit day for Brad. It started off badly and just seemed to go from bad to worse. The sales meeting was as excruciatingly tedious as ever and the interview with the police was not pleasant. Brad was interviewed about the road-rage incident. Apparently, several witnesses had called them with his description, and the number plate of his company BMW had pinpointed him to this address. Witness statements described the attack as violent and without mercy. As van man had not actually thrown a single punch and Brad had thrown several, it looked like Brad had been the aggressor. The situation had been made much worse by him throwing his *victim's* keys away and leaving him unconscious. And there was also no record of him calling the emergency services. It wasn't looking good.

"You claim to be the victim in this," one of the policeman said. "But what sort of man beats another man unconsciousness and leaves the scene without calling for medical help and without so much as a second thought? You also do not appear to be in the least bit remorseful about what you have done."

The policeman had a point. Brad knew that he should be concerned, but he wasn't; in fact he had barely given the matter any thought at all. He didn't harbour any ill will towards van man, neither did he care whether the man recovered or not. The reasoning part of Brad's brain was telling him that this was not right, but it still didn't change the way he felt. Brad was arrested and taken to the police station where he was charged with assault and criminal damage. Van man was apparently still unconscious and there were concerns about whether he would make a full recovery, or even regain consciousness. After spending several hours in the police cells, Brad was released and told that he would be contacted by the police the following day. It was now 3.00 pm and he remembered that one of his main accounts was expecting him to drop off a supply of a new asthma drug.

Brad called in to Kings Road Surgery on his way home. By the time he had finished the impromptu clinical staff meeting called by the senior partner, it was a little after 5.00 pm before he was back in his car and heading for home. His route took him past the spot where he had the confrontation with the van driver that morning and everything looked the same as it ever did. Driving past he felt no emotion, no adrenaline rush, nothing at all.

Gina greeted him on the doorstep of their respectable but small house in the suburbs of Sanderswick. It was not Brad's first choice of home; he didn't care much for the style of the property, but it had been reasonably priced and was in an up and coming neighbourhood. Gina looked good tonight, but then she always did. At thirty-eight, she was younger than Brad and looked much younger. She had dark brown almost black, hair and dark brown eyes almost certainly due to the Italian blood in her recent ancestry. She was five foot three and had great legs which she showed to their best advantage by wearing short skirts and dresses most of the time. On the rare occasion she wore jeans they were the sort that hugged her like a second skin and accentuated her perfect figure. Tonight, Gina was working and looked elegant in a blouse and knee-length skirt. "There's salad and some of that hand-carved ham you like in the fridge. I'm running a bit late, and this party is at the other side of town. Don't wait up!" she said as she kissed Brad dryly on the cheek and got in her car and sped off without waiting for his reply.

"So how was your day, Brad? What's wrong with your hand, Brad? Why is it bandaged up, Brad?" He growled under his breath as he stormed inside and slammed the door behind him.

He was hungry. In fact, he was starving hungry and realised he hadn't eaten at all that day.

Opening the fridge door, the ham was screaming at him to be devoured instantly and he couldn't resist its siren song. He ate the whole lot whilst looking for something more to eat. He remembered that there was steak in the freezer; he took out a neatly labelled packet containing two reasonable-sized rump steaks and put them in the microwave to defrost. Brad liked his steak on the rare side, but today he didn't even bother to cook them and set about eating the steaks as soon as the microwave pinged. Two barely thawed, lukewarm steaks later, he showered and set off to meet Lauren.

***

Lauren was dressed in a tight short black skirt that just about covered her modesty. Her long-tanned legs were on display to Brad's hungry eyes. He had never wanted a woman as much as he wanted her right now. She stepped into his car, and they drove to a pub out of town, in an area that he didn't usually frequent, to avoid any embarrassment. The conversation was remarkably relaxed considering that this was almost a blind date. Brad knew that he should be feeling guilty for what he was doing and what he was planning to do, but he didn't. Lauren leaned across the table and whispered, "Let's go somewhere a little more private."

Brad knew the area well and a short drive later, he pulled off the main road onto a single-track road that led to an abandoned quarry. The quarry had been a major source of gypsum, a material widely used in the construction industry, until the vein was exhausted in the seventies. As a boy, Brad had a keen interest in rocks and minerals and his father had taken him here many times with his geologist's hammer and cold chisel, hunting for rocks and minerals to add to his collection. He switched off the engine and with the lights off, the night closed around them like a velvet glove. Everything outside of the car was blotted out by the darkness and it felt as if they were all that existed in the world.

For a moment or two, they both just sat there keenly aware of the mounting tension that crackled like static electricity in the air surrounding them, each enjoying this moment of calm before the inevitable storm that was sure to follow. Brad broke the moment by getting out of the car and walking around to Lauren's side and opening the door. As she started to get out, he pulled her into his arms and kissed her fiercely. Their bodies pressed against each other and Brad was instantly aroused. Apart from his impromptu arousal at the minor injuries unit, he couldn't remember the last time he had had an erection, and it felt good. In fact, it felt a lot more than good as Lauren ground her hips into his hardness. Lauren was the first to break off, and taking control pushed him back and sank to her knees unzipping his trousers.

Sex with Lauren was without doubt the best he had had in a very long time, possibly ever. There had been little in the way of conversation, but still they managed to communicate their needs and desires to each other. Leaning through the driver's window when he dropped her off, Lauren kissed him passionately on the lips. "You are not like other men Brad; there's something different about you that I just can't put my finger on. Oh, and for the record, I've never done this kind of thing before," she said as she turned and walked away into the dark night. Returning home, Brad showered and went to bed. Gina was not home yet, and he was asleep before his head hit the designer pillows that she had insisted they *simply must have*.

Looks like a fucking pimp's palace! was his last thought before he fell blissfully asleep.

Chapter 10
Brad and Gina

Brad had been having more trouble than usual sleeping recently and he put this down to the stress of his job. This morning, however, he had woken early after a deep dreamless sleep and he felt good. In fact, he felt more than good, he felt amazing! He spooned Gina who was still asleep and facing away from him. He could feel his cock getting hard as he pressed himself against her. Gina only ever wore a t-shirt to bed, annoyingly usually his favourite t-shirt, but never any underwear. She stirred as Brad discarded his boxers and was instantly fully awake as he pushed himself into her from behind. Although surprised, Gina responded by grinding into him. Brad was oblivious to her needs and used her for his own pleasure. He was alive and felt amazing, better than he had ever felt.

They rarely sat down and ate breakfast together, but today was different. Gina made them both bacon sandwiches and Brad made the coffee which was as shit as always. Gina didn't care much for coffee and always bought cheap stuff and this morning Brad was acutely aware of just how bad it was. "That was a little unexpected," Gina said, between sips of coffee, "it's been a while since we last made love I know, but you seemed different."

"Different?"

"Yes, maybe it's just because it's been so long. I'm not being funny but…"

Here it comes! thought Brad.

"It's just that it seemed so, well, rough, like you were just using me. You are always so gentle and considerate when we make love. But you fucked me hard, without considering my needs, it wasn't like you at all. If I didn't know better, I would be suspicious! But it really turned me on, it made me feel sexy that you wanted me so urgently and just took what you wanted."

For the last year or so, their sex life had been all but non-existent as Brad had had difficulty in getting and maintaining an erection. It was starting to affect their marriage. He would avoid any situation that could lead to intimacy and would go to bed later than Gina and get up before her in the morning. On the odd occasion, they had made a conscious effort, it ended the same way, disappointing for both of them. Gina tried to be understanding, but she had needs too and Brad's lack of libido left her feeling frustrated and unattractive. She tried to hide her frustration but occasionally she took it out on him. She knew this didn't help him, as it only added to his performance anxiety, but she couldn't help herself.

The previous Saturday, it had been her best friend's hen night and matters had gotten a little out of hand. A lot of cocktails were consumed and Gina ended up having a one-night stand. It was a pretty tawdry affair. He was a builder, strong and muscular and had been paying her attention all evening. His van was parked nearby and the rest was inevitable. Although she was drunk, she knew precisely what she was doing and used him every bit as much as he used her that evening. She had given him her mobile number and was flattered by the passion in his texts and ended up seeing him again. In fact, last night Gina hadn't been working at all.

***

Brad's working day wore on pretty much the same as it always did. Except that his sales were considerably better. He put it down to the fact that he felt so good that nothing was going to get in his way. Brad's mobile rang, "Hello, Bradley White speaking."

"This is DC Pengelly calling about the incident you were involved in yesterday. You have to come to the police station before 5.00 pm today," the voice at the other end of the telephone commanded.

"I can be there at 4:30 pm," Brad replied.

"Report to the main desk and ask for me."

Brad was a punctual man and arrived at the police station five minutes ahead of the allotted time and reported to the front desk as instructed. Ten minutes later, DC Pengelly arrived and ushered him into an interview room. "It would seem that you have luck on your side, Mr White. The man that you assaulted yesterday regained consciousness and does not want to press charges. Did you threaten him Mr White, because I don't understand why anyone who took a beating like that wouldn't press charges?"

"No, I didn't threaten him. In fact, I was the one that was threatened by him."

"I just don't get it," DC Pengelly continued, "in your statement you claim to have acted in self-defence, but there isn't a mark on you and you half killed this man. You have no prior convictions for assault, but this was a savage attack. I don't consider you to be any kind of hero, if what you say is true, and if I had my way I would lock you up."

Brad sat there looking on, detached from any emotional involvement, barely even aware of the others presence. He could hear the sounds of the city outside the police station and the gentle hum of the air conditioning.

"Are you listening to me, Mr White? This is a serious matter and you don't seem to be showing any signs of remorse. Fortunately for you, he regained consciousness later yesterday and as I said he doesn't want to press charges and the witness statements are vague. So we can't charge you. I don't like your kind Mr White, and I can tell when something is not right."

"So are you going to charge me with something or not? Because if you are, get on with it. If not, I'm leaving. Either way I'm not going to sit here and take a lecture from you. Do you understand me, you judgemental piece of shit. You are an officer of the law and not the fucking law. I don't give a fuck what you think." The words came unbidden from his mouth in a low and menacing tone. Brad could hear the words and the malice they were soaked in, but felt no regret as he glared at the policeman. He could feel his muscles bunching, ready for action. Surely, he wasn't going to attack this man?

DC Trevor Pengelly reacted as most people do when insulted and stood up in anger to face down his aggressor. He didn't have to take this and had the full weight of his position to back him up. Before Brad could even think about what he was doing, he was on his feet and ready to attack. In the same strange detached way, he was certain that any aggressive movement from the policeman would provoke a violent reaction from him that he would not be able to prevent. "Don't fucking move." Brad hissed, as much for his benefit as for the policeman's.

Trevor Pengelly served in the army when he was younger and during this time had seen active service in various conflict zones around the world. Rumour had it that he had killed more than one enemy soldier in the defence of the realm, although Trevor never talked about this with anyone. He was always the first on the scene when a fellow police officer was in trouble, and was not a man to be easily scared. But today, he was afraid. There was something about this Bradley White that was very wrong. He couldn't quite put his finger on what it was, and outwardly White was nothing out of the ordinary.

The two men stood facing each other and time seemed to be standing still, as if it was an onlooker, waiting to see what would happen. Just then and only for the briefest of moments, Trevor saw what looked like zig-zagged, orangey-red coronas that hinted of a deadly power around the pupils of the man that stood before him. Trevor Pengelly instinctively knew that White was dangerous and capable of anything, and he found that fear had rendered him unable to move. On later reflection, it may have been a self-preservation instinct, because he was convinced that the slightest movement on his part would have provoked an attack from White. He stood motionless, save for the beads of perspiration that were gathering on his brow. His heart was beating rapidly and his fingertips were tingling. His legs felt like rubber and his vision became tunnelled as anxiety gripped him in its iron clasp. Long moments passed and slowly, after regaining some control of his trembling legs, he sat down.

Brad turned and walked out of the interview room without a backwards glance. DC Pengelly watched him go and said nothing.

As he walked back to his car, Bradley White was relieved that nothing had happened. He was, however, convinced that had the policeman laid hands on him, he would have attacked him, and he was equally certain that he would not have been able to stop himself. *What is happening to me?* This was totally out of character and he knew that it should concern him deeply, but it didn't. He reasoned that it wasn't, that he didn't give a fuck about other people and had suddenly turned into a callous thug. It was that starting with the van man confrontation, he now felt detached when in a conflict situation. His reaction seemed to be almost clinical in nature, that his body was ready to do whatever was needed to protect him, at any cost to the other. Yes, that was it. After considering what had happened during the confrontation with white van man, it seemed to Brad like his *flight or fight reflex* had changed into *fight until your opponent is incapable of fighting back*. But unlike the *flight or fight reflex* there was no adrenaline, just this odd detachment.

During the short drive home, Brad relived the events of the last two days. Something had definitely changed inside him and he was not entirely sure it was for the good. The way he had beaten van man and threatened the policeman were just not like him. Getting off with Lauren was the stuff of fantasies but had never been something he had ever come close to experiencing in his life before. Even his sales success of today was not something he was used to. But what bothered Brad the most was this mental disconnection, the detached feeling that took control of him during these events.

He pulled into his drive, still trying to work out what was wrong with him. The front door opened before he had even switched off his car's engine and Gina stood there, tightly wrapped in her bathrobe. She kissed him passionately and half pulled him into the hallway of their home. Stepping back, she opened her robe and let it fall to the ground. She was wearing a nurse's outfit. Not standard NHS issue, the outfit was so short the tops of her black fishnet hold-ups were clearly visible. It was tight and unbuttoned enough that Brad could see an indecent amount of cleavage. He kicked the door shut behind him as they kissed each other hard. Such was their need to satisfy their lust that they didn't make it to the bedroom and ended up rutting like animals, half-way up the stairs.

They eventually found their way to the bedroom and started again. This time more gently but every bit as intense. It was almost 8.00 pm, when both hungry, they drove to their local fast food outlet. Gina had her usual medium sized chicken strip meal, but Brad was ravenous and ordered two large burger meals. They went to a nearby beauty spot that overlooked the sea to eat their food.

It was a warm evening and still relatively light as they ate in silence. The only sounds were those of crickets and other insects in the nearby field. "I think you should make an appointment to go back and see Dave Rogers," Gina said, breaking the silence. Dave was Brad's doctor and Gina's previous employer.

"What makes you say that, Gina," Brad replied.

"I'm concerned that your blood pressure may have gone up again. It's great that you've got your libido back, more than great actually, but something's not right."

"I'm not quite with you, how do you mean?" Brad asked. Gina hated this expression of his.

"This is a little embarrassing, it's about your cock."

"My cock?" Brad retorted incredulously. Gina flushed.

"It felt bigger when you were inside me and I've never seen any cock as hard as yours has been today. Don't get too big-headed stud, you're no porn star but we should get this checked out, it could be a symptom of very high blood pressure."

"Embarrassing for you, Gina? What do I say to Dave, 'Hi Dave Gina wanted me to see you because my cock seems to be stiffer than normal.' If he doesn't piss himself laughing, I'm going to die of embarrassment on the spot!"

"Indulge me," responded Gina, "just go there and ask to have a blood pressure check, okay? And when did you last eat? I can't believe that you just ate two full size meals. You'll get fat, Bradley White!"

Brad did not sleep well that evening; his dreams were feverish and disjointed. He woke up several times in the night and each time his t-shirt was drenched in sweat.

Chapter 11
Greenhaven

Brad set the alarm clock to wake him up at 6.00 am on weekdays and it invariably did, as he was never awake before it went off. He had a five-minute snooze button which was always pressed the maximum three times. Brad was not his most energetic or enthusiastic first thing in the morning. Today, however, he had been awake for about an hour before his alarm rang. Surprisingly though, he felt wide awake and refreshed, although he dreaded to think just how little sleep he had actually had last night. *I'm going to feel it later today,* he thought. *Great and just in time for the fucking weekend.*

"Wakey wakey, Gina!" Brad said as he pressed himself against his wife from behind.

"Not again!" she sighed, more asleep than awake, but her actions belied her words as she ground into him.

Sometime later, Brad reached for his glasses. He always kept them in the same place; on his bedside cabinet, so that he could find them easily in the morning. He had been short sighted ever since he was thirteen and without his glasses, his world was indistinct and blurry. But this morning, everything was sharp and clear. Thinking that he must have put his glasses on without realising it, Brad nearly poked himself in the eye when he felt his face to check if he had them on, but he didn't. *Must be a trick of the light,* he thought as he stumbled out of bed and headed for the bathroom, leaving his glasses on the bedside cabinet.

He was shaving a little absently as he couldn't stop thinking about the impossibility of his vision suddenly returning to normal. It had been twenty minutes since he had first noticed the change and he was expecting to be returned to his blurry world at any moment, but it didn't happen. He was so distracted that it took him a while to notice that something wasn't quite right with his reflection in the mirror. It took a moment or two for him to realise what it was; his perfectly reflected image didn't have any grey hair. He stopped shaving and examined his hair, moving it first to one side and then the other, then scraping it back and forth. After a near manic examination, he couldn't find a single grey hair. *That's fucking bizarre,* he thought. *What the fuck is going on?*

"Gina, Gina, come quick, you've got to see this!"

Gina who was still in bed, called back, "Good try Brad, but don't you think I've seen enough of it for one day?"

"No, seriously Gina, something's wrong."

Gina got out of bed too quickly and fought a wave of dizziness as she rushed across the short landing to the bathroom.

"Look, can't you see?" Brad was jabbing his finger towards his head like an idiot as he paced the short landing, clearly agitated. The absurdity of the spectacle was not altogether lost on Gina. "What on earth is the matter with you Brad, and why are you pointing at your head like that?" It was all she could do to stop herself from laughing out loud.

"Can't you see my hair Gina, look at it!"

"Ah, I can see what you've done, you've dyed it!"

"No Gina I haven't, that's just it."

"Good one! Are you having me on, Bradley White?"

"No Gina. I woke up this morning and I can see perfectly without my glasses and now this. What the fuck is going on?"

Gina inspected Brad's hair closely. "It is strange. I've heard of people whose hair turned grey overnight, but I've never heard of grey hair disappearing overnight. Have you made that appointment with Dave Rogers yet?"

"No," replied Brad. "I wasn't going to because to be honest, I've never felt better."

"I really think that you should. I just want to be sure that all of this isn't a strange side effect of some illness or other."

"You are not making me feel any better, Gina!"

"I'm sorry Brad, but please indulge me and see Dave?"

"Okay, I guess a chat with Dave won't do any harm."

Brad was still preoccupied with this when he entered the shower cubicle. Showering was a simple joy that he never tired of. As he was washing with Gina's new shower gel, his had run out days ago, he noticed that his stomach felt different to his touch. It was usually soft, and he could definitely *pinch more than an inch of fat*, but not today. Today his stomach was hard and flat as he prodded it and it felt like he had a *six-pack*. Looking down he could see his cock, but even that was remarkable because his stomach normally got in the way. This was the first time he had seen his cock without sucking his stomach in, for five or more years. Then, he noticed his legs, his thigh muscles were a bit bigger and more defined than he remembered and gone too were the small varicose veins that had started to appear in recent years. Brad jumped out of the shower and ran into the bedroom, still naked and wet so that he could examine himself in the full-length mirror. He couldn't believe what he saw; it looked like he had lost about a stone and a half in weight, if not more, and his muscles were well defined as if he had been working out. He looked better than he done had in years.

He saw the reflection of his hand in the mirror and realised that he had forgotten to make an appointment to go back to the minor injuries unit to have it plastered. The bandage was dirty, so he unwound it and took it off. Discarding it onto the floor he flexed his hand. There was no pain and both the swelling and bruising had completely gone. It was as if his finger had never been broken in the first place. *This is impossible,* he thought, *bones can't mend that fast.*

When Brad finally left the house, he was running late. Normally, this would have caused him stress and anxiety and would most likely have ruined his whole day. Today he felt good, no better than good, today he felt terrific and he didn't give a fuck about anything else.

***

His day wore on pretty much as it had done yesterday. His sales were at record levels, and his newfound confidence seemed to be the reason. Mid-afternoon found Brad in one of the more remote areas that he covered. Most of his accounts were pretty central but he had the odd country practice that he looked after. He had had such a good day that even though it was barely after 3.00 pm, he was going to call it a day and go home. It had, after all, been a busy week!

His mind began to wander as he recalled the events of the last three days. In particular, he thought about the changes he had noticed in himself which were both physical and emotional.

There was no doubt that he had changed. He had not only regained his libido, he had more stamina and capacity for sex than he had ever had. Better still, his wife found him sexually attractive again. And never in his wildest dreams, would have hoped to bed a woman as young and attractive as Lauren.

His newfound detached confidence in the face of adversity however, was worrying; he had stood up to a thug and threatened a police officer. He didn't seem to have any control over the violence that appeared to follow if he was threatened or attacked. And the changes he had noticed this morning were also unbelievable; his grey hair had completely gone, he no longer needed glasses and his body had become toned overnight. "*What is happening to me?*

Brad was battling with this question when his attention was caught by a road sign that said, 'Greenhaven 3 Miles'. It was an out of the way place, that although only thirty miles or so from his home, he had not really noticed before. That is until a fortnight ago. For some reason, that day stood out in his mind, but he was having trouble remembering why it did.

He pulled up outside the corner shop he had visited on that last trip and went inside and bought a bottle of cola like before. Despite the rain, Brad decided that he would go back to the Chemist shop he had visited the last time he was in Greenhaven. He suddenly realised that he hadn't given his meeting with the strange Chemist a second thought, but he should have.

Fragments of the meeting came to him in rapid succession. Could the strange tablets he had been given be responsible for the changes he was experiencing? He couldn't remember taking them and must have done so without thinking about it. Why had he been so compliant: agreeing to take tablets that were new, unproven, and without knowing who they were made by or what they contained? He of all people should know better.

It was then that he remembered the black bands that had been placed on his wrists, or as he now recalled, the bands that he was forced to wear. There was no way that they could possibly be part of any treatment. So what on Earth were the bands doing to him and why couldn't he see them? He rubbed at his wrists, there wasn't the faintest of signs that they were there and yet somehow, for reasons he could not explain, he knew that the bands were still there, even though he couldn't see them. Brad had a lot of questions that needed answers urgently and he was certain that only the Chemist could provide them. At the thought of meeting the Chemist again he felt an involuntary shiver go through him. There was something very wrong about that man. And those eyes, Brad had never seen eyes like them.

He was still deep in thought when he arrived at the chemist shop. It was closed and looked like it had been abandoned years, or even decades ago. The large old fashioned pharmaceutical bottles in the shop window that were full of brightly coloured liquid before, were still there, but the liquid had faded to an unattractive brown colour and the bottles themselves were covered in cobwebs and a thick layer of dust. This was impossible, how could the chemist shop have become so run down in only two weeks? Believing that maybe there was another chemist in the village, and he was looking in the wrong place, Brad walked from one end of the village to the other, checking out the myriad of side streets and even the back alleys as he did so.

It was raining, and he was soaked through and growing increasingly angry. He went back to the corner shop and asked the assistant for directions to the chemist as his sodden garments dripped onto the wooden flooring. "There's no chemist in this village," came the reply.

"You must be mistaken; I was here two weeks ago and went to a chemist just over there." Brad pointed over his shoulder.

"I've lived in this village for over fifteen years," the shop assistant retorted, "and in all that time the chemist shop you are pointing to has been abandoned."

"Is there a chemist in the next village on the road to Stokingley?" Brad asked, thinking that maybe there were two very similar villages close to each other. Yes, that was it, he must have confused the two.

"Phah, do you mean Lower Greenhaven? Because if you do, that village is so small it barely qualifies to have its own village idiot! There's no chemist or much of anything there." Brad glared at the shop assistant. "Is there anything else you want?" she asked.

"No," he replied flatly as he walked out of the shop.

Brad retraced his steps. He recognised every detail from before; in fact, his recollection was as clear as a photograph in his mind. *This is definitely the right place,* he thought, *so where is the fucking chemist?* He trudged back towards his car, trying to make sense of it all when he noticed an old man who was hunched over, and unsteady on his feet, shuffling towards him. As they drew level with each other, the old man stumbled and fell without warning. Instinctively, Brad grabbed him by the arm to prevent him from falling to the pavement. Seemingly to steady himself, the old man grabbed Brad by the wrists. His grip was impossibly strong and icy cold, *just like...no it couldn't be, could it? Was it the Chemist?* Their eyes met and Brad was transfixed by the zig-zagged, orangey-red coronas around his jet black pupils. He tried to break away but found that he could not, he couldn't even open his mouth to speak. He was paralysed.

The old man smiled humourlessly and Brad felt a sensation like an electric shock in both of his wrists where the icy grip held him fast. The pain was excruciating. Within a matter of seconds, it spread up his forearms and then through his entire body. The pain was accompanied by a sound like the crackle of static electricity and the zig-zagged, orangey-red coronas of the old man's eyes pulsed in time to a silent rhythm. The pain was so intense that Brad thought he would die. His vision started to mist over and fade, and everything was becoming distant, apart from the pain which was very real and very present. Just as he was about to pass out, the old man released his grip and hit Brad hard in the centre of his forehead with the palm of his hand. Brad's world erupted as a blinding white light ignited his vision. It became brighter and brighter, and pulsed with the intensity of a thousand laser beams. Vertigo swept through him and the last sound he heard as the light went out and darkness engulfed him utterly, was the old man's voice as he whispered, "Awaken!"

Chapter 12
The Destiny of Zoryn

Sanjin Dakor knew that his brother had a dark side to his personality. In fact, everyone who had ever met Zoryn quickly found this out for themselves. There were strong hints of it even as far back as his early childhood. Zoryn was a spiteful child who showed a total disregard for others. He grew into a moody aggressive teenager and then into a vicious young man with no compassion or respect for his peers. Because of this Zoryn stood apart from others and was feared and avoided whenever possible. It was hoped that Zoryn would grow out of this behaviour. But he didn't, and the Council of Elders felt it unlikely that he could ever be allowed to lead the peoples of the Five Lands.

Zoryn Dakor despised his brother Sanjin who was the first-born and was groomed to be the King of the Five Lands from birth. Sanjin was strong, intelligent and respected by everyone. Everyone that is, except his sibling.

From as far back as he could remember, Zoryn knew that he should be the King of the Five Lands. He believed that the kingdom had become bloated and lazy as a direct result of the past decades of peace and had become weakened as a result of it. Under his leadership, the size of the military would be massively increased. No longer would it be a defensive force, it was time that the military became much more. He developed secret plans to invade their nearest neighbour Kazendia whose mines were rich with mineral and metal deposits. This would make a fine prize and would massively increase the wealth and power of the Five Lands. Kazendia, however, was heavily protected and its fighting force was renowned for its military prowess, but Zoryn felt the risk was worth taking. He wanted to build a kingdom, the like of which had never been seen before.

Zoryn became aware of the existence of Black Metal by chance, or to his way of thinking, by destiny. His frustration in being next in line to the throne, but probably never to lead the Five Lands, slowly ate away at him. By the age of twenty-five, Zoryn felt like he couldn't take any more and had to do something. He believed that he was destined for greatness and that he would rule the Five Lands and beyond. All would acknowledge him for who he really was, and men would bend their knee and swear allegiance to him. Of this he never had any doubt.

Zoryn was training with an Arch Mage from the Eastern Realm, Draxan Longseer, in the central training ground of the Great Citadel. The Mages were warrior magicians from the Dyroshin, a secretive race of people the men of who devoted their lives to the art of magical fighting. The training went well and Draxan was impressed with the abilities of his student. As they were leaving the training ground, he turned to address Zoryn. "This is the second time that we have trained together and each time you have fought with a fury that I have only ever witnessed in battle. There is a lot of frustration and pent-up aggression in you." His voice deep and heavily accented. "This is not a criticism; your fighting spirit is impressive, but your frustration is holding you back from being the fighter you were born to be."

Zoryn was not used to being criticised so openly and looked the Arch Mage deep in the eyes. "You are right," he responded finally. "Politics and an accident of birth have thus far denied me of the right to rule these lands. To say I am frustrated is a fucking understatement." The years of frustration were reflected in his tonality as he spat the words out.

"Then you need to find your purpose, young master."

"I have a fucking purpose."

"Do you really? Or are you just hoping and waiting? That would frustrate me too if I was in your position and all I did was wait."

"You are in danger of going too far with this, mage. Do you forget so easily who you are addressing?" Zoryn's eyes narrowed menacingly.

"I do not mean any offence. I am paid to train you, to make you the best fighter that I can, but if you have an inner conflict that prevents this, I would be failing in my duty to you and the Five Lands if I did not bring this to your attention."

"So what exactly are you saying?"

"There is a place in the Krendyran Mountains called the Lake of Visions. Have you heard of it?"

Zoryn had heard of the mythical lake but had discounted the stories as rumour and fantasy. Legend had it that the Renshaw Mine was not the only source of the magical White Metal. It was thought by some that it was more plentiful and that there were deposits, deeper underground in other locations. The water in the Lake of Visions was believed to come from a spring deep underground at the source of the magical ore and had become suffused with its power.

"Yes, I've heard the tales," Zoryn replied.

"It is said that the lake only responds to those that destiny has called upon. If you are correct in your assertion, then the lake will reveal the way to you."

"You really think that I should travel all the way to the Krendyran Mountains to bathe in a lake that probably doesn't exist and wait for my destiny to be revealed to me?" Zoryn's tone was mocking.

"I most assuredly do, young master."

"And what makes you so fucking sure that I will agree to such nonsense?"

"Because I have bathed in the lake and that is why I was compelled to come here to train you. It's time for change Lord Zoryn, and you will be at the centre of it."

***

Several months passed and during this time, the words of Draxan Longseer kept replaying themselves in Zoryn's mind. He decided that he would make the journey to the Lake of Visions and find out, once and for all, if there was any truth in what he had been told. He had not seen Longseer again during this time, but oddly the night before he intended to set off, the man appeared from the shadows across the other side of the training ground and walked towards him. "So, you have decided to bathe in the Lake of Visions, young Master?" Draxan said as he approached Zoryn.

"How the fuck do you know that?" Came the reply.

"Destiny has made me your guide. I would be a poor guide if I did not arrive at the appointed time. Meet me outside the main keep at first light tomorrow." Draxan turned and walked away without waiting for Zoryn's reply.

***

The journey took four weeks and passed largely without incident except when a group of five men thought they would steal Zoryn and Draxan's horses and kill their owners. Zoryn cut the first man to the ground with his broadsword before the man knew what had happened. Two of the others tried to rush him, attacking wildly as they charged forward. Zoryn held his ground and parried the first man's attack and he slammed into his partner as his strike was deflected. Without pausing, Zoryn brought his shorter sword to bear and thrust his blade between the man's ribs, piercing his heart. Ducking to avoid a wild slash from the other man's sword, Zoryn countered with a slash of his own broadsword, slicing the man through his midsection and badly cutting his assailant's sword arm in the process. Bringing his own sword back up, Zoryn finished the man with a two handed downwards thrust with the point of his sword. The man's life ended where he stood.

Draxan Longseer was confronted by the other two men. The first man held a small throwing dagger in each hand and threw one with deadly accuracy at the Arch Mage's chest. Inches from its intended target, the knife hit an invisible barrier and fell to the ground where it glowed brightly and then burst into flames. The man that had thrown the knife stared slack jawed at the burning blade. His momentary distraction was to be his downfall. Still some distance away, Draxan punched at the air in front of him with his right fist. His would-be assailant reacted as if he had been punched in the chest. Such was the force of the strike that he was thrown back several feet and landed hard on his back, the wind completely knocked out of him. Draxan Longseer chanted and a ball of what looked like lightning, appeared between his hands which he held close to his chest. With a shout from him, the ball shot towards his fallen adversary with tremendous force and engulfed his body in lightning-like flames as it burnt him to death in an instant.

The remaining attacker managed to get behind Draxan and thrust his dagger with all his might between his victim's shoulder blades. The knife was stopped by the same invisible shield his partner's throwing knife had struck earlier. The shock of the impact travelled up the man's arms and he dropped the blade, doubling over and clutching his shattered arm. The last thing he saw was Zoryn's blade, as it burst through his stomach from a savage thrust right through his body from behind. Zoryn kicked the man in the back as he pulled out the blade, leaving his opponents lifeless corpse to collapse to the ground.

As luck would have it, the men must have been more successful with other unsuspecting travellers as they had five horses tethered to some trees in a small copse, a few hundred feet away. The horses were well fed and much fresher than those belonging to Zoryn and Draxan, so they took them and set their own horses free as they continued on their journey.

***

This was the first time that Zoryn had been to the Lake of Visions. He had heard the stories as had most people, but he never really believed that such a place existed. Nobody he knew, or had heard of, had been there, and expeditions that set out to find it were always unsuccessful. And yet here he was at the crest of a hollow that looked as if it had been carved out of the mountains by the hands of a giant, gazing down on a lake with water that was blacker than his own heart.

When they first crested the hollow, the lake was not visible. Draxan Longseer chanted in a language that Zoryn didn't recognise and as he did so the waters of the lake were revealed to their sight. Tendrils of mist hung suspended over the lake and looked like they had come from its unfathomable depths. It was an eerie sight.

The hollow was nestled about three quarters of the way from the summit of one of the mountains of the Krendyrans. It was enormous and was one of many that made up the range. For the most part, it was devoid of vegetation apart from thorny bracken that grew to waist height and tore at the traveller's clothing and any exposed skin as they forged their way through it. There were a few paths up the mountain, which although quite steep, could be traversed by foot. The paths were animal trails used by the hardiest of small game that were able to survive on the meagre nutrition provided by the bracken. The temperature was much lower this high up the mountainside, and the presence of low-level clouds with their accompanying mist enveloped the place in a preternatural gloom.

So well hidden was the lake, that it would be impossible to locate unless you had been there before. Zoryn was beginning to believe that maybe the Arch Mage Draxan had been here before and had been telling the truth. "So, what happens now?" Zoryn asked Draxan, who stood beside him.

"Now young master, you discover your destiny," Draxan said as he began the short descent to the lake. He didn't look to see if Zoryn was following him. For the first time in his life, Zoryn followed another without question.

Standing by the lakeside, the first thing that struck Zoryn was the utter silence of the place. Although it was getting late in the day, there had been birdsong as the travellers climbed their way up the mountainside. But now there was silence, a thick cloying silence that permeated everything around them. The sense of expectation was intense, it was as if the very mountain itself was holding its breath, waiting for something to happen.

Zoryn walked over to the edge of the lake and stood transfixed. The water was black. Where there should have been reflections, there was nothing; the lake absorbed everything that touched it. "Be aware of this, Lord Zoryn," Draxan began, "the visions are representations, of what might, or might not become reality. You cannot force the lake to show you what you want to see, it is capricious by nature and will reveal what it will." Zoryn nodded in response.

"You must not enter the lake until you see the sign, young master. If you do and the lake rejects you, the shock to your body will kill you."

Zoryn heard the words, but they did not register. The lake held his attention as surely as it held anything else that came too close to it. He felt compelled to enter the water to become one with it. The hypnotic siren call of the lake played across his senses and before he realised what he was doing, Zoryn discarded his clothes and launched himself into the lake.

The shock of the ice-cold water brought Zoryn back to his senses with a jolt. He tried to scramble back to the edge of the lake, but despite his every effort, he remained exactly where he was in the water, unable to get any closer. Reaching down with his feet, he tried to touch the bottom of the lake, in an effort to walk out. He could not feel any ground beneath his feet and strangely could not sink below the surface to test the depth of the water, despite several attempts. It was then that he felt a strange calmness which seemed to come from outside of his body. With it came warmth as it wrapped itself around him, enveloping him completely in its soothing balm. Zoryn felt an overwhelming urge to lie back in the water, and as he did so, the first vision came to him in the instant he closed his eyes.

Zoryn could see himself riding through the courtyard of the Great Keep in Gaardsholme on a powerful jet-black warhorse. It was a warm, sunny day and he felt good, no not good, he felt victorious, triumphant even. He could see around him and feel everything even though he was an observer, detached from the actual events. It was a strange sensation. His brother's wife, Kaiya, was riding by his side on her dapple mare looking beautiful and regal. Flanking either side of the courtyard were men that were loyal to him. They were wearing full battle dress and his personal insignia of the snarling black wolf's head. It was clear from the appearance of the men, many of whom were injured, that they had just come from a battle. This, however, was a victory parade and his men were paying homage to him, Zoryn Dakor, their new King. As Zoryn reached the centre of the courtyard, he saw himself dismount from the horse. Terryn, High Lord of the Council of Lords, approached him and fell to one knee, his eyes cast downward as he offered up a great broadsword to Zoryn. "My Liege," Terryn said, as he raised the ceremonial sword of command to Zoryn, "by the time-honoured right of succession, I proclaim you the King of the Five Lands. According to the authority vested in me as the leader of the Council of Lords, I pledge the allegiance of the Council to your rule."

Zoryn took the sword. It felt good and right in his hands.

"How quickly your allegiances change." Zoryn glared at the other with open disgust in his eyes as he spat the words, "You are, however, correct about one thing; I will have your fealty."

"My Lord!" Terryn began to protest.

Zoryn smiled as he watched the vision of himself hit the man hard with a back handed slap to the face, knocking him off his knees and into the dirt.

"Get this man out of my sight," the vision of Zoryn commanded.

The vision faded and was quickly replaced by another. Zoryn saw an old man and Kaiya in a place that he did not recognise, but on some instinctive level he knew that it was not his world. The old man didn't look like him, but he knew that it was. He could see himself on his knees looking exhausted and Kaiya was beside him with her slender arms around him. "Are you sure about this one, Zoryn?" Kaiya knew that it was dangerous even for her, to question Zoryn's decisions. His back was turned to her as she asked the question, but he spun around to face her with an almost supernatural speed that belied his apparent age. The orangey-red, zig-zagged corona's surrounding his midnight black eyes pulsed to the beat of his barely contained rage. He stared at her for a moment longer before replying.

"I have made this weakling kill another for that which he holds dear. I will fashion him into my weapon and he will do as he is commanded. The time is approaching for us to leave this accursed place and make ready for the return to our land to claim what is rightfully ours." He turned his face to the sky and in a voice rumbling with distant thunder said, "Enjoy your last few weeks of life Sanjin my brother, and then witness all that you hold true fall."

In the next vision, the image of Zoryn was sat at a table with another man. He could see himself clearly, but the other's back was turned to him and he could not see his face. However, as he started to talk, the man's voice was familiar to Zoryn, but he couldn't quite place it. "So, you can supply me with this Black Metal that you talk about?" The vision of Zoryn asked.

"Yes, I can young master, but the price is high."

"What is your price?"

"For my people, I want independence from the tyranny of the reign of the Five Lands."

"And for you…what is it exactly that you want?"

"Ten million gold when you become king and a share of the spoils when you expand your kingdom."

"That is indeed a high price," the vision of Zoryn sneered, "so why should I agree to your outrageous terms?"

"You understand the power of White Metal and why it is so highly treasured. Black Metal is a far more destructive and dreadful power. Whereas White Metal is well known for its positive and constructive powers, Black Metal will tear down and destroy, laying waste to all that stands in its way. Such is its power that even a novice magic wielder equipped with Black Metal, will defeat all but the most experienced and powerful magician. Just a small amount enhances the body's healing and recuperative powers and makes the individual stronger and more powerful. I believe that it can also be used to open portals between worlds."

"What do you mean by other worlds?" Zoryn asked incredulously.

"Lord Zoryn, there are many worlds other than our own. Some are primitive compared to ours, but many are much more advanced. The opportunities to conquer and plunder, for one so inclined, are almost limitless."

"And why would you want my help to do that? Why can't you do it for yourself?" Zoryn asked.

"My people have no interest or desire to conquer and grow mighty. They are content with what they have."

"But you are not?"

"No, I'm not content to live this way anymore. I used to be, but I have a hunger deep inside me that cannot be satisfied by the way that my people would have me live. I am happy for them and want them to live as they wish. But for me, I want more, much more."

"So why turn to me?" Zoryn demanded.

"I have been following your progress for a long time. You are not like others from your nation. I see in you an appetite for power that is even greater than my own. You are ruthless, a man that will stop at nothing to get what you want. You were born to lead, and men will follow you even if it costs them their lives. But most of all, you have the legitimacy of the Dakor blood that runs through your veins. With your help, I can take control of the lands of my people and all others in the Eastern Realm. With you as King and me as their leader, maybe I can wake my people from their apathetic slumber."

"And how do you know this?"

"It has been revealed to me in a vision, Lord Zoryn." The man said this as he stood and turned away from the vision of Zoryn who still sat at the table. The image of Draxan Longseer looked up, and as if he could see Zoryn through the veil of the vision, asked in his thickly accented voice, "Do we have an agreement, Lord Zoryn?"

The icy cold of the water returned in an instant, bringing Zoryn back to his senses. This time he could move and quickly scrambled back to the shore of the lake.

"You…!" Zoryn said, as he pulled himself up to face Draxan. "It was you."

"Yes, Lord Zoryn it was me," Draxan replied softly.

Vertigo overcame Zoryn as his world went black and Draxan caught him as he fell.

Chapter 13
Zoryn and Kaiya

Kaiya had never found Zoryn more attractive. Physically, he looked like his brother, Sanjin Dakor the King of the Five Lands, but that's where the similarity ended. Sanjin was a hard man but fair in his dealings with others. Zoryn was not. His violent temper and viciousness was only tolerated because he was the King's brother. In another person, the magistrates would have denied him of his liberty, or worse, many years ago. Those that voiced concerns over Zoryn's behaviour seemed to either disappear or meet an unexpected fate. Everyone feared Zoryn Dakor, but it was this cruel side to his nature that attracted Kaiya to him. Whenever they met in secret, their lovemaking was feral, like two wild animals rutting. Zoryn didn't have any concept of the subtleties of sensual love, or if he did he didn't care. He just took what he wanted. For a strong woman who had easily controlled her previous lovers, the abandonment to Zoryn's total domination was like a drug to her and she had become addicted.

They had been in this place now for three weeks and it had been an interesting experience. In their world, magic although tightly controlled by the state, was used extensively for providing luxuries for the affluent and for more basic needs, like healing the sick and injured. Some individuals had innate magical abilities, which ran in their families. Others could only access magic through direct contact with White Metal which was very expensive and licensed by sheriffs directly appointed by Sanjin Dakor. There was, of course, a black market in White Metal, but more often than not, its quality was inferior or it had been depleted to the point of having little value.

Zoryn had innate magic. He was an empath but not like others with the same gift. Whereas most empaths became healers, or councillors, Zoryn used his abilities against people. He wasn't a mind-reader, but he could predict with uncanny accuracy how his opponent would react in a fight, and he always won. He was also able to project fear into the hearts of those that opposed him, and many battles were won without Zoryn needing to raise his sword. However, when he did he showed no quarter to his enemies which added to his reputation for viciousness.

Kaiya did not have any innate magical ability but didn't need it. She was sharp, quick-witted and totally amoral. Like Zoryn, she could read others, but the qualities that she drew on were those gained over years of experience of dealing with and deceiving people. Kaiya may not have killed and maimed her opponents in the same way that Zoryn did, but she was equally as dangerous in her own way. She also had the patience to wait for the right time to strike at her enemies, never directly, always through a proxy but with razor sharp accuracy. Kaiya knew, from as far back as she could remember, that she would rule the Five Lands and her life up to this point had been building towards that truth. She could not tell the future and had never seen any point in trying to locate the fabled Lake of Visions to see what the future held for her, but somehow she had always known.

The world Zoryn had transported them to was different to their own. There was no magic here. In its place the people had built strange devices to do the things that magic did back in their world. Many of the devices amused Kaiya, in particular those that were used for cleaning and other domestic matters. She couldn't understand why anyone would want to make the life of servants, whose job it was to attend to such matters, easier. It just didn't make any sense to her. Transport, however, was another matter altogether. She marvelled at the carriages called cars that seemed to be used by everyone in this strange place to travel vast distances with amazing speed. Her world had nothing close to this.

When they first arrived, and she finally accepted that they had indeed travelled an incalculable distance from Zendyros, Kaiya thought that Zoryn would transport them back straightaway, but he did not. Instead, he said that they would stay there for a few days. In part to let any disturbance caused by their disappearance to settle, and also because he was convinced that this was a world that he could conquer. Even Zoryn wasn't so egotistical to believe that he could do it alone, although with his command of the power of the Black Metal he doubted that there was anyone in this world that could possibly stand against him. He would need an army to conquer this place.

Zoryn told Kaiya little of his plans to seize control of the Five Lands from her husband, Sanjin Dakor the King. But she knew him well enough to know that he must have a plan. They had been on this world for two weeks and Zoryn had spent every day gathering intelligence about this strange place. The first couple of days were spent finding somewhere where they could sleep at night and would become their base. Their clothing marked them as different and they stood out. Kaiya was the King's wife and wore garments of the finest silks and other rare and exotic materials. On the evening of her translocation, she was wearing a pale lilac gown that was drawn in around her tiny waist. Zoryn had been in a coma and wore only a loose-fitting cotton gown. The inhabitants of this world wore clothing that Kaiya could only describe as drab. When they walked into the first small village they encountered, the oddly dressed couple were the subject of much curiosity, with people openly staring at them.

As they approached an alleyway, away from the main road, two young men looked over at them from the other side of the road.

"What happened, mate?" one of them called over. "Have you just escaped from the mental hospital?" Both men laughed and walked towards Zoryn and Kaiya. Zoryn stopped as both men approached, and Kaiya took a step back giving her lover plenty of room, knowing only too well what was coming next.

"We don't want nutters like you in our village." The taller of the two jeered, as he stopped in front of Zoryn, who for his part looked down at the ground and said nothing.

"Looks like this twat can't talk either," the other man said as he also drew nearer. "Let's have some fun with this guy and then her."

"Well twat, what have you got to say for yourself, you fucking nutter?" The first man was inches from Zoryn's down-turned head as he shouted. It was the last thing he would ever say.

Zoryn lifted his head up and stood a full foot or more taller than his would be attacker. He smiled at the man, but there was no hint of humour in the smile which dripped with malice. The man stared in open astonishment and shock as he looked into Zoryn's eyes. The zig-zagged, orangey-red coronas around his unnatural eyes pulsated and screamed of savagery and intent. With almost supernatural speed, Zoryn hit his assailant with a straight punch to the solar plexus. The man doubled over in excruciating pain, his arms folded across his body in a vain attempt to block a further strike. Zoryn didn't hesitate and grabbed the man by his hair, lifting him up slightly and to the side as he smashed his right knee into his temple with bone-crushing brutality. The man's eyes rolled back into his skull as he fell to the ground lifeless.

The other man's view of the attack had been partly obscured by his friend's back. But seeing his friend on the ground unmoving, the second attacker realised that he was in trouble. In an effort to save himself, he launched his own desperate attack, swinging a wild haymaker punch with his right fist at Zoryn's head with every ounce of strength he could muster. The second attacker was taller and broader of chest than his accomplice and the force and speed of the punch would have stopped a bull in its tracks. Zoryn stood his ground, and at the last moment, and with breathtaking speed, blocked the punch with his left arm. Before the man could retract his arm and launch another attack, Zoryn moved his arm in an outwards arc, trapping his attacker's fist and arm in a straight-arm bar. Instead of exerting pressure to force his opponent to yield, Zoryn slammed his upturned palm into the man's arm from underneath, dislocating his shoulder and shredding ligaments with the force of the blow. The man would have screamed in pain and fear had Zoryn not stepped forward in that instant and smashed the man's jaw with a savage right elbow uppercut to his chin. Such was the savagery of Zoryn's blow that it fractured the man's skull, and he was dead before he too fell to the ground.

"Now that you've had your fun," Kaiya whispered to her lover, "I think you should drag their bodies into this alley out of the way, before we draw any more attention to ourselves."

Zoryn said nothing as he dragged the lifeless bodies into the alley. Both men were smaller than Zoryn and their clothes would have been of little use to him, but he searched the bodies anyway and found purses of a strange textile, that contained an assortment of coins and what he assumed was paper-based currency.

If anyone had witnessed the attack, there was no sign of it and Zoryn and Kaiya quickly slipped into the shadows of the alleyway that were forming as night came.

They spent that evening taking shelter in a small shed that was full of hand held agricultural tools. The shed was at the bottom of an unkempt garden at the back of a property that unlike all those around it, did not have any lights on. It was strange to Zoryn that night fell a good deal slower in this world. In his world, twilight lasted for a matter of no more than a few minutes, whereas here it had already lasted much longer, and it was still nowhere near full darkness. Zoryn quickly cleared a space for them and was pleased to find a pair of wicker chairs. They were far from comfortable, but the shed was for the most part dry, and gave them somewhere to rest away from the prying gazes and unwanted attention of others.

The next morning, Zoryn ventured to the back door of the dwelling. It was locked and refused to yield despite the considerable force that he exerted in his effort to prize it open. For the first time since he had arrived in this land, Zoryn summoned the magic of the Black Metal. He was confident that he could, even here where magic did not exist, so confident was he of the magic that was now a part of his very being. The magic came to him quickly and easily. If anything, the biggest problem that he faced was containing its might. It felt like trying to restrain a colt that refused to be harnessed. By sheer strength of will, Zoryn directed his magic into a small ball which floated above the palm of his hand briefly before he sent it slamming into the locking mechanism. So focused was the bolt of magic that it destroyed the lock with barely a sound and made little damage to the door itself. Zoryn entered the property and after several long minutes, he emerged and beckoned Kaiya to join him. Inside the property looked like it had probably not been inhabited for some time as a layer of dust covered everything.

After a brief walk around and seeing that the property had indeed been abandoned, Zoryn and Kaiya made it their base.

At the front of the property was a large glass window behind which sat two large bottles of a brownish liquid on a recessed shelf. It was clear that this was the premises of a merchant and after a closer inspection of the many shelves and cabinets, Zoryn was certain that the merchant was a dealer in pills and potions. Such merchants plied their trade in his world and catered for those who could not afford a magical healer. He doubted the efficacy of such potions, but in a world such as this, where he couldn't feel the presence of any magic, he guessed that it was all that they had. Something that surprised Zoryn was that he could understand what the pills and potions were for, even though he couldn't read the markings on them as they were written in an alien language that consisted of strange symbols. He mentioned this to Kaiya but all she saw were the odd markings and couldn't interpret their meaning. Zoryn believed that his ability to understand came directly from the magic of the Black Metal.

There was living accommodation above the store, consisting of a small room that had a bed and some furniture in it, a larger room with more comfortable furniture, and a room that was similar to one of the royal bathrooms in the palace at Gaardsholme. It was much smaller but contained strange pumps that dispensed a seemingly endless supply of water. On a table in the larger room, there was a striking picture of an elderly man and woman. What was so remarkable about the picture, to both Zoryn and Kaiya, was how lifelike it appeared. The artist that painted it had made every detail appear real, and there wasn't a single brushstroke to be seen on its shiny surface. In a chest of drawers in the bedroom, Zoryn found some clothes that he managed to get into. They were a little on the small side but infinitely better than the loose-fitting cotton gown he had been wearing since he entered this world.

Zoryn had only used the magic of the Black Metal, whether intentionally or otherwise, for destructive purposes, but he instinctively knew that it was capable of much more. While Kaiya explored the rest of the property, he picked up the picture. Imprinting the image of the old man into his mind, Zoryn closed his eyes. He slowed his breathing and concentrated, willing the image to take shape over his own features. A warm feeling formed in the pit of his stomach and radiated outwards until his whole body was immersed in its warmth. It lasted a few moments and then it was gone. Zoryn knew that his appearance had changed even though he didn't feel any different. Kaiya called to him from the ground floor of the property, saying something about an object that she had found. She looked up as Zoryn entered the room and was so startled by what she saw that she dropped the ornately decorated vase she had been holding. It fell to the floor and shattered into thousands of pieces. With the agility of one used to the subtle art of knife-fighting, Kaiya pulled a blade that was strapped to her thigh and launched an attack at the man as she shouted for Zoryn. Her opponent moved with a speed that belied his years and swatted the knife from her hand. He then stepped back and laughed.

"You call for your lover and yet you try to kill him!" The voice was Zoryn's.

"What enchantment is this?" Kaiya demanded. "What have you done to him?"

"Do you not recognise the man who stands before you, proud Kaiya?" The amusement in his tone was not reflected in his eyes which were aflame with a terrible orangey-red fire.

"Zoryn, what has become of you?"

"This, Kaiya, will be my disguise for the duration of our stay here. The bodies of the men that attacked us yesterday will have been found by now, and I am sure that whatever serves for law in this place will already be hunting for the two strangers."

"Can you revert back to your own form?"

"Anytime I want to. Does this body displease you?" he asked mockingly.

"Ask me again after," Kaiya replied as she approached her lover, not attacking like before but every bit as dangerous.

Chapter 14
Sarah

"Are you okay?" It was a concerned female voice that sounded like it came from a long way away. Brad opened his eyes. He was sodden wet, laying face down on the pavement. Pulling himself part-way up onto his knees, his head felt like it was about to explode.

"What happened?" he croaked.

"I saw it all," came the reply. "You were walking down the road and then you slipped and fell down. I don't know if you hit your head, it happened so fast. Here, let me take a look at you," she said as she helped him to his feet and examined his head.

He could not remember falling. His last memory was of trying to find the chemist shop. The woman studied him and said that she had some training as a first aider. Brad felt dizzy weak and nauseous, but somehow managed to reassure the woman that he was okay. She was smartly dressed and must have been in her early thirties and Brad couldn't help but notice that she was very attractive. She was little over five foot with slender limbs and soft brown shoulder-length hair; her eyes were so brown that they were almost black, and she exuded self-confidence. "You seem okay, but that was a nasty fall and you are soaking wet. I only live down the road. Come with me and I'll make you a hot drink and get you dried out."

"Thanks, I could really do with that!" The woman helped him to his feet and led him a short distance down the street and stopped outside the abandoned chemist shop.

"Do you know anything about this shop?" Brad asked her as he peered through the dirty glass of the shop front, trying to see into its dim interior.

"Not really," she replied. "The owner is a very private man and is not the easiest person to engage in conversation."

"It's just that I was here a couple of weeks back and the chemist shop was open, I'm sure of it. But looking at it now it looks like it must have been abandoned decades ago."

"Oh dear! You really did take a nasty fall back there and may even have a concussion," the smartly dressed woman said as she put her key in a door to the side of the shop frontage. "Come in, let's get you patched up."

Once inside, she took his arm as they ascended a short flight of stairs to a flat above the shop. Brad was still very shaken and needed the help but also welcomed her closeness. She sat him down at a table in the kitchen and took off her coat. She was wearing a white blouse and a tight short black skirt. Brad found it difficult to concentrate as she led him to the bathroom. She suggested that he take his clothes off for her to dry them while he warmed up in the shower. She left the bathroom to give Brad some privacy and asked him to call out when he was in the shower and she would come in and get his clothes and leave her husband's dressing gown for him to wear. The hot shower felt good and Brad took his time.

Refreshed and feeling much better, he joined his rescuer in the kitchen and was greeted by the smell of a sweet hot drink that he couldn't quite place. "Here, try this," she said as she handed him a steaming cup of the sweet-smelling liquid. She beckoned for him to sit at a large breakfast table in the centre of the room. His hands were still shaking as he took the cup.

"It tastes lovely," he said after taking a sip of the brown liquid. "I've never had it before, what is it?"

"It's called draema and I would be surprised if you had tried it before! It comes from a land, a long way from this place. It's said to have restorative powers, so you should feel like new in no time!"

With each sip he took, Brad could feel his strength returning, just as she said it would. It tasted amazing too and he soon drained his cup and put it on the table in front of him, his hand now steady. All thoughts of his encounter with the Chemist somehow seemed a little less important. "It was worth falling down just for this amazing draema, or whatever it is you call it," he said.

"And is that all?" she asked as she came around to his side of the table to top up his cup.

"And for meeting you," Brad replied as he grabbed her by the waist. Pulling her to him, he kissed her full on the mouth. She broke away and taking his hand in hers, led him to her bedroom.

Kaiya Dakor had made the draema stronger than was needed to restore his strength. In higher concentrations, it had a sedating effect and she had calculated the dose at the right level to ensure that he would fall asleep. She made certain that their lovemaking ended quickly so that he would relax and the draema would do its work. Brad fell asleep as expected and she went through his pockets until she located his wallet. The Chemist stood beside her and examined the contents of the wallet. "I believe this to be the address of the place where he lives," the Chemist said, "you have done well, Kaiya. I will go there and find out more about this man so that we can be assured of his compliance."

Brad woke up to see that the woman he had met for the first time a few hours ago was already dressed and was laying his freshly dried clothes on the bottom of the bed. He was captivated by the woman's eyes. They were dark-brown, almost black and were mesmerising. She laughed and the moment was gone. "Well, that's a first for me!" she said. "I've never picked a guy up in the village where I live before, talk about too close to home for comfort!"

"I guess I should take that as a compliment!"

She ignored him and continued, "Look, I know that we've only just met and it's pretty obvious that we are both married, but my husband is away on business for a few days and I wondered if you wanted to meet up again tonight and get better acquainted?"

"My wife is picking our son up from university tonight and is staying at his place, so it would appear that I am also free!"

"Good," she said. "Pick me up outside at 8.00 pm. We can go for a drink and stay at the motel just outside town; it's less complicated that way." Brad nodded his agreement.

Driving home he felt conflicted; he couldn't wait to see the woman whose name he realised he didn't even know again that evening, but the whole Chemist thing was deeply disturbing. The tablets he had been given by the man had only lasted for a few days and by all accounts, even though he couldn't remember taking them, any toxins they may have contained should have flushed out of his body by now. Were the tablets responsible for the changes to his body and to his behaviour? He felt certain now that they were the cause. But how could that be possible as he was equally certain that there were no tablets on the planet that could do that? But assuming the tablets were the cause of these changes, on the whole they had been for the better, except for what appeared to be his new propensity for violence. Perhaps, this was a side effect of the drug? But still, none of this made any sense. The Chemist was not what he appeared to be and there was something very wrong about the man. Brad was certain that whatever the motives of the Chemist, they had nothing to do with Brad's health. He was equally convinced that this had not yet fully played out and he had a growing sense of apprehension about what would happen next.

Brad noticed that his wrists felt warm to the touch, which was all the more remarkable because his hands themselves were cold. *What the fuck is in those black bands?* he thought. *This has to be because of them.* Brad spent the remainder of the relatively short drive reliving his first encounter with the Chemist, searching for clues.

It was nearly 6.00 pm, and he was usually home by now. Gina was going to pick their son, David, up from university and would be leaving soon to start the three-hour drive. They normally went together, but on this occasion Gina wanted to spend some time with David alone and had arranged to take him out for a meal and stay over near the university campus, driving back the next day. Brad's cell phone started to ring. Being on the road as much as he was, he always had his bluetooth headset on and was able to take the call while driving.

"Where are you?" Gina's tone was terse.

"I'm about thirty minutes or so out. My last appointment lasted longer than planned. What time are you heading off? "

"I'm leaving now, Brad. You should have told me you would be late."

"Sorry Gina, I guess I must have lost track of time. What time are you planning on coming back with David tomorrow?" Brad could feel the inevitable argument brewing, but decided that avoiding it was the best policy.

"I won't be rushing back, somewhere around 3.00 pm, that is if you can be bothered to be there. I don't know what's going on with you Brad, but for the last few days or so even when you have been with me, it's like you are somewhere else. Are you having an affair?"

"Don't be ridiculous," he replied. "You know how stressful my job is and how things have been recently. What do you expect?" Brad could feel his own temper rising.

"I just don't care much for your attitude at the moment. Things need to change, Brad; we will talk about this when I get back tomorrow." Gina ended the call without giving him the chance to reply.

Brad was furious. Gina knew what buttons to press to get to him. He let out a howl of anger and punched the windscreen in rage. This was his way of letting off steam and invariably resulted in bruised knuckles and a fair amount of pain, but no damage to the car. For just a split second, as Brad hit the windscreen, he thought he saw a flash of light, like the approaching headlights of a car that had just gone over a bump in the road, and then the windscreen shattered into a million pieces. *"Fucking great,"* Brad snarled.

He pulled over and called the mobile glass fitting service that came with his company car insurance. True to their advertising claims, they arrived within the hour and fitted a new windscreen. "You say that a stone kicked up by the car in front of you did this?" the fitter said. "It's just that normally we would expect the windscreen to shatter, but still be in place. But it looks like yours was hit with tremendous force from

72

inside. But that still doesn't explain this," he said as he handed a few fragments of the glass to Brad. "If you look at the edges of the fragments, you will see that they are not sharp as you would expect them to be, they look rounded as if they have been melted. Shattered and melted, most bizarre smashed window I have ever seen." Brad stared at the fragments and said nothing.

Brad reckoned that he must have been about twenty miles outside of Greenhaven and it was already a quarter past seven. It wasn't worth going home just to get a change of clothing; he would never get back in time for his date. So, he pulled off the road at the next junction and headed back towards Greenhaven.

Arriving ten minutes ahead of time, he parked up in the centre of the village. He walked over to the abandoned chemist shop. The rain had stopped and although it was still light, the overcast sky gave a spectral look to the village.

"You look like a man who's lost something, Bradley White." The voice came from behind him and belonged to the woman he had first met those few short hours earlier.

He turned and was more than a little surprised that he had not heard her approaching and yet there she was, standing before him in this spectral landscape. "I guess I am that man," he replied. "How embarrassing is this? I appear to be at a disadvantage; I don't seem to know your name."

"At a disadvantage, are you?" she responded. "You didn't seem that interested in my name earlier."

Brad was taken aback by the sharpness of her response. "Please excuse my bad manners; you could say I was somewhat distracted at the time! This sort of thing never happens to me and I could have behaved better. Please accept my apologies."

"That all depends," she replied. "I like the name Sarah, so why don't we run with that?"

"I take it that's not your real name?" She said nothing. "Sarah it is then! And for what it's worth, I think that the name suits you! I'm Brad. It's not a name I would have chosen for myself, but you could say that I have grown into it!"

"You do understand that we only have this one night together, don't you? I'm not looking for a relationship. I just want to have a little fun; this place is so dull, and I have been left to fend for myself."

All thoughts of the Chemist were forgotten as Brad looked at her. She was dressed more casually this time, wearing a short summer dress and a light jacket. The dress clung provocatively to her every contour and accentuated her impossibly perfect body. Brad really couldn't believe his luck and wasn't about to talk himself out of this by questioning her motives. "That sounds like a plan I can work with!" he replied.

They walked back to his car in silence. It was a short drive to the motel and they checked in as Mr and Mrs Smith, not terribly original, but it appealed to Brad's sense of humour. He paid with cash as Gina handled all the banking and credit card bills, and a receipt for a double motel room, so close to home while she was out of town, would take some explaining!

Before they went up to their room, they went to the fast food restaurant that was next to the motel. Brad could not recall when he had last eaten and made quick work of consuming the largest meal he could find on the menu. Sarah did not eat and made small talk while he finished his meal. Brad knew nothing about this woman and realised that it was unlikely he ever would. They walked back to their motel room and closed the door on the world behind them.

Chapter 15
Raymond Oliver

Raymond Oliver was not a good man and had a long criminal record filled with convictions for violence and just about every other crime. Standing over six-foot-tall, he was a big man, weighing sixteen stone and with fists like a stonemason's hammers. He looked every bit as intimidating as he was in reality. He had a fearsome reputation for violence and had never been beaten in a fight. In fact, he didn't fight as such because that would imply that his opponent was able to fight back, he would just keep hitting his victim way after they lost consciousness and would only stop when he felt like it or if there were enough people around to drag him off.

All the clichés applied to Oliver; he grew up on the wrong side of town, his father was a convicted criminal who was absent for almost all of his formative years, and his mother was a heroin addict who funded her addiction by opening her legs for whoever would pay. Raymond loved his Mother and metered out his own version of justice to her more violent clients. He had not seen his Father since he broke his jaw in three places when he was seventeen.

It was Friday evening and Raymond Oliver was doing what he did every evening; sitting in his seat at his local pub. Even on the busiest of evenings, his seat was always empty and waiting for him. He would think nothing of *twatting someone*, as he put it, for sitting in his seat. This had happened too many times for anybody to be stupid enough to sit there.

Raymond stood up and walked to the bar to get another pint of strong ale. When he turned to walk back to his seat, he saw that an elderly man was sitting there. Not a respecter of anyone, let alone the elderly, Raymond saw red and walked over to the old man.

"Get out of my seat, you old cunt."

"No one was sat here," replied the old man without even bothering to look up.

"I'm telling you for the last time to move or I will break your fucking neck." The pub had gone completely silent as Raymond snarled at the old man. Nobody dared to speak for fear of reprisals.

"No, you won't, you worthless piece of mother fucking shit," the old man said as he sprang to his feet impossibly fast.

Raymond swung his right fist at the old man's face, hard enough to smash stone. The old man laughed a dry humourless laugh as he ducked to the left under the attack and punched him in the ribs hard, causing him to buckle over in pain. With astonishing speed, the old man followed up with his left fist, hooking the punch in an arc and down into Raymond's jaw.

Raymond Oliver was on his knees gasping in pain, fighting to remain conscious as he searched for the old man through the blackness that was crowding at the edges of his vision. The last thing he saw was the old man looking down at him like a predator about to strike. Something was wrong, in fact the whole thing was wrong, this couldn't be happening. Raymond's vision cleared just for an instant and in that instant, he saw the other's eyes. The zig-zagged, orangey-red coronas around the old man's pupils pulsated and burned into his very being. Raymond felt like he was sinking, drowning, suffocating and for the first time in his miserable life, he felt fear. The old man raised his fist again and Raymond Oliver's world went black.

**

"Hi Mum, come in." David greeted his mother at the door of his room in the halls of residence at the university. David was Brad and Gina's only son, and they loved him dearly. It was a real wrench for them both when he left home to study at the university. It was the first time they had been separated from him, for more than a few days, since he was born. David was a good-looking, popular young man and was rarely without an attractive girl on his arm. Growing up, he was a regular visitor to the doctor's surgeries where his father peddled his wares and he spent most of his school holidays accompanying his father on his travels. He was fascinated with all things medical and it was hardly a surprise to anyone when he decided to study to be a doctor.

"What's wrong, Mum?" David could tell that something was troubling his mother.

"Oh, it's nothing really," she replied.

"I've seen that look before, Mother and don't believe you for a minute."

"Me and your Dad had an argument before I drove up, and it's just put me in a bad mood. He knew that I was coming up tonight and hadn't come back from work by the time I left. It's not really a huge issue, but he should have been there. I don't know what's wrong with him at the moment, but I'm sure there is something wrong; he seems different."

"Different?"

"For the last few days, it's like he was somewhere else. Did you know that he got into a road-rage incident on Wednesday and beat some thug unconscious? Mercifully, the man didn't press charges."

"Why didn't you tell me this before?"

"I didn't want to worry you unnecessarily and fortunately your father was released with a caution."

"No wonder you seem stressed Mum. This thing with Dad is worrying. We all know that he can get wound-up when driving, but for him to beat someone so badly that he got cautioned by the police is just not like him. Is he stressed at work? I know that sales is a tough way to make a living, and that drug sales is about as hard as it gets, but dad has been doing this for a long time now and is pretty good at it."

"I don't think it's his job, David, because his sales this week have been his best ever. The odd thing is that despite all that has happened, your father has said next to nothing about it. It's as if he doesn't care about what he did. I considered the possibility that he was having an affair, but I don't think he is."

"How do you mean, Mum?"

"Well, if he was having an affair I would expect him to at least be happy! The only word I can use to describe your father is that he seems detached. Yes, that's it. It's worrying because it's just not like him, David; it's just plain odd behaviour."

"It does sound strange, Mum. Have you tried to talk to him about it?"

"That's the thing, David; I had planned to talk with him this evening before setting out to come here. I know that he wasn't planning to come up, but I was hoping that maybe he would, and we could talk on the way up, but the selfish bastard couldn't even be bothered to get home in time."

75

"Would you like me to talk to him when we get back tomorrow, Mum?"

"No David, I don't want you to get involved. Anyway, let's not spend any more time talking about your father, let's go for this meal. I'm starving!"

***

Raymond Oliver woke up. He was disorientated and as he pushed himself on to his knees, he felt a sharp pain in his side and realised that at least one rib was broken. "You have a job to do, you piece of shit," came a snarling disembodied voice from the blackness that surrounded him.

***

As the door closed behind them, Sarah grabbed Brad with a strength that surprised him and pushed him up against the door. She kissed him hard and pulled at his clothes. Brad was a little taken aback by the voracity of Sarah's actions and had never been with a dominant woman before. For just a moment, he wondered what he had got himself into, but all such thoughts left his mind as her persuasive hand made contact with his manhood.

***

Gina and David went to the same restaurant that they always patronised when she came to visit. It wasn't the most upmarket of restaurants, but they were always assured of an excellent meal there and the staff were genuinely helpful and always made them feel welcome. Their conversation was a little subdued as the argument with Brad had left Gina feeling not at her most sociable.

The restaurant was only a short walk from David's halls of residence and they decided that they would walk back and stop for a quick drink at the pub that was on the way. As they walked the short distance to the pub, they were deeply engrossed in conversation and did not notice the unsavoury character who had been watching them from across the road.

***

Raymond Oliver knew exactly where to find them; they were just where the old man had said they would be. *This should be easy money,* he thought as he watched them enter the pub.

***

Sarah was unlike any woman Brad had ever been with before. In fact, she was unlike anyone he had ever met. She seemed perfect in every way, almost too perfect, but there was something about her that didn't seem right. He had the strangest of feelings, a sense that she didn't belong here. And despite their intimacy, there was a coldness about her. He didn't doubt it when she said that she would use him. But why him when she could have any man that she wanted? Something was very wrong about all of this, but he was enjoying himself so why not just go along with it and see what happens?

76

The hotel room was basic. It was a typical overnight motorway stop for people travelling to somewhere else. The facilities reflected this utilitarian theme, consisting of a kettle, a few small milk cartons and two tea bags. Sarah walked over to the kettle, unabashed by her nakedness and Brad followed her delicious form with his eyes. "Are you watching me?" she said, still with her back to him.

"Just enjoying the view!" he responded.

She was filling the kettle when she felt the presence of Zoryn Dakor and looked into the mirror that was on the wall in front of her. His appearance in the glass was striking, even in his guise as the old man, and she still felt a flush of excitement every time she saw him. He was the strongest of their kind and completely ruthless, everyone on their home world feared him. "It is done, Kaiya. You can dispense with this charade." The words were heard by her alone.

Brad saw her gazing into the mirror and came up to her silently and grabbed her by her waist.

"Enough of this, our time together is at an end," she hissed as she wheeled around to face him, kneeing him in the groin hard as she did so. Shocked by the sudden turn of events and in excruciating pain, Brad tried to straighten up, but in so doing left his head exposed and Sarah smashed the kettle into the side of his face and slammed her perfect knee into his nose as he fell. "Your race makes me sick with your self-obsessed arrogant selfish and pathetic ways. Well, your life is about to change." Her words dripped with vitriol. Darkness crowded at the edges of his vision and Bradley White's world turned black.

***

Kaiya left him where he lay as the old man appeared in the bedroom, still faintly glowing from the release of magic that had transported him there. "All the pieces are in play," he said as his strange eyes burned with a feral intensity that made the hairs on Kaiya's neck stand on end. Still naked, Kaiya linked hands with the old man as he chanted. An eerie green light appeared around them, encasing them with tendrils of wicked power as it increased in intensity. It pulsated to the rhythm of the old man's chanting, flared once in a blinding flash and then they disappeared.

Chapter 16
The Hospital

Brad could hear his mobile phone ringing, but it seemed distant and not relevant to him. His mind wandered and he fell asleep again without having fully woken up in the first place. His phone rang a second and then a third time and it wasn't until the fourth ring that he managed to rouse himself from his stupor and stand up. He was naked and had been lying on the floor of the hotel room where Sarah had left him the previous evening. He had no idea what time of day it was, except that the light escaping from the edges of the curtains in the bedroom suggested that it was daytime. His mobile stopped ringing before he could get to it. He checked the missed call log and it showed that a caller withheld number had tried to call him eight times. It must have been something important judging by all the call attempts, but as Brad could not return the call, he put his phone down and walked into the bathroom.

He splashed water on his face to help clear his head which felt like it was full of cotton wool and there was dried blood on his nose. His recollection of the previous evening's events hit him with the force of a breaking tsunami as he remembered the way that Sarah had turned on him and the violence of her attack. "Did that really fucking happen?" He asked his reflection out loud as he tried to make sense of it. One minute they had been having sex and the next she literally beat him up. Something was seriously wrong.

The memory of his first encounter with the Chemist played out in his mind and then he remembered the second time he saw the man, just before he met Sarah. Brad was certain that somehow Sarah was a part of whatever was happening, there were too many coincidences to be ignored.

For fuck's sake, he thought to himself, *how could this have happened and what the fuck is the matter with me? The chemist was fucking weird; there is no chemist shop like that. Why didn't I just walk out? I took unlisted drugs without a second thought and without having a clue what they would do to me. How could I have been so fucking stupid? And why did I not remember it after? What the fuck is wrong with me and what the fuck did the Chemist do to me, and who the fuck is Sarah?* The questions multiplied in Brad's mind like bacteria swarming in a petri dish.

Instead of feeling anxious, like Brad would have felt in the past, he was furious. Each question fuelled his anger until he was practically incandescent with rage. Snarling with fury, Brad screamed at his reflection in the mirror and raised his fist. It was then that he saw his eyes in the mirror, the edges of his irises burned with an iridescent zig-zagged, orangey-red corona just like those of the Chemist. He let out a howl of rage and despair as his fist struck the cold hard marble of the washbasin. As the blow struck, he felt heat in his right wrist and looked down. The remains of the marble washbasin lay in a pile of fragments and dust at his feet. He had completely destroyed it. He examined his fist which was glowing, but it showed no sign of any injury. Looking into the mirror, his eyes looked perfectly normal again. "Did I imagine all that?" he asked himself, and then he looked at the floor again. "What the fuck is going on?"

Brad's mobile phone rang. "Is that Mr White?" asked the voice at the other end.

"Yes, it is," he replied.

"This is the hospital in Port Cuthbert. You need to come here right away. It's about your wife and son."

The journey to the hospital was a three-hour drive from the hotel Brad had stayed at and it seemed to take an eternity to get there. All the Sunday drivers in creation were either going the same way, or determined to get in his way. More than once, he had sounded his horn to move somebody out of the way or hurry them along. At one point, the driver of the car in front got out of his car and walked over to Brad's door intent on a confrontation. Brad wound down his window and glared at the man, his seat belt already unbuckled and his hand on the door ready to spring out. The man saw the look on Brad's face and then he noticed his eyes. They were burning with a rage he had never seen before; in fact, he had never seen eyes like it, with their zig-zagged, orangey-red coronas pulsating with a malign intensity. His blood turned to ice in his veins and he knew that he had picked a fight with the wrong man. "Get back in your car and fuck off," Brad snarled.

Brad arrived at the hospital and the signs said that all the hospital car parks were full.

"Fucking typical," he cursed. Turning into a small service road in the grounds of the hospital, he abandoned his car to the mercy of the wheel clampers.

The hospital was a sprawling mass of wards, but Brad quickly found the private room that his son was in. David was sat up in bed and there was a policeman and woman in attendance. He looked up at Brad. His face was a mass of bruises and his left eye was so swollen it was almost closed His hands were also heavily bandaged. Oblivious to the presence of the police, Brad's eyes filled with tears as he went over to his son and cradled his head in his arms as he asked, "David who did this to you, what happened?"

"I don't know, Dad." David's voice was thick with emotion. "We had been for a meal like we normally do when Mum comes up, and we stopped at the pub just off campus for a quick drink before going back. There's an alleyway just past the pub and as we walked past, a man sprang out of nowhere and grabbed Mum by the throat and pulled her into the alley." Tears flowed as David relived the events of the previous evening. "The rest is still a blur, but I can remember shouting for help and struggling to try to get Mum away from the man. I thought he was going to kill her." David's voice was trembling and little more than a whisper. "Why would anyone do this to her?"

Brad listened in stunned silence, his right fist clenching and unclenching.

"The police believe that I was hit in the head with a weapon because the next memory I have is waking up in an ambulance and seeing…the paramedics trying to resuscitate Mum… Dad I thought she was dead. She was just lying there hooked up to all these machines."

"Where is Mum now?" Brad asked.

"She's in intensive care, but nobody is telling me anything. The police haven't left my side since I first got here. I'm really worried about her, Dad."

Brad felt sick to his soul. *How could anyone do this to his wife and son, and why would they?* His head was spinning as each thought multiplied and took on a life of its own. Brad couldn't shift the feeling that this was somehow to do with him, because of him, and that his son and wife had been deliberately targeted to get to him.

"What happened to your hands?" Brad asked as he stared at the mass of bandages.

"I can't feel them, Dad. The consultant said that my hands looked like they had been repeatedly beaten with a hammer or other heavy object. Every bone in my hands and wrists has been broken. He is going to operate later today but said I will never regain the full use of either hand. I'm never going to be a surgeon, Dad." David broke down and wept openly as his father cradled him in his arms, rocking him gently as his own tears flowed.

Brad was incandescent with rage and hurt for what had been done to his wife and son. Gently placing David's head on the pillow, he kissed him on the forehead. David looked up at his Father and recoiled in terror as he saw his eyes. "Help me!" David screamed. "Get him away from me."

The policeman was instantly on his feet. "What's wrong?" he asked David.

"That's not my father...look at his eyes." David was cowering as far away from Brad as he could get within the confines of the bed, as he pointed to his father's eyes. The policeman looked at Brad, bemused.

"There's nothing wrong with your father's eyes, David," he said.

"David it's me. I think you're having a panic attack," Brad said. David looked up at his father and seemed to relax a little.

"Mr White, can I have a word with you please, outside?" the policeman asked.

"I don't want to leave my son on his own."

"PC Sharon Mendez will stay here with your son."

The policeman extended his arm in the direction of the door.

"I will be right back, David," Brad said to David as he accompanied the policeman.

"Mr White, I have some very bad news for you. Your wife was violently attacked and is fighting for her life in intensive care."

"I need to go there now."

"I completely understand Mr White, I will take you there."

Intensive care was on another level in the hospital and the walk seemed interminable to Brad.

"Do you know who did this to my family?" he demanded.

"We are following a number of lines of enquiry, and we have DNA evidence and are pretty sure we know who is responsible. We have some CCTV footage from a nearby camera which coupled with your son's account, places a man that is well known to us at the scene."

"Do you have this man in custody?"

"Not yet, but we are closing in on him and I am confident that he will be arrested soon."

"What sort of fucking animal could do this?" Brad could feel his rage starting to build again.

"Do you have any enemies, Mr White?"

"What do you mean?"

"This attack seems very personal to me. If the man we think it is did this, it is out of character for him. He's a petty criminal with a long history of violent attacks, but this looks like it was planned rather than being a random event. Whoever did this wanted to destroy your family, Mr White."

"I don't have any enemies that I am aware of, and I am certain that neither my wife nor my son do either."

"You have been involved in trouble recently though, haven't you Mr White?"

"This has got fuck all to do with that. For a start, the incident you refer to happened fucking miles away and secondly, from what I can make out the guy involved is probably still eating his fucking meals through a straw." Brad was furious.

"I understand that you are upset, Mr White," the policeman continued, "but we are only trying to help you and your family and arrest the animal responsible for this attack."

"I'm sorry," Brad replied. "Seeing my son like that, I just don't have the words to describe how angry I am. I want this animal to suffer the way my son is suffering. I want to kill the fucking cunt."

"We are doing everything that we can to find him. As upset as you are, we take any threat seriously and the law takes a very dim view of revenge Mr White, so I suggest that you concentrate on being there for your family and leave this scumbag to us. I will ignore your previous comment."

"Just get the fucker."

Arriving at the intensive care ward, the policeman pressed the buzzer and they waited for a member of staff to let them in. Brad had never been in an intensive care ward before and it was nothing like he imagined. He expected to see lots of doctors and nurses milling around each bed and to hear the whirl and hum of life support machines. Instead, the ward seemed peaceful and calm. There were no more than six beds and there was light music playing in the background with barely any machine noise to be heard. There was a dedicated nurse per bed and mostly they appeared to be just monitoring their patients.

Gina was unconscious. Brad could see from one of the machines that her pulse, blood pressure and oxygen saturation levels were being constantly monitored. Although Brad had no formal medical training, he had some basic knowledge that he had acquired during his many years' experience in the pharmaceutical industry, and to his untrained eyes, Gina's levels seemed normal. He sat in a chair at the head of the bed and gently took her tiny hand in his. Resting his head on her hand, Brad wept uncontrollably, the spasms of his grief wracking his whole body as he let go to its embrace.

Looking back later, he could not recall at what point he fell asleep, but he was roused by a gentle hand touching his shoulder as a nurse offered him a cup of tea.

"Thank you," he said as he gratefully accepted the steaming brew. "What exactly is wrong with my wife?" he asked the nurse.

"You need to speak with the ward Sister, Mr White, she's the best person to talk to. I'll go and get her for you."

Brad returned his attention to Gina. She had a thin tube which entered her mouth under an oxygen mask and there were two half full bags of blood on a stand by the side of the bed that were connected to her by a thin clear tube attached to a vein in her left arm. It was clear that she had also been hit in the face with a lot of force because her left cheek was badly bruised and swollen and there was a row of stitches above her left eye. Brad's stomach churned at the sight of his wife like this and he felt sick to the very core of his being.

"Mr White?" came a gentle voice. Brad looked up. "I'm Katie Parson, the ward Sister. Will you come with me to my office please?"

"Please sit down Mr White," Katie said as she closed the door to her office which had large glass windows to three sides so that she had an uninterrupted view of the ward.

"I know about the injuries to your son and can't begin to know how you must feel. Please be assured that your wife will receive the very best of care and you can contact me or any member of my staff whenever you need to."

Brad swallowed hard on the emotions that were threatening to overwhelm him as he whispered his thanks.

"This won't be easy for you to hear, but your wife has been badly beaten. She also has several lacerations and she has stitches in three areas, the worst of which is above her left eye as you have seen. Your wife was unconscious when she was admitted yesterday evening and we are keeping her in a drug induced coma until the swelling to her brain has reduced."

Brad could not stop the tears which tracked their progress down his unshaven face.

"How bad is her head injury?" Brad asked in a voice thick with emotion.

"Honestly Mr White, we don't know for certain, but the next twenty-four hours will be critical. She has a fractured skull and there was some inter-cranial bleeding. The surgeon managed to stop the bleed and we just have to wait now. It is the swelling to her brain that is causing us the most concern."

"Is she going to die?"

"Your wife was admitted very quickly after the attack and thanks to the skill and experience of the paramedics that attended the scene, our consultant neurologist was paged and the theatre ready as soon as she came to us. If there had been a delay, your wife's chances would be very slim. We are hopeful that she will recover, but the next twenty-four hours will be critical. I wish I could give you better news, Mr White. I really do."

Brad stared at Katie, incapable of speech.

"Was Gina taking birth control?"

"I, I don't know what you mean," Brad replied.

"You do know that the attacker raped your wife, don't you Mr White?"

***

Brad returned to David's ward and sat with him until he was taken to the operating theatre. The surgeon told him that the operation would take around five hours and their aim was to save as much as they could of each hand and restore some nerve function. He was confident that they could make significant improvements but told Brad not to expect too much as the injuries were severe.

The rest of the day was an endless round of going from David's ward to intensive care and waiting for his son to return from theatre. When David did return, he was so heavily sedated that he remained asleep. Brad was reminded of how David looked when he was sleeping as a child and sat by his son's bed and wept.

"You need to get some rest, Mr White," the nurse said as she gently touched his shoulder. "Your son probably won't come around fully until tomorrow. You really should take this opportunity to get something to eat and get some sleep." Brad acknowledged her with a silent nod of his head as he rose to his feet and left the ward.

Chapter 17
Revenge

Brad walked out of the hospital and quickly found his car exactly where he had abandoned it earlier that day. Sure enough, there was a triangular yellow clamp on one of the rear wheels and a notice had been stuck on his windscreen. The sight of the clamp instantly re-ignited Brad's rage and he was furious that anyone could clamp his car at such a time. But oddly enough as he kicked the clamp, he felt his anger focus almost like how a laser beam concentrates a beam of light, and as his foot made contact with the clamp, he thought he saw a flare of light and then the clamp shattered. Picking up one of the pieces, it felt hot to the touch and it looked like it had been cut with a welder's torch as its edges were rounded over. *Must have been a flaw in the metal,* he thought as he chucked it and the other pieces over a nearby hedge closely followed by the penalty notice he had just ripped off the windscreen.

Brad drove to the nearest motel he could find as he wanted to be close to the hospital. After checking in, he went straight to the restaurant and ordered the largest steak that he could find on the menu which he washed down with a bottle of house red. For some reason, a conversation in muted tones from a table behind him attracted his attention.

"Oliver's in big fucking trouble now."

"It was always going to happen, he's fucking nuts," came the reply.

"That he is, but are you gonna tell that psycho son of a bitch that to his face?"

There was no reply.

"I thought not. So, do you think he did it?" the first speaker asked in his nasally tone.

"The filth are looking for him that's for sure and funny how no one has seen him since."

"Where do you think he's holed up?"

"Nearby, travel will be impossible with all the filth on the streets looking for him."

Instinctively, Brad knew that the men were talking about the attack on his wife and son.

"We should keep a low profile too for a while. With our names so closely associated with his, we need to be careful. If they find him through us, we are dead men."

"Okay, I don't pretend to be a brave man, I'm a fucking thief not a hitter, let's go away for a while." With that, they both stood up and left the restaurant, leaving their half-finished drinks on the table. Brad followed them out to the car park.

Brad walked up to the nearest of the two and without saying a word, punched the man with a clean right cross that connected squarely with the point of his chin. He was unconscious before he even realised he had been hit and fell to the ground without breaking his fall. The other man stood rooted to the spot in shock of the suddenness of the attack and before he could react, Brad grabbed him by the throat and lifted him off the ground, shaking the man like a rag doll. Brad slammed him into a small utility van and held him there pinned by the throat.

"You are going to give me the name of the man you were talking about back in the restaurant and you will tell me where I can find him, or I will break your fucking neck. Do you understand me?" Brad snarled into his face.

Black dots were crowding the man's vision and he felt his grip on consciousness sliding away.

"Raymond Oliver," he barely croaked.

"Where can I find him?"

"N, N Newtown."

"Give me your mobile phone," Brad demanded.

The man fumbled in his pocket and withdrew his phone. Brad loosened his grip a little to allow the man to give him the mobile's password.

"What's your fucking name?" Brad tightened his grip again.

The man knew that if Raymond Oliver traced this back to him, he was dead for sure and shook his head in defiance.

"Fucking tell me," Brad howled with rage.

"I can't, he will kill me if he finds out." The man's expression turned to one of horror as the orangey-red, zig-zagged coronas around Brad's pupils burned into his very being. "It's Chris Donleavy."

Brad let the man go and walked over to the other man who lay face down in a pool of his own blood. He may well have been dead, but Brad was unconcerned as he searched his pockets for his mobile. Finding it, he ripped the battery off and stamped on the SIM card until it was incapable of being used.

Chris Donleavy had made good his escape and was nowhere to be seen as Brad walked over to his car. Glancing over his shoulder, he saw that a couple were stood in the doorway of the restaurant. He did not know how long they had been there, but as soon as they saw him looking at them, they scurried back inside. Clearly they had seen at least some of what had happened. Brad decided to leave his car where it was and went back to the unconscious man and found a set of keys with a fob control in his pocket. He walked around the car park, pressing the button until he found the man's car. It was a black BMW convertible that instantly roared into life when Brad started it. He sped out of the car park heading for Newtown.

***

Raymond Oliver had done what the old man had demanded of him. He was no stranger to violence, but always in the past there had been a reason for it, at least in his mind anyway. But this time, he had done what he was told to do, what he was ordered to do, and he hated that. He did not feel guilty or give a fuck about the lives of those he had just ruined. But what he was consumed with was that he had no choice in the matter, that he had been forced to do the bidding of the old man. The woman and boy had been exactly where the old man had told him they would be and at the precise time. Oliver knew this part of town well and had used its many alleyways in the past. By the time the woman and boy had spotted him, their fate was already sealed. He knocked the woman to the ground with a single punch and was on the boy before he could call for help. The boy was no match for him and despite landing a punch on Oliver, he was easily beaten unconscious with the reign of terrifying blows that was Oliver's trade mark. Remembering what the old man had told him to do, Oliver went to work on the boy's hands and wrists with the baseball bat he had brought with him. And then, he dragged the unconscious limp body of the woman deeper into the lane and raped her.

His mobile phone vibrated twice alerting him that he had received a text message.

'U ok mate?' It was his friend Chris, if you could call him a friend. Raymond Oliver did not really have friends, but there were plenty of low-life petty criminals that found that an association with him could be useful. If nothing else, it gave them a degree of protection, because no one in their right mind would pick a fight with a friend of Raymond Oliver.

'The filths been sniffing around mate looking for u. No one said nuffin. Just thought u should know.' The texts were sent by Brad from Chris Donleavy's mobile.

'I got u some food and you can take me mate's beemer which is full of gas.' Brad texted.

'I ain't dun nuffink. What u doing this for?' Oliver replied. He hated texting with a vengeance.

'Don't care if u dun it or not mate. We boys from Sanderswick look out fer each ovver and I know you would do it fer me.' At that, Oliver, who was not known for having a sense of humour, laughed out loud. "Fat fucking chance of that, you stupid twat," he said to himself.

'I'll leave the beemer unlocked outside the side entrance to the cemetery in Brook Street. The key will be under the passenger seat.'

'I'll need sum cash too,' Oliver replied.

'The car will be there after 10.00 pm'

'Right.'

"Got you, you fucking cunt," Brad said to himself as he put the mobile down.

It was a little after 9.00 pm and to make this work, Brad had to get the car over to the cemetery now and find somewhere to conceal himself.

Arriving at the cemetery at 9.30 pm, Brad needed to disable the car somehow so that Raymond Oliver could not escape if things went wrong. He didn't have any tools on him, but he lifted the bonnet and grabbed the positive connection on the car's battery and yanked it hard. He didn't expect to break the lead, but his wrists started to glow and he pulled the terminal clean off the battery. He didn't have time to consider what he had just done, so he shut the bonnet and jumped over the low wall that surrounded the cemetery. He lay still and waited.

Raymond Oliver was by nature a cautious man. With his colourful past, you had to be. But he also wanted to get far away from this place. This time he was in real trouble. Raping the woman meant that the police had his DNA. There was no way he was going to walk away from this one, even with the skills of his silver-tongued brief. He needed to get away, a long way from here and the offer of a fast car that wasn't linked to him and some cash, was too good an opportunity to ignore.

The cemetery was a short walk away but he wasn't taking any chances. He hadn't gone home since the attack and spent the last twenty-four hours moving from one place to another, keeping his head down and blending into the background as much as possible. It was a little after 1.00 am when he finally arrived at the cemetery. Even then, he walked passed the car, suspicious it may be a trap, before coming back fifteen minutes later.

Brad sprang over the wall and landed a couple of feet in front of Raymond Oliver. The jump was an impossible one and Oliver was caught completely by surprise. Brad stepped forward and punched Oliver with a right straight to the centre of his chest. The blow connected, breaking bone as Oliver staggered back. Without pause, Brad kicked the side of Oliver's right knee, shattering it and disabling his opponent. Oliver was on his feet still, but only just, which was what Brad had intended. "Why did you attack my wife and son?" Brad howled at him.

"Fuck you," came the response. Brad slapped Oliver hard across the face with the back of his hand. Oliver fell to the floor stunned, his face burning. Brad grabbed him by the lapels of his jacket and hauled him to his feet head butting him in the nose as soon as they drew level. This time he did not let Oliver go. Looking him in the eyes, Brad repeated the question. Oliver looked down and sensing danger, Brad twisted his body hard to the right instinctively, narrowly missing being stabbed by a long thin knife that Oliver had in his hand. Brad grabbed Oliver's wrist and squeezed. Impossibly, he could feel the bones in Oliver's hand break under the pressure. Raymond Oliver howled in pain, but Brad did not release his grip. The blade started to glow in Oliver's hand and Brad could smell flesh burning as the blade grew hotter and hotter. Brad let go of Oliver's hand and as the knife dropped to the floor, he stamped on it, shattering it into a thousand pieces of burning metal.

"Who, who are you?" Oliver stuttered. But then, he caught sight of Brad's eyes for the first time, seeing the same zig-zagged, orangey-red coronas he had seen in the eyes of the old man and he recoiled in terror.

"You, the old man, you're the same."

"What do you mean?" Brad snarled as he advanced on him.

"Those fucking eyes, you ain't normal, neither is he. He made me do it."

"Do what?" Brad was nose to nose with Oliver now.

"He made me attack your wife and told me exactly what to do. He 'ad sum strange powers I 'ad to do it or he wud 'ave killed me."

"So, you admit that you beat my son and raped my wife?"

"I 'ad to, it was nuffink personal."

"Where is the old man now?" Brad's voice was barely a whisper.

"I dunno, never told me how to contact 'im; he could be anywhere." Brad pushed him back like a rag doll and howled with rage and frustration as he slammed his open hand into Oliver's chest. Light flared from Brad's wrist as Oliver's body flew backwards, landing broken several metres away. Raymond Oliver was dead before he hit the ground.

Brad looked around and was surprised that no one had heard what had just happened, the street was silent and empty. He knew that there was a licensed all-night diner a half mile or so down the road, and he could do with a drink and some food. After that, he would get a taxi back to the motel and catch a few hours' sleep before going back to the hospital. Brad knew that he had killed Raymond Oliver the second his life ended. Despite his anger, he had experienced the same detached feeling he had in the incident with the van man a few days earlier. He knew that he should feel remorse, or at least something, having killed Oliver, but he felt nothing at all. What was really troubling him was the Chemist and Sarah. They were clearly involved in all of this. Maybe they were testing him? He didn't know. He also had no idea how to find them, but he would leave no stone unturned in his search for them and for answers.

Chapter 18
Departure

Brad was so deep in thought that he nearly walked past the diner. It was empty, so he had his choice of tables and selected one towards the back of the room and chose a seat that faced the door. An attractive waitress, with an impossibly short skirt came over and took his order. She was less than half his age, but he found her flirting a welcome distraction from his dark thoughts. "There's been a major incident over by the old cemetery," she said as she came over with his ice-cold lager. "Lots of police."

"Well, let's hope it's hungry work for them!" Brad jokingly replied. "Because it's dead in here and you could do with the business."

"See that light above the door over there," she said, pointing.

"Yes."

"That means that your breakfast is ready. It's time to get you fed, sir!" she said mockingly.

"Better add another lager to the order," Brad said as she turned her back and went to collect his food. When she came back, Brad set about devouring the enormous breakfast systematically. After a third pint of lager, he started to unwind a little.

Three men in their mid-twenties entered the diner noisily and took a table just in front of where he sat, oblivious to his presence. The waitress came over to take their orders and it was clear from their banter that they also found her attractive. Their orders took longer to cook and by the time the waitress returned with their food, they had already consumed three rounds of drinks. The banter took on a harder edge and without warning one of the men grabbed the waitress by the waist and pulled her onto his lap forcibly. She was no match for him and the more she struggled, the more he appeared to enjoy it. Her skirt was riding up which only made him more determined, to keep her on his lap.

"Let her go," Brad shouted before he realised what he was doing.

The man holding the waitress let her go. "And what's it to you?" he snarled in reply.

Without thinking, Brad sprang to his feet and grabbed the guy and as he did so, he felt a stinging sensation in his shoulder. He caught sight of the dart and wire as the policeman holding the taser gun discharged the weapon.

Brad could feel the electricity coursing through his body, but it had no effect on him. The man that he still held, however, was convulsing so Brad let him fall to the floor. It was then that he saw that the policeman who held the weapon, was also convulsing as the charge from the gun had somehow been reversed and was coursing through his body, but at a much higher level. The policeman couldn't turn the weapon off. Brad knew instinctively that the man would die if he didn't do something quickly, so he grabbed the wire that was still attached to the dart and yanked the taser gun from the policeman's hand. The policeman fell to the floor unconscious. Two more officers rushed to the aid of their fallen colleague and more were entering the diner. To avoid any risk to the other policemen, Brad lay face down on the floor with his arms and legs spread and did not resist his arrest.

***

"You're entitled to a phone call," the duty sergeant said as he walked Brad to a holding cell in the bowels of the Victorian police station.

"My son has just undergone major surgery and my wife is in a coma. I have no one to call," Brad replied. The sergeant nodded and showed him to his cell.

"The duty solicitor will be coming to see you early because you will be standing in front of the magistrate at 9.00 am; so if I were you, I would get some sleep while you can."

Brad was locked in a cell and left in silence. Despite the seriousness of the situation, the police had treated him well and with a degree of respect. The man that he had killed was well-known to them and had many convictions for violence. He was also the prime suspect in the attack on Brad's family. Any family man could understand what had driven Brad to attack him and they couldn't but have some empathy with him. Brad's quick thinking had also undoubtedly saved the life of one of their own. No one in the station had ever heard of a taser shocking the handler; it was an impossibility that seemed to challenge the very laws of physics. And yet, if Brad had not yanked the taser gun out of their colleague's hand, he would almost certainly be dead.

Brad lay on the thin mattress and instantly fell into a dreamless sleep. He was woken a few hours later by a knock on the door to his prison cell and the gruff voice of a younger policeman telling him his solicitor was waiting to see him. It was 7.00 am and the police station was quiet as they walked to the interview room. Brad was wearing handcuffs due to the seriousness of the charges he was facing. It appeared that there were two people waiting for him in the interview room, a man and a woman, but both were facing away from him when he entered the room. It wasn't until his escort left the room and locked it behind him that the two figures turned to face him.

"You, who the fuck are you? What the fuck is going on?" Brad shouted at the pair.

"So, you do remember me then?" taunted the old man.

"Of course I fucking do, you're the Chemist from that odd shop and you..." he glared at Sarah. "Fuck knows who you are."

"You still don't fully remember. Here let me help you." With that, the old man closed the gap between them and grabbed Brad by the head in an impossibly quick movement. Brad felt like he had been kicked in the head and his world span at a sickeningly fast rate and then the old man released him and he fell to the floor. It took several moments for the room to stop spinning and then Brad's incomplete memories came back to him in an avalanche with one memory falling over another and then another and another. He remembered it all vividly as if the memories were brand new. He remembered the events that led up to his going to the chemist shop and could even remember the detached way he had felt during so many of the strange things that had happened to him recently. A veil had been lifted from his mind and he was seeing things clearly for the first time in weeks. What had happened to him? What had been done to him? What had possessed him to do the things he had done? What had been done to his family? Why had this all happened? He was locked up in a police station for killing a man. Reeling more from the realisation of what had happened, than the vestiges of the vertigo he had felt earlier, Brad groped for a chair and sat down.

For long minutes, the old man and Sarah said nothing as Brad sat there staring into space while he tried to make sense of it all.

"Who are you?" he said at last, as he looked up at the old man.

"Who I am, who we are, is not important. It is what you will do that is important."

"I don't understand?"

"I don't care whether you understand or not. But let me make one thing very clear right now. All that you hold dear will be made to suffer even more and will be destroyed if you don't do exactly as I tell you."

"You fucking bastard," Brad screamed. "You are responsible for what happened to my wife and son, aren't you?"

"Yes, and even now I hold their lives in my hands."

"And you Sarah, or whoever the fuck you are, what was your part in all this?" Brad spat through gritted teeth.

'Isn't it obvious?" came the reply in her sensuous voice. "While you were fucking me and being unfaithful to your wife, she was being raped and your son was being beaten. What sort of man could do that to his family, Bradley White?" she asked mockingly.

"I will kill you both for this." Brad was already on his feet.

"Enough of this," the old man said as he pointed a bony finger at Brad. Inextricably, Brad found that he was paralysed and could not move. "You have a job to do Bradley White, and be in no doubt you will do exactly what I tell you to do. Should you disobey me, your wife will never wake up and your son will be subjected to more pain than he can endure for as long as it pleases me, and then they will both die. I will kill you too, but only after you have witnessed their suffering. The same fate awaits you if you fail to complete your task. And don't think that your newly developed strength and skills are a match for mine. I gave them to you so that you may complete my task, but you are no match for me in any way. Try to attack me again and I will crush you and your family.

You are going to a land that is a very long way from this place. A land from which your only hope of return is the completion of your task. You are going to kill a man, which is something you have already shown that you can do. This man will be harder to kill and access to him will be difficult, but you will kill him. I have equipped you for this task and you will learn more when you get there. I have spies everywhere and I will know your every movement. Do not make the mistake of underestimating me; my reach has no boundaries. You cannot hide from me in the place I am sending you to or anywhere else. Goodbye, Mr White."

The old man reached into his pocket and withdrew a small green ball about the size of a ping-pong ball and threw it at Brad's feet. The ball hit the ground and more green liquid than it could possibly have contained, quickly spread in a circle around his feet and boiled and pulsated as if it was alive. Snake like tendrils grew from the wicked green circle and wrapped themselves around Brad's legs, climbing higher and higher as more and more appeared. Unable to move, Brad could only watch on as the old man started to chant. The sound was like nothing he had heard before and it took on a dark and sinister tone as it increased in volume and rose in pitch. Brad could feel the air moving around him in a circle and within the space of one or two heartbeats, the speed of the wind was at hurricane force as it howled with savage intent. The green tendrils completely covered Brad, forming a skin around his body which should have suffocated him, but somehow, he could still breathe. His world had taken on a green hue and through this haze the walls of the building looked like they were shaking, no not shaking, the walls were pulsating, throbbing to the unearthly howl of the chanting.

Brad could see a brilliant white light emanate from the old man which pulsed and with each pulse it intensified. It looked like a sphere with the old man at its centre. But then it detached itself from the old man and moved slowly towards Brad. The howl of the wind intensified, and the sphere of light moved towards him inexorably, until without warning Brad was inside it. His world suddenly went silent, and he started to fall.

The police station lay in ruins. Everyone that had been inside had perished, except for two lone figures; an old man who was on his knees exhausted from his massive expenditure of magical energy, and a beautiful young woman who had her arms around him.

"Do you think he will survive the journey to our world, Zoryn?" she asked the old man.

"He will Kaiya, my once and future queen," came the reply.

The old man stood up and as he did so, the years fell away from his visage and his body straightened. In the old man's place stood a handsome, powerfully built man. His strength was returning and he stood with the relaxed but ready poise of a fighter. He was dangerous, and power radiated from him in waves that were palpable to every sense. Lifting his face to the sky and in a voice full of menace Zoryn Dakor shouted, "Enjoy your last few weeks of life Sanjin my brother, and then witness all that you hold true fall."

Zoryn Dakor and Kaiya held hands and Zoryn once more chanted as they disappeared.

Chapter 19
Gina White

Gina slept fitfully in her drug-induced coma. The medical staff could not understand the unusually high level of brain activity. It was like she was dreaming, but how could that be possible with the amount of sedatives coursing through her veins? Whether she was dreaming or not, something was causing her to be distressed and agitated.

She was running as fast as she could, trying to get away from whatever it was that was pursuing her, hunting her like an animal. She didn't know what it was, or why it was chasing her. All that she knew was that it was there behind her, relentless in its pursuit of her. She also knew that if she stopped or faltered, it would catch her. She was running for her life in an ancient forest that was dark and sinister and stank of decay. It was not at all like the warm and welcoming woods that she remembered playing in with her friends when she was a child. This was a place that was cut out from the very fabric of nightmares and she was trapped, caught-up in her own living nightmare.

How did she get here? She didn't know. All she could remember was leaving the pub with her son, David, and then...and then they were attacked. It happened so fast that she didn't have time to react, didn't have time to save herself or her son. She could still picture the rotten teeth and could smell the rank breath of her attacker as he bore her to the ground. His hands grabbing and ripping at her clothing and then blackness as he struck her a second time. She knew what he had done to her even though she had been unconscious at the time. But strangely, the hatred that she should feel for this animal of a man was absent. Something inside her told her that he was dead, that he had been killed and his death had not been without pain and suffering. He had got what was coming to him and it was her husband who had avenged her. How she could be so sure of this – she didn't know, but she was certain that he was dead and that gave her some degree of comfort.

Whatever was following her was soundless in its pursuit. She had not seen or heard it, but she could sense its malevolent presence behind her and it was gaining on her rapidly. Gina snagged her foot on a tree root and fell to the ground hard, the force of the fall knocking the wind from her chest, leaving her seeing stars and gasping for breath.

It was then that her pursuer struck, emerging from the gloom like a wraith. Pulling her to her feet in one motion, yanking her arm as he did so, the hand holding her released its vice like grip and she fell to her knees. It was a man that stood above her, but this was no ordinary man. He appeared to be in his late thirties and was dark skinned with jet-black hair, and he was powerfully built. In different circumstances, she would have described him as handsome, but his face was twisted into a terrible snarl and she was afraid. Evil power and malign purpose radiated from him and she felt utterly powerless as he eyed her with the hunger a predator viewed its prey. "Get up," came a voice as hard and cold as the moss-covered granite rocks that littered the woods, "how did you get to this place?"

Gina looked up at him and was instantly drawn to his eyes which burned into her very being. Around his midnight black pupils were zig-zagged, orangey-red coronas that pulsated wickedly. She was transfixed; she couldn't move.

"Answer me."

"I, I don't know. Where is this place?"

"This is a place far from where you live out your miserable existence with your pathetic husband and son. The question is how did you get here?"

"I don't know. This must be a dream; this can't be happening, one minute I was…" Gina couldn't complete the sentence as she recalled the horrors of her attack.

"Well, I guess however you came here, you might as well know the fate that awaits you. Your husband has been sent away from you and your precious son to do my bidding. If he fails, you will all die." The man said tormenting her with his words.

"Who are you? What have you done to him?"

"That is none of your concern. All that you need to know is that I can reach you, wherever you may choose to hide yourself, even in this place."

"And if my husband does what you want, what happens to us then?" Her question barely a whisper as she fought to control the panic that was threatening to engulf her. He laughed a humourless laugh as the iridescent zig-zagged, orangey-red coronas surrounding his pupils pulsated and blazed.

"If your husband does what I command, you and your son may yet live."

"And what of my husband?

"Your husband is already dead to you and will never return."

Gina felt the horror of his words wash over her, drowning her in their vitriol, as the forest swam before her eyes, spinning in a vortex of muted colours and decay until darkness consumed her.

Part II
Preparation

Chapter 20
Translocation

For a long time, Brad fell, tumbling and spinning. There was light and colour, but he was moving so fast that the colours melted into each other. It felt like he was inside a never-ending kaleidoscope. Wherever he was, it was cold, numbingly cold in fact. He could breathe, but there was no mist from his breath and no wind or breeze despite the apparent speed of his movement. He lost all sense of time and space and could have been tumbling for a minute or a year, he couldn't tell. As terrifying as the sensations should have been, Brad did not feel fear, rather he felt a detached cold acceptance. It was as if he knew that this would end, that he was in transit, but to where?

Just when he thought his body couldn't take any more, he hit solid ground. The force of his landing was such that the air was knocked out of his lungs and his vision exploded into stars that swirled around, threatening to engulf him in their vertiginous dance. He was dimly aware of a sound like thunder rumbling in the air around him and his skin was itching all over as if he was covered in a swarm of biting ants.

His head eventually cleared a little and he hauled himself to his knees and looked around to get his bearings, but the horizon was still tilting at a dangerous angle. He did not know where he was, but he was definitely not at the police station. Brad felt a wave of nausea course through his body with the inexorable force of a tidal wave and he threw up and was consumed by darkness.

He was not sure how long he had slept but he awoke with a start and a banging headache, but at least the vertigo had passed. Tentatively, he stood up and was relieved that the ground beneath his feet felt real. Scanning his surroundings, he could tell that he was at the bottom of a valley where once a river had cut its way through a low hilly area. There was no water here now and by the look of the scorched rocks and desiccated soil, there had not been any water here for many years. By his reckoning, it was around midday as the sun was almost directly overhead and it was hot, so hot that unless he found shelter and water soon, things were going to get uncomfortable.

But, where was he? What was this place and how did he get here? His encounter with the old man and Sarah, or whoever the fuck they were, was etched onto his brain. He should be inside the police station or at least somewhere recognisable, but he wasn't. In fact, he had no idea whatsoever where he was. Squinting up at the sun, he noticed for the first time a blueish tinge. Brad was no expert on the sun, but he had never seen this phenomena before. He glanced at the sun again briefly and the blueish tinge was still there. It also appeared to be larger than it should be. "I must've taken a hit on the head when I fell down." He muttered to himself.

"Oi you." An aggressive voice broke the silence of his thoughts. Brad looked to the source of the voice and saw an old man standing a few metres away from him.

"Are you talking to me?" Brad replied tersely.

"Who the fuck else is here?"

"Where is this place?" Brad's recent experience of old men had not been good and he was wary as the other approached. Old men were not always as they appeared to be.

"All in good time," came the response. "Did anyone see you arrive?"

"I have no idea. I was too busy throwing up."

"The sound of your arrival will attract unwanted attention. We don't get thunder and lightning like that from a clear sky." The old man was less than a couple of metres away now.

"Stop where you are," Brad commanded as he felt his anger rising. "Before you take another step forward, you will tell me who you are and what you want."

"You are in no position to command me. Have you forgotten so soon the words of Lord Zoryn?"

"Who the fuck is Zoryn?"

"The man who sent you here."

"The old man with the beautiful woman?"

"Yes, but he isn't old like me. It's just a disguise," the old man sneered.

"So who is this man and why should I do anything he fucking tells me to." Brad could feel his anger rising once more.

"He is Zoryn Dakor, the brother of our exalted King Sanjin Dakor, a man of dreadful power. Did he not demonstrate his power to you in your world?"

"What the fuck do you mean by my world?"

The old man chuckled. "Look up to the sun you fucking idiot. Does the star that warms your world and breathes life to all that lives there burn blue?" Brad looked up and saw again the blueish tinge to the sun. "No! I thought not." The old man took a step closer to Brad. He smiled, but there was no warmth in his smile as he opened his hand to reveal a small green ball. Brad instinctively recoiled, but it was too late. The old man had already thrown the ball and it hit Brad between the eyes without a sound. A green mist enveloped his vision as vertigo once again claimed him, and he lost consciousness.

Chapter 21
Captive

Brad came awake in a dimly lit room. His head was pounding, and his mouth was parched as if he hadn't drunk anything for days. He was lying down on what looked like a crude sleeping pallet which consisted of little more than a rough blanket that had been thrown over a few inches of straw on a cobbled stone floor. For a moment or two he felt disorientated, this wasn't right, where was he and how did he get here, wherever here was? Then he remembered his encounter with the Chemist at the police station. But when was that, days ago, weeks ago?

"So, you are awake at last?" came a voice from somewhere close by. Brad tried to stand up to move towards the noise but found that his body would not respond to his commands.

"Don't even try to move because you can't," the voice said mockingly. "Until you and I are better acquainted, you aren't going anywhere."

Brad recognised the sneering tone to be that of the old man he had spoken to in the valley before...before he had hit him with some strange green ball.

"You fucking bastard," Brad spat from behind gritted teeth. "Fucking let me go now."

"Not a chance," came the reply. "Here take this; you're going to need it." The old man stepped into Brad's field of vision and handed him a roughly cut wooden cup that contained a perfumed smelling liquid. Brad found that he could move his hands and arms just enough to take the cup.

"What is it?" Brad said as he inspected the contents of the cup suspiciously.

"Do you remember leaving your world?" asked the old man.

"For all I know, this is my world. I don't know what you and this Zoryn are playing at but I want some fucking answers."

"Well let me tell you this much Bradley White, you are in a different place to where you think you are and right now you have a serious problem. In fact, you have a life-threatening problem, and if you don't listen to me you will die soon."

"What the fuck do you mean?"

"You remember the blue sun you saw when you looked up? Well, it emits a certain light that is strongest in this part of the land. Those that come from other lands quickly die unless they are treated. You are not from any land that I know of and you too will soon die. The liquid you hold in your hands will reverse the process and hold it at bay, protecting you."

"I don't buy in to all this shit," Brad said as he threw the cup and its contents across the room. "You and this Zoryn are full of shit. I'm not on another world; he is not some all-powerful being, and none of this is real. What's really going on here? You better fucking start being honest with me or I will beat the fucking shit out of you."

"Is that right? Okay beat the shit out of me. Try getting off your bed?"

Brad was incandescent with rage and tried to get off the pallet. His legs failed to obey the simplest of commands, the smallest of movements. He had full sensation in his legs, but it was as if something was blocking the signals from his brain.

"Of course, to beat the shit out of me, you will need to be able to stand up which you can't. It's a shame you threw the elixir on the floor. I won't have any more until tomorrow. Looks like you will be having a pretty rough time of it until then. Maybe then you will be a little more co-operative." The old man turned and walked away.

Brad lay where he was, unable to get up; he resigned himself to the fact that at the moment there was little that he could do. He was unsure how much time had passed since he had arrived in this place. He glanced at his wrist and saw that he was still wearing his watch and remarkably; it was working. The time was 6.00 pm but he had no way of telling if it was still Sunday. All that he knew was that his headache was worse and his skin felt hot all over and itched unpleasantly. Brad felt weary and against every instinct, he closed his eyes and instantly fell asleep.

His sleep was fevered and troubled and he awoke in pitch darkness, wet with perspiration and shivering. His skin was hot and his body ached with fever. The itching sensation he felt earlier had turned from unpleasant to painful. He felt ill. Attempting to sit up straight on his pallet, Brad felt the room lurch despite not being able to see it. He leant over just in time to stop the violence of his vomiting from fouling his clothing. Lying down once more, it felt like his bed was spinning but somehow he fell sleep.

Brad woke feeling no better, but at least it was light. The whitewashed walls of the place of his confinement took on a blueish hue from the first rays of the morning sun. He was lying there for some time before he heard sounds of movement from another part of the building.

"So, you made it through the night then?" The old man's sneering voice preceded his arrival.

"No, I fucking died you stupid cunt." Brad's reply was as thin as a whisper.

"I should make you suffer some more. I don't like you and watching you die would be entertaining, but sadly I have a job to do." With that, the old man walked off and came back with the same rough wooden cup and more of the strange elixir.

"Just so that you understand your situation, Mr White; this is all of this stuff that I could get. If you waste this dose, you will die before I can get any more. Personally, well you know how I feel. It's up to you, take it or die." The old man was about to offer the cup to Brad when he paused. "Oh, just one more thing: take a look at your hands."

Brad looked at his hands and could see several of the angry looking sores on the back of each of them were moist with pus. He had not noticed them before but as he stared at them, the affected nerve endings seemed to come alive and felt as if a naked flame was being applied to them. The stench from the sores was suddenly overwhelming and reeked of pestilence and decay.

"Pretty, aren't they?" sniggered the old man. "Soon your body will be covered in them, but most people die in agony before then. You though, Mr White, have been made stronger and I suspect your suffering will last a lot longer. So, what's it going to be?" He handed the cup to Brad who accepted it with numb fingers. Holding the cup to his mouth, Brad said nothing and drank the liquid in one go.

As soon as the liquid hit the back of his throat, he knew that something was wrong, very wrong. The liquid was physically cold, but it burned his throat like acid as he swallowed it. Impossibly fast, the burning sensation enveloped him completely. Brad could feel every part of his body at once, from the tip of each hair on his head to the inside of his eyelids. His whole body was on fire and the sheer scale of the sensations hitting his brain simultaneously, overwhelmed him. He could hear buzzing, like the chatter of a swarm of insects and his vision was obscured by ghostly phosphenes. Before he lost consciousness, he heard the scream of an animal crying out in pain and realised, as his grip on reality faded, that the sound was coming from his own tortured vocal chords.

Chapter 22
Recovery

The next few days passed quickly for Brad. When he first came around after taking the elixir, he felt much better. The headache had all but gone and the open sores on his hands had dried and no longer caused him any pain. He was however, more tired than he had ever felt in his life and drifted in and out of consciousness. Occasionally, his slumber was punctuated by the old man providing him with some basic food, which consisted of little more than water, a tough but not unpleasant tasting unleavened bread and a sharp tasting hard cheese. The water had an odd sweet taste and Brad had no doubt that something had been added to it, but he had gone past the point of caring. If they had wanted him dead, he had no doubt in his mind that he would already be dead. Besides, they clearly appeared to have some purpose for him, and had gone to some considerable effort to bring him to this place.

The time he spent awake increased steadily and he spent these periods in silence trying to make sense of what had happened. He worried about Gina and David and desperately wanted to see them and be reunited with them. Where was he, how could he get away from wherever here was and more importantly, how could he get back to his wife and son? Each question chased the previous one and ran around and around inside his head, over and over again, until he felt dizzy trying to make sense of it all.

Although the safety and wellbeing of his wife and son dominated his thoughts, Brad kept hearing the words of Zoryn Dakor in his mind as clearly as if they had been spoken only moments earlier. In truth, he could not say when they had been spoken because he had completely lost track of the days he had been in this place. What he did know was that this *Zoryn Dakor* was clearly a mad man. A dangerous mad man who had managed to get others to believe in his delusions. Whatever he was planning, there was no doubt in Brad's mind that he was serious. He wanted Brad to kill a man. He had said as much, but the whole thing seemed ridiculous to him. But then so many strange things had happened to him in the last few weeks that ridiculous had become the norm.

Brad continually ran through these events in his mind; from the road-rage incident, his newfound confidence, the attack on his wife and son, killing their attacker and then his subsequent transportation to wherever he was now. How could all this have happened? Was Zoryn Dakor really the cause of it all? How could he escape from this place and rescue Gina and David? He had plenty of questions, but he didn't have any answers.

"Time to get your sorry ass off that bed." Brad was roused from his reverie by the unfriendly tone of the old man who had entered the room and stood near the head of his pallet.

"And do what precisely?" Brad sneered in response.

"Well for a start, you smell like shit." Brad's only exposure to water over the last few days had been the odd sweet tasting water he had been given to drink. He was handed a bucket when he needed to relieve himself and was given some small squares of rough cloth.

"There's a room out back that has a bucket of water in it and some soap. I suggest you use it. And there's some clothes there too. Apart from the fact you stink like a pig, you will attract too much attention dressed like that. Don't go getting any ideas. The effects of the magic I used to bring you here have yet to wear off, until they do, your actions are limited to those that I allow."

"I want to see my wife and son."

"Then you had better do what I tell you."

"Where am I being held?"

"Zoryn didn't tell you, did he?" The old man chuckled. "You are far from the world you know, Bradley White. In fact, far from anything you know."

"What the fuck does that mean?"

"Even if I wanted to explain it to you I couldn't, because in truth, I don't know where your world is. All I know is that to reach it you have to leave this world and as far as I know, Zoryn and Kaiya are the only people that have ever done it. Now follow me."

The water was icy cold and the soap smelled like disinfectant, but Brad felt much better after he had washed. He would have welcomed the opportunity to shave off the beard that he had grown during his captivity, but he doubted that he would be allowed the use of a knife. The clothes that were laid out for him were simple and clearly homemade and consisted of a pair of loose-fitting heavy cotton trousers that were held up with a leather belt and a grey cotton type shirt. The shoes were made from thick leather and had obvious signs of age and wear. He was also provided with thick woollen socks and a thin tan leather sleeveless jacket that appeared to be even older and more worn than the boots.

Chapter 23
Training

From what Brad could make out the building he was being held captive in, consisted of four rooms; the room that he had been confined in for the last few days, the washroom, a kitchen and a small living room. The old man did not appear to sleep in the building. There were windows in all the rooms, and when Brad looked through them the view was the same from each one; grassy fields with hills in the distance. The dwelling was in a remote location and any chance of his being rescued was similarly remote.

"It's time to start your training, put these on." The old man entered the washroom and threw a pair of rectangular leather pads at Brad that had ties on each corner.

"What the fuck are these for?" Brad demanded as he caught the pads.

"These pads, Mr White, will give your arms some protection," came the reply. "Now put them on."

"Why the fuck should I."

"Because if you don't, I will break your fucking arms during your training."

Brad lunged at the old man, but as soon as his hands reached his throat, he found that he was paralysed and was unable to move. The old man easily sidestepped the next attack when Brad regained the use of his legs. Brad was unable to move in time to avoid the kick that the old man aimed between his legs. As the old man moved a little away, Brad could move once more but the pain in his testicles was so intense that he fell crashing to the floor, retching violently.

"That was fun!" laughed the old man. "Let's try that again." Furious, Brad who was still on the ground, rolled over in his own vomit and kicked out at the old man's legs as hard as he could in an attempt to topple him and bring the fight to the ground. His kick missed its mark and the paralysis struck again. This time the old man did not laugh and bent over the still paralysed Brad and punched him hard on the side of his jaw. Surprisingly hard for an old man. Unable to move, Brad took the full force of the blow and his vision erupted into shooting stars. "I really don't like you," the old man said as he hit Brad a second time with a harder blow. Brad didn't feel the third blow and was unconscious before his body regained enough movement to slump on to the hard cobble-stoned surface of the floor. "Looks like your training is over for today," the old man said to Brad's unconscious body as he kicked him hard in the ribs and walked off.

Brad came around some time later, with the taste of dried blood in his mouth and his clothes covered in vomit. He was still lying on the cobblestoned floor, and when he rolled over onto his knees to get up, he felt a sharp pain in his ribs. *That fucking cunt must have kicked me in the ribs,* he thought to himself. *When I get free of whatever is stopping me from moving, I will rip his fucking throat out.*

The shadows were long and he realised that he must have been unconscious for quite some time. Although his jaw was a little stiff and he had some pain in his ribs, he seemed to be in remarkably good condition. He thought back to how quickly his broken finger had healed. The old man could only have punched and kicked him a matter of hours ago and already he was healing. Perhaps, this was one of the things that Zoryn Dakor had been referring to in the police station?

Brad walked back to the room that had been his sleeping quarters. There didn't seem to be any sign of the old man in the property. Curious, Brad went into each of the rooms in turn. They were sparsely furnished and basic. He got the impression that this building wasn't anybody's home, as it showed no signs of being lived in. There were two doors to the property, one at either end. It was impossible to call them front or rear doors because the orientation of the property was vague. Brad selected the door that was furthest from his room and tried the heavy wrought iron handle. To his surprise, the door opened with a loud click as the mechanism responded. Brad stood motionless, listening intently and waited to see if he had attracted any unwanted attention.

After several long moments it was still silent so he opened the door. The grassy fields and hills in the distance looked surreal in the fading light of the day. Brad could see the final stages of a sunset between the distant slopes, but it was a sunset unlike any he had seen before. Where the sky and wisps of cloud should have been streaked with dazzling reds and orange, there was pale blue that was shot through with flashes of a deeper, darker blue. Brad was so taken with the strange vista that he did not hear the footsteps behind him.

"See that picket fence about a hundred yards from here?" Came the old man's voice from the shadows. "Well, that's as far as you would make it. One step further, and you will experience the very worst pain that you could possibly imagine. Why don't you try it and see for yourself?"

Brad ignored him and watched the sun set. The blue colours in the sky darkened as the light that fuelled them faded and darkness fell upon the land with more speed than any sunset he had ever seen back home. Within a matter of minutes, the land was plunged into darkness with the only light coming from the faint luminosity of the stars in the sky above his head. He was about to go back inside the property when he noticed an area of total blackness in the sky where there were no stars. He thought the stars may have been obscured by a cloud, but on closer inspection, there was no sign of any clouds in that part of the sky.

"Why are there no stars there?" he asked, pointing.

"That part of the sky is called Dakor's Darkness and is why Lord Zoryn is so feared," came the reply.

***

Brad did not fall asleep until late that night, as he once again churned over the events of the last few days in his mind. He was in no doubt whatsoever that he had been transported to a strange place, a different world even, and that his wife and son were in real danger. Either that or he was having some form of paranoid delusion, but he quickly dismissed this as everything about him was just too real. He decided that for the time being at least, his best chance of helping Gina and David was to play along with whatever was demanded of him. Besides, if he did manage to escape from this entrapment, where was he to go and how could he get back to his own world? Without a way home he couldn't protect his family.

The next morning, Brad sat up on his pallet and flexed his muscles. Physically, he felt good. The ache in his jaw had completely gone, as had the pain in his ribs. He dressed quickly in the simple clothes that had been left out for him. The old man joined him in the kitchen and handed him the same food and drink that he had been given on every other occasion. He had barely finished when the old man handed him the pads that he had produced the previous day.

"If you know what's good for you, put these on and tie them securely to your forearms."

Brad did not bother responding but did as he was told.

"Now follow me."

The old man led Brad outside the building to a small flattened area covered in sand just inside the picket fence. In the centre was a circle of black sand about two metres in diameter. "Go over and stand in that black circle and wait there for me there," said the old man. Brad did as he was instructed.

As soon as he stood in the circle, Brad felt a little lightheaded and his vision swam. It only lasted for a few moments and when his vision cleared he felt good, better in fact than he had ever felt. Even his vision and hearing seemed improved. His sense of smell was sharper too. Shocked by the sudden onslaught to his senses, Brad stood motionless.

"Feels good, doesn't it?" the old man asked in his mocking tone. "Strong enough to take on the world maybe? But not strong enough to leave that circle though?"

Brad responded to the old man's challenge but as soon as he tried to leave the circle his legs were no longer his own and they failed to obey his commands. He could move within the strange black circle, but every time he tried to leave it, he simply couldn't move.

"Your training starts here Bradley White, and during your training, you will not be able to leave the circle until I release you. Now defend yourself; let's see what you've got."

The old man walked over to the picket fence and came back with two wooden staffs that had been leaning against it. He tossed one to Brad. It was about a metre in length and made of an intensely black hardwood like ebony, but even darker. It was smooth and felt surprisingly warm in his hands. It must have weighed about a kilo and was five centimetres thick. But the most striking feature of the staff was that although the sun shone brightly above, there wasn't the slightest hint of a reflection from its smooth surface. The staff was like nothing Brad had ever seen before.

For the next several hours the old man swung his staff at Brad from different angles. The attacks seemed fast to Brad, but the old man referred to them as *half-speed*. Each strike would have struck had Brad not defended himself by blocking the attack with his own staff. The stamina of the old man was such that he never paused or relented in his attacks, and Brad had no time to launch any counter attacks of his own. Whenever Brad lost concentration he was struck by the other's strikes, which did not stop and inflicted much pain.

It must have been Brad's enhanced senses that saved him as he sensed rather than saw the full-speed attack from the old man. At the last moment, Brad dropped to a crouch and brought the staff up to protect his head. The impact sent shockwaves up his arms but he managed to hold onto the staff. Unnaturally quick, the old man attacked again, this time a swinging strike aimed at Brad's ribs. The attack was so fast that Brad barely had time to move the staff which caught the blow, but it was too close to his body and this time the shock winded him and he let go of the staff. Brad sank to his knees clutching his side, gasping trying to get some air back in his lungs. He managed to look up and saw the old man smiling and out of the corner of his vision saw the swinging attack that was sure to kill him. Instinctively, he brought up both arms to shield his head. The old man's staff slammed into Brad's left forearm and despite the pad tied there, he felt the sickening snap as the bones in his arm broke.

Pain coursed through his arm and his defences fell. The old man entered the black circle and held his staff above his head to deliver another blow. Despite the pain, Brad leapt to his feet and head butted him under the point of his jaw. It was not a particularly hard strike, but it caught the old man by surprise and stunned him momentarily. Kicking the old man's staff away from him, Brad sensed victory and swung his staff with all his might at the other's head, determined to kill him. Cat-like, the old man dropped to the ground and rolled outside of the black circle easily dodging the attack. "Not bad for your first training session. Now leave your staff in the circle and follow me," the old man said as he got up and walked back to the house.

Brad stepped outside the black circle and as he did, he felt his energy level drop a little. Oddly enough, the pain Brad felt in his arm was already diminishing. In its place was a warm, not unpleasant, sensation. By the end of the short walk back to the house, Brad could flex his fingers and turn his wrist over. The bones appeared to have healed already. "How is this possible?" Brad asked as he stared at his hand.

"Zoryn has infused you with magic to make you more than you are. He has enriched the area of black sand so that injuries heal rapidly. There is also some magic in the training weapons. You will be injured many times before this is over and we cannot waste time waiting for your bones to mend," the old man said without bothering to turn around. "My niece has prepared some food which is set up inside. First you eat and then we continue with your training. You will need all the energy you can get."

There was no sign of the old man's niece when they sat down to eat their meal. It was simple fare, consisting of dried meat, a better tasting cheese and some fruit that Brad had never seen before. After the subsistence rations metered out by the old man, this was a veritable banquet and Brad attacked the food like a starving animal. They ate in silence and washed the food down with what appeared to be some kind of fruit juice. It was sour, but amazingly thirst quenching and had a warming effect that spread throughout his body, energising him.

"Right, time to resume your training," announced the old man as he pushed his own plate and cup into the centre of the table.

"What am I being trained for?" Brad asked.

"Without training, you will fail in your mission and will be killed quickly and easily. With training you may survive, but only time will tell. If you get killed, or fail your mission, Lord Zoryn will have no further use for your beloved family and they will be killed. Does that answer your question?" the old man sneered.

The training continued in much the same way as it had earlier with one notable exception, the old man held back some power on each winning strike. Instead of breaking bones, the strike would cause sharp pain or knock Brad to the ground. The old man however, was relentless in his attacks, never giving Brad chance to recover or mount a counterattack. Brad was not being taught anything other than how to minimise the beating he was being given.

On one occasion, Brad made the mistake of turning his body away from the old man and curling into a ball, to protect his face. The old man howled in rage and beat Brad senseless, reining blow after blow at every part of his body that he could reach. Brad longed for the wings of unconsciousness to take him away, but the preternatural healing powers of the black circle only served to prolong the beating. After what seemed like an eternity, Brad managed to raise his left arm to stop the blows to his head just long enough for him to raise his own staff and fight back. His counter blows did not get close to connecting with the old man, but they did manage to buy him just enough time to defend himself to some extent, rather than just remaining a target for the old man to beat. Several times, the old man intensified his attacks and Brad gave ground, but he would never again turn his back and cower in the face of an attack.

"If you ever turn your back on me again, I don't care what plans Lord Zoryn has for you, I will kill you myself. In this land such an act goes beyond cowardice, it is an insult to your opponent and they will kill you." The old man spat the words out with vitriol and disgust, and Brad knew that he meant every one of them. "Your training is over for today. Leave your staff here and do what the fuck you want. But remember you cannot leave this place." He turned and walked back to the house leaving Brad tired and bruised despite the rapid healing. It was already late in the day and Brad sat in the black circle for some time, feeling his strength return as he watched another stunning blue sunset.

Chapter 24
Garan Smithson

Garan Smithson felt the weight of his years rest heavy on his shoulders as he walked back to the house, leaving Bradley White behind. He had had enough of the man for one day and didn't give a fuck what he did for the remainder of it. He hated having to train him and hated the purpose behind the training. Of all people, he had every reason to want Sanjin Dakor dead, but not at his hands or those of someone he had trained for that purpose.

He had no choice in the matter. Zoryn Dakor had recruited him in the early days of his scheming, long before his true intent had become clear.

Garan had been dishonourably discharged from his position as head trainer of Sanjin Dakor's Elite Guard. Although he was fifty years of age at the time, his close quarters fighting skills were legendary.

His training methods were brutal but incredibly successful. He never relented or gave his students the opportunity to give up during sparring. His mentality was that your enemy would not back off if they had the upper hand in a fight, neither would they let you rest to catch your breath. Sparring was treated as if it was real and students were expected to go for the killing strike every time. In fact, the session was never allowed to end as a stalemate; there always had to be a victor, just as there would be in a real conflict situation.

Despite the daunting reputation of his training, there was never a shortage of applicants. This was despite the fact that to be eligible to apply for Elite Guard training, an applicant had to pass a gruelling series of physical endurance tests as well as being recommended by their commanding officer.

The weapons that were used for training were made of a very dense hardwood that was capable of inflicting great pain when blows were not blocked correctly. Students started with a hardwood staff and progressed to training with a variety of swords and daggers. Night training was made possible by the faint blue glow given off by some of the weapons. The rationale being that you could see the attack but not as clearly as you could during daylight hours.

Tempers often became frayed during training and this was not discouraged as too much good feeling often led to half-hearted attacks and sloppy defences. The training weapons were infused with magic which meant that they never chipped or blunted and were always as new. The magic also made it impossible to kill with one of these practice weapons, but they could still inflict serious injuries, and broken bones and deep cuts were common.

It was rare for a sparring session to end without either or both combatants acquiring a significant injury, due to the fact that submission was not allowed under any circumstance. Trainees learnt to their peril that to stop fighting and admit defeat was seen as the ultimate insult to their opponent as they would be robbed of a clean kill. Instead of accepting the submission, the dominant fighter would go into a frenzy, beating their opponent senseless and in most cases abandoning their weapons to use their fists. Even in sparring sessions, the beating would almost always carry on until the losing fighter had lost consciousness.

Garan Smithson had only been put on his ass, in training by a very small number of people. The most notable being; Sanjin Dakor the King of the Five Lands, Zoryn Dakor and Farric Clearwater who later became the closest thing that Smithson had to a friend.

***

Zoryn Dakor was utterly ruthless and never showed any mercy to his opponents. His style of fighting suited Smithson's training. On occasion, Zoryn would visit Garan and his niece Hania at their home that was only a day's ride from the garrison. "Your niece is such a delicate creature Garan, and I can see how close you are," Zoryn said on one of his impromptu visits, "you must take great care of her, something so rare and delicate cannot be replaced."

Hania was nineteen at the time of Zoryn's first visit. Her mother and father had been caught up in the Great Incursion five years ago and had perished in the battle between the armies of the Five Lands and the invading forces. The Five Lands won an overwhelming victory and Sanjin Dakor was hailed as the greatest warlord the kingdom had ever known. Garan, however, held him personally responsible for the deaths of his beloved sister and her husband, Hania's parents. He believed that more could have been done to protect the villages from the invaders, and on more than one occasion he had got a little too drunk and voiced his displeasure in the inns that served the garrisons. Each time, he ended up sleeping it off in military detention. Word of this reached Sanjin Dakor.

Over time, Garan's pent up anger manifested itself in self-destructive ways. His drinking became more of a problem and most inns wouldn't serve him. When he did manage to get his hands on grog, or any other alcoholic drink it always ended the same way, one or more badly injured individuals and Garan sleeping it off in detention. To begin with Sanjin was lenient with him as he was not blind to his suffering and he kept any punishment to a minimum. He spoke with Garan on more than one occasion, encouraging him to stop drinking, and later warning him of the consequences if his destructive behaviour continued. The outcome was predictable; Garan didn't pay any attention and ended up being imprisoned for six months for beating two men half to death during a game of cards. Sanjin stripped him of all military honours and discharged him from service. He had no choice.

Without his role as military trainer, Garan Smithson had nothing to live for except to look after his beloved niece, Hania. He still drank, but only in the evenings and never left his home when he had been drinking. Money was tight for Garan and Hania. As he had been dishonourably discharged from the military, Garan did not receive a military pension and the only money they had was from selling plants and vegetables that he and Hania grew on the small parcel of land attached to the house.

Merchants would engage his services to collect debts from bad payers. Usually debtors paid without question when Garan knocked on their door. Occasionally those that were not aware of his reputation, offered some resistance, but they always paid whether he left them conscious or otherwise. Garan Smithson enjoyed these commissions and was always a little disappointed if the debtor paid up too quickly.

On one occasion a debtor awaited Garan's arrival and had a friend with him for company. Both were ex-military and each man had a reputation for violence, particularly when it came to women. The property looked empty when Garan

108

approached, but he knew better than to take any such sign for granted. Instead of knocking on the front door, he circled the house and hid just out of sight of the rear windows of the property. He waited for over an hour until he heard the front door open and the sound of gruff voices. Garan jumped to his feet and ran the short distance to the rear door and kicked it by the handle, shattering the locking device and forcing the door to open. Both men rushed to face the intruder and instantly regretted the decision. Smithson left the men beaten half to death and went through every room looking for anything of value. He found some knives and swords that the money lender would accept in settlement of the debt and took whatever else he found for himself.

He returned home later to find that Zoryn had been there earlier. "Zoryn called to see you Uncle," Hania said with her soft voice. "He didn't stay long when he realised you weren't coming back soon, but he said that he had some work for you that would pay well and he would call on you again soon."

Garan feared that this day would come. He knew Zoryn only too well, and that the offer of work was not a request. He was not afraid of Zoryn, but he knew what he was capable of and feared for the safety of his beloved Hania.

Chapter 25
Farric Clearwater

Farric Clearwater was having a bad day. It started off badly when he realised that the whore who had been so eager to please him the previous night had stolen one of his money bags, despite the fact that he had kept it well hidden. *The bitch was good,* he thought. *But not that fucking good.*

Events took a turn for the worse when his horse decided to go lame on him. If he ever had the good fortune to meet the man who sold him that useless animal, he would teach him a lesson in honesty that he would never forget. Farric dispatched the horse cleanly with a double-handed blow from his sword. He took no pleasure in doing this, but the horse would have died of starvation had he left it where it was. Farric Clearwater was not a happy man. It was a long walk to the nearest tavern and his mood had darkened still further by the time he got there.

The food at the tavern was simple but wholesome and tasted good. He attacked the meat stew with a passion born of hunger and wiped the plate clean and dry with the rustic slab of bread that came with the meal. The ale was dark and strong and not like the watered-down shit that was served in most towns. After his third tankard of the brew, he started to relax. *Maybe today won't be as bad as I thought it would be,* he thought to himself.

Farric always sat with his back to a wall, facing the entrance, whenever he visited a tavern and where possible, he preferred to stay in the shadows. His clothing was typical traveller garb, consisting of stout leather walking boots, dark-brown cotton breaches and a weathered dark-tan long coat that may once have been made from leather. He did not stand out from the crowd which was precisely how he liked it. In his line of work, the ability to blend in was essential. Farric was a mercenary, a sell-sword, a man with no allegiances, who would sell his services to anyone who could afford him. He was expensive to hire, but despite that his services were always in demand.

What singled Farric out above others who plied the same trade, was his total lack of fear. He wouldn't describe himself as brave, because he had never experienced fear, which made bravery a concept that he didn't understand. Growing up, he was always the child that would take on the dare that no one else would attempt. Not just to show-off, but because he wasn't shackled by the constraints of the fear that held others back. It took many broken bones and countless concussions before Farric started to learn his limits. But these weren't imposed on him by fear, these were physical limits which delineated that which was possible and that which was not, even for him.

Farric served for a short time in the Five Land's army but never fitted in. He wasn't a team player and had little respect for anyone. Taking orders was not for him and he left the army after the twelve months compulsory service that all men and women had to do when they reached the age of eighteen. Many stayed on and served the Five Lands. Farric Clearwater however, couldn't wait to leave. Not that he had a lot of choice in the matter, as he spent most of his time in the brig for a series of minor offences, mostly to do with insubordination. He enjoyed the combat training and after he left service, he practically camped outside the door of the legendary trainer and fighter Garan Smithson until he agreed to teach him in exchange for his labour.

It was at this time that he met Smithson's niece Hania, who he instantly fell deeply in love with. Sadly for Farric, his love was unrequited despite his many attempts to win her over. Hania liked Farric and was attracted to him, but she was saving herself for another. Just who that was, she had no idea, just a strong sense that she would know him when she met him. Such was her conviction that most of the local men had given up on her, despite the fact that she was the most attractive young woman that any of them had ever seen.

"I think he's a pig farmer," came a voice from across the room. "Coz he sure smells like shit!" Other voices joined in the laughter. Farric looked up from his tankard and took in the scene; there were three men sat at a table across the room from him. They were all thickset and had the appearance of men that worked on the land from their burnished skin and their heavily muscled arms. Farric avoided eye contact with the speaker and looked back to his ale, quietly pushing his chair back a little as he did so.

"Seems like he's ignorant as shit too." The voice of the other grew louder. "Too high and mighty to mix with the likes of us."

"Please Dared, don't start anything," the innkeeper pleaded from behind the bar.

"Just fuckin' keep out of this."

Farric was unconcerned about the situation that was escalating around him and took a long slow drink from his tankard.

"Ignorant as shit, smells like shit; that makes you shit in my opinion, stranger." His companions laughed at the last comment that was addressed directly to Farric.

This time Farric did look up and even from across the room, all three men saw the unmistakable flash of anger in his eyes. This man was not intimidated by them. There was also something about him that hinted at danger. Realising a little too late that maybe this wasn't going to be quite as one-sided as it had been with all the other strangers stupid enough to enter the tavern, the three men said nothing as Farric pushed his chair back and stood up.

The loud-mouthed man was the first to try his luck and met Farric in the middle of the room as the two men advanced on each other.

"Fancy your fucking chances, do you?" the fat man snarled.

Farric said nothing and stood less than three feet from the other man, relaxed but poised and maintaining eye contact. The other two men got up and stood to either side of their companion a little further back. Farric saw a flash of steel as the fat man reached into a sheath that was strapped to his right leg and attempted to pull out a knife. Closing the distance between them in an instant, Farric moved slightly to his right and as he did so he smashed his right fist with brutal force into the side of the mans' jaw. The fat man staggered forward, the knife still partly drawn from its sheath. As he did so Farric grabbed him by the head, wrenching it down hard as he hammered his knee into the other's face with concussive force. The fat man dropped like a dead weight, unconscious before he made contact with the hard floor.

Farric had positioned his attack well and was directly in front of another of his assailants, the bulk of the fat man separated him from the third man. The man he was in front of appeared to be in shock from the speed and violence of Farric's attack on his friend and looked at Farric slack jawed. Without hesitation, Farric kicked the man hard between his legs, too fast for the other to block the attack. The man's knees buckled and as he went down, Farric swung his right elbow in a descending arc that caught the man in the side of his jaw. So hard was the blow that two of the man's rotten stubby teeth were propelled to the floor before his unconscious body joined them.

Farric took longer dealing with the second man than he intended to and only just saw the third man's attack out of the corner of his eye. He didn't have time to block it, or get his in first, but he correctly gauged the angle of the attack and managed to move his head just enough so that the punch raked across his right cheek rather than hitting him square on. The third man had obviously put all he had into the punch, and Farric's vision swam from the impact even though he had avoided the main force of the punch.

Farric Clearwater was a mercenary. He was reputedly the best there was and his training, and years of experience kicked in. His attacker had overbalanced himself and as he lurched forward, Farric grabbed him around his bull-like neck, locking his fingers together behind the man's head. The third man was already off balance and Farric yanked him hard to his left, leaving him teetering on one leg, before he yanked him brutally to the right with a whip like action, all the while not letting go of him. Still holding him fast, Farric drove his right knee into the man's groin hard, then taking a half-step back he kicked the man hard in the crutch. As his attacker doubled up in pain, Farric grabbed him by the hair and pulled him down hard as he drove his knee up with explosive force into his face. The farmer was unconscious before he fell to the ground.

The first of Farric's attackers moved slightly, and suspecting that he may be about to regain consciousness, Farric bent down and lifted the man's head just enough to punch him hard in the face. He may have hit him harder than he planned as he felt bones break as he made contact. *Oh well,* he thought. *I never started this.*

The tavern had been empty except for Farric, the three farmers and the innkeeper. Scanning the tavern, Farric noticed that the innkeeper was nowhere to be seen. *Must have gone to get the local militia*, he thought to himself.

Farric searched through the clothing of each man and quickly found what he was looking for. Each man had a small leather draw string purse. None of the purses was particularly heavy but he took them anyway. Not wishing to have any dealings with the militia, Farric took the rear exit from the tavern which was through a small kitchen behind the bar. The kitchen was filthy and Farric regretted having eaten in this place.

Once outside, Farric spotted a small cart with two tired looking horses tethered to it. Lifting the tarp, he saw that the cart appeared to be full of vegetables in rough hemp bags. He knew better than to take anything at face value, so he rummaged around and found a dozen or so well made oak barrels. His eyes lit up as he realised that they almost certainly contained the legendary mead from the Isle of Akandia. Farric rapped each barrel with his knuckles and was treated to the dull sound that signified that the barrels were full. Farric smiled as he secured the tarp and pulled himself into the driver's seat of the cart. *This is turning out to be a pretty good day after all* Farric thought as he led the horses away from the tavern.

Chapter 26
Hania

Brad's enforced training continued every day at the same level of intensity. He had been at this place for about a week when he first saw the girl. He suspected that the old man had not been the one that prepared the food each day. The first time he saw her, she was leaving the kitchen area of the house as Brad and the old man returned from a day's training. She turned as they entered the room and smiled as her eyes met Brad's. For the briefest of moments, they looked at each other and then she turned and said something to the old man. Her voice was soft and lilting and contrasted with the guttural sound of the old man's reply.

She was about twenty-three years of age, five feet four inches tall and she was dressed in simple clothing that consisted of a long-woven skirt and a shirt like top finished off with a leather waistcoat. Her hair was strawberry blonde and her features were finely sculptured and delicate. But it was her eyes that held Brad captive. Even from across the room, he could see that they were a striking emerald green and burned with an intensity that melted his heart. He was so dazzled by her beauty and piercing eyes, that later that evening when he thought about her, he couldn't recall if he had returned her smile or just stood there staring. He suspected the latter! He had never seen eyes like hers; no one had eyes like that. His sleep that evening was interrupted many times by emerald dreams and when he awoke the next morning, his heart ached for another glimpse of the girl with the emerald eyes.

"Keep away from that one, Hania," Garan Smithson told his beloved niece as he walked with her to the outbuilding that was just the other side of the picket fence that surrounded the house. The outbuilding was not visible from the main house as it was obscured by trees. Garan had designed it this way. He had trained a number of people over the years and made it a rule to keep his work away from his family life. Most of the people he had trained were assassins or other unsavoury characters. He never discussed his work with Hania. Although he thought that she probably knew what he did, Hania never asked her uncle and he was happy to leave it that way.

"He seems different to the others, Uncle," Hania replied.

"He comes from another place."

"Where does he come from?" Hania asked.

"Just another place," Garan's reply left no room for further questions and they finished their short walk in silence.

The training continued, with each day being similar to the one that preceded it. It seemed strange to Brad that even though there was much repetition, he did not get bored with it. The truth was that the intensity of the training, and the fierceness of the old man's attacks, left little time for thought. When he did get a few moments to himself his thoughts were about his son and wife and the girl with the emerald eyes.

Several days had passed since he first saw the girl and he was beginning to think that he would never see her again. It was getting late one afternoon when the old man sent Brad back to the house to pick up some water. Opening the door, he was deep in thought as he looked up and was greeted by the sight of the girl preparing their evening meal. She smiled at him in a relaxed and friendly way, and in that moment he felt like he had known her forever.

"I'm Hania," she said in a voice as gentle and refreshing as spring rain.

"I'm Bradley White." The words sounded alien to him, as if they came from another.

"Well Mr White, I am pleased to make your acquaintance." There was humour in her voice, but it was good-natured.

"Where's that fucking water?" Garan Smithson's gruff voice from outside cut through the moment like a rusted blade through the finest linen, destroying all in its path.

"Sounds like Uncle is as grumpy as ever!" Hania laughed as she handed the water jug to Brad. For the briefest of moments, their hands touched and it felt like an electric shock passed through her fingertips and into his body. In that instant he felt a connection with her, it was like he had known her all his life. He felt sure that she had felt something too, as her smile turned contemplative for the briefest of moments as she looked at her hand before looking up again and smiling at him.

Convinced that he had not imagined it, Brad was looking at his hand when Hania enquired, "You are not from around here, are you?"

"No, I'm not," replied Brad. "To be honest Hania, I don't even know where here is."

Hania looked at him quizzically for a moment then said, "You better take the water to Uncle, Bradley White; he doesn't like to be kept waiting!"

While Brad had been getting the water, the old man had reduced the size of the black training circle by half. "It's time to move your training up to the next level," he said as he picked up a staff and threw it to Brad.

The old man's speed was astonishing; no sooner had Brad caught the staff then the old man picked up another and launched a fearsome double handed downward strike to his head. Brad managed to get his staff up enough to absorb the main force of the blow but was too slow in moving his body to the side. The momentum of the attack brought the staff down hard on his right shoulder and he felt his collarbone break. Without pausing, the old man shifted his hold on the staff, levering it upwards and to the side this time, smashing the other end of the staff into Brad's ribs. It felt like a red-hot poker had been thrust into Brad's rib cage.

It was only sheer force of will that kept him on his feet. Twisting his body and leaning back slightly, the old man brought his staff up in a smaller arc and hit Brad under his chin with the opposite end. It was only a short movement, but the strength and speed of the attack was concussive, and Brad knew that he was in trouble. Darkness crowded the edges of his vision and he could hear buzzing in his ears. One more strike like that and he would be unconscious and completely at the mercy of this sadistic old man.

He knew that he was no match for this man and that he stood no chance of winning this fight, but he was not going to lay down and die when his wife and son needed him. Drawing on reserves he didn't know he had, he summoned what remained of his strength and attacked the old man with a right slash, followed by a left cross with the staff. The old man instinctively moved back a little, then a little more as Brad attacked again and again. Every attack he launched wracked Brad's body with pain, but he did not relent. The old man was sweating freely as Brad pushed him back with each attack, and despite his superior skill, all the old man could do was defend himself. Brad swung

114

his staff in a crushing downward blow, determined to cave the others skull in and finish this for good. The old man held his staff above his head with both hands. Brad heard a savage roar and realised that it was coming from him. The two staffs met with such force that both men felt the shock wave of the impact racing up their arms. There was a blinding flash of light and a sound like thunder as the old man's staff shattered into a million pieces. Brad's staff looked like it was on fire as it blazed a brilliant clear white in his hands just for a moment before flaring once and returning to its midnight black colour.

For the briefest of moments, the old man looked surprised as he and Brad stood less than a metre apart staring at each other, neither one moving, both stunned by what had just happened. Finally, the old man broke the silence. "Training is over for today. I will arrange for your injuries to be taken care of." He turned and walked back to the house.

Brad managed to stay on his feet until the old man was out of sight and then his knees buckled beneath him and vertigo claimed him as he fell to the ground.

He woke later; how much later he didn't know, but it was dark. Somehow, he was back in his room lying on the rough pallet that served as his bed. His breathing rattled with congestion and he tried to sit up, but the intense pain in his side from his injuries was too much to bear and he gave up trying. It would appear that either his injuries were greater than could be healed by the restorative magic of the black sand of the training circle, or its power had been diminished when the old man reduced its size. Either way, Brad knew that his injuries were bad.

"You took some beating today by the looks of it," came a voice out of the darkness. "You either really pissed him off or he may actually like you! Uncle is a complicated man!"

The darkness receded a little as Hania walked into the room holding a small candle. Even in the flickering light, Hania seemed to glow as if she had light of her own.

"I don't know why you are here," she continued, "but I do know that your training has lasted longer and has been more intense than I have ever seen before."

"He does a lot of this?" The pain in Brad's side reducing his voice to a rasp.

"Yes. Some people farm, some people make things, uncle teaches people how to fight. And if the rumours are true, there is no one better in all the Five Lands."

Brad started to feel light-headed, despite the fact that he was lying down.

"Let me look at your injuries, Bradley White," Hania said as she put the candle on a small table beside the pallet.

"How did I get here?"

"Uncle carried you in; he's never done that before."

Hania opened his shirt and gently touched his shoulder. Brad felt an electric shock like he had the first time they had touched, but this time her hand lingered and the energy that passed between them felt soothing and familiar to him. Hania kept her hand on his shoulder and closed her eyes. Brad was dimly aware of her soft and gentle chanting as sleep wrapped him up in its gentle balm. "You feel it too, don't you Hania?" He said as he lost consciousness.

A soft glow enveloped Hania's hand as she worked her healing magic into Brad's broken collarbone. In her mind's eye, she could see the broken bones and tissue damage, and she used her healing magic to knit the bones back together and repair the worst of the damage. She then turned her attention to his ribs. Here the damage was much worse. Only two ribs were broken but they were a mess and one had punctured his lung. If she didn't stop the bleeding and drain the blood, he would die. "Uncle did a good job on you," she whispered to Brad's unconscious form. "And who are you and why do I feel such a connection to you, to a man I barely know? I know you can't hear me but yes, I too feel something when we touch. I believe I have waited all my life for you, Bradley White."

Hania worked steadily through the night, and it wasn't until the first faint blue rays of dawn started to lift the gloom, that she was satisfied with her work. Brad's breathing was steady and much quieter. He had moaned in his sleep several times during the night and at one point had become feverish. She dealt with his fever like she had with all his other injuries. One thing puzzled her; the strange sensation she felt in her hand the first time they had touched and again last night, was something that she had never experienced before. There was magic in him, power in his touch, of that she was certain, but it was a power, a magic that was alien to her. Could this stranger have some innate magic that she had not encountered before? Exhausted, she left Brad sleeping peacefully and went back to the outhouse where she fell onto her bed, falling instantly into a deep dream filled sleep.

Chapter 27
Coercion

Brad woke later than usual that morning, it was a little after 9.00 am. Somehow, his watch had survived his translocation to this place and his first day's training, after which he had left it under his sleeping pallet. Although his watch had virtually no meaning in this place, it was his only link with his home world. He had not really tracked the days much but if his watch was correct, today was the 15th June which meant that he had been here for two weeks and two days. It felt that he had been here much longer.

He felt okay and tentatively sat-up, expecting the wounds in his collar bone and ribs to scream out in protest, but there was no pain. He pulled his shirt up, expecting to see heavy bruising around his ribs, but there was no bruising. Brad quickly dressed in the simple clothes that had been laid out for him and was surprised to find that both the shirt and trousers seemed a little tighter than they had previously. It would appear that Zoryn Dakor had been telling the truth about further transformations, although he suspected that the changes had been brought about by the old man's fierce training regime.

He was thinking about Hania and whether he had imagined her with him the previous evening tending his injuries, and didn't notice the arrival of the old man until he stood at the foot of his pallet. "You survived then." The old man smiled humourlessly as he spoke.

"It would appear so."

"There's food on the table. I suggest that you make the most of it because you leave here today on a long journey and food may not be as plentiful on the road."

"Where are we going and why the fuck should I go anywhere with you?"

"Do you forget so easily the words of Lord Zoryn?" the old man asked sarcastically.

"I remember," Brad hissed between clenched teeth.

"Well, Lord Zoryn wants to talk to you anyway."

"Where is he?" Brad was instantly on his guard. The old man opened his hand to reveal a small green ball. Brad flinched instinctively as he threw it against the wall to the side of the pallet.

The ball hit the wall noiselessly and a wicked green glow sped from the point of impact rapidly, covering the whole wall which pulsated in time to a silent rhythm. For a moment, nothing else happened, and then Brad could make out some shapes and colours. The shapes quickly coalesced and became clear. The image was of the hospital room that his son was in and he could see David sat up in bed talking to a man that Brad did not recognise. The man appeared to be in his thirties and was dark-skinned, with jet-black hair and was powerfully built. He was wearing dark glasses and Brad could not see his face. But as he started to speak, Brad instantly recognised his voice; it was the Chemist.

117

"Leave my son alone, you fucking bastard," Brad screamed at the vision. David couldn't hear him but Zoryn Dakor clearly did and turned to face Brad and smiled. This was the first time that Brad had looked into the real face of his enemy, and his blood ran cold in his veins and every one of Brad's senses told him that this man was both immensely powerful and dangerous. "Has your Father been in to see you recently?" Zoryn was still looking at Brad as he asked David.

"No, I haven't seen him for a week, or it may even have been two weeks. It's difficult to keep track of time in here."

Zoryn turned back to face David and said, "You do understand that the infection in your hands will get worse until it kills you slowly and painfully, don't you David? Have the doctors told you this?"

"What do you mean? Who are you? I thought that you were a doctor."

"No, I'm not a doctor, but I know precisely what's wrong with you and I alone can end your suffering, for the better or worse. The choice is down to your father."

"If you hurt my son I will kill you, you fucking bastard." Brad raged at the image of Zoryn.

"Dad, is that you?" David could hear his father's voice.

Fighting to keep his emotions in check and not wanting to show any signs of weakness in front of Zoryn, Brad responded, "Yes David it's me. Don't listen to this man; he is twisted and evil."

"He also holds your life in his hands and that of your mother," Zoryn added.

"Where are you, Dad? Why can't I see you?"

"He is a very long way from here," Zoryn replied. "Your father has a job to do for me. If he succeeds, I may let you and your Mother live. If he fails you will both die slowly and painfully, and your Father and everybody else in your world, will be powerless to help you."

Brad screamed at the image but was helpless to do anything more. Zoryn removed his dark glasses and David screamed in terror when he saw his eyes, with their zig-zagged, orangey-red coronas savagely ablaze. Zoryn laughed and the vision flared once and then vanished.

Brad turned to the old man. "What sort of man are you to work for him?" he spat in anger and hatred.

"The same sort of man that you are," the old man half whispered the words before composing himself and added, "Now get ready and eat; we leave soon."

Chapter 28
Journey

Brad paid no regard to the food that had been laid out in front of him. In his mind, he replayed every detail of his encounter with Zoryn Dakor. He had to find a way of getting Gina and David away from him, somewhere safe. But where could they ever be safe from a man like Zoryn? There was no doubt in Brad's mind that Zoryn was a dangerous and powerful being. The fact that he had transported him to this place, with its strange blue sun and where magic existed, was testament to the power that he wielded. Zoryn had a dangerous and powerful magic that he seemed capable of wielding in both realms. What was the extent of his power? Where did the power come from? How could he stand up to such a man? And even his new-found strength had been given to him by Zoryn, and Brad had no doubt that he could take it away again whenever it suited him to do so.

He knew that he couldn't trust Zoryn to keep his word to leave David and Gina unharmed when this was all over. And that was assuming that he somehow managed to kill Zoryn's enemy. For the first time since this began, Brad thought about the man he was supposed to kill and why Zoryn, as powerful as he was, needed someone else to do it for him? Why couldn't he do it himself? Did the man wield the same power that Zoryn did and if so how was Brad to defeat him? He didn't have any answers but was convinced that this information would give him with some much-needed leverage.

One thing was clear to Brad and that was that Zoryn had to be killed. The seemingly impossible task that confronted Brad was how could he keep David and Gina safe long enough for him to get back to them and find a way of killing Zoryn? But then, even if he could go home, how could he kill a man with the power Zoryn possessed? Despair swept through Brad's body in a merciless, inexorable black wave that threatened to drag him under and drown him.

But he didn't drown. He couldn't stop the despair, but somehow he managed to detach himself from it just a little. It was this detachment that saved him and brought him back to himself. If he gave in now, Zoryn would kill his wife and son and he would also be killed. No, the only chance of survival for his family was for Brad to find a way to fight back. As impossible as this seemed, he would fight back; he had to fight back.

Brad knew that his only hope was that some opportunity may present itself to him. He swore to himself that if he spotted even the smallest opportunity to fight back, he would throw everything he had at it, even if that meant risking his own life. Any chance was worth taking. In the meantime, he would go along with events as they played out, but he would stay alert and ready to strike. With a resolve forged from the flames of determination, he was ready to see this through. Keeping his mind focused and his body strong would be essential to any chance of success, no matter how slim. He ate all the food that was set out in front of him.

"It's time to go, here drink this," the old man said as he handed a cup of perfumed liquid to Brad.

"The last time I drank that shit, it knocked me out." Brad eyed the cup suspiciously.

"You were weaker then and the potion had more work to do. This is the last time you will need to take it, but if you don't, you will die. The choice is yours."

Brad drank the liquid and once again, his senses were assaulted. The liquid was physically cold, but it burned his throat like acid as he swallowed it. As before, the burning sensation enveloped his body completely and it felt like he was on fire. His vision was obscured by ghostly phosphenes and he felt dizzy. This time, the sensations ended abruptly and in a matter of moments his vision cleared and he felt okay again. The old man handed him a heavy backpack.

"Where are we going?" Brad asked.

"Even if I told you where we are going it wouldn't mean anything to you. How could it? You don't know this place; you have never been here."

Brad followed Garan outside the property. It was a warm day and the pale blue sun was climbing in the sky overhead.

"I'm taking you to meet someone who will accompany you on a journey to the Eastern Provinces. You will collect an item and bring it back here and you will be gone for many weeks. I warn you now that any attempt to escape will be futile. You have nowhere to go, no way of getting back to your world and nowhere that you and your family can escape the reach of Lord Zoryn. I heard what he said to you. Your only chance of getting through this is to do his bidding. I believe that he will honour his word and free your family, but if you cross him, don't expect any mercy or a second chance. I have seen first-hand what he is capable of and witnessed the fate of fools who believed they could oppose him."

Brad stood for a moment in stunned silence. It wasn't the words themselves that caused his surprise, it was the fact that this was the most the old man had said to him since they had first met. Sure, it was a warning, but it hadn't been delivered in his usual threatening tone.

Two horses were tethered to a post just outside the back door of the property. They were both in fine condition and snickered gently as Brad and the old man approached them. The horse selected for Brad was as black as midnight except for a white diamond on its forehead. He had never really liked horses and had only ridden a horse once when he was younger and hated every minute of it. But there was something different about this horse that caught his attention and almost without thinking, he gently rubbed the horse on its flank. Brad could feel the strength of the horse through his touch and sensed a calm intelligence.

"This is Hania's horse," the old man declared. "He is strong and swift but has a placid temperament. I doubt you have any skills as a rider, which is why this horse was chosen for you. He is called Lightfoot and will do the work for you provided you treat him with respect." The horse nickered as if voicing his agreement.

They mounted the horses and the old man led the way. When they reached the picket fence at the perimeter of the property, Brad saw a gate that he hadn't noticed before. The old man dismounted and led his horse through the gate and Brad followed. "I thought you said I couldn't cross the picket fence?" Brad said.

"You shouldn't believe everything you are told then, should you?" came the response.

There was a small copse immediately in front of them that was so dense that they could not go through it and had to ride around it. On the other side was a small dwelling and as they approached it, Hania came to the front door. Brad's breath caught in his throat at the sight of her. Hania was beautiful, but her beauty was not limited to her physical appearance; it radiated from her very being. She said hello to her uncle and smiled at Brad. He felt lightheaded as he returned her smile. Hania's striking emerald green eyes held his gaze for a moment longer than was seemly and something unsaid passed between them. In that instant, Brad knew what had been missing from his life and he couldn't imagine a life without Hania being a part of it. He had heard of love at first sight but had never believed it was possible. Lust at first sight yes, but love? This was not the first time he had seen Hania, but each time it felt like the first time and yet, in a way he couldn't explain he felt like he knew her already.

"Have you prepared the saddle bags, Hania?"

"Yes Uncle, I'll go and get them."

"Bradley White will help you."

Brad dismounted and followed Hania into the dwelling. A short hallway led to a small utilitarian kitchen and the saddlebags were on top of a solid wooden table that was positioned against a wall to the left of the room. Hania stood in front of the table as she turned to Brad and said, "I don't know where Uncle is sending you, but please be careful, Bradley White." Hania looked at him with her piercing emerald green eyes before she turned to the table to pick up the saddlebags.

"Hania." Brad's voice was little more than a whisper.

She turned towards him, eyes cast down, not daring to meet his gaze, unsure what to do, how to react. Brad reached out to her and pulled her to him gently. She was powerless to resist as he drew her into his arms. She looked up at him and he kissed her. As their lips touched they both felt the by now familiar shock-like sensation pass through their bodies. Brad pulled Hania's soft and yielding body even closer to him until they were so close it was impossible to tell where one ended and the other began. Hania responded to the urgency in Brad's kiss and was as hungry for him as he was for her.

"I will come back for you, Hania," Brad whispered in her ear, his face pressed against hers as he slowly pulled back from her.

"I have waited for you to come to me all my life Bradley White. I will be here when you return."

Part III
Krendyra

Chapter 29
Rendezvous

Brad and the old man rode for the rest of the day. Stopping briefly every few hours to rest their horses, or drink water from the supplies that Hania had packed for them. There was no conversation between them except the barest minimum to make each other understood. Brad had no interest in talk, he was deep in thought, reliving every precious moment he had spent with Hania that morning.

He had never thought of himself as a romantic and had only really been in love once. He was old enough and cynical enough to be able to tell the difference between love and physical attraction. But with Hania, it was different.

He felt a connection with her that he had never felt with anyone before. It was a feeling, a sense of knowing her, even though he hardly actually knew her at all, and he was struggling to make sense of it. He also couldn't understand why he wasn't feeling guilty for thinking and feeling this way about another woman, when his wife and son were in such grave danger. He didn't believe in destiny, and yet somehow he knew that he was meant to be with Hania, that they belonged with each other. From what she had said to him it was clear that she felt the same way.

Brad was so caught up in his thoughts, that he only realised how late in the day it was when the sky started to become darker and the blueish light from the sun was turning the edges of the clouds into a paint box of almost every shade of blue. He had seen the sight many times since he had entered this land, but was in awe every time he saw it. He knew that the transition from sunset to night happened quickly and was somewhat relieved to see what looked like a small town ahead.

Arriving at the town, Brad could see the flicker of candlelight in some of the outlying buildings. There was a road, which was little more than compressed dust, that meandered its way through the town. They had seen a few other people since they entered the town but these people only paid them scant regard. It seemed to Brad that they were used to seeing strangers in their midst.

The old man led them towards what appeared to be a tavern. As they got closer, Brad could hear a mixture of voices coming from inside and it was clear that this was the focal point of the town. There was a paddock to the side of the tavern with a large open fronted barn in the middle of it with several horses in its stalls. The old man led them to the entrance of the paddock where they were greeted by a barrel-chested man of indeterminate years.

"Well met Garan Smithson," he said as the travellers approached, "we've not seen you in these parts for some time."

The old man dismounted and walked over to the man, slapping him hard on his shoulder and replied, "I'm surprised you had time to notice Regin, if the rumours I hear about the House of Secrets opening up here are true!"

"Oh the rumours are true, Garan. My wife wonders where all my money goes and why I only bother her in bed at the end of the week when I run out of money!"

Garan Smithson laughed as he handed the reins of his horse to Regin. "Take care of our horses and make sure that our bags are taken straight to our room."

Regin led the horses to the barn as Brad and Garan Smithson walked over to the tavern. It took Brad a moment or two for his eyes to adjust to the dim light when they stepped inside. Although there were candles dotted around the room, the lighting was subdued by the smoke that rose from the pipes of the occupants. The smoke had a sweet tinge that was not unpleasant. Judging by the looks on the faces of those inside, Brad was convinced that whatever it was they were smoking had a narcotic effect.

Garan walked over to the bar. A man of forty plus years with broad shoulders greeted them.

"Welcome back to the best tavern in Tyria, Garan Smithson!" he said.

"And the only tavern," replied Garan in his usual gruff tone. "Is my usual room free tonight?"

"Yes, it is."

"Is Farric Clearwater here?"

"No, I haven't seen him in a while, not that I really want to anyway."

"Why's that?" Garan asked

"Farric has landed himself in a whole heap of trouble as usual. Surprisingly, it wasn't fighting this time; although I suspect there will be a fight when he shows up. This time he managed to get the local militia leader's daughter pregnant."

"Apart from the obvious, why's that so bad?" Garan asked.

"She was engaged to marry the only son of the town's wealthiest landowner who will be disinherited if he so much as sees her again. The militia leader's family have little or no wealth and this was the perfect match for their daughter. Nobody will marry the poor girl now. It may not come as a shock to you that Farric disappeared soon after her father demanded that he make an honest woman of her!"

"I am beginning to see the problem here!" Garan replied.

"The militia leader must have taken a bang on the head if he really thinks that Farric could make an honest person out of anyone. Farric has no fucking idea what honesty is. If he is stupid enough to show his face around here, he would be well advised to keep a low profile."

There were rows of barrels on a shelf behind the bartender and he filled two large metal tankards with beer from a scruffy looking barrel that was situated midway along the shelf. Brad was intrigued why the bartender poured their beer from such a scruffy looking barrel when the ones on either side seemed so much more appealing. "What's in the other barrels?"

"That's the over-priced piss we sell to strangers like you!" The bartender laughed as he set the tankards in front of the two men. The beer tasted like lager, but the quality and taste went well beyond that of any lager that Brad had ever had before. He took another long draught then another and as he raised the glass a third time, he felt Garan's hand on his arm restraining him.

"This beer is a lot stronger than the piss you are used to. If you fall down drunk, you stay where you fucking fall, because I'm not dragging your body to the room."

The bartender roared with laughter. "You always spoil my fun Garan, your friend looks like the quiet type and they never fail to entertain when they have too much to drink."

"He's no fucking friend of mine," Garan grumbled in reply.

"I will arrange for some food to be sent over to your table."

Brad and Garan sat at a table to one side of the bar in silence while they awaited the arrival of their food. They didn't have to wait long. A serving girl brought them each a steaming bowl of meat stew and a crusty loaf which they broke apart with their hands. The stew was well seasoned and despite its hard crust, the bread was fresh. Brad, however, was so hungry that he would have eaten whatever was put in front of him. As the empty dishes were being collected, a wiry man about six-foot-tall, with a dark complexion and an air of confidence, entered the bar. He quickly spotted Garan and walked over to where he was sat with Brad. "Well met Garan Smithson," he said as he approached them.

"Farric," Garan replied.

"Perhaps we should go somewhere more private to talk?"

"Yes, I understand that you have upset the local militia leader, and we could do without him interrupting us."

"Quite!" replied Farric. "Although the word *upset* may not quite describe the depth of his feelings towards me! Rumour has it he is not best pleased that he will soon become a grandfather. There is of course some good news; at least the ugly cunt will have a good-looking grandchild!" Garan grunted in response and stood up and led Farric and Brad to their room.

"I understand that you want me to escort your companion to Krendyra?" Farric asked Garan.

"Yes, that is exactly what I want. My *companion,* as you have described him, will collect an object that he is to return to me. Your job is to make sure that the meeting takes place and he returns with the object."

"And you?" Farric turned to Brad. "What is your name?"

"My name is Bradley White," Brad replied. Farric gave him a long appraising look. "That's a strange name. You are not from these parts, are you?"

"No."

"Looks like this is going to be a long journey!" Turning to Garan, Farric said, "Our usual arrangement applies Garan, half the cash up front and the rest when we return."

Garan walked over to the nearest bed where the saddlebags had been placed and reaching inside, pulled out a fat looking leather drawstring money bag and dropped it on the table. Farric smiled broadly, as he picked it up. Hefting it in his hand, he was rewarded by the distinctive chinking sound of coin on coin. He opened the bag and pulled out a dull yellow metal coin. "Gold works for me, Garan. I don't trust any other currency. Any coin made of cheap metal is not worth rat shit." Farric checked the contents of the bag before putting the coins back. "We will head out the day after tomorrow. I need to tend to some matters here and pick up some provisions for the journey. When are you heading back to your place, Garan?"

"I will be leaving at first light tomorrow."

"Okay, well as much as I've enjoyed your company, I have somewhere to stay tonight where the company is much more to my liking and so much better looking, so I will bid you both farewell! Bradley, I will come back here later tomorrow afternoon to finalise our plans."

"I suggest you get some sleep," Garan said to Brad after Farric left. "I will be leaving at first light and will take the horses with me. It would appear that you will have the day to yourself tomorrow. There is some coin in your saddlebag to buy food. The people in this town are used to strangers, but you stand out even by the standards they are used to. Keep a low profile and wait for Farric to return. Do not draw any attention to yourself. I'm sure I don't need to remind you what is at stake." Brad did not reply.

Chapter 30
Forest

Brad was aware of Garan Smithson's departure at first light. In fact, he had no choice but to be aware as Smithson made so much noise that he had woken him up and it was impossible to sleep through it. Brad feigned sleep, not wanting to give Smithson the satisfaction of knowing that he was awake, besides he was glad to see the back of the man. Eventually he left and Brad drifted back to sleep.

His sleep was feverish and his dreams incoherent. And then, he heard his name being called. The voice was familiar but so distant that it was only just audible. Did he hear the voice or sense it? He was called a second, and then a third time, and each time he felt himself being pulled in the direction of the voice. The force was gentle but compelling and he could sense a power and purpose behind it and doubted that he could resist its siren call even if he wanted to.

One by one his fevered dreams fell in jagged tatters and were replaced with a single crystal-clear dream. Brad dreamt that he was walking through a dark sinister forest. So vivid was the dream that he could feel the springiness of the leaf litter under his feet and hear the cracking of small twigs as he stepped on them. Even the dank fetid smell of the Forest was real to his senses.

The tree canopy blocked out any sunlight and it was impossible to tell what time of day it was as the forest was wrapped in a preternatural gloom. There was something not right about this place and the feeling made his flesh crawl. It was at the edge of his senses, like something you see out of the corner of your eye that disappears when you look directly at it. Brad continued walking, knowing that he had to get someplace and meet someone, but not knowing where or who, or even why.

It felt like he had been walking for a long time, nothing much changing, until he heard movement. The forest had been silent up to this point save for the sound of his walking and breathing. The sound was feint at first. It sounded like someone was walking towards him. He looked in the direction of the sound and could just make out a darker object against the gloom. The object took on form as it got closer, and then it coalesced into the form of a person, a woman, Gina.

She stopped when she was about ten feet or so away from him. It was Gina that stood before him, but she appeared insubstantial, ethereal, wraith-like. He was so shocked that he just stood there, rooted to the spot, unable to move or speak. Gina looked at him and smiled sadly. "This is no ordinary dream, Brad," she said, her words hurried. "We don't have long."

"Gina, is that really you?" Brad's voice was thick with emotion.

"Yes, it is me, or at least some part of me I think. I don't understand how Brad, but I believe that this is really happening and that we are together in a kind of shared dream."

"Do you know what's going on?" asked Brad.

128

"Yes I do; well some of it anyway. I know that you are being made to do something against your will by an evil man. I've met him in here Brad; he's powerful and dangerous."

"He is very dangerous, Gina. It's a long story and sounds like madness to me but I have to kill a man and if I fail, you and David will be harmed. I have to go along with this because I don't know where I am Gina or how I can get back to protect you both. Somehow, I've been transported to a place that I am certain doesn't exist on our world." His words sounded incredible to him. "Are you still in hospital, Gina? Has he come to you there as well?"

"Yes, I'm still in hospital and I'm in a coma. I can hear the doctors and nurses talking but cannot move or communicate with them. I can't think clearly when I'm there. It's like I'm wandering in a fog and can't break free from it. I don't know if he has been there. The coma prevents me from seeing things, but the fog that clouds my mind lifts when I am here in this place."

"I know that he has been to see David," said Brad. "He made sure that I knew, that I could see the strength of the hold that he has over you both, to make sure that I do exactly what he demands of me. The man responsible for all of this is called Zoryn Dakor."

"Well, I think he may have made his first mistake. He wasn't expecting to find me here in this forest, and that must be significant in some way. What he doesn't know is that I can call you here Brad, like I've just done."

"You called me here?"

"Yes, but don't ask me how; I just knew that I could. I have tried many times before but couldn't reach you. And then, I tried again just now and felt your presence and called you to me. I can't explain it; none of this makes sense, but sometimes I dream of you. The dreams are jumbled but I can sense you. It's weird but it feels that wherever you are, we have some sort of connection."

"But how will any of this help us?"

"I don't know; you'll have to figure that out. There's one more thing, Brad."

"What's that, Gina?"

"Your eyes have changed; they look the same as his."

"At first I thought that it was just my imagination, but sometimes I see his eyes when I look at my own, but they are not like it all of the time."

"We can't stay here any longer in case this Zoryn comes back. He mustn't know that we can meet each other here. Now go, Brad."

"I can't leave you Gina, I can't do this." Brad could sense the forest fading around him. The dream becoming fine tendrils of smoke between his fingers as it slipped from his grasp.

"You must, Brad." Gina's voice was no more than a whisper as the dream faded altogether.

Chapter 31
An Evening at the House of Secrets

Brad slept on until mid-morning, his sleep deep and untroubled. He awoke surprisingly refreshed and got up and surveyed the room. It was basic with just two beds, four chairs and a table. The furniture was made from a dull brown wood that he didn't recognise. It was plain and unfussy, but well-made and durable. A shiny hammered metal pitcher of water was sat in a large earthenware bowl on the table with four finely turned wooden cups arranged around it. He poured himself a cup of water, which although at room temperature was surprisingly refreshing. Pouring himself another cup, he drank it as he walked around the room, stopping at a window that faced towards the street at the front of the tavern.

The street was busy but not crowded. People were heading in both directions, most were walking, some were riding horses and there was one horse and cart with a weary looking driver. Since he had arrived in this land, Brad had not seen any evidence of mechanisation. The town reminded him of those from the Wild West movies back home. There was no sign of electricity or gas and horses seemed to be the only form of transport.

But this land, or the people that lived here, had something that his home world did not have and that was magic. He had first-hand evidence of its existence, as he had seen Zoryn use it several times and even Garan Smithson seemed to have some limited use of it. Brad wondered if everyone could use magic but suspected not. If the use of magic was that common, keeping order and some degree of control would be all but impossible. He assumed that magic must be a limited commodity that he suspected commanded a high price, if indeed it could be purchased. Perhaps, magic was the reason why there was no mechanisation. Maybe they just didn't need it and this civilisation had developed without it.

He was deep in thought when there was a loud knock on the door. He opened the door and was surprised to see a pretty serving girl. She was carrying a tray of cold meats, cheese and small cakes. "Shall I put your breakfast on the table, sir?" Her voice soft and lilting.

"Yes, please do." Brad moved aside to let her enter the room. As she walked past him, he noticed her perfume, a sweet, flowery fragrance that reminded him of summer fields back home. She was in her early twenties and was short, with medium length brown hair, an easy smile and intelligent eyes. Her clothing was simple, consisting of a long flowing skirt that was drawn in tightly about her small waist. She was wearing a blouse that hugged her ample breasts and revealed a scandalous amount of cleavage. As she sat the tray on the table, she looked up at him. "Would sir be requiring anything else of me?" Her meaning was obvious and her seductive smile was unmistakable. He closed the door and walked over to her. Wordlessly, he pulled the drawstrings of her blouse and without effort, her breasts were revealed to his hungry gaze.

"Twenty sentars and you can do what you want. One silver and I'll do all the work."

Brad had no idea of the value of this land's currency and at this moment in time, he really couldn't care less. He rummaged through the saddlebags Smithson had left him and with his back to the serving girl, found two leather drawstring money bags. A quick survey of their contents revealed many bronze coins, a goodly number of smaller silver coins and some gold coins. Taking a silver coin, he turned to the serving girl and placed it in her hand.

She was as good as her word and despite not knowing the real value of the silver, Brad felt like he had had excellent value for his money! At some stage, he must have fallen asleep, but he instantly came to his senses when he felt her leave the bed. He feigned sleep as she gathered her clothing from the floor and quickly dressed. She headed straight for the saddlebags. Brad waited until she reached inside and withdrew one of the money bags and then leapt out of bed and snatched the bag from her hand. She turned to face him, the shock evident in her pretty features.

"I think it's time that you left, don't you?" he said. She looked at him, a flash of defiance in her eyes as she left the room without a word and without looking back.

Brad sat at the table, still naked and ate the food, not realising just how hungry he was until the plate was empty. Pouring the remaining water into the earthenware bowl, he washed.

***

It must have been around midday when he went down to the tavern. He quickly found the bar keeper who assured him that the room would remain untouched until he left the following day. As a precaution, Brad had already taken both moneybags and these were tucked securely into his clothing.

The town was not very big and was laid out in a linear style, with all the shops on the one road that led straight through the town. Brad spotted what must have been a hardware store judging by the assortment of buckets, brooms and various sized barrels that were arranged outside of it. He went in and looked for something to shave with but there were no razers or similar objects.

A shopkeeper emerged from a room at the back of the store and Brad asked him if he had any shaving equipment. The shopkeeper laughed. "Folks around here shave with a knife and soap," he said as he pointed to a pile of hard-looking, green soap bars. "We don't go in for any of that fancy shit they use in the East." There was more than a little sarcasm in his tone. Brad ignored him and picked up a bar of the soap. He also managed to find a knife with a six-inch blade that was incredibly sharp.

"That'll be twenty bronze," the shopkeeper said as Brad placed the items on the counter. He paid the man and returned to the tavern.

The soap foamed up well and had a surprisingly pleasant smell, despite its stark green appearance. After a little practice, Brad found that he could get a close shave with the knife without cutting himself too many times. He didn't have a mirror, but the shiny metal water pitcher gave him just enough reflection to see what he was doing. Satisfied with his shave, he splashed water on his face and left the tavern once more.

He spent the next couple of hours walking around the town and to an extent, enjoying his new-found freedom. In reality, he was far from free, but it felt good to be alone and to do whatever he wanted to do. The sunlight felt warm on his face as he walked.

From what he could make out, the town was in a small valley between two hills and was probably built on an old riverbed. There was no evidence of a river now and Brad suspected that the town got its water from boreholes, or naturally occurring springs from the hills. There were many some houses dotted around either side of the main road. One building in particular, caught his attention. It stood out because it looked new and there was a sign on the front apex that was clear even though he was a few hundred metres away. It was a simple sign composed of two parallel vertical white lines. By now it was late in the afternoon and the light was fading fast so he headed back to the tavern.

It was another hour or so until there was a knock on the door. "Open the door Bradley, it's Farric," the voice proclaimed. Brad opened the door, and Farric entered the room.

"We leave at first light, but not from this place. You stand out a little too much and I don't think staying here another night is such a good idea. Besides, I think you're going to enjoy where I'm taking you! Now let's go."

Brad didn't have chance to reply as Farric turned to go. It only took a moment for Brad to stuff everything into the saddlebags and follow him out.

Farric led them to the new looking building with the strange sign he had noticed that afternoon. "I saw this place earlier," said Brad. "What is it; it looks new?"

"It's called the House of Secrets," replied Farric. "It's an old business, but new to this town. The women that work here are the finest you will see anywhere and they will not steal from you, nor will you catch anything unpleasant from them. Treat them well and they will make this a memorable evening!"

They stood in front of the building and Farric knocked twice and waited. The door opened and an attractive woman of about thirty-five wearing a loose-fitting black filmy robe that was gathered around her small waist, stood before them.

"Greetings, Selicia." Farric smiled as he spoke.

"Farric Clearwater no less!" she replied, the warmth of her smile was echoed in her words. "And I see you have brought a friend with you." She extended her hand in greeting which Brad accepted. "Won't you gentlemen come in?"

The first thing that Brad noticed was the opulence of the interior of the building. From the outside, it looked pretty well like all the other buildings in this town except that it was much newer. Inside, however, it bore no resemblance to the tavern. Where the furniture in the tavern had been sturdy and utilitarian, the furniture in this building was ornate, made of a richer wood and was highly polished. Intricately woven rugs covered the floor and fine paintings adorned the walls. Brad was taken aback; it was not at all what he had expected. Selicia clapped her hands and two men appeared. "Take our guest's belongings to their rooms."

Brad was still holding his saddlebags and resisted, as one of the men attempted to take it from him. "Relax," said Farric. "This is one of the few places where you can trust the people not to steal from you. Let him take your bags."

"Farric, I think that your friend could do with a drink to relax him a little. Won't you both join me in the lounge?"

Selicia showed them into a side room that was sumptuously decorated. They sat down on large, well cushioned armchairs. She left them to enjoy the opulence of their surroundings and they were immediately attended by serving girls who provided them with light refreshments and large tankards of the same beer that they had had in the tavern. Brad couldn't resist the urge to gulp down the ice-cold beverage and almost instantly felt the pleasant light-headedness that accompanied it. The combination of the soothing environment, the blissfully relaxing armchair and strong beer, helped him to relax for the first time since he had been transported to this land.

Selicia entered the room a short time later. "I have selected one of our new girls for you, Farric. She has a lot to learn but has a wild untamed streak which is why I thought of you." She clapped her hands and a woman in her early twenties entered the room. She was dressed in a similar loose-fitting robe to Selicia's except that hers was white and much shorter and was gathered in the right places to accentuate her perfect body. Her skin was pale and flawless and her hair was a radiant blonde colour. Farric was clearly impressed with Selicia's choice and rose from his chair to meet her.

"This is Lisandra, treat her well!" Selicia said. Farric didn't reply and Brad doubted that he even heard her, as Lisandra led him away.

Selicia turned to face Brad. "In his eagerness, Farric didn't introduce you."

"My name is Bradley White, Brad for short."

"Please follow me, Mr White."

Selicia took him to another room and once inside closed the door behind them. Where the previous room was all about relaxation, this room was clearly about pleasure. There was a sunken bath in the middle of the room that was already full of hot water, with tendrils of fragrant steam rising from its welcoming depths. Brad could smell a subtle but seductive fragrance which came from a small incense burner. But what really caught his attention were the illuminated globes that hovered just below the ceiling without any visible means of support. They gave off a soft warm glow that provided the perfect lighting for this intimate setting. They clearly weren't powered by electricity and he suspected that the source of their illumination was magic.

Selicia walked towards the sunken bath and as she turned to face him, her robe slipped from her body, as if by itself, leaving her naked form revealed to his hungry gaze. Her skin was soft and flawless and every inch of her perfect body hinted at the pleasures that awaited him. She was confident in her nakedness and smiled unflinchingly as Brad stood there staring in wonder. "Won't you join me?" she said as she stepped into the bath. He quickly discarded his clothes leaving them where they fell. He was so entranced by this vision before him, that he barely noticed his own arousal as he stepped into the bath.

There was a ledge that was about a foot below the surface of the water that ran around the bath. Selicia sat on the ledge and beckoned him to sit next to her. The water was warm and soothing as he eased himself into its fragranced depths. Without saying anything Selicia straddled him. He could feel the heat from her body where it touched his as she impaled herself on him without using her hands. Slowly at first, she ground her hips into him. And then faster and harder as her rhythm increased in tempo to satisfy his need for release.

They remained in the bath and continued to bathe until they were interrupted by the arrival of two male servants bearing heaped platters of food. Brad didn't realise just how hungry he was, until he saw the quality and freshness of the meal. It consisted of generous slices of perfectly cooked ham, beef and other meats, a selection of fine cheeses and a basket of the finest assortment of breads that he had ever seen. The servants laid the food out on a wooden table to one side of the room. For a brief moment, he thought back to his home world and the desperate plight of his wife and son and felt guilty for enjoying himself.

"You seem a little distant," Selicia said as they rose from the bath and were wrapped in thick, soft white towelling robes the servants held ready for them.

"I was just thinking about home."

"And what land is your home, Brad? Because there is something very different about you and you are clearly not from any of the Five Lands of this kingdom."

"Where I come from is a long way from here Selicia, a very long way," he said as he gazed into her beautiful eyes, wary to reveal too much about himself or to trust anyone in this land.

"I think that you speak in riddles to tease me, Mr White," she replied, holding his gaze and smiling as she spoke. "But no matter, let's enjoy the meal that has been laid before us. You can tell me all your secrets later. You have a story to tell Bradley White, and I am determined to wrest it from you!"

Brad felt pleasantly light headed and suspected this had more to do with the incense than the beer. The rest of the evening was a blur. He remembered the fine food and being massaged by Selicia later in the evening. He must have fallen asleep at some stage, but he had no recollection of when. All he could remember clearly was a feeling of total relaxation, at a level that he would not have thought was possible.

Brad was woken early the next morning by a sharp knock on the door to his room. Selicia was not in the bed and must have left at some time during the evening, but her delicate fragrance remained.

Chapter 32
The House of Secrets

The history of the House of Secrets was only known to a very few. Its roots went back over two hundred years, maybe longer, no one knew for certain. It started out as a small brothel in Gaardsholme, catering for the needs of the military garrison. It recruited only the most attractive women and soon became the most popular brothel in the city, even though it charged more than any of its rivals.

The founder of the House of Secrets, Nadina Heartswood, was a shrewd businesswoman who put most of the profits back into the business. She knew that the more luxurious the surroundings, and the prettier the girls, the more she could charge for their services. She named her brothel the House of Secrets because all the girls who worked there were sworn to keep any information they acquired from their clients secret. Secret that was from their wives and mistresses and the outside world, but not from Nadina!

Over the years, Nadina became very wealthy and opened many houses in different towns and cities across the breadth of the Five Lands. With her increased wealth and the compromising information she had learnt about her clients, many of whom held high positions, came power. She enjoyed making officials and others squirm and didn't hesitate to wield her power over them if they didn't acquiesce to her increasingly unreasonable demands. This was ultimately to be her downfall. Having made many enemies, it was only a matter of time before someone took their revenge.

Her end came swiftly and without mercy one summers evening. Nadina had a voracious sexual appetite and was still very attractive for her age. Three men, new to the town, had sought the pleasures of the by then legendary House of Secrets and expressed a preference to share the same girl. Nadina, usually provided guests with a choice of girls, but this evening her own appetite got the better of her and she escorted the men to her private chambers. As soon as she closed the door, she felt the cold hard steel of the blades of the assassins. The men left her where she fell and met little resistance from the security guards, cutting them down easily and making good their escape.

The House of Secrets continued to thrive despite the untimely death of Nadina Heartswood. However, the next few decades were quite turbulent, as different factions sought for control over the organisation and the houses became independent of each other. That all changed when a young woman called Myreena Farrower joined the House of Secrets.

Myreena was twenty-one and was the youngest daughter of a blacksmith. She was quick-witted and heartbreakingly beautiful. She also possessed a rare and potent gift; Myreena had the ability to mind-skim.

Few in the Five Lands possessed truly innate magic. Almost anyone could wield magic, at least to some degree, if they had White Metal, but only a small number could summon magic without it. When Myreena was intimate with someone, she could sense

135

their dominant emotions and pick up some of their thoughts. She wasn't able to sense everything that they were thinking, and would not have wanted to even if this was possible, as it would have been overwhelming. By using her abilities, she could satisfy her lover completely. Myreena kept her ability a secret, and by using it to read the dominant thoughts and desires of others, she quickly rose through the ranks of the House of Secrets. Sleeping with both men and women, she used the information she gathered to further her position in the hierarchy. Nobody knew of her gift and when she assumed control she was not challenged, as all agreed that she was the obvious choice.

Myreena set out to bring the other houses together and over time she achieved her goal. She personally interviewed all the new applicants for each house. By asking a series of questions, she soon discovered that the ability she had to mind-skim was not unique, it was not common, but there were others like her. Those with the ability she swore to secrecy and over time she had at least one mind-skimmer per establishment.

She referred to these employees as agents, and in return for higher wages and other privileges, they were to share all knowledge they gained from their clients with her and her alone. Myreena, however, did not make the same mistake of her predecessor Nadina Heartswood. Instead of using the information for blackmail and personal gain, she formed a secret alliance with the King, to supply the crown with information. In return the crown turned a blind-eye to the operation of the House of Secrets and discreetly dealt with those identified by it as being of danger to the state. And so the House of Secrets, the largest privately owned intelligence network in the Five Lands, was born.

Chapter 33
Selicia

Selicia was deeply troubled. As with others of the House of Secrets, she had the ability to mind-skim and could sense the dominant feelings and thoughts of a man or woman she was intimate with. What troubled her was that she was not able to catch even the smallest fragment of any of Bradley White's thoughts. She couldn't even sense his dominant emotions, which even the least skilled of her order could do with little or no training. He was completely closed and unreadable. She had never experienced anything like this before.

She took another client that same evening, something that she never did, to see if she could read him, to make sure that she hadn't lost her talent. Within moments, she knew more than she cared to know about him and could hear his dominant thoughts as clearly as if he had spoken them aloud. Armed with this knowledge, she gave him sexual relief in the way he most wanted it and in so doing brought matters to a swift conclusion so that she was free to spend time with her thoughts.

When she left Bradley White's room, she felt deeply fatigued and a little light-headed. It didn't last very long and passed soon after she left his chamber, but she had never felt that way after sex, regardless of how vigorous it had been.

Selicia did not sleep that evening. She knew that the head of her order, Katzin, would want to know about this strange man. *It may be nothing,* she kept saying to herself. *But there is something unusual about this Bradley White. It's like he's not from this place, this land even. The whole thing just feels odd, not right. And why can't I sense any of his thoughts?* Selicia left her room and headed for her study that was at the top of the building.

Nobody but Selicia was allowed to enter the room, in fact nobody but her could enter the room due to the magical wards that had been put in place. She stopped before she reached her study and went looking for Lisandra.

It was still early and the house was quiet, but she wasn't prepared to wait any longer so she knocked on Lisandra's door.

"Who is it?" came the sleepy reply.

"It's Selicia, I need to talk with you now Lisandra. I'm coming in," Selicia said as she walked into the room.

"What's the matter Selicia?" Lisandra asked, now wide-awake as she sat up in her bed.

"The man you slept with last night, Farric Clearwater, what did you get from him?"

"Not much," replied Lisandra. "He's travelling to the Eastern Realm with that other man he arrived with to collect something and take it back to Gaardsholme."

"What is it they are collecting, Lisandra?"

"I don't know. I don't think that he knows. All I could make out was that he was being paid to escort this man, to make sure that he got there and that the whole thing goes ahead."

"Who's paying him?"

"A man named Garan Smithson. I think he's a friend of his," Lisandra replied.

"What does he know about his travelling companion?"

"From what I could tell, I don't think he knows very much about him at all, except that he is not from around here. He doesn't like him; that much is clear."

"Do you know where they are going?" Selicia asked.

"Yes, they are going to Krendyra. Annoyingly, the route they are going to take was Farric's dominant thought even while he was having sex with me!" she exclaimed.

"Do you know how long the journey will take?" Selicia asked.

"Farric seems to think that it will take them about four weeks."

"Thank you, Lisandra. You have done your job and served our order well."

"Is everything okay, Selicia?" Lisandra asked. "You've never asked for my report before our normal morning meeting."

"Yes, everything is fine Lisandra, try to get some sleep."

With her ebony hair and pale skin, Selicia looked like a wraith as she hurried down the corridors of the House of Secrets to her study. The first light of day cast an ethereal quality to her beautiful features. She reached her study and closed her eyes as she reached out in her mind to release the magical lock on the door that barred entry to all but her. The door immediately responded to her quiet summons and opened soundlessly. Selicia entered the room and closed the door behind her, locking it as she did so.

Although it was still early, there was just enough light from the large window behind her desk to illuminate the room. She reached into the deceptively deep drawer of her heavy wooden desk and withdrew an object that was covered in an intricately woven cloth of the finest silk. She removed the cloth to reveal a small rectangular block of an opaque white substance. It felt light in her hands and warm to her touch, as if it was alive. Selicia smiled as she held it in her hands and closed her eyes.

***

The secret to using a Zindaw Stone was to calm the mind and let go of any thoughts other than those of the person you wished to contact. It took both innate magical ability and a strongly disciplined mind to make the magic of the stone-work and most who tried failed.

Wherever White Metal ore was discovered, there was a surrounding layer of an opaque white substance. It had the appearance of a finely grained stone but was much lighter and was always warm to the touch. To extract ore from the ground, miners had to cut through this strange stone which was not easy, as it was much harder than the surrounding stone and more resilient to their cutting tools.

The material did not appear to have any magical properties and although decorative to an extent, the difficulty in cutting it meant that it was seen as a waste product and generally discarded. It was Selicia who first discovered the power of what later became known as a Zindaw Stone.

One of her clients had fashioned a small rectangular block of the stone as a present for her. Selicia was used to receiving presents from her clients, particularly those that had been visiting her for some time. But this gift was different to the others. She cared little for the man that gave it to her but nonetheless she always carried it around with her. It felt good in her hands, always warm to the touch and comforting.

One morning Selicia was relaxing with a hot infusion of sweet herbs that were known for their calming effect. She liked to start her day this way, and today she felt particularly good. She was due to prepare her weekly report for Katzin, who was the head of her order and insisted on weekly reports of all mind-skimming activities, no matter how insignificant they may appear.

Selicia sat with the stone in her hands as she often did and was thinking about what she would report to Katzin, when she felt a tingling in her hands where they made contact with the stone. In that moment, she felt the presence of another in her mind.

"Selicia?" A faint voice sounded in her mind, barely a whisper. "Selicia, is that you?" The voice repeated. This time Selicia recognised the voice, it belonged to Katzin. Selicia knew that she was not imagining this and was acquainted enough with magic to realise that some form of magic was at work.

"Katzin, can you hear me?" Selicia replied out loud.

"Yes, I can hear you, but only just." Katzin's response was immediate. "Where are you?"

"I'm sat in my study about to write my daily report. I sensed your presence Katzin; it's strange, I've never experienced this before."

"I suspect that magic is involved, Selicia."

"Yes, I do too, but I don't understand how. I haven't done anything different, except that I am holding a small stone I was given as a present from one of my customers. It's strange Katzin, but ever since he gave it to me I have held it in my hands. I like the feel of it, and it feels warm to the touch." As she spoke to Katzin, Selicia lifted the stone and could see a faint glow emanating from within it.

"Selicia, I want you to wrap the object in a thick cloth and bring it to me straight away. We don't know what we are dealing with here and I want to get it checked out before we use it anymore."

"Yes Katzin, I will leave immediately."

***

Selicia took a deep breath, and as she slowly exhaled she released all the pent-up tension that was in her body. She felt the familiar and seductive warmth of the magic from the Zindaw Stone flowing through her fingertips, up her arms and through her entire body, enveloping her in its soothing, almost sensual embrace. The stone started to glow and she pulled her thoughts deeper inside, as she called the image of Katzin to her mind.

Nobody knew for certain how the Zindaw Stone worked. To initiate contact, the individual had to hold the stone and visualise the person they wished to speak with. But the strange thing was that the receiver could hear the thoughts and respond without having a stone of their own. However, if the link was broken, the receiver could not re-initiate contact themselves unless they also had a Zindaw stone. The receiver had to be a willing participant. If they did not want the contact, or if the timing was inconvenient, all they had to do was ignore the caller.

Katzin was beautiful and was the most independent and confident person Selicia had ever met. But it was her kindness towards others that drew Selicia to her. Selicia loved Katzin in a way that went far beyond the simple love that friends felt for each other. It was not difficult for Selicia to call the image of Katzin to her mind, and within a few seconds she could feel her presence. "Selicia, this is earlier than usual." Katzin's voice was full of sleep. "Is everything alright?"

"I don't know Katzin, I really don't. We had two guests here last night; one who is well known to us, Farric Clearwater."

"Yes, I also know of this man," Katzin interjected. "He is never far away from trouble."

"Yes, Katzin. But it's not him that's the cause of my concern; it's his travelling companion, a man by the name of Bradley White."

"Strange name," remarked Katzin.

"The troubling thing is that I couldn't read him," said Selicia.

"Don't you mean that one of your girls couldn't read him?"

"No," Selicia replied. "I noticed something strange about him the minute I first saw him and decided that I would be his partner for the evening."

"What was it that caught your attention?"

"It's difficult to put into words, but he just looked like he didn't belong, like he was out of place. I know it sounds strange, but that was the impression I got."

Katzin knew that prolonged contact with the Zindaw Stone heightened any innate empathic skills in the user, whether they were in contact with the stone at the time or not. Selicia was a natural empath and the stone seemed to be making her ability stronger every time she used it.

"When you say *from someplace else,* what exactly do you mean?"

"Like he didn't belong in this land. That's why I decided to be his partner last night. I spent the evening with him and learnt nothing at all from him. He was very tense when he arrived and said little. I couldn't sense anything from him; no thoughts, no emotions, nothing Katzin. At one point, I thought that I must have lost my abilities and I took another client after White had fallen asleep. This other man I read like a book. There is something else, but it's probably nothing."

"Tell me Selicia, often that which appears inconsequential, is the most important."

"I felt unusually weary after I had been with him, it soon passed when I left his room, but it felt like I had been drained of my energy in some way, it was a strange feeling."

"And what about Farric Clearwater?" Katzin asked.

"One of the other girls was his partner, a smart girl called Lisandra."

"Yes, I've met Lisandra, a good match Selicia. I'm sure that he would have been well pleased with your choice for him!"

"From the look on his face and Lisandra's tiredness this morning, I would have to agree with you! Lisandra read Farric well. It would appear that he has been paid to escort White to Krendyra to collect an object and bring it back with him to a place near Gaardsholme. Clearwater doesn't know what the object is and doesn't seem to care much either. He's only doing it because it pays well. He doesn't like Bradley White and has only just met him and knows nothing at all about him."

"Do you know who's paying Farric to do this?" Katzin asked.

"Yes, apparently it's a man called Garan Smithson who lives near Gaardsholme."

"That's not a name I've heard for some time. You were right to bring this to my attention, Selicia. I will speak with the King and will come back to you. In the meantime, I do not want you to discuss this matter with anyone. If you discover anything else, no matter how insignificant it may seem, you are to call me immediately."

"I will." Selicia felt Katzin's presence withdraw from her mind, and she was left alone with her thoughts as the glow from the Zindaw Stone slowly faded.

Chapter 34
The Militia Leader

Bradley White was woken early the next morning by a sharp knock on the door of his chamber. Selicia was not in the bed and must have left during the evening, but her delicate fragrance remained. "It's time to get going, Bradley White, fuck it, I'm just going to call you Brad, its far fucking easier," Farric's voice came from behind the door. "I've settled our account here and you owe me a gold coin. Meet me at the livery yard in ten minutes, we have a long journey ahead of us and need to get moving." Brad grunted in response.

He didn't bother to wash and he got dressed quickly, eager to get on with whatever had to be done, to see an end to this whichever way it turned out. For a moment his thoughts drifted back to Hania. He could see her clearly in his mind, her pale skin, strawberry blonde hair and those piercing emerald green eyes. Would he ever see her again?

Brad checked his saddlebags. Oddly enough, he hadn't bothered examining the contents before. He found the two leather drawstring moneybags and there was a change of clothing. There was also a small metallic water bottle, a thick rough woollen blanket and a flint and file and some tinder for making fire.

"So you managed to drag your sorry ass out of bed then?" Farric taunted Brad as he arrived at the livery yard.

"Yes, it would appear so," Brad replied, matching the sarcasm in Farric's tone. Farric was inspecting the small cart and horses in preparation for their journey. He had acquired the cart from two farmers he had met a few days earlier at a tavern. It had come with bags full of fresh vegetables and several barrels of mead. Farric had given the vegetables to a poor woman he had seen begging by the roadside, and sold all but one barrel of mead. The remaining barrel he kept under the tarp securely lashed to the cart. Farric lifted one corner of the tarp just enough to allow Brad to put his saddlebags inside.

"We have a settle to score, Farric Clearwater," came a voice from behind one of the horses across the yard from them.

"Seems to me that you owe my family a lot of money after fucking up my daughter's wedding plans." The voice belonged to a man who stepped out from behind the horse. Brad assumed that he must have been the militia leader. At that moment, five men appeared from different places in the livery yard where they must have been hiding.

"It doesn't look like you've come to discuss a financial settlement." Farric moved to one side of the cart as he responded, facing the men who were about fifteen feet away. He quickly assessed the situation and could tell at a glance that these were no ordinary thugs; they had the look of militia men. The militia was made up of non-serving soldiers who all had some level of military training, which made them dangerous but predictable.

"Oh, there will be a settlement today. I'll settle for your dead body." The militia leader's men sniggered at the threat.

"Interesting terms." Farric's eyes narrowed as he stared at his adversary. "Now, here are my terms; you are a fat cunt and after I deal with your men, I will break every fucking bone in your body. These terms are not negotiable, so let's get this settled now, shall we? That is of course assuming that your men are not cowards like you?"

During the exchange, Brad took in the scene and despite Farric's apparent confidence, he was hopelessly outnumbered. Maybe he was playing a dangerous game of bluff? He quickly dismissed the thought as Farric took a few paces forward to confront the men. There was no way that this was going to end without bloodshed. If Farric was killed, Brad knew that his chances of getting out of this land and rescuing Gina and David, were practically non-existent. And even if he managed to find his way back to Garan Smithson and Hania, what then? He didn't believe that Zoryn Dakor would give him another chance. Brad realised that this was also his fight.

One of the men broke ranks with the others and charged at Farric, a knife in his hand as he closed the distance between them. Farric looked relaxed, almost to the point of indifference as the man bore down on him, not moving to defend himself. Sensing an easy win, the man thrust his knife forward, using his momentum to deliver the killing blow. With the knife looking certain to pierce his chest, Farric moved slightly off centre at astonishing speed, just enough to avoid the fatal thrust. As he did so, he hit the man hard with a short left hook that caught him just below the ear. The combination of the attacker's inertia and the force of the blow sent the man sprawling to the ground. Farric glanced down at the man quickly to see if he was still a threat. The man moved slightly and Farric stamped down hard on the back of his head. He didn't move again.

The next attack was more coordinated, as two men approached Farric with a little more caution. Neither man appeared to have a weapon. As they got closer, they separated so they could attack him from different sides at the same time. Farric didn't wait this time and launched a pre-emptive attack of his own.

Brad was astonished by Farric's speed, as he threw a feint jab at his would-be attacker. The man raised both his hands instinctively to block the attack which enabled Farric to move in close as he smashed his fist into the man's ribs with bone shattering force. Farric twisted his body to the right and hit the man hard under his chin with a powerful upward elbow strike. Before the man could fall to the ground, Farric slipped behind him and gripped him in a blood choke. Using the inside edge of his wiry forearm, he squeezed the man's neck tightly, stopping his ability to breathe and starving his brain of blood.

The other attacker sensed his opportunity and charged at Farric from his left side with a short-bladed dagger in his hand. Still holding the other man firmly in the choke-hold, Farric turned to face the attacker and thrust forward using the man as a shield. The attacker had no time to stop and his dagger pierced his partner's chest killing him instantly.

Farric let go of the now lifeless body and pushing it to one side, kicked the remaining man hard between his legs. As he slumped to his knees Farric grabbed him by knotting his hands in his long hair and slammed his knee into his face, yanking his head down to meet the upwards strike with devastating force. Blood poured from the man's broken face as he fell to the ground.

Throughout the attack Brad, who was on the other side of the cart, watched on. It all happened so fast that there was little else he could have done. He had never seen anyone fight with the skill and savagery of Farric and it looked like he could deal with all the men without his help. There should have been three men remaining, but Brad couldn't see them. He quickly moved to the front of the cart and it was then that he saw movement just a few feet behind Farric. The militia leader was advancing on him with as much stealth as he could muster. Brad realised that the leader of the militia must have known about Farric's fighting skills and had used his men to keep him distracted while he waited for an opportunity to strike without risking his own life. Farric was right about this man, he was a coward. But where were the other two men? He didn't have time to consider this, as the militia leader threw a large rock at Farric.

Farric had his back to the man and didn't see the attack. The rock connected with his undefended head, stunning him. As he turned to face the threat, the militia leader was upon him and struck him cleanly on the chin with a swinging punch. Farric fell to his hands and knees. Sensing his opportunity, his attacker pulled a blade from a sheath that was strapped to his leg and smiled as he drew his arm back to strike.

Brad scanned the area for the other two men as the militia leader threw the stone. He knew that the others were probably lying in wait and would attack him if he came to Farric's aid. But if he didn't, Farric would be killed. Brad ran at the militia leader, but was still too far away when he saw the blade. Shouting a warning to Farric, Brad leapt at the Militia Leader.

Farric reacted by falling forward and rolling to the side. The speed of Brad's attack gave him enough momentum to reach his target. He fell on the man, driving the point of his elbow down with tremendous force into the top of his head, rendering him unconscious. The Militia Leader fell onto his own blade which pierced his beating heart, silencing it.

Brad helped Farric to his feet as the two remaining men struck. With astonishing speed, Farric dropped to the ground kicking hard at one of the assailant's legs. The kick was so hard that the man fell without breaking his fall and blood poured from the back of his head where it hit the bone hard ground.

The other man managed to blindside Brad and hit him in the side of the head with a punch that stunned him, giving his assailant sufficient time to put him in a rear headlock. The man yanked Brad hard to the side using his neck for leverage, unbalancing him and using him as a shield, should Farric attack. Brad started to feel light headed as the oxygen giving blood was starved from his brain.

Where he would have previously been overcome with panic and fear, he felt the now familiar detached feeling he had experienced so many times recently. Brad dropped like a dead weight seemingly unconscious. His attacker stumbled forward, momentarily off balance, which was all the advantage Brad needed. Turning sharply to one side, he struck the man hard in his ribs with his elbow, feeling them break with the force of the blow. His assailant released his hold, and as Brad turned around to face the man he head-butted him full in the face. Blood streamed from his attacker's broken nose as his eyes rolled back into his skull. Brad slammed an open-handed palm strike into the man's chest to gain some distance and to launch another attack. As his hand made contact, blinding crimson fire flared from his wrist and the force of the blow lifted the man off his feet and propelled him several feet backwards where he fell to the ground lifeless. Brad stood there stunned as he stared at his hand in disbelief.

"Maybe we are going to get along after all!" Farric's voice jolted him back to his senses and despite the carnage around them, he couldn't help but laugh.

"Please don't tell me you've made any other women pregnant," Brad said as he pulled himself up onto the seat at the front of the cart. Farric didn't reply as he untethered the horses and jumped up beside him.

"So, what happens now, Farric? Do we report this to the local authority?"

"That was the local authority and I don't think they'll bother us again for a while, do you?"

***

"Katzin, can you hear me?"

"Yes Selicia, but I wasn't expecting to hear from you again so soon. What's wrong?"

"I've just witnessed a disturbance at the livery yard that you will want to know about," Selicia replied.

"What kind of disturbance?"

"It involved Farric, Bradley White and the local militia leader and some of his men. From what I can see from here there are several fatalities?"

"Do they include Clearwater and White?

"No, they are unharmed. I wouldn't have called you back so soon just to tell you about a street fight, even where one of the protagonists is of interest. I would have included it in my next report, but I thought that you would want to know that Bradley White may be a whole lot more dangerous than we had thought, Katzin. I've just seen him use a strange magic to kill one of the men."

Chapter 35
On the Road

They spent most of the day in silence each wrapped up in their own thoughts. The day was uneventful and they saw only a few other travellers on the road. Brad noticed that in practically all cases, they travelled in groups of three or more. The travellers gave them a wide berth as they passed by and only made eye contact with them if it was unavoidable, and it rarely was. The nervousness and caution apparent in their demeanour, made it clear to Brad that travel in this land was far from safe.

They stopped to eat a meal of dried meat and fruit at midday and then continued their journey until it started to get dark. Night fell quickly in this land, something that Brad was still getting used to, and he knew that they would have to find somewhere to spend the night soon.

Farric led them off the road. He didn't follow any discernible track that Brad could make out in the fading light. They continued on for about a half a mile until they reached a small copse of dense trees and the ruins of a small dwelling. Its crumbling walls stuck out of the ground like the bones of this strange land. There was no roof to offer them any real shelter, but the remains of the walls afforded them some protection at least.

"There won't be a fire tonight," Farric broke the silence. "It's not safe here, and we may still run into some militia from Tyria."

"They really don't like you very much, do they Farric?" Brad replied.

Farric turned to face him, his features hard and unreadable in the darkness. For a moment, Brad thought that this may not end well and readied himself.

"Ha, you could say that!" Farric broke the tension as he roared with laughter.

"You could have left me there," Farric said after his laughter subsided. His tone now serious. "I was in no position to stop you if you decided to run off. I don't know what hold Garan Smithson has over you, but it's pretty obvious to me that you're doing this against your will, and yet you stayed. It's not my business to know, I'm being paid to escort you to Krendyra and ensure your safe return and nothing else. It may not have ended well for me back there without your help Brad. I can't remember the last time that someone had my back, thank you." Farric turned away before Brad could respond.

The night was cold and the thin blanket that Garan had supplied was less than adequate. Brad managed to get some sleep, but the combination of the hard ground and the cold was enough to interrupt his sleep on more than one occasion. Farric, however, appeared to have slept well, at least if his snoring was any indication.

Brad thought that Farric must be used to living this way, and for the first time since they had met, he found himself wondering who this man was and why Garan had hired him? He suspected that it had a lot to do with the man's fighting ability which, was the best that he had ever seen. What made it even more impressive was that Farric had been outnumbered and had been fighting for his life against trained men. Farric Clearwater was clearly a very dangerous man.

They woke early and ate a cold breakfast of dried fruit and a strongly flavoured hard cheese which they washed down with water from some skins that Farric took from the cart. Although the rations were meagre, Brad was surprised at how full he felt.

"How long will it take us to get to this Krendyra?" Brad asked as they climbed up onto the cart.

"Four weeks, if we make good progress, maybe longer. Why, do you have somewhere else to go?" Farric replied good-naturedly.

"I guess not, for the time being at least," Brad murmured more to himself than to his companion.

They made good progress that day, stopping once around mid-morning for a light lunch of dried meat and some more of the strongly flavoured hard cheese. Again, Brad was surprised at how full and satisfied he felt after eating such a small meal. "What is this cheese?"

"I know an old woman near Tyria who makes it," replied Farric. "She infuses it with magic to enhance its restorative qualities. Small amounts will sustain you on a long journey and keep you strong. Few know of its existence and it's very hard to come by. It doesn't taste too bad either!" They continued their journey and as night approached they reached a small village.

It was dark when they arrived and the absence of streetlights made it difficult for Brad to make much out. Farric, however, seemed to know where he was going and before long they reached a tavern in the centre of the village. There was a small access lane by the side of it which led into a gated courtyard where they left the horses and cart.

It was gloomy inside the tavern, with the only light coming from a small fire and some candles that were dotted around the room. The air was full of smoke, partly from the fire but mostly from the pipes of the occupants, who each seemed to be engulfed in a cloud of their own making. Nobody bothered to look up when they entered the room, and it seemed to Brad that they were used to strangers in this village and paid little heed to them. Farric spoke with the innkeeper and arranged for a large room with two beds for the night and were soon sat down with brimming mugs of ale.

"So what is your connection with Garan Smithson?" Farric asked, as direct as ever.

"I'm not sure I fully understand the connection myself," replied Brad. "Smithson is working for someone else, and I am somehow caught up in it."

"Why don't you walk away?"

"I wish it was that simple, but I can't," replied Brad.

Farric took a long appraising look at him before he spoke again. "You are not from these parts, are you?"

"No, I'm not," Brad replied. "I don't even know where *these parts* are."

"I don't understand, what do you mean?"

"All I know is that one minute I was in my world, and then the next I was here."

"Can't you go back?"

"I don't know how to, or even where my world is in relation to this place. Wherever it is, I am certain that it can't be reached by horse or ship."

"So how did you get here in the first place?"

"You won't believe me if I told you."

"Try me," replied Farric.

"If it didn't sound so ridiculous, I would say that I was transported here by magic."

"Do you consider magic ridiculous?" asked Farric.

"We certainly don't have it where I come from."

"Would it surprise you if I told you that we have magic here?"

"I've seen some strange things in the last few weeks and nothing very much surprises me anymore."

"Not everyone here has the use of magic. It's mostly reserved and protected for those of *noble birth* or those who have the money to buy it. I'm not in either group and I wouldn't want to have magic even if I was."

"Why's that?" Brad asked.

"I don't trust it. I've seen what magic does to a person, and I don't like it. It's unpredictable and it makes the wielder lazy. I wouldn't want to gamble my life on it working when I needed it most."

Their conversation was interrupted when a serving maid arrived with two steaming bowls of meat stew. Brad and Farric ate their meal in silence, both hungry and weary from the day's travel.

***

Their journey continued for the next two weeks in much the same way and without incident. They stayed where possible, at inns and slept under the stars at other times. Brad was slowly getting used to the speed at which night fell in this land, but still marvelled at the blueish light from this world's sun. It was eerie but strangely beautiful. The only people they spoke with were the serving staff at the inns.

After another day's travel, they made camp a half mile or so off the road and had their usual meal of dried meat and the strange tasting hard cheese. Farric felt that it was safe to light a campfire and Brad was thankful as the evenings were cold in this land, despite the heat of the days. Neither man craved conversation and were content for the little there was, both deep in their own thoughts. Brad fell asleep quickly that evening.

Chapter 36
Connection

"Brad." Gina's voice called out to him in his sleep. "Brad, come to me."

In his dream, Brad could feel himself being pulled towards something or somewhere, drawn by some unseen force. Slowly at first and then faster and faster. He knew what was happening to him, but last time the force had been gentler. This time it was much stronger, and he doubted that he could resist its inexorable summons. He was moving so fast now that all around him was a blur, punctuated only by kaleidoscopic flashes of light that disappeared almost as quickly as they appeared.

Then without warning, his feet connected with the soft leaf litter of a forest floor and he was standing on his feet, a little unsteady as the vertigo of his transportation faded. He was back in the forest and Gina was standing in front of him, wraithlike and pale as a ghost. She looked as beautiful as the day they had first met, but her beauty was as delicate as her presence was ethereal. Brad went to her, and despite her apparent lack of substance she felt real to his touch, to his senses. He wrapped his arms around her, she returned the embrace and as they held each other, he wept.

For long moments, they stood without talking, taking comfort from the presence of the other.

"Have you had another visit from Zoryn?" Brad eventually asked, punctuating the silence.

"No, I haven't," Gina replied. "I don't think he will come back, he doesn't need to. I think he just wanted to demonstrate his power and make sure that I understood our helplessness."

"If I could only get you and David away from him, maybe we would stand a chance."

"He's too powerful to take on directly Brad; he would crush us without a second thought. And I believe him to be evil beyond anything I have ever imagined."

"All I can do is go along with what he wants, at least until I can figure out some way of getting you and David away from him," said Brad. "If it comes to it, I will kill him if that's what it takes to escape from him."

"No Brad, you mustn't kill anyone for us. I can't let you take another's life." Gina's voice betrayed the emotions she was feeling.

"But I've already killed a man. The man who crippled my son and raped my wife."

"I know, Brad." Gina's voice barely a whisper.

"How could you possibly know that?"

"I heard the police talking to each other when they came to my bedside. They said that a man called Raymond Oliver had been beaten to death and had strange burn marks on his chest."

"I've never felt anger like it before Gina, I went looking for him and I killed him."

"Do you understand that he was just a puppet of Zoryn?" Gina asked.

"Yes, but I don't regret it and I would do the same thing again if I had to."

"You've changed, Brad, you would never have done anything like this before."

"I know. Zoryn has done something to me, changed me somehow. I am stronger now than I was in my twenties and I don't feel any fear when I get into a fight. In fact I don't really feel much anymore and never gave killing Raymond Oliver a second thought. I still don't feel any remorse and doubt that I ever will."

"You have changed, Brad."

"I think that something has been implanted in my wrists, Gina. I don't know what it is, but I think that it is the source of the power that has changed me. Maybe if I could find a way of using that power, we could use it against Zoryn."

"I'm growing tired and can't keep you here any longer. Take care my love." Gina's already ethereal body evaporated in front of him as the forest went black and he returned to his dreams.

Chapter 37
Magic

The next morning Brad was awake early, ready to move on and face whatever came his way. He wanted to get this over with. He had been a victim for too long, helpless and trapped by Zoryn and unable to see any way of fighting back. But something inside him had changed last night and he felt stronger because of it. Seeing Gina had given him the inner strength that had been lacking since he had been transported to this land. He felt something else too, but it had been so long since he had felt it that he barely recognised it for what it was, he felt hope.

"We will be staying somewhere far more hospitable tonight, Brad," Farric announced as they packed the cart ready for the day's travel. "Tonight, my travelling companion, we stay at The House of Secrets." Farric could barely contain the enthusiasm in his voice.

"You mean…"

"Yes, Brad, that is exactly what I mean!" Farric interrupted before he could complete his sentence. "I don't know this one as well as the one in Tyria, but I do know that the welcome will be just as good!"

Brad couldn't help but smile, not just at Farric's infectious enthusiasm, but at the prospect of a soft warm bed and the other comforts that The House of Secrets had to offer.

As they continued their journey, Brad thought back to his meeting with Gina the previous night. Only a few weeks or so ago when his life was normal, he would have thought someone insane if they had told him that they had met someone in their dreams and that they could talk to them and feel everything as if it was real. But he knew that his meeting with Gina had been real, that they had met in a forest and that they had held each other close. After all, so many strange and seemingly impossible things had already happened to him in the last few weeks, that a dream meeting seemed perhaps the least strange of all.

They travelled for the rest of the day, mostly in silence, each locked inside a world of their own thoughts. Stopping briefly for their usual lunch of stale bread and the rejuvenating strongly flavoured cheese, they made good progress and arrived at the next town before nightfall.

All the towns that Brad had been to since his transportation to this land, looked very similar and he would be hard pushed to tell one from the other. He had not been interested in place names before, but he was beginning to realise that if he stood any chance of defeating Zoryn, or at least getting his family to safety, it was important that he knew his way around this land.

"What's the name of this place?" Brad asked Farric, as they rode into the centre of the small town.

"It's called Dumas and is the last town of the Western Provinces," replied Farric.

Nearing the centre of the town, Brad saw a well-kept property that had a sign with two parallel white vertical lines on it. It was the same sign he had seen on the House of Secrets in Tyria. As they drew up outside the building, a smartly dressed middle-aged man opened the door and approached them before they had chance to get off the cart.

"Would you gentlemen be staying here this evening?" he asked, in a confident, well-educated voice.

"Yes, we will," replied Farric.

"In that case, may I tend to your horses and arrange for your belongings to be brought to your rooms?"

"Yes. That would be most gracious," said Farric with a flourish of his arms as he glanced over and smiled at Brad, who for his part was trying not to laugh at Farric's theatrical response. The man clapped his hands and a younger man appeared at the doorway and proceeded to take their bags from the cart.

"Please, follow me inside," bid the older of the two men as he led them into the House of Secrets.

Inside the property was remarkably similar to the House of Secrets in Tyria. *No not similar*, he thought, *identical, with its large opulent reception room*. They were greeted by a woman in her thirties with a dazzling smile and hypnotic gaze.

"Welcome gentlemen." Her greeting as warm and effusive as her smile. "My name is Myrinia, please follow me into the lounge where you can relax and enjoy some refreshment while we make preparations for your enjoyment."

They were led into an equally opulent room which had been designed to relax guests with its soft lighting and sumptuous furnishings. There was a subtle but seductive fragrance that emanated from a small incense burner to one side of the room and this reminded Brad of his evening with Selicia.

His mind wandered back to that evening and his reverie was only broken when a strawberry blonde-haired girl in her early twenties offered him a frosted glass of the same ice-cold beer that he had in Tyria. Brad was so caught up in his daydream, that he didn't notice the arrival of the girl, or the disappearance of Farric. He realised then that the incense was a mild drug that was probably used by the House of Secrets to intensify their guest's experience, or to make them more compliant and easier to deal with. Either way, it appeared to be working.

Looking up at the girl, he was immediately struck by how much she looked like Hania. She had the same flawless skin, the same strawberry blonde hair, only her eyes were different. Where Hania's eyes were a striking emerald green, this girl had pale blue, almost translucent eyes. He felt his passion rise and knew that he had to have her.

"My name is Iolanthe, is there anything else you require master." Her voice soft and playfully mocking, teasing him and hinting at the pleasures to come. He said nothing as he pulled her to him. She didn't resist as his mouth found hers and he kissed her hard. He parted her filmy robe and was rewarded by the touch of her naked flesh.

Afterwards, she led him to his room which had a luxurious sunken bath in the middle of the floor. The water was comfortably hot and she sat behind him wrapping her long legs around his body. She gently massaged his neck and back and used delicate soaps and oils to bathe him.

"She must be very special," Iolanthe said as she continued.

"What do you mean?" Brad replied.

"I have slept with many men, and I am used to their desires and needs, but for you I was someone else. It doesn't concern me, because your stay here is all about your pleasure, but the passion you feel for this girl is strong. She must be very special; you must care very much for her."

"Yes, she is special Iolanthe, and I do care deeply for her, even though I hardly know her at all." Brad didn't dream at all that evening and awoke the next morning feeling completely rested and full of energy. He suspected that this was all part of the House of Secrets experience, and that his deep sleep may be due at least in part to the intoxicating incense. Turning over in the soft luxuriance of his bed, Brad was not surprised that Iolanthe had already left. He smiled as he remembered their night together and how much she reminded him of Hania.

***

Iolanthe made her report to Myrinia. "What did you discover about this stranger?" Myrinia asked her.

"Nothing, his mind was closed to me. How can this be possible?"

"I don't know Iolanthe, he is a strange one. I will report this to Selicia straight away. If you recall anything else about this man that may interest her, no matter how insignificant it may seem, let me know without delay."

"Well it sounds odd, but there was something else. I felt completely drained of energy when I left his room and couldn't have taken another client. But once I was away from him, I started to feel better almost immediately."

"I will ensure that Katzin receives a full report."

***

Brad could easily have stayed in the warmth and comfort of the bed all day, but a loud knock at the door soon put paid to that.

"Get your lazy ass out of bed Brad," came Farric's less than dulcet tone. "We need to get going."

Instead of heading straight for the cart, Farric took them to a scruffy looking tavern in a side street off the main road. Inside it was equally as scruffy and smelled of stale beer. Farric walked up to the bar and ordered two large breakfasts, to be sent over to a table at the side of the room.

"Doesn't look like much, does it?" Farric said to Brad, "but this place serves the best food this side of Gaardsholme."

"I thought you were in a hurry to leave," replied Brad.

"I was in a hurry to eat something!" And besides, this may be the last hot meal we get to eat for quite some time."

"Why's that?"

"We are approaching the Eastern Realm and bandits operate in this area. You will need to be on your guard at all times. There will be no camp fires now so make the most of this."

A short time later, a plain looking serving girl brought them each a steaming plate piled high with thickly cut meat, sausages, eggs and coarse-grained white bread. The meal was accompanied with a pot of sweet smelling hot liquid. Brad poured himself a mug and sniffed at it tentatively.

Farric laughed. "Have you never had draema before?" He asked.

"Yes, I have." Brad recalled his first meeting with Sarah, or Kaiya or whatever she was called.

He took a sip of the draema and was surprised at how refreshing it was and how good it tasted.

152

"Apart from its great taste," said Farric, "draema has strong rejuvenating properties and provides the body with instant energy. It also helps combat the sluggishness most feel after a large meal and it will help you keep your wits about you. At least we can but hope that it will!"

"Very funny."

Brad drank some more, and as he did so he noticed that a man at the other side of the room was watching him intently. Holding his gaze for a few seconds, he felt uncomfortable by the other's scrutiny of him and looked away. Farric was saying something, but Brad was not listening, as he was certain that he was still being observed. He looked up and again made eye contact with the man. This time, he could see the hostility in the other's stare and knew that this wasn't going to end well.

"Who the fuck do you think you're staring at?" shouted the man from across the room. Farric turned in his seat to see where the voice had come from and turned back to Brad smiling.

"Seems like you don't even need to light a campfire to attract unwanted attention!"

Brad couldn't help but laugh despite the seriousness of the situation.

"So, you think it's funny, do you?" the man said, as he stood up.

"I apologise for whatever offence I seem to have caused you." Brad replied in a low voice that carried across the room. "Why don't you let me buy you a drink and allow us to finish our meal, so that we can leave this place in peace?"

The man chose to ignore him as he crossed the room and stopped less than two feet from where they sat. Brad looked up at him, this time making deliberate eye contact.

"You ain't fuckin' going nowhere, you cunt," said the man, "least wise not unless it's in a fuckin' box."

The man was tall and thickset with a fat neck and hands like shovels. He had the swarthy look of someone that spent their working day outside in all weathers and judging by his build he was clearly used to heavy work.

In his previous life, Brad would have tried to talk his way out of a situation like this, trying to lose as little face as was possible without the other realising just how scared he really was. Most times he succeeded and rarely had events like this escalated into a fight. Even on those rare occasions when they did, he escaped serious injury by either being lucky enough to strike first and make good his escape, or others had intervened. This time, like so many other times in the last few months, Brad didn't feel any fear, the detached feeling once again enabling him to think and act deliberately, rather than reacting out of fear or anger.

"I told you to sit down," Brad growled, still maintaining eye contact.

"Fucking make me," the other howled as he attacked.

With astonishing speed, Brad pushed his chair backwards. His attacker was unable to stop in time and momentarily lost his balance as he swung his hammer like fist at where Brad's head had been just moments before. Brad jumped to his feet and slammed his knee into the man's chest. The blow was not as hard as it could have been because Brad pulled it slightly, as he had no desire to cause the man permanent harm. It was, however, hard enough to take the wind out of his attacker, who fell to his knees gasping for breath.

"Now fuck off and let us finish our meal in peace."

Farric remained seated and continued to eat his breakfast, seemingly oblivious to the chaos that was going on around him. Brad looked up and saw his reflection in a filthy mirror on the wall in front of him and for the briefest of moments thought he saw the zig-zagged, orangey-red corona around his irises that he was certain he had seen before. The man on the floor squirmed with pain where he lay. But it wasn't the pain that was making him squirm, he was trying to locate a dagger that was concealed within his clothing. Too late, Brad looked down and saw the glint of steel as his attacker regained his feet and thrust upwards with the blade.

The knife should have penetrated Brad's body between his ribs, and with the upwards angle of the attack, it would have found his heart and killed him. He felt the blade pierce his clothing but as the cold steel made contact with his flesh, there was an eruption of blinding crimson light that seemed to come from within his body. His attacker dropped the knife to the ground with the shock of the impact, his shattered wrist hanging limply. Brad was transfixed by the sight of the dagger glowing red hot on the floor. It was only then that he noticed that his own wrists were also glowing, as if they too were red hot. He touched them, expecting to be burnt, but they were the same temperature as the rest of his body. Brad was barely aware of his surroundings as Farric kicked the man in the face rendering him unconscious.

"We have to get out of here now," Farric hissed as he yanked Brad away.

Chapter 38
Katzin

"Katzin, can you hear me?" Selicia called out to the leader of her order. She sat in her study with the Zindaw Stone in her hands.

"Yes, Selicia I can hear you, what do you have to report?" The sound of Katzin's voice always reminded Selicia of the time that they had been intimate.

"I received a message from Myrinia, our agent in Dumas. One of her girls slept with Farric Clearwater last night and confirmed that he is heading to Krendyra with Bradley White."

What else did she tell you?"

"Clearwater knows little about White but feels that there is something odd about the man."

"Odd in what way?"

"He doesn't know where he comes from, but he knows that White isn't from these parts or any of the Five Lands. Clearwater is being paid a lot of money to escort White and he believes that whoever is behind this must have a very good reason for doing so. Clearwater also thinks that White is being forced to do this." Selicia replied.

"How do you mean forced?"

"He thinks that there is a reluctance in White to go to Krendyra. White hasn't said anything, but Clearwater suspects that he is being threatened, or that whoever is paying him has a hold over White."

"What about White himself? What did they find out from him?"

"Nothing at all. A girl called Iolanthe slept with him and had the same problem that I did and couldn't skim Bradley White's thoughts or feelings."

"Did Iolanthe report anything else?"

"Yes, she said that White was distracted during their moments of intimacy."

"Distracted, Selicia? What did she mean by that? Did she explain?"

"Yes, she said that even without being able to skim his thoughts, it was clear that he was thinking about someone else when they were together. She asked him about it and he said that there was a woman he cared deeply about."

"What makes you think that is important?" Katzin asked. "It's not unheard of for men to visit us even when they have a loving relationship of their own."

"Yes I know, but at least we are building a picture of who this man is. Iolanthe also said that she experienced the same fatigue that I did when I was with White."

"Nice work, Selicia. I will speak with Sanjin and see what he wants to do. I suspect that they will stop at our house in Krendyra. Maybe we can find out some more then. Get an urgent message to our head of house in Krendyra and tell her to expect company."

"Yes Katzin, I will let her know and I will ensure that our guests are well attended to there."

"Yes, Selicia," Katzin couldn't help but laugh, "and make sure that they report everything that they learn no matter how small the detail. We need to know much more. I have a bad feeling about this."

They spent another half an hour or so going over recent events with Selicia providing Katzin with her usual report and snippets of information that the House of Secrets was so good at obtaining.

One of the reasons that Sanjin Dakor was such a successful ruler was that he knew what the most powerful and influential amongst his subjects were thinking. The power of this information was beyond calculation. It enabled Sanjin to motivate where necessary and deal with any problem at an early stage before it had chance to take root and cause the Five Lands any real harm. Used in this way, the House of Secrets had helped their society function in a well and controlled manner and it had very much been a force for the greater good. Sanjin often thought how dangerous a weapon it could be in the hands of his brother Zoryn. He had no doubt, whatsoever, that if Zoryn controlled the House of Secrets, he would extort those whose own secrets left them vulnerable to blackmail and worse.

Chapter 39
The Krendyran Mountains

"What the fuck happened back there, Brad?" Farric demanded. They had left the town in a hurry and were now a few miles outside of its border.

"I was attacked by a fucking twat is what happened." Brad was not in the best of humours.

"That's not what I meant. You have magic, don't you?"

"I honestly don't know. That blade should have killed me, that much I know for sure, but what happened and how it happened I don't know."

"Well, I've seen magic used more times than I care to remember and it was definitely magic that saved you." Farric continued, "But not like any magic I've seen before. It looked like it came from inside you rather than from an object in your possession. The question is how did you do it?"

"I don't know," Brad said truthfully. "It happened all by itself."

"You must have done something?"

"No, I didn't but this has happened before."

"What happened?"

"I hit a man, back where I come from. There was a bright flash of light when I hit him, and the force of the blow was much greater than should have been possible and it killed him."

"I saw what happened in Tyria," Farric said.

"You saw what happened there?" Brad asked incredulously. "I didn't think you did, you didn't say anything."

"I only half saw it and dismissed it as being impossible. You don't look like the type that would have magic and the way you used it was different. But what happened back there in Dumas showed that you do have magic and that I wasn't mistaken."

"So, what does all this mean?" asked Brad.

"I don't know but one thing's for certain, people will have seen what happened in both towns which means that you will be talked about and will attract attention. This is the last thing that we need right now. And there's something else I think you should know."

"What's that?"

"Your fucking eyes change colour when you use this magic you say you know nothing about.

My advice to you Brad is not to make eye contact with anyone if you get yourself into another fight. Better still stay out of fucking trouble. Smithson has a fucking lot to answer to when I see him."

***

The next week and a half passed without event, much to Brad's relief, as they continued their journey to Krendyra. They didn't pass through any towns or villages and as Farric had said before they left Dumas, they didn't light any campfires and ate their meals cold.

The land itself was changing the further east they travelled. When they set off from Tyria, the land was mostly flat with grass, light vegetation and the occasional wooded area. The landscape in front of Brad was far from flat, with a mountain range on the horizon that seemed to stretch as far as he could see in either direction. Even at this distance, it was an impressive sight and looked impenetrable.

As if reading his mind, Farric said, "That's the Krendyran Mountain Range you see in front of you. We will be there by mid-afternoon tomorrow and we'll make our camp about a mile or so away from them. The way through the foothills is too narrow to take the cart, but the horses will make it. Our passage will take a full day and is too dangerous to attempt at night. I've seen that you can take care of yourself in a fight, but these are dangerous lands. Tonight, and tomorrow night, we will take turns keeping guard, so don't expect a lot of sleep."

Farric was true to his word when they stopped for the day and insisted that Brad took the first watch. "Wake me when the moon appears over that mountain to the east," Farric said pointing to a mountain peak made barely visible by the last of the day's light. "I'll take over from you then."

"What if it rains and the moon is obscured by clouds?" protested Brad.

"Then my friend, your watch will last even longer!" Farric laughed, as he rolled over in his blanket falling asleep almost instantly. Brad couldn't help but smile, Farric was the closest thing he had to a friend in this land and despite himself, he found that he liked him. Sure, he was a mercenary and cared only for himself, but unlike Garan Smithson, Farric seemed to be independent of Zoryn.

Even though Brad liked Farric, he didn't trust him. He couldn't afford to trust anyone in this place, except maybe Hania. His thoughts returned to her. He had hardly spoken with the girl and yet felt a bond, a closeness to her, which he had never felt with anyone else, not even with Gina. As ridiculous as it was, he realised that he was in love with Hania.

Brad looked to the east and noticed that the moon had risen above the mountain range and it was a truly wondrous sight. Glowing a pastel shade of blue from the reflected light of the long set sun, it was much larger than the moon he was used to back home. Its beauty however, was almost eclipsed by the darkness Brad could see a short distance to the west of it and a little higher in the night sky. What made the darkness so profound was the total lack of stars within its indistinct boundaries. Where the rest of the sky was punctuated by millions of pinpricks of light, this area had none.

Brad was mesmerised by the sight and felt the hair on the back of his neck rise in response to the uneasy feeling that it provoked within him. He knew instinctively that something was not right, not natural about this. It looked like the stars that should have been there had been destroyed or consumed. He recalled Garan Smithson referring to this part of the sky as being Dakor's Darkness. What manner of being was Zoryn Dakor and what power did he wield, that made him capable of creating such a thing?

"Time to get some sleep, Brad," Farric said, appearing out of the darkness like a wraith.

"What do you know about this Dakor's Darkness, Farric?" Brad asked, still looking at where the stars should have been.

"Not much, I don't think that anybody does, except maybe our beloved leader Sanjin Dakor."

"So, there's another Dakor? That's all I bloody well need."

"I may have my differences with Sanjin Dakor," Farric laughed, "but he's nothing like his brother. I believe that you've met Zoryn Dakor?"

"Yes, I've met him," Brad replied between clenched teeth.

"The story goes that he discovered a powerful and deadly magic from antiquity, and unleashed its power ripping a hole in the sky." Farric handed Brad a small cup of mead. "Drink this, it will help you sleep."

Chapter 40
Outlander

Farric was right, the mead did help Brad sleep that evening and he did so without dreaming. He awoke the next morning feeling surprisingly refreshed but with some apprehension. It felt like something was about to happen, but he didn't know what. It was a strange feeling, made more so by the fact that he felt it so keenly. He couldn't shrug it off and put it down to the fact that it was hardly surprising that he should feel this way, bearing in mind the situation he was in and that he and Farric were getting very close to their destination. There was nothing that he could do about it so he packed his gear and made ready to leave.

Farric was feeding the horses as Brad loaded his meagre possessions onto the cart.

"The guys that gave me this cart sure did us a favour," Farric said smiling as Brad approached.

"Why do I get the feeling that they may not have parted with it willingly?" Brad replied.

"You may have a point there, I guess!" said Farric. "Still, it's not a bad cart and the horses have held up well." They loaded up and continued their journey.

In the light of the day the mountain range they were approaching was imposing, and was made even more so by the flatness of the land that surrounded them. They looked like the bones of the land and stretched as far as Brad could see in either direction. The mountains were dark to the point of being black, creating an unnatural silhouette effect as they seemed untouched by the rays of this land's strange blue sun.

As they made their way toward the mountains in their small cart, Brad could see that they were much closer to them than it had appeared the previous evening. They looked impenetrable, like an enormous wall of solid rock and he wondered how they were going to be able to pass through them.

"It's an impressive sight," Farric said as if reading Brad's thoughts.

"Can we really get through those mountains in just one day?" asked Brad.

"We have to. They stretch out for many leagues in either direction, like a massive barrier across the land. They are narrow at the point that we will enter, but they fan out on both sides."

"What's so dangerous about them?" asked Brad.

"The weather can change very quickly in the Krendyrans, going from extremes of temperature to some of the worst winds and storms you can imagine and the terrain itself is treacherous. There's so much loose rock and shale up there that it doesn't take much more than a gentle breeze to bring tons of rock crashing down on top of you. Parts of the range are favoured by outlaws and other scum. Most have made their homes further south, but lack of food and the lure of wealthy travellers, draws them here. They wouldn't think twice about slitting your throat for a loaf of bread or a wineskin."

"Have you ever encountered any of these people yourself?"

"Yes, on more than one occasion."

"And what happened?"

"Let's just say that they don't like the taste of steel very much!" Farric laughed. "Some say that there are magic wielders amongst these people. I haven't seen any and I don't know if I believe them, but some strange things have been reported about this place. And of course, the fabled Lake of Visions is supposed to be somewhere up there, but I don't know anyone that has ever found it."

"What is the Lake of Visions?" asked Brad.

"They reckon there's a lake somewhere in the mountain range. It's supposed to be fed from a spring that passes through a vein of White Metal that they say is the purest in the land, and this is what gives the lake its power."

"What is White Metal?"

"It's the refined version of the magical ore from which magic users get their power. You really are a stranger to this land, aren't you?"

"You could say that," replied Brad. "So, what does this *Lake of Visions* do?"

"If someone bathes in its waters, they are supposed to see their future in a series of visions." Farric replied. "However, it doesn't always work out well for the person."

"How do you mean?"

"Apparently, not everyone gets the visions, some do and the others die."

"So maybe not the most popular of places to visit!" quipped Brad.

"On the contrary, there are regular expeditions to the Krendyrans by those trying to find the lake. Mostly, they are highborns with money to burn. They never find the lake and some never return. Whether that's because of the bandits, or the lake itself, who knows."

"Would you go to this lake if you could find it?" asked Brad.

"Not for the visions, that doesn't interest me at all," Farric replied.

"So, what would interest you?"

"Taking my own expeditions there and fleecing all those stupid enough to pay me. Now that really would interest me!"

***

They rode in silence until around midday. Farric brought their cart to a stop in a small wooded area in the foothills at the bottom of the mountain range which was now towering over them. It offered them scant cover, but it was the only cover within sight.

"There's a spring just ahead where we can get some fresh water," said Farric. "You can search for some firewood while I fill up the wineskins." Brad nodded his response.

Farric made his way through the foothills and was soon out of sight. Brad looked up at the mountains in front of him. Even this close to them, they still looked black and forbidding, their presence alien in this otherwise flat landscape.

Brad managed to find a good armful of dry wood and as he returned to the cart, he glanced up to where Farric had entered the foothills. For just an instant, he thought he saw movement a little further up. He couldn't be sure because it happened so quickly and whatever it may have been, disappeared as quickly and soundlessly as it had appeared.

Maybe there are some animals up there? He thought to himself.

He stared intently, but after several long moments saw no further movement and looked away, putting it down to a trick of the light.

Farric returned soon after, with their wineskins fat with cold fresh spring water.

"I thought I saw movement over there while you were gone," Brad said pointing to the foothills.

"You probably did," Farric replied. "Did you get a close look at whatever it was?"

"No, it was in shadow and vanished almost as soon as it had appeared."

"It may have been one of the small animals that live up there, but it was most likely one of those people I warned you about earlier."

"Do you think they know we are here?"

"We've kicked up enough dust coming here that they could hardly have missed seeing us. Yes, they know that we are here alright."

"Will they attack?"

"It's unlikely unless we are stupid enough to enter their *kingdom* during the night. We can have a camp fire tonight; in fact, we will have a big fire, one that they are certain not to miss."

"Why would we want to do that?" Brad asked incredulously.

"They are more likely to attack us if they have darkness to cover their approach. These people are only loosely held together and do not have the stomach or the organisation for an all-out fight. Sure, they will slit your throat and take everything that you have if they can get away with it, but they won't engage in combat unless they have no alternative."

"How safe is the passage through the mountains during the day?" asked Brad.

"It's not safe at all!" Farric laughed as he replied. "But at least the light will make it harder for them to ambush us. Tonight, one of us will need to be awake at all times to guard the camp. We will take watches of four hours each and you'll take the first watch starting from now."

"But how will I know when the four hours is up?" Brad protested.

"Because that's when I will wake up and take my shift!"

"How can you be so sure that you will wake up in time?"

"I served for a while in Sanjin Dakor's so called *Elite Guard* and that's where I learned all about four-hour watches. Believe me, when you go out on patrol for three months at a time and you are unfortunate enough to be continually picked for watch duties, you quickly learn how to wake up in time for your shift. If you don't then when it's your partners turn to wake up and take over, they will make you wait much longer than four hours and there's fuck all you can do because you can't leave your post unmanned."

"Is that where you met Garan Smithson?" Brad asked.

"Yes, Garan was Sanjin's head trainer at the time."

"So how did you become friends?"

"It's a long story Brad but let's just say that Garan and I had a somewhat interesting sparring session during my combat training."

"Somewhat interesting?" repeated Brad.

"Yes, you could say that! I put Garan on his ass!"

"I would imagine that didn't go down very well with him?"

"No," replied Farric. "But after another ten minutes or so of sparring, we kind of reached an understanding you could say!"

"I would have loved to have been there!" said Brad.

"I still feel sorry for the poor bastard that got to spar with Garan afterwards. I can still see the look of sheer terror in his eyes when he realised he was next!" Farric roared with laughter, as he found somewhere to sleep for the afternoon.

Brad had his wristwatch so could tell when his four-hour watch was about to end. He hadn't considered that an hour in this world may be longer, or shorter, than back home. Farric did indeed rouse himself to take over at the allotted time, so Brad reasoned that an hour must be the same in both worlds. It was just dark and Brad managed to find a relatively soft place to sleep. He must have fallen asleep instantly, because the next thing he knew was Farric waking him by nudging him with his boot.

"Your turn," was all Farric said.

Brad sat beside the fire that Farric must have made whilst he had been sleeping. Although it wasn't the biggest of fires, it took the chill off the evening air and Brad was thankful for that. Farric had instructed him to sit to one side of the fire and not to look at it directly, to keep his night vision sharp. Brad looked toward the mountains, but they were just a darker smudge against a dark sky that was pinpricked by a myriad of stars. He turned his attention upwards and scanned the night sky to see if he could recognise any stars. He had been keen on astronomy as a child and knew many stars and constellations, but this sky was alien to him. Although the stars looked just like any others, the patterns were not recognisable. Wherever this place was, it must be an unimaginable distance from Earth.

From the moment Brad arrived in this land and saw the blue sun, he knew that he was a very long way from home. But where in the Universe was he? Or was he even in the same universe? With his basic knowledge of astronomy, he reasoned that he must have been countless light years from Earth. But even then, surely there would be at least some constellations that would look familiar? If he was that far from home, the power needed to transport him there would be beyond comprehension. Brad felt certain that this wasn't the case, that he hadn't been flung half-way across the Universe. Instead, he believed that he may have been transported to another universe altogether, maybe a parallel universe of some kind, but surely, that was just the stuff of science fiction?

He looked at his watch and according to the dial; it was 14th July. If he had got his maths right, then he and Farric had been on the road for exactly four weeks and a day. The days in this place were a little longer than back home and on several occasions, he had had to change the time on his watch. He set it by making the assumption that the sun set at 6.00 pm. At first, he didn't want his watch to be out of sync with the time in his home world, but the differences in the time shown on his watch and the apparent time of his surroundings was confusing and ultimately unnecessary, so he decided to keep pace, as best as he could, with the time here.

Brad was deep in thought when he heard a faint sound behind him. The evening was calm and there was no wind to cause the leaves on the few trees around their camp to rustle, and there had not been any animal sounds. He turned towards the noise and jumped to his feet when he saw a woman, scarcely four feet away from him. She was difficult to age, as she appeared to be younger than her grey hair would have suggested. At her temples, even from the meagre light of the campfire, he could make out streaks of midnight black. Her smile was friendly as she advanced a few paces toward him with her arms outstretched and her palms facing upwards to show that she wasn't holding a weapon. "I didn't mean to startle you, Outlander." Her voice was soft, but Brad could sense strength behind her words.

"Who the fuck are you and what do you want?"

"Who I am is not important," her piercing blue eyes cut into his very being as she spoke, "my people know who you are and have been aware of you long before you entered our land and became Zoryn Dakor's unwilling assassin."

"How could you possibly know anything about me?" Brad was beginning to feel uncomfortable in this woman's presence.

"We know this by the same means that you will learn of your destiny and the plight of this land. You will soon have choices to make Outlander, choices that will shape this land for good or ill for many generations."

"What do you mean?"

"Zoryn Dakor is a powerful man and if he succeeds with his plans, nobody will be able to stand in his way. He is without compassion or restraint, seeking only that which he wants, that which serves his purposes. Some say that he is evil and will not be content until he destroys everything around him."

"So why are you telling me this?" Brad snapped. "What the fuck has any of this got to do with me?"

"Because Outlander, Zoryn Dakor must be stopped and fate has made you this land's only hope."

Chapter 41
The Lake of Visions

"What the fuck do you mean I'm the land's only hope? And you still haven't answered my question, who are you?" Brad demanded.

"My name is Velhanna and I have been asked by my people, the Dyroshin, to be your guide. We have seen glimpses of the future and cannot let Zoryn come to power."

"Then why don't you fight him?" Brad asked.

"We are too few in number and could not stand up to his might and that of those who stand with him. We are also sworn not to interfere directly with events in the Five Lands."

"There are others?"

"Yes, Outlander. Zoryn has allies who also plot against his brother."

"Why would I want to get involved in any of this?" Brad demanded.

"You already know the answer to that," Velhanna replied calmly.

"What do you mean and what can you possibly know about me?"

"We know a little, Outlander. It is clear to us that Zoryn sent you here for a reason. What that reason is we don't know and why you were specifically chosen, is also not known to us. We do know that Zoryn has found the long-lost Black Metal and that he has been building his power for some time. He is a warlord and would have selected you for a specific talent or ability that you have."

"Well, I don't have any *abilities* that would be of any use to a warlord, or anybody else for that matter.

So how can I possibly stand against this Zoryn?"

"Your destiny is complex and nothing is certain. But what we do know is that your future and that of the dread Lord Zoryn are intertwined. Whether this is for good or ill has not been fully revealed to us, but what is certain is that you will play a major part in whatever happens."

"And what if I refuse to have anything to do with this?"

"Can't you see that you are already involved and that you are playing your part even as we speak, Outlander? Whatever you decide to do now or in the future all forms part of your destiny, a destiny that fate has inextricably linked with that of Zoryn. Even if you were somehow able to go back to where you came from, that too would have an effect here."

"So why are you telling me this? What do you want from me?" Brad demanded.

"There is a place not far from here, a lake hidden in the mountains, where your destiny, or some part of it at least, may be revealed to you. What you learn there may help you make the right decision when the time comes."

"Why should I trust you?"

"You can't trust anyone here except maybe for one person."

"And who is that person?" Brad asked. "Is it you?"

"You already know the answer to that, Outlander."

An image of Hania came to Brad's mind unbidden. *She must be talking about Hania, but how can she possibly know anything about her?* He thought to himself.

"And if I go with you, what about my companion? What will happen to him?"

"Don't worry about your friend," the woman said, "he will remain as he is until you return."

"I didn't say that he was my friend."

"He may not be now, but your friendship will deepen."

"How can you be so certain that he will remain here and not wake-up and come after us?"

"My people have the ability to make a moment in time last for several hours, or even longer if required. It takes a tremendous amount of energy to do it and it is through the collective strength of my people that they have taken us both out of time and we will remain that way while we go where we must."

"I don't believe you," Brad said flatly.

"Then look up and see for yourself."

He looked up and saw a night bird, one of the few that he had seen since he had entered this land. It hung about ten feet or so above his head, motionless, impossibly suspended in mid-air. Brad stared at the bird in disbelief, what he was seeing was impossible. He glanced at his watch, the second hand was motionless and no amount of shaking would restart it. Then he looked at the fire and knew that this strange woman was telling the truth. The flames were frozen in their reach for the sky and where there should have been a crackle and burn as the wood combusted, there was silence.

"As far as your friend is concerned, we will be gone for less than the blink of an eye. He wouldn't know what happened, even if he had been wide awake and talking to you as I appeared."

Brad looked at the woman and something about her made him believe that she was speaking the truth. He thought back to his last dream meeting with Gina. She had said to him that their ability to meet may be an advantage and may be something that they could use against Zoryn. Surely, knowing more about his so-called *destiny* must also help them? Besides, what did he have to lose anyway? As if she was able to read his thoughts Velhanna said, "That's why it is even more important that you come with me to the Lake of Visions, Outlander. We have found out all that we can and still it is not enough to oppose Zoryn. If the Lake reveals even a fragment of your future to you, this extra knowledge may help us and others frustrate his plans."

"I thought you said there weren't many of you?"

"That is the truth, my people are few in number, but there are other groups and other people who fear the life that they would be forced to endure under a savage dictator. Please Outlander, you must come with me now. It takes a lot of energy for my people to hold this instant in time, we must get going now."

"Fuck it, what have I got to lose?" Brad asserted rhetorically, as he turned his back to Velhanna and faced the ominous black of the mountains that stretched out in front of him.

In a voice, barely a whisper Velhanna muttered, "There may yet be hope." As she walked past Brad, taking the lead.

***

They had been walking in silence for an hour or longer. To begin with, they had followed a well-worn trail, picked out by the bluish light of this world's moon. Later, however, they left the main path and had to force their way through some tough bracken like vegetation before they found another much less used trail. This trail was so feint, he doubted whether he would have been able to follow it even in full daylight. Velhanna, however, led with the confidence of one who was certain of their way.

Their path took them close to the granite rock-face of one of the mountains. Its surface was so hard and impenetrable that only the hardiest scrub had managed to get a toe-hold on its rugged surface. It was otherwise unremarkable except that the surface of the rock was giving off a faint ethereal glow. There wasn't much light, just enough for Brad to see the objects around him a little clearer.

"I've never seen rocks that glow before," he said, more to himself than to Velhanna.

"It's not the rocks that are glowing; it's the thin film of vegetation that lives on the rock that gives off the light. During the day it just looks like a thin covering of green, but at night it gives off light," Velhanna replied.

"Is it on all the rocks here?" Brad asked still intrigued by the strange organism.

"Yes, it is on practically every rock surface in the Krendyran's but it only glows like this in certain places."

"Why's that?"

"It draws on moisture from the air and in places where the rock is more porous. The water in the rocks originates from the water in the lake that we are going to."

"Oh!" said Brad with a little more sarcasm than he intended. "That would explain it!"

They continued walking along first one, then another and yet another trail that only Velhanna could see. It was surreal that they were still living in the frozen instant that Velhanna and her people had created with their magic, and yet at the same time it was palpable to Brad's senses.

Throughout their journey, it was clear that they had been ascending and his aching legs attested to the fact that they had been walking for some time. Velhanna had not slowed her pace throughout their ascent, but seeing that Brad had fallen further behind, she stopped and waited for him to catch up to her. She carried a small pack on her shoulders and took it off. Reaching inside, she pulled out a small wineskin and offered it to Brad.

"Here, drink some of this," she said. "It will restore your strength."

Brad did as she bade and drank deeply from the wineskin. Almost instantly, he felt a warming sensation in his stomach that quickly spread throughout his body. The feeling did not last long and when it subsided he felt amazing. The ache in his legs had gone and he felt truly invigorated and full of energy. Turning her back on Brad to resume their journey, Velhanna said, "I told you it would restore your energy."

"Thank you," he replied, "do you want the wineskin back?"

"No Outlander, keep it, you may well have need of it again before this night is out."

They continued without stopping for what felt like another two hours until they reached the crest of a hollow that looked as if it had been carved out of the mountain by the hands of a giant. Looking down into the hollow, Brad was dismayed that they had still not reached the lake and inwardly groaned at the thought of having to walk even further.

Velhanna held up her hand, beckoning him to stop. She started to chant, the words indistinct and alien to his ears. The hairs on the back of his neck stood up and his skin itched as a static charge built in the air around them. He knew that Velhanna was using magic and felt something deep within him stir, something that he had no name for. Velhanna sensed it too as she glanced at him momentarily before continuing with her otherworldly chant. Moments smashed into each other and time had no meaning, as the charge about them intensified and then, without warning, Velhanna fell silent.

At first, Brad didn't notice it, and then as he looked again at the hollow before him, he saw a still blackness that moments before hadn't been there. In the dim blueish light of the moon, he found his gaze captivated by the sight of a lake below him. A lake with water that was so black it absorbed all light and reflected nothing from its calm surface. Tendrils of mist hung over the lake, moving slowly, rhythmically, like wraiths dancing upon its ebony surface. It was an eerie sight and Brad's pulse quickened in anticipation of what was to come.

Chapter 42
Destiny Revealed

Brad's reverie was interrupted by Velhanna as she said, "Come Outlander, let us climb down to the lake." As they descended, she continued, "Remember this, the visions are shadows of what might, or might not come to pass. You cannot make the lake reveal its secrets to you; it is capricious by nature and will show you what it will. You should also be aware that events never play out exactly as you see them portrayed here. The lake provides glimpses of its own reality, but not interpretations or insights. These are matters that you will have to work out for yourself."

The descent was short and much easier than their journey through the undergrowth to reach this place had been. The Lake looked impressive from his previous vantage point, but now that Brad was standing by the side of its still black waters, he was completely mesmerised. He had never seen anything like it, had never seen anything as black, it was eerily beautiful. The water was perfectly smooth, without the merest hint of a ripple or other disturbance. "Wait for the sign Outlander and then enter the water. If you do not see a sign you must not enter, or you may die." Velhanna's voice was feint to his ears, like a whisper lost in a fog. He heard her words, but they didn't register in his conscious mind. Right now, only the lake existed to him. He felt it calling to him, tugging at the edge of his senses, inviting him to enter its waters and join with it, to be one with it. The call of the lake was seductive and even if he wanted to, Brad could not resist its siren call. Stepping forward, he entered the Lake.

The shock of the ice-cold water brought him back to his senses immediately. He tried to scramble back to the edge of the lake, but despite his best efforts, he remained exactly where he was. He tried to touch the bottom with his feet in an effort to walk out of the water, but he couldn't sink below the surface to test its depth. Brad should have felt fear but all he felt was calm. The calmness was unlike anything he had experienced before and seemed to come from outside of his body. With it came warmth as it wrapped itself around him, enveloping him completely in its soothing embrace. He felt an overwhelming urge to lie back in the water and as he did so the first vision came to him the instant, he closed his eyes.

"Brad how did you do that?" It was Gina and they were in the Forest again, but how was that possible?

"What do you mean Gina, how did I do what?" Brad was still trying to work out what had happened. How could he be in the Lake of Visions in one instant and in the forest with Gina the next? It just wasn't possible.

"Before when we've met here, I've been here first and when I call out to you, you appear, but this time it's different. I was asleep in the hospital bed and could hear you calling my name, and then I was here. Something has changed."

"I didn't call out to you, Gina," said Brad, "I walked into a lake in that other place and then I was here. I just don't get it."

"Think hard Brad, what did you do differently? I think this could be important."

"But that's just it Gina, I didn't do anything different, except for…"

"Except for what, Brad?" asked Gina. "What was different?"

"This lake I am in is called The Lake of Visions and is supposed to be magical, showing visions of the future to some that enter its waters. I know it sounds crazy Gina, but then all of this is fucking crazy."

"Maybe that's what it is, Brad. Maybe all of this is a vision, your vision."

"But if it's my vision Gina, why are you here with me?"

"I wish I knew the answer Brad, but I'm convinced that you are having a vision now."

"I don't know, it all seems pretty real to me."

"But how can it be?" Gina protested. "For a start, I'm really in a hospital bed and as for you Brad, no one knows where you were before you even went into this Lake of Visions. I think that if this lake really does show the future, that you have been sent here now for a reason. I believe this is important and that it means something, we just have to work out what that something is." Gina and the Forest started to fade before he could call after her.

As soon as the first vision faded, another one came. This time he could see a company of ten or more armed men surrounding him. They all wore the same uniform with the insignia of a brown hawk swooping in for the kill with its talons extended, emblazoned on their tabards. It was clear from their bearing that they were military men. It was strange to see himself from this detached viewpoint. His image was in the middle of these men and although not bound, he was clearly their prisoner. So too it would seem was Farric, who walked beside him.

"Looks like I misjudged you Bradley White, you must have done something pretty bad to warrant this number of guards being sent to take you to our beloved King. Sanjin Dakor must really want to talk with you!"

Farric had a number of cuts and bruises to his face and his left eye was closed over from an angry looking swelling that reached half-way down his face. As if sensing his thoughts, Farric looked at Brad and said, "I let my guard down back there Brad, I'm sorry."

"How could you have known?" The spectre of Bradley White replied. "How could either us have known that we had a traitor in our midst?"

The vision was quickly replaced by another, as he saw Zoryn Dakor standing on a platform atop a tower that had a low black granite wall encircling it. Brad could sense a massive build-up of magical energy and could see tendrils of power reaching from the smooth surface of the granite and enveloping Zoryn. As if in slow motion, the midnight black of the granite wall shattered as it discharged all of its pent-up might to the dark warlord. Zoryn staggered for a moment, as if his body couldn't absorb all that magic and then he straightened. Brad couldn't hear what Zoryn shouted as he raised his fist to the dark sky above him, but he saw the bolt of blinding crimson fire that blasted from his fist. The massive discharge of power lasted several long moments as the bolt of fire rent the firmament asunder, leaving an inky black void in its wake.

Brad drifted for a time before the next vision came to him. This time he was back in the house that he was held captive in and Garan Smithson was sat at a table eating with Hania. Hania, his heart leapt at the sight of her. He had only spoken to her a couple of times and even in such a short space of time, he knew that he had fallen in love with her. She was the most beautiful and delicate creature that he had ever set eyes on. The colour of her hair reminded him of long summer days and those crystal-clear emerald eyes, and her beautiful delicate pale face, made his whole-body ache with longing for her.

"You must forget about him," Garan scolded her, "he is not from here and will be gone for good soon enough. Keep away from him, he is dangerous, Hania."

"But how can you say that uncle?" Her voice like a zephyr playing across a summer's meadow.

"Zoryn has brought him here," came the reply. "And nothing you or I can do will change whatever plans he has for him."

"What could Zoryn possibly want from him?" Hania asked.

"I don't know and Zoryn's not about to tell me either, but whatever it is, it isn't going to end well for him that's for sure."

"You have to help him uncle, you have to protect him, you're the only one who can."

"And stand against Zoryn Dakor? Have you completely taken leave of your senses girl?"

"Zoryn will kill Bradley White when he's finished with him, won't he?" Hania's voice was barely a whisper.

"Yes Hania, I have no doubt of that."

"How can you just stand by and let that happen, Uncle?"

"I can't stand against Zoryn, no one can."

"Maybe if you were to defy him others would join you?"

"And he would kill every one of them."

"Is he really that bad uncle?"

"He is Hania, and those that fear him do so for good reason. Zoryn has my loyalty, he saw to that many years ago."

"What do you mean, Uncle? What did he do?"

"He came here and found you Hania," replied Garan. "From that moment he knew that I would do whatever he wanted." The vision faded.

"This knife cannot be detected by ordinary magic," said the burly dark-skinned man, in the next vision. The object was obsidian black, a shadow in the spectre of Bradley Whites hands, midnight on midnight. In his vision Brad could sense his shade's thoughts as if they were his own. *He expected the knife to feel light, but it had a weight to it that belied its appearance. It had the feel of a well-balanced, throwing knife and it felt good in his hands, right almost, as if this was where it belonged. It was a strange feeling.* Brad stared at the knife in wonder, despite its lack of decoration, there was an otherworldly beauty in its simplicity and something about it hinted at power.

"The knife has no magic itself," the dark-skinned man said as if sensing Brad's thought. "But it will absorb some of the magic used by others in its presence which is why you must never use magic near it."

The man was lying, somehow Brad could tell. The knife did have magic, everything about it screamed of raw and savage power. So why was he lying? What was he hiding?

"I don't have any magic," Brad responded.

"You don't have any magic?" The man responded angrily. "Do you take me for a fool?"

"No, but I don't have any magic, I'm not from these lands and where I come from magic doesn't exist."

The man looked at the spectre of Bradley White appraisingly. "I believe you are speaking the truth. The truth that is, as you see it, but you do have magic, Outlander." He laughed as the vision faded.

The next vision was of Gina holding a small baby, which judging by its size, could only be a few weeks old. She was at home and her older sister was with her. Gina was cooing softly to the child who was warmly wrapped in a pink fleece blanket.

"She is so beautiful Gina, so perfect and it's a miracle that she survived the horrors that you have been through." Alice's eyes were filled with tears of joy for the baby and tears of sadness and compassion for her younger sister. "Have you settled on a name for her?"

"Yes, she is called Hope," Gina replied.

Alice couldn't hold her tears back as she sobbed, "That's so beautiful," composing herself a little she added, "I believe that he will return to you, Gina."

Gina did not reply as she bent down to kiss her daughter. As she tucked her in, the way that only a devoted parent would, Hope White opened her eyes and looked straight at him, through the veil of the vision. Brad was certain that she could see him, could see through the vast distance between them and the impossibility of it all, with her midnight black pupils surrounded by their iridescent zig-zagged, orangey-red coronas.

The icy cold of the water brought Brad back to his senses with a jolt. He was not far from the shore of the lake but was still further out than he could remember going. Scrambling back, he hauled himself out. "Did you see anything?" Velhanna was waiting for him as he reached dry land.

"Yes, I saw many things," he replied, trying to make sense of what he had seen.

"Good. You mustn't tell me any of what you saw Bradley White, the visions were for you and not for anyone else."

Chapter 43
Suspended Time

The descent from the Lake of Visions seemed to take even longer than their journey there. Brad couldn't put his finger on the reason until Velhanna stumbled and would have fallen, if he hadn't caught her arm in time.

"Thank you, Outlander," she said as he gently helped her stand up. Even in the pale light of the moon, Velhanna looked exhausted.

"Would you like to rest for a while before we continue?"

"No, you have to get back to your companion soon. We cannot hold this moment in time for much longer. As you can see the magic takes its toll on those who wield it."

He nodded and continued to walk, but this time by Velhanna's side.

"Does all magic do that?" Brad asked.

"Yes, it does. The strength of the magic is determined by the strength and skill of the person who wields it. Prolonged use of magic will weaken an individual until they either stop or they die."

"Why would anyone let it get that far?"

"The use of magic is seductive and intoxicating and gives the person who wields it the sense that they can do anything," she replied. "For some, the intoxication is all consuming and they can't stop until they are consumed by it. Many pass out long before then, but every now and then someone will push just that little bit too hard."

"Can everyone in this land use magic?" Brad asked.

"In order to use magic, the wielder must have innate magic or White Metal."

"What is White Metal?"

"It is a much-coveted material that is scarce and its scarceness makes it valuable. It is a natural source of magic. It looks pretty much like any other metal and can be cut and moulded into shapes and designs. It's only when you touch it that you realise it is profoundly different. It's warm at all times and those that have innate magic can sense its power," Velhanna replied.

"Does White Metal run out of power? Can it be drained?" Brad was fascinated.

"Yes Outlander, eventually it does run out of power, or at least almost. It draws its energy from the rocks and land from which it was formed and can never be exhausted entirely. When its energy has been depleted, it is returned to the land and like a wick dipped in lamp oil, it slowly draws the natural magic from its surroundings unto itself until it is restored. The process is slow and it takes a very long time before it can be used again."

"Where can this substance be found?" Brad asked.

"It's rare and despite repeated attempts to find new sources, there is still only one mine. It is from this single mine that deposits are still being extracted."

"I guess whoever has control over that mine must be extremely wealthy and powerful," Brad mused.

"Very little White Metal is extracted and the state controls what little is produced. Because of its power, it is only sold or traded under strict crown control. Sanjin Dakor fears that if too much of it falls into the wrong hands, the consequences could be dire."

"I can see why," Brad said. "Is that what this is all about?"

"How do you mean, Outlander?" Velhanna asked.

"Is Zoryn looking to gain control over the source of this mine?"

"Some in my order believe this to be true," she replied.

"Is this what you believe?"

"Yes, but I fear that Zoryn has other plans for White Metal. There are signs that he may have found a way to pervert the purity of the metal, turning it black in the process, or else he has rediscovered Black Metal."

"What's does that mean? What is Black Metal?"

"Black Metal is much more powerful than White Metal. It draws its power from the wielder, but it can also take power from other sources which means that its power is potentially unlimited. And, it draws on this power much faster than its white counterpart. This is what makes it so dangerous."

"Can White Metal be turned into Black Metal?" Brad asked.

"We believe that it can however, some Black Metal must be used in the process."

"Where would someone get this Black Metal?"

"Some of the oldest legends of the Five Lands tell how it was discovered by chance hundreds of years ago. Only one piece was found but managed to find its way into the hands of a hated ruler named Jal Chindo. He used it's might to lay waste to his enemies' lands and all that opposed him. His rule lasted for almost half a century.

"What happened to Jal Chindo?" Brad asked.

"No one is certain. He went hunting alone one morning, safe in the knowledge that he had Black Metal with him and he never returned. They never found him or the Black Metal."

"Are there any other tales about this stuff?" Brad asked.

"No there aren't, but there are those that believe in the tale of Jal Chindo and many still search in the hope of finding what was once his."

"Do you believe the tale?"

"Yes, I believe in Black Metal and my people have sensed its use recently," she replied.

"Sensed its use?" Brad demanded, "but I thought you said that it had been lost centuries ago?"

"Yes, it was lost but now it would appear that Zoryn may have discovered it."

"What makes you think that?"

"For a start, you have been brought here by Zoryn from a distant place and there isn't a magic here that's strong enough to do that. And then there's also the matter of Dakor's Darkness."

Chapter 44

A Long Evening

They continued back to the camp in silence. When they got there, Brad looked up and the night bird was still motionless about ten feet in the air above his head, exactly as it had been when they left.

"What happens now?" He asked.

"That Outlander, only you can determine. You have seen parts of your destiny that might or might not come to pass. Your fate and that of the Five Lands of Zandyros is in your hand," she replied.

"How can you say that, when Zoryn holds the lives of my wife and son in his hands. How can I possibly stand against such a being? What chance do I stand?"

"Zoryn Dakor underestimates you, Bradley White," she replied, using his name for the first time.

"And what makes you say that?"

"I believe that you have innate magic and that Zoryn does not believe that this could be possible. The Lake has shown my people glimpses of your world and it would appear that magic does not exist there."

"And you don't believe that?"

"I don't know for certain, but I can sense magic in you. Or to be more precise, magics."

"How do you mean?"

"I am certain that you have at least some Black Metal inside you. That would account for how Zoryn was able to transport you here in the first place. That he must have planted it inside you is clear to me."

"I think you are right, at least about the Black Metal," Brad replied. "When I first met Zoryn, he tricked me into putting bands of the strangest black material I have ever seen around my wrists."

"Where are they now?"

"They seemed to catch on fire and then vanished without leaving a mark."

"What you are describing is almost certainly Black Metal and I believe that it has been absorbed into your body. You must not reveal this to anyone. The substance inside you is so rare and powerful that many would kill you to extract it."

Brad shuddered at the thought.

"There's another reason why I am convinced you have Black Metal inside you."

"And what's that?"

"Your eyes, Outlander. When you first came out of the lake, there was something very wrong about your eyes, about the colours and strange shapes around the centres of your eyes and the way they seemed to pulse. There was something vaguely familiar about them and it's taken me until now to make the connection."

"And that is…?" Brad asked.

"Jal Chindo. I remember reading some ancient text where the cruel King's eyes were described. It is only mentioned in that single text. To make eye contact with someone such as he was strictly forbidden, even when he addressed somebody directly. But clearly, some scribe had either seen his eyes, or had been given a reliable account by someone that had, and he recorded it. The way he described Jal Chindo's eyes is exactly the way your eyes appeared as you walked out of the lake."

"I think I might know what you mean," Brad said. "I thought I saw something strange about my eyes, a couple of times before I was transported to this place. But each time, it didn't last long. Are my eyes like it now?"

"No, your eyes appear quite normal now. I suspect it is a reaction to the magic of the Black Metal and only reveals itself when you are accessing its power."

"So, if it is so powerful and I have it inside myself, why can't I just stand up to this Zoryn Dakor and beat him at his own game?" Brad asked, a hint of irony in his voice.

"Well maybe you can, but if you did, you would need innate magic which Zoryn believes you do not possess.

"So, to use this magic against Zoryn, I have to find and develop magical skills that the people of my world don't possess," Brad said incredulously, "I never realised it was going to be so easy!"

"I'm sorry Outlander, but I do not have the answers you need."

"If you can't get directly involved with the problems facing this place Velhanna, aren't you somehow breaking the rules by telling me this?

"My people cannot interfere directly with the events that take place in this land for reasons that I cannot explain to you."

"If that's the case, how do you explain the Lake of Secrets? Surely, that counts as interfering?"

"The Lake is a natural resource, a part of this place and its visions provide glimpses of what is and what may never be. But you are right, we have interfered by taking you to the Lake. We took you there by way of reparation."

"What do you mean by reparation?" Brad asked.

"Our people divided into two factions, for ideological reasons, centuries ago. I cannot go into detail now, but the other faction sees benefits to the Five Lands being ruled by Zoryn Dakor. We do not share this belief. Zoryn was taken to the lake of Visions by Draxan Longseer, the leader of the other faction. We have done the same for you to help counter any advantage that Draxan's interference may have given to Zoryn."

"So, what happens now?" Brad repeated the question.

"Now you get some sleep and continue on your journey tomorrow," Velhanna replied.

"Do you really think that I can prevent Zoryn from becoming the ruler of the Five Lands Velhanna?"

"I cannot answer that, nobody can, but I can tell you that the fate of the Five Lands and your own are inextricably linked."

"Thank you for taking me to the Lake of Visions Velhanna. You have given me at least some small amount of hope and that's something I haven't felt for a very long time."

"It was my destiny, Bradley White. My time here is rapidly ending, but before I go I need to ask you about the forest."

"What do you mean?" Brad was instantly on his guard.

"You are right to be wary about who you talk about this with," Velhanna said, as if reading his very thoughts, "it is a place between worlds that I believe is a construct of the Black Metal, a side-effect so to speak. Zoryn can enter it, as he has command over the magic of the Black Metal. He does not know that you too can enter this place at will. He must never know this, Outlander." Her image was becoming insubstantial. "Farewell."

Before Brad could reply, Velhanna literally disappeared right before his eyes. At the exact same moment, the night bird was freed from its suspended animation and Brad heard the flutter of its wings as it flew off. Not that he needed further proof but was curious anyway, Brad looked at his watch. The second hand remained motionless. "Typical, now my only link to home is broken, back to the fucking reality of this place," he muttered under his breath, "phah, if any of this really is real?"

As long as the night had already been for him, no time had actually passed, which meant that he still had several hours of his watch left before it was time to wake Farric. The time however passed quickly as Brad relived the evening repeatedly in his mind. With a seemingly uncanny accuracy, Farric woke up and took over the last watch. Brad found an area that was relatively flat and without too many rocks and rolled into his blanket. His last thought before he fell asleep, was how he wished he could tell Gina about the visions.

Chapter 45
The Magic Within

He was back in the Forest with Gina. "I heard you call my name again, Brad," Gina said, her features pale and ethereal in the twilight gloom of the Forest.

"I really need to talk with you, something beyond strange happened to me this evening and now I know that I have to go up against Zoryn."

"You can't Brad, he will kill you."

"I have to Gina, I don't have a choice. I have to break Zoryn's hold over us. He believes that I am powerless to stand against him, so he doesn't think of me as a threat. In his mind, the worst that I can do is not kill his brother. I was taken to a place called the Lake of Visions and saw glimpses of my future; I may not be as alone in this as I first thought I was. There may yet be some hope for us."

"I know about one of your visions Brad, it was real and we did meet here and talk. But how can you possibly know if anything else that you saw was real? Can you trust the person that took you to the lake?

"You're right Gina, I don't know anything for certain, but I trust this woman Velhanna who took me there. I believe that her and her people are somehow on my side in all of this, something about her just seemed right. It's difficult to explain, but the people in this place aren't like people from our world. They look like us but they are harder, untrustworthy and deeply mistrusting of others. I didn't get the same feeling about Velhanna. She has her agenda I'm sure, like everyone else I have met in this wretched place, but she seemed genuine and I believe her," Brad said. "Shit Gina, all this talk about magic and a Lake of Visions must sound like I've completely lost my fucking mind, but this place is real and these things really are happening."

"Is she attractive, Brad?" Gina's tone was flat, her eyes as hard as flints.

"You must be recovering, Gina!" Brad laughed. "You have no reason to be jealous, Velhanna is trying to help, but she is not doing it for me, she is doing it for her people and the others that live here. I don't really understand, but I'm beginning to think that there is more at stake here than just David's, yours and my freedom."

"I know Brad, but you are a long way from home!" Gina held Brad in her unwavering gaze for a moment longer and then laughed. The sound was a healing balm to his frayed senses. There had been little to laugh about for months before Brad's translocation and certainly, there had been nothing to laugh about since.

"How do you propose to break Zoryn's grip, Brad?"

"I doubt whether I can, I doubt whether anyone can. I want to kill him, but I'm not naïve enough to believe that you can simply walk right up and kill someone that has that much power. That's supposing I can even get close enough to him in the first place, and I have no idea where he is, or how to find him. I have only seen an image, a vision of him since I came here. The last time I saw him in the flesh was in our world."

"If you do manage to break the link he is bound to know," said Gina, "and then he will come after you, I'm certain of that."

"Yes, I'm sure you're right which is why the timing will be critical."

"But if you break Zoryn's link to our world, you will be stranded where you are Brad and we will never see you again."

"If I can break Zoryn's hold over you and David, then staying here is a price I'm prepared to pay."

"Do you think you can do it?"

"I don't know Gina, but I'm beginning to think that it may be possible."

"What makes you think that?"

"It was something I saw in one of the visions and something that Velhanna said. She told me a story about some mythical Black Metal that is supposed to have very strong magical properties. Apparently, this stuff is from legend and nobody knows whether it is real or not."

"Does she believe it's real, Brad?"

"Yes she does. Velhanna doesn't strike me as someone who would waste her time telling me about something if she wasn't convinced about its existence."

"But even if it is real Brad, how will it help you?"

"I think that Zoryn has got this Black Metal and that is how he was able to reach into our world, and I think that I know why he did it."

"I thought that we already knew that it was so that he could get someone to kill his brother?"

"Yes, well that's what he told us. But there must be more. Think Gina, why would he take someone from our world, using all that energy in the process, when he could find someone closer to home to do his bidding? From what I've seen since I've been here, there is no shortage of people who will kill someone for money. So why go to all the bother of taking me from our world?"

"I don't know," said Gina.

"I didn't either, until I entered the lake, but now I think I do," Brad replied. "It was something that was said to me in one of the visions when I was handed the black knife that I am to use to kill Zoryn's brother. The man that gave it to me said that I must not use magic around the knife as it absorbs some of the magic of others. In the vision, I said that I didn't have any magic, but the man didn't believe me."

"I'm struggling to see how any of this helps us, Brad?" Gina questioned.

"I think that the reason Zoryn came to our world was because it's a world where there is no magic and where people do not have any magical abilities. I'm convinced that the knife is made of Black Metal."

"And Zoryn doesn't believe that you would know about its power because you come from a world without magic?" Gina asked.

"Precisely! And that's the whole point. If this Black Metal does have the power that Velhanna believes it does, Zoryn is placing this power in my hands!"

"Do you think that you could use its magic, Brad? Do you think that you really do have any magical powers? It all sounds pretty unlikely, don't you think?"

"Yes, it does, but I've seen some pretty strange shit since I've been here. I have seen magic being used and it can do things that shouldn't be possible. It seems to break every law of physics, but it must have its limits. I don't think that Black Metal has the same restrictions as other magic. Zoryn used it to reach out to our world which must be an incredible distance from here. At night, none of the stars are familiar to me and this world even has a fucking blue star as its sun. If Zoryn can make a link between worlds so vastly distant, then there must be a way to break that link using the same Black Metal that created it. I just need to find out how to do it."

"But what if you can't?"

"We have nothing to lose. Zoryn will kill me when I'm no longer any use to him, and I fear that he may come after you and David as well. But I think that's less likely to happen."

"Why do you think that?" asked Gina.

"You and David are his leverage against me, his insurance that I will do what he demands. After I've gone, you and David are no threat or use to him and it's possible that he may just leave you alone, but there's no way I'm going to leave that to chance."

"I don't know why I think this, but maybe this Forest holds some of the answers, Brad."

"How do you mean, Gina?"

"That's just it I don't know, but this place is definitely a link of some kind between the two worlds. If Zoryn doesn't know that we can meet here, then we must have some advantage. At the very least, we can communicate with each other. It's also strange that when you entered the Lake of Visions I was brought to this place again, without being called by you first."

"Can you enter the forest whenever you want to?" Brad asked.

"Yes I can, well most of the time anyway."

"Velhanna also seems to think that this place is important."

Gina started to become less substantial and he knew that this heralded her departure. Before either could utter another word, she had gone and Brad fell into an uneasy and troubled sleep.

Chapter 46
Blackreach Wolves

Brad and Farric ate a breakfast of dried meat and fruit and some of the strange tasting hard cheese that was infused with restorative powers. They only had warm ale to wash the food down with but were glad of the refreshment it provided.

Farric pulled the tarpaulin off the cart and reaching inside, pulled out two short-swords that were sheathed in utilitarian dark brown leather scabbards, each complete with a heavy belt and metal buckle. "Here, take this," Farric said as he threw one over to Brad. "You better put it on. If we encounter any bandits, they will be armed. Have you ever used a sword before?"

"No, but I get the general idea of how they work!" Brad replied sarcastically, as he strapped the sword to his waist.

"Ha, that's all I need; a smartass companion who can't use a fucking sword." Farric roared with laughter. "Let's hope that we don't need to put your *skills* to the test!"

They had little in the way of possessions and quickly emptied the cart. Farric had a back-pack which he filled as best as he could and managed to get most of what remained in Brad's saddlebags which he slung over one of the horses. What was left was superfluous to their requirements and they left it in a small heap by the cart.

"The cart and this stuff," Farric said, as he nudged the pile with his foot, "will be gone by nightfall, of that you can be certain!"

Although the horses seemed to be quite docile, Brad was somewhat relieved when Farric, sensing his apprehension, handed him the reins of one and said that he believed it to be the *better behaved* of the pair.

It had been a long night for Brad. With Velhanna's suspension of time, it had lasted twice as long, maybe longer, for him than it had for Farric. However, despite his tiredness he felt surprisingly good. He thought that it may have been the effects of the cheese but then it dawned on him, he had hope for the first time in as long as he could remember. It wasn't hope that things would end well for him, he didn't really believe they would. His hope was that maybe he could save Gina and David. But even then, any chance they had depended on the possibility that Zoryn had miscalculated, that he had made mistakes in his assumptions, that his reasoning was flawed. Could a being as powerful as Zoryn really make mistakes like that? It seemed unlikely to Brad, but maybe, just maybe Zoryn's arrogance could be his greatest weakness. Brad clung to this thought as he and Farric wound their way through the foothills of the Krendyran Mountains.

Their passage was similar to the route that Brad had taken only a matter of hours before with Velhanna. But the odd thing was that try as he might, he couldn't see any trace of the paths they had taken, maybe this was why the Lake of Visions was so hard to find? The path that Farric took was much lower in the mountain range. It was well worn and in a number of places, it was much narrower, as the rock of the mountains hemmed them in on both sides. In these places, they were forced to ride in single file.

Mindful that they were vulnerable to ambush, Farric scouted a short distance ahead and called Brad to follow when he was satisfied that the way forward was clear. The day wore on and Brad began to feel weary. They rode in silence for much of the day, stopping infrequently for food and drink. Their passage was shrouded in gloom, as the high walls of the mountains blocked out most of the day's light and the transition from daylight to dusk was barely noticeable.

"Shit!" Farric hissed, his voice low and feral.

"What's wrong?" Brad's response was barely more than a whisper.

"We have company," Farric replied as he signalled for them to stop.

"What do we do now?"

"We wait. The path opens up ahead and is not defensible. This spot isn't ideal but we can make a stand here."

"What makes you think there will be trouble?" Brad asked.

"We are close to the edge of the mountains, and no one in their right mind would attempt a crossing from the other side this close to nightfall, except bandits."

They dismounted quickly and quietly and stood in silence listening intently, their eyes focused on the path in front of them. Each drew their sword and stood crouched and ready to fight.

The transition from dusk to night happened quickly in this world and it was soon dark. There wasn't any moonlight and it should have been completely dark but the ethereal luminosity emanating from the rock around them gave a little light. There was just enough for Brad to make out objects within a few feet or so of where he stood. He tested the steel of the blade in his hand. It was a plain short sword with no markings, but it was a good weight and felt balanced. The edges were razor sharp and it was clearly made for just one purpose. He wondered if he would be able to put up much of a defense with it if they were attacked.

The attack came without warning. Brad heard an animal growl but could only watch as Farric slashed his sword wildly at a massive wolf-like beast as it sprang at him. Even in the relative darkness, the beast looked enormous, easily standing four feet tall, heavily muscled with massive shoulders. Its maw was gaping open revealing row after row of razor sharp teeth. But what struck Brad the most were the creature's eyes. Even at this distance, he could see a flicker of intelligence and a burning hatred. This was no ordinary beast. But there was something else about the animal's eyes that he couldn't quite make out clearly from where he stood. Farric's sword caught the beast across its shoulder and slashed into its right flank. Raising his sword again, he delivered a crushing downward blow to the animal's skull ending its life.

Although only a matter of seconds had passed, Brad's attention had been diverted by Farric's plight and he didn't hear the second animal as it charged at him out of the darkness. Unlike the other wolf, it didn't make a sound and it was only Brad's heightened senses that saved him.

The beast was upon him in a heartbeat and he only just managed to raise his arm in time to stop the animal from taking him by the neck. The strength of the wolf and the force of the impact momentarily knocked Brad off balance which was just long enough for the creature to sink its razor-sharp teeth into his forearm. Its teeth ripped through the tough leather of his jacket and sank into the flesh of his arm as the wolf tightened its grip. The great beast thrashed its head from side to side in an effort to force Brad to the ground. Searing pain, made worse by the thrashing of the creature, coursed through Brad's savaged arm and threatened to overwhelm him. He knew that if he panicked and the animal was to take him to the ground, his chances of survival would be slim. Summoning all his strength, he stood his ground, forcing the wolf to face him.

It was then that he saw the wolf's eyes clearly for the first time. Around its pupils was the same zig-zagged, orangey-red corona that he had seen in Zoryn's eyes and his own. Looking into the beast's malice filled eyes, Brad felt as if he was face to face with Zoryn. Howling with rage and renewed strength, he slashed at the animal's snarling maw with his sword, his blade biting into the beast with each strike. Every time he struck, a further wave of pain ran through his damaged arm, but he was oblivious to it and continued slashing at the beast until he had a clean strike. He ran his short sword into the beast's skull killing it where it stood.

Brad felt lightheaded and checked his arm for blood loss. It hung loosely at his side and was clearly shattered. He was bleeding, but not enough to cause the dizziness that was increasing by the second. Black spots crowded his vision, and the last thing that he saw was Farric lunging with his sword at yet another creature as it charged at him.

***

"You should be dead. Nobody survives a bite from a Blackreach Wolf, nobody Brad but you it would seem."

"Where are we?" Brad's mouth was parched and his voice was as dry leaves in a breeze.

"About two hours ride from the eastern side of the Krendyran's," came the reply.

"How did I get here?"

"After the wolves left us in search of easier prey, I slung you over the back of your horse and got us out of there. I reckoned that if I delivered your body to Krendyra, I would have upheld at least part of my end of the deal and would be paid something. I wasn't expecting you to survive."

"What happened, was I poisoned?" He was weak, the effort of talking draining what little strength he had.

"You could say that, you were bitten by a Blackreach Wolf."

"What's a Blackreach Wolf?" Brad asked.

"It's a beast about twice the size of a normal wolf and its bite injects a lethal venom that nobody has ever survived. But of all the dangers that we might encounter, I wasn't expecting it to be Blackreach Wolves."

"Why's that?"

"I've never heard of them hunting this far down in the mountains. Something must have caused them to come down. Their hunting ground is the Blackreach forest high up in the mountains that stretches between the three highest peaks of the Krendyran's. The forest is ideally suited to wolves because it is overshadowed to a large part by the face of the mountains that shield it from direct sunlight, making it dark. So dark in fact that the wolves have even been known to hunt during the day. It is rumoured that there is plentiful game up there and there are those that are foolhardy enough to go there in search of it. "

"Foolhardy?" Echoed Brad.

"Yes. The wolves are very protective of their hunting grounds!"

"Ah, I think I understand!"

"But what you don't know is that the bite of a Blackreach Wolf contains a fast-acting venom that renders its victim helpless within seconds and dead within minutes. If the venom doesn't kill you, the wolf, or the rest of the pack, will. But not you Bradley White, you were unconscious and close to death, but you didn't die."

"I've never heard of a wolf's bite containing venom," Brad said.

"Only Blackreach Wolves have venom. The grass the animals eat in the Blackreach Forest is plentiful; hence, the large amount of game that lives there, but it contains a poison that taints the meat from the game. If you eat it, it would make you ill and you would be puking for days. It doesn't affect the wolves in the same way, but I believe it is the source of the venom which becomes concentrated inside the wolves' bodies."

"You seem to know a lot about them?"

"I've been there and managed to get out, my travelling companion was not so lucky."

"I'm sorry to hear that."

"Don't be. If the wolves hadn't killed him, I would have!" Farric replied with his customary grin softening his hard features.

"Do you have any water?"

"Sure, take this." Farric handed him a water skin as he continued.

"What I still don't understand, is why the wolves ventured so low in the mountains. Something must have attracted them there."

"What do you think it was?" asked Brad.

"Beats me, I have no idea."

"So, what happened back there, Farric?"

"We killed a few wolves between us but I reckon it was only a small hunting pack, any more and we wouldn't have made it. I managed to drive the other two wolves off. It was fully dark by the time I led our horses out of the foothills and I figured that it would be wise to put some distance between us and the mountains, so I kept riding with your horse in tow. There was nothing I could do for you and I didn't want to stick around so close to the mountains. An hour or so later, I looked back to see if you had died and your whole body was glowing."

"Glowing?" repeated Brad.

"Yes, your whole body was fucking glowing a weird crimson colour. Weirdest thing I ever fucking saw, really freaked me out. I very nearly left you there. Some magic was at work, that much was obvious, but none that I've ever seen before. We were still too close to the mountains, so I carried on with you in tow for another hour until we came to this spot."

"How long have we been here?" Brad could feel his strength slowly beginning to return.

"About three hours I reckon. It must be somewhere around midnight. You stopped glowing soon after we got here, which was a fuckin relief believe me. You have magic Brad, whether you believe it or not, and something is protecting you. Without it, you would already be dead. First, you escaped that blade in Dumas and now you survive the bite of a Blackreach Wolf. Somebody wants you kept alive Brad, at least for now I guess."

They didn't have much food left but Farric managed to make a small cold meal of what remained. Brad was ravenous and devoured his food within minutes.

"Fuck it Brad, I have a little Akandia Mead left over. It doesn't look like I'm going to get any sleep tonight, so we might as well finish it off and make the most of a shitty evening!"

Brad laughed as Farric passed him the small barrel. He took a large mouthful of the delicious amber drink and handed the barrel back to Farric. The combination of the after effects of the venom, fatigue and alcohol hit Brad like a sledgehammer and he fell asleep where he sat.

Farric left Brad to sleep as he guarded their camp for what was left of the night. He was tired himself but had grown to like Brad over the course of their travels and didn't feel it would be fair to wake him up to take his turn guarding the camp. From a practical standpoint, Farric didn't think that Brad would have stayed awake during his watch anyway, which could have put them both at risk. Besides, he had survived the bite of a Blackreach Wolf and deserved a little rest.

The next morning was bright and warm and Brad woke early. The effects of the venom had gone and he felt remarkably good. Farric, however, looked haggard and very much like a man who had been awake all night, which indeed he had. Brad tried to make light conversation but Farric's grumpy responses were a clear sign that he didn't want to talk. They packed their meagre belongings and mounted their horses with Farric leading the way.

They had finished their supplies the previous evening and rode in silence, stopping only once during the morning to relieve themselves. The temperature was much hotter since they passed through the Krendyran Mountains and the landscape had taken on a more desert like appearance. The vegetation was sparse and the ground was sandy where the soil had been blown or burnt away by the heat. It was not a very hospitable place and when they stopped, the horses found little vegetation to eat.

"We're about a day's ride from Krendyra and there won't be anything to eat or drink until we get there," Farric said as he turned in his saddle to face Brad. "It's gonna be a long fucking day."

"What's Krendyra like?" Brad asked.

Farric laughed, It's like no place you've been to before, Brad."

Chapter 47
Travelling Light

It was a risky strategy but there was no other choice. They only had a small amount of water left and what little they had they agreed to give to their horses. Logically, it made sense, Krendyra was at least a full day's ride away and without horses, at least two days walk in what had now become the searing heat of this arid landscape. Either way, they could make it, but two days walk in this heat would be torturous. They rationed their meagre supply of water between the horses as best they could and just hoped that it would be enough.

They stopped for the day, late in the afternoon. Farric broke their self-imposed silence as he set-off to scavenge for anything that they could burn for their campfire. Brad had every intention of helping him, but he was hypnotised by the setting sun. He had seen the sun set many times since he had entered this land and it never failed to fill him with awe. During the day, the blue colour of the star that heated this planet was barely perceptible and he had gotten so used to it that he didn't really notice it any more. But when the sun set, the sky took on every imaginable shade of blue and being so low in the sky, it was possible to look directly at the pale blue orb. Unfortunately, it wasn't a sight that lasted very long, as the transition from twilight to darkness happened within minutes in this strange land.

"The fire's shit," Farric declared, "but at least it'll give us some warmth. I take it you haven't been in these parts before Brad, so let me tell you this, it gets fucking cold in the evenings here! Tell me Brad, where exactly do you come from?"

"I don't know how to answer that," he replied.

"Seems a simple enough fucking question to me," Farric snorted, "one thing's for certain, you're not from anywhere I've been to."

"What makes you say that?"

"You look the same as other people but you act differently and I just get the impression that pretty well everything about this place is new to you, and then there's the magic."

"I thought that magic was commonplace here?" Brad replied.

"It is, but I've never seen anyone with magic like yours."

"What do you mean?"

"I saw you use magic in Tyria and Dumas and again after you were bitten by the Blackreach Wolf, and each time it was different. That's not how it normally works. I've met many people who have the use of magic and in each one their ability is restricted to one area. Yours is different, I've seen you use it to attack a man, save you from what should have been a fatal blow and heal yourself when you should have died.

I've never heard of anyone who could heal themselves when they were already unconscious."

"I don't understand any of it either," Brad replied, "where I come from, magic doesn't exist and I certainly didn't have magic there, nobody does." He gazed into the campfire for a moment and said, "I come from a place distant from here, that much I do know but I have no idea in which direction, or even how far away, it is."

"Is your home like this place?"

"In some ways it's similar, but in other ways it's totally different."

"How do you mean?"

"Our sun is white, yours is blue. In your land there is magic, in ours magic doesn't exist. You travel between places on horseback, we have machines that take us great distances much faster than a galloping horse."

"Sounds totally fucking different to me," Farric replied. "I've never heard of any place like that. So how did you get here?"

"I honestly don't know." He was not about to tell Farric about Zoryn.

"Well I know fuck all about magic, other than what I've seen with my own eyes, but it sounds like a powerful magic must have been used to get you here."

Changing the subject Brad asked, "What do you know about me?"

"Next to fuck all. I was hired to make sure that you got to Krendyra and then to get you back to Garan Smithson's place near Gaardsholme."

"Who hired you?"

"I wouldn't tell you even if I knew, but as it happens I don't know for certain."

"But surely someone is paying you?"

"Yes, and the money came from Garan, but that old bastard never had that kind of money and if he did, he would drink himself dead!" Farric replied.

"And if I didn't agree to go with you…"

"I was hired to get you there whether you wanted to go or not." Farric cut Brad off mid-sentence.

"I kind of thought as much."

"You clearly don't want to go, so tell me how come you haven't put up any resistance?"

Brad paused for a moment before answering. How much could he trust Farric? He didn't really know him at all despite having spent the last few weeks in his company. He liked him and in another time and place, they could be friends, but Brad doubted that this was the time or the place. The only person he felt he could trust was Garan Smithson's niece Hania but even then, he knew practically nothing at all about her either.

"I reckon that we both know who's really behind all of this," Brad said at last, "and I have no doubt that you know far more about him than I do. If that's so, then you'll know how he gets people to do his bidding. I never had any choice."

"And what happens then?" Farric asked.

"How do you mean exactly?" Brad responded

"Well reading between the lines, this someone seems to have gone to a lot of trouble and expense to make sure that you get to Krendyra. Surely it doesn't end there, does it?"

"No Farric, it doesn't."

"So where does it end Brad, and how does it end?"

"I don't know," Brad replied truthfully, or at least as close to the truth as he was prepared to go at this time.

"Ha! We have more in common than either of us would admit to, Bradley White. I may even grow to like you if you survive this."

"I don't know what frightens me the most," Brad said without smiling, "facing whatever is waiting for me in Krendyra or the prospect of becoming your friend."

Farric roared with laughter.

***

Brad didn't sleep well that evening. It was a combination of apprehension for what awaited him in Krendyra and the bitter cold. The fire didn't last much past midnight and Farric was right about this place, the evenings were cold. Zoryn's plans for Brad had seemed a million miles away whilst he was staying with Garan Smithson, even though he was being held a prisoner. In a strange way, his journey with Farric had felt like he was putting some distance between himself and Zoryn, but that couldn't be further from the truth. And now that Krendyra was less than a day's ride away, Brad felt more trapped by Zoryn than he had when he had first set foot in this accursed land.

***

"We leave everything here," Farric announced as he stood next to his horse strapping his short sword to the saddle. It was morning and time to move on. He gave the horses the last dregs of water from the wineskins and tossed them to the ground.

"Won't we need them for the return journey?" Brad asked.

"We can get new ones in Krendyra. If we don't lighten the load by as much as we can, these horses won't make it and I for one don't want to walk there. Besides, if the horses survive we might just be able to sell them!"

They rode in silence. Both men were hungry, thirsty and exhausted and the last thing that either wanted was to talk. The land was bone dry and desert like, without a hint of a breeze. It seemed to Brad as if even the air itself could not survive in this place.

As the afternoon wore on, Brad noticed a subtle change in the environment. It was still baking hot, but here and there were small patches of low growing hardy looking vegetation. He doubted it would provide any nourishment and even the horses didn't bother to stoop down to eat the plants.

It was impossible to be certain what the time was, but the blue sun was noticeably lower in the sky and the temperature, although still very hot, was not quite as unbearable as it had been earlier. The air tasted different to Brad's parched mouth and it reminded him of something that he couldn't quite place. And then he realised what it was, he could taste salt in the air, they were getting closer to the sea.

The horizon began to change shape. Whereas all day, the demarcation between land and sky had been blurred by the heat rising from the ground, now Brad could make out shapes which coalesced in front of his tired eyes into buildings and other man-made structures. The closer they got, the more distinct the shapes became.

After another hour or so, they reached the outermost edge of what was clearly a large city. The sun was by now very low on the horizon and night would fall quickly as it always did in this land.

"Welcome to the ancient city of Krendyra." Farric announced as he turned in his saddle to face Brad. "Your destiny awaits you!"

"I can't wait." Brad scowled in response.

"You lack a sense of adventure!"

"So, what happens now?"

"Tonight, we find a tavern and eat and drink!"

"And tomorrow?"

"Tomorrow you meet Draxan Longseer."

"So that's the name of the man I am to meet. What do you know about him?"

"I know where we have to go to find him and that's about all," Farric replied.

Farric led them to a tavern on a side road off the main route into Krendyra. There was a small paddock to one side of the tavern and as they approached, a young boy ran out to greet them. Farric tossed the boy a copper and told him to take care of the horses as he dismounted and signalled to Brad to do the same. Brad was stiff from riding all day and thought his legs would buckle under him as he handed the reins to the boy. What he needed more than anything else right now was a hot bath to relieve his aching muscles.

The tavern was small and Farric chose a table off to one side, where they would be relatively inconspicuous and where he could keep an eye on those entering and leaving.

"Are we expecting trouble?" Brad asked in a hushed voice.

"I always expect trouble," Farric replied. "We should be okay here but it's better to be safe than sorry, don't you think?"

They didn't have to wait long before a sour-faced woman of middle years put two large tankards of a yeasty smelling brew in front of them. "Would you gentleman be wanting food to go with your ale?" she asked in a nasally voice.

"Yes, what do you have?" Brad asked. Farric had a mouth full of ale and nearly choked with laughter as the woman scowled at him and stormed off.

"What's so funny?" Brad asked as Farric regained his composure.

"I don't know what food you get in taverns where you come from, but here its meat stew and hard bread. She thought you were taking the piss. I wouldn't be at all surprised if your bowl has just a little more piss in it than normal!"

When the stew arrived, it smelled good and Brad devoured the contents. Farric left the table and returned a short time later. "I've got us a room. It's shit as you might expect in a place like this, but it'll do for tonight." Brad nodded in agreement, as Farric gestured that they should go to the room. He had no idea what time it was but suspected that it must still be early in the evening, but he didn't care. All he was interested in right now was finding somewhere soft and warm to lay down and sleep. "Oh, one piece of advice Brad, don't be tempted to sample the delights of any ladies that may knock on our door later. This is the poorer end of the city and the girls here aren't too choosy, it won't just be a fuck you'll get if you sleep with one of them!"

"I'm so knackered I doubt I could manage it even if I wanted to!" Brad replied.

Chapter 48
Krendyra

Brad woke early the next morning and was surprised to see that Farric was already up and dressed. "Let's get out of this shithole," Farric said. Brad nodded in agreement and quickly got up and dressed. The room was every bit as Brad had suspected it was the previous evening when darkness had shrouded its interior. It smelled unpleasant, whether it was the room or himself and Farric that smelled was difficult to tell as neither man had bathed since their visit to the House of Secrets in Dumas.

They made their way through the poorer part of the city, along a wide dirt road which was already busy with the hustle and bustle of people going about their day. Smaller arterial roads branched off but Farric kept to the main route. They continued for about half an hour and as they did so, Brad noticed a gradual improvement in the quality and condition of the houses which were interspersed with the occasional store and tavern. He suspected that Krendyra was a seaport and that the poorer parts were inhabited by seamen and stevedores, with the merchants living in the more opulent parts of the city. The road angled to the right and without warning, Brad was met by the stunning vista of the port of Krendyra which stretched out in front of him as far as he could see in either direction. He was so taken aback by the sight that he literally stopped in his tracks.

"Yeah, it had the same effect on me when I first came here," Farric said.

"It's certainly better than the other places I've been to since I got here," Brad replied. "How long are we staying here?"

"One night, maybe two, it all depends."

"Depends on what?" Brad asked.

"If the man, we are to meet, is easy to find."

"But I thought that you knew where to go to meet this man?"

"Yes I do, but I've never met him before and the description I have been given of him is a little vague. I doubt that he will be at the meeting place anyway and suspect that we will be sent somewhere else for the actual meeting."

"Do you think there will be trouble?" Brad asked.

"Brad you should know by now that I always expect there to be trouble wherever I go!"

"Funny thing that Farric, that is certainly how it seems to end up!"

Farric roared with laughter as he led the way deeper into the city.

The houses gave way to more and more stores and taverns as they ventured deeper into Krendyra. Each property was more lavishly built and decorated than the one before it. They eventually stopped outside a building that stood out from the rest. Unlike the others that surrounded it, it was detached and sat on its own piece of land. Brad suspected that like in his home world, land near the centre of a prosperous city came at a premium. Whereas, the surrounding properties were lavish and immaculately painted, this property was proud of its bare timbered simplicity which emphasised the quality of its remarkable construction. It was a stunning property.

A sign was attached to the front of the building. It was simple but well-crafted and appeared to be made out of metal. It was black with just two parallel white vertical lines. Brad had seen this sign before and smiled, as he knew what it meant. Farric had taken them to the House of Secrets.

Oh well, He thought. *Whatever else happens in Krendyra this part at least is going to be pleasant!*

Before Farric could knock on the door, it was opened by an immaculately groomed man of middle years.

"Welcome to Krendyra gentlemen," he greeted them, "and to the House of Secrets. May your stay with us be memorable."

"I'm sure it will!" Farric replied, as he slapped Brad on the back and headed inside. Brad did not need a second invitation and quickly followed.

They were taken to a reception room where they were given a tray of small, but exquisitely made cakes and steaming mugs of draema. The high sugar content of the cakes and the restorative powers of the draema soon helped to dispel the fatigue from so many weeks on the road. They devoured the cakes in short order and were ready for a much larger meal, as they hadn't eaten since the previous evening.

"Our chefs have been instructed to prepare your meal gentlemen, but first may I invite you to enjoy our spa?" Came a voice as light as a zephyr dancing on summer meadows and as rich as the finest of meads.

Both men turned to face the speaker. For a moment, they were silent as they took in the beauty of the woman who stood before them. She was five foot five, probably in her early thirties and of a slender frame. Her skin was dark and her eyes darker still. The white filmy gauze dress she wore accentuated her curves and provided the perfect contrast to her skin tone. She wore her shoulder length hair loose and its midnight lustre made it shine despite its jet-black colour.

"As always, the fabled House of Secrets never fails to anticipate the needs of its guests! We are hungry and weary from weeks of travel and we could do with soaking off the dust from the road." Farric responded.

"I am Nyree, head of this establishment and I will personally see to it that your every need will be satisfied during your stay with us. May I enquire how long your visit will be?"

"Two days, maybe longer."

"Rooms have been prepared for each of you and your clothes will be washed whilst you bathe." Nyree clapped her hands and two girls appeared from the doorway behind her. Each girl was wearing a silk gown of the purest white that contrasted with their burnished skin. The gowns had been designed to accentuate their feminine bodies and provided little in the way of concealment.

"May your stay here be memorable, gentlemen." Nyree's honeyed voice conveying more than any words ever could as she turned and left the room, leaving Brad and Farric alone with the girls.

The House of Secrets at Krendyra was a well-run establishment that was dedicated to the pleasure of its guests. Brad was bathed and massaged by his beautiful companion and was not left wanting when his arousal became obvious. By the time he left the private bathing area he was clean, relaxed and satisfied. The girl led him to a room that was his for the duration of his stay here. It was immaculately clean, and the bed was firm but comfortable with clean sheets that smelled faintly of lavender. What a contrast he thought with the tavern that he and Farric had stayed at the previous evening.

Brads thoughts turned to his life before he was taken away from it by Zoryn. It still seemed bizarre to him that he could have actually left his world, but there was no doubt in his mind that he was on another planet, maybe in a different universe altogether. There was a certain irony to the fact that his world had technology and from that perspective was much more advanced than this place, but yet totally incapable of achieving what Zoryn had done with no technology whatsoever.

He had been away for at least a couple of months and the only contact he had had with his home world had been the meetings with Gina in his dreams. Despite the impossibility of these meetings, Brad believed that they were real.

His thoughts turned to his son David. How was he? Was he still in hospital? Had Zoryn been back to torment him? David knew that his father was involved in something sinister when Zoryn had posed as a doctor and threatened his life. Since then Brad had had no way of contacting his son. What must David be thinking? Did he think that he had abandoned him? When he thought about his son and how powerless he was to help him, it felt like a knife was being turned in the pit of his stomach.

Brad's thoughts were interrupted by a knock on the door. He opened it and was greeted by the sight of the girl who had bathed him so intimately earlier. She smiled and handed him his clothes which had been freshly laundered in an impossibly short period of time. Brad suspected that magic had been used. She informed him that lunch was ready and that she would accompany him to the dining area as soon as he was dressed.

Farric was already eating when Brad entered the small but immaculately decorated dining room. Apart from the serving staff, they were alone.

"Sit down and enjoy the food, it's the finest either one of us is going to eat for weeks after we leave this place." Farric announced between mouthfuls of food that he continued to chew as he spoke.

Despite the splendour of the food in front of them, both men wolfed their meals down, as their empty bellies were no respecters of quality.

"Right Brad, let's get on with this, it's time we found out who it is I have been paid so much to take you to."

"Yes, let's get this over with," Brad replied through clenched teeth as both men rose and left the table.

Chapter 49
The House of Secrets in Krendyra

It was late in the afternoon as they wound their way through the busy streets of Krendyra. At one point, their path took them through a large open-air street market. Brad's senses were bombarded by the bright colours of the stalls and the heady aroma of spices, some of which smelled familiar to him and others did not. There were stalls selling fine meats and exotic fruits, and others that displayed all manner of prepared food and delicacies. He wished he had time to explore the market and sample some of the produce but Farric's pace allowed no time for pause.

Eventually, they arrived at the harbour itself. By now, the sun had set and night fell with its characteristic eagerness to erase any trace of the day. There were many inns and taverns along their route and each one was illuminated inside and out by oil lanterns which provided enough light for them to continue their search.

"Do you actually know where we are going?" Brad asked.

"Yes, but the last time I was here, it was daylight and it was some time ago."

"How long ago would that be?"

"Must be five or more years I guess."

"Oh great," replied Brad. "This is going to be a long night!"

"It better not be; I have plans for later and they don't involve you." Farric snapped in response.

"That comes as somewhat of a relief!"

Farric ignored him as he continued moving from one building to the next. He stopped at several taverns and peered inside as he gestured to Brad to stay outside.

Just when Brad thought they would still be searching at the break of day, Farric stopped outside a tavern that didn't have a lamp outside as if it seemed to prefer the anonymity of darkness.

"This is it," Farric announced as they stopped outside. All the other taverns nearby had signs hanging from their façades depicting various scenes. Some had strange lettering on the signs in a style and language that Brad had not seen before. The tavern that Farric had brought him to had no such sign and was clearly not interested in drawing attention to itself.

"Stay close to me when we go inside and don't make eye contact or speak with anyone unless they speak to you first," said Farric. "I know the type of men that go to this place and they place little value on the life of a stranger."

Brad nodded in agreement and said nothing as he followed Farric inside.

The tavern was dimly lit, and it was clear that the patrons of this establishment valued their privacy. A seaport the size of Krendyra must have a black market where contraband was traded, and Brad suspected that a fair amount of such business was transacted here. There was a dozen or so men in clusters of two or three sat around small tables in hunched discussion. Each cast a wary eye in the direction of the strangers but quickly looked away and continued their quiet murmurings.

They made their way to a solid wooden bar that ran in one long piece along the entire length of the rear wall. It was easily six inches thick and must have taken a dozen or more men to secure it in place when the tavern was constructed. The bar had been constructed in such a way as to afford those serving some degree of protection should trouble break out, and Brad had no doubt that trouble was a frequent visitor to this establishment.

"Two tankards of ale," Farric growled at the man serving behind the bar.

"Will you be joining us for some meat stew as well?" the barman replied.

"No, we won't be staying here long."

Brad was thirsty from the walk from the House of Secrets and readily accepted the tankard when Farric offered it to him.

"Take your time with it, Brad," Farric said below his breath. "This ale is strong, and I don't want to carry you back."

Brad took a mouthful of the ale and was surprised at just how good it tasted, but then he figured that if the men were as rough as Farric warned him they were, it would be unwise of the tavern to serve them shit beer. He heeded Farric's warning despite the overwhelming urge to drain the tankard and slake his thirst.

"So, what brings you gentleman to Krendyra?" The barman asked.

"Business," replied Farric, "isn't that why everyone comes here?"

The barman, a rough looking man of indeterminate age held Farric's unflinching gaze for a moment then laughed.

"And would that business be of any benefit to an honest hardworking barman?" the man said in a hushed tone, as he leaned conspiratorially closer to Farric.

"I doubt it," Farric replied.

"Why's that then?" The barman's tone was not quite as friendly now.

"Because I find honest hardworking men make poor business decisions, don't you agree?"

The barman paused as if in thought before he answered. "You have me there, I've never met one so I wouldn't know!"

Farric reached into his pocket, pulled out three gold coins and handed them to the barman discreetly as he raised his tankard to drink the ale. "Get word to Draxan Longseer; tell him that Garan's friends are here."

"And what if I don't know this Draxan Longseer?" The barman sneered.

"Then friend, you have just received a very generous tip," Farric said as he put his half-emptied tankard on the bar, turned his back on the man and walked out of the tavern with Brad close behind him. The men in the tavern didn't look up as they walked past, but Brad was certain that all eyes were on them as they left the tavern.

"Do you think he knows this Longseer?" Brad asked, breaking the silence, after they had walked about a mile from the tavern.

"Without a doubt," Farric replied without turning.

"So, what happens next?"

"One of his people will get a message to us with a date and time for a meeting."

"How will he know where to find us?"

"The chances are he knows we are here already and Garan would have assumed that I would head straight for the House of Secrets anyway. Besides, the man following us will tell him."

Brad went to turn around but Farric stopped abruptly and grabbed him by his leather jerkin preventing him from turning. "Make out that we are arguing Brad, I don't want Draxan's henchman to think we have spotted him. Besides if it isn't one of Draxan's, we want surprise to be on our side, wouldn't you agree?"

Without warning, Brad punched Farric on the chin but at the very last moment, he pulled the punch just enough to avoid any real damage but hard enough to send Farric sprawling to the ground.

"You insult my sister again you fucking twat, and I'll break your fucking neck!" Brad shouted loud enough for anyone nearby to hear. Then in a lower voice for Farric's benefit, he added. "Is that convincing enough for you?"

Farric pulled himself to his feet and exaggerated a swaying motion as he did so. "Twat?" he repeated under his breath. "What the fuck is a twat?"

"It's an insult where I come from," Brad replied.

"I think I may like it there. We don't have twats here, but I think I shall adopt this word, it sounds pretty insulting to me!"

"Believe me Farric, there are plenty of twats in this place," Brad replied.

Their walk back to the House of Secrets passed without further incident and once they were inside Farric said. "We were followed all the way from the tavern. If that wasn't one of Draxan's people, then somebody else is taking an interest in you."

"Will it be safe to stay here?" Brad asked.

"This is about the safest place there is. The local officials and military leaders spend a lot of time here and nobody in their right mind would launch an attack on this place. Besides, the men that work here act as bodyguards and you may not believe it to look at them, but they are skilled fighters. We are safe here Brad, now if you don't mind, I'd rather get laid than talk with you."

The two girls, that Brad and Farric had spent time with earlier that day, appeared from a side room. They each wore a translucent black garment that left nothing to either man's vivid imagination and all thoughts of pursuit and attack disappeared as the girls led them away.

When Brad reached his room, the girl opened the door, but instead of entering, she turned and kissed him on the cheek and bade him enter the room without her. He was a little surprised and disappointed that she wasn't going to join him. The room was thick with the smell of incense which had the immediate effect of making him feel a little light-headed but good.

"Won't you join me for a glass of wine?" Came a voice as soft as velvet and rich with promise.

"Nyree," replied Brad, "I am honoured that you have paid me a visit."

"The honour is all mine. We don't often receive guests that have travelled as far as you have."

The effect of the incense was definitely stronger this time and he felt a little more muzzy-headed than he had the last time, but it was a warm and comforting feeling and he was happy to give himself up to it. Nyree held Brad's gaze for a long moment without speaking and as he looked into the fathomless depths of her eyes, he wondered what she had meant by her comment. Did she know where he came from? Or did she mean the journey he had undertaken with Farric to get here?

She's fishing for information, he thought to himself, *but why? Why would she want to know about me?* Although he didn't believe that Nyree worked for Zoryn, he wasn't about to tell her anything about himself. He still didn't know who to trust in this place and perhaps Farric was right when he had told him that no one could be trusted.

Nyree smiled and poured him a glass of wine from a finely crafted crystal decanter that reflected the light in kaleidoscopic colours. "Here, try this," she said, as she rose to her feet and handed him the glass, "it comes from the finest cellar in this great city of ours and as well as tasting wonderful, it is renowned for its other quality."

"And what would that other quality be?" he asked, as he accepted the glass.

195

"It is said that it has the ability to prolong the moment of release during lovemaking," she said as she sank to her knees in front of him and tugged at his belt. Brad drank deeply from the glass.

In some ways, Nyree reminded him of Selicia, who he had met the first time he had been to the House of Secrets. Both were very intelligent and exuded natural confidence and inner strength. They were also stunning and skilled in the art of love and seemed to enjoy their work as much as their patrons did. There was no hurry, no urgency and their ability to sense what their clients wanted and to satisfy these desires, was a powerful combination. Brad had never before experienced the intensity of feeling and complete satisfaction that he experienced with Nyree and Selicia. And Nyree was right about the wine, if he took that back to his home world and sold it, he would be very wealthy indeed.

Nyree lay with him after he had fallen asleep. She was troubled. Despite the intensity of their lovemaking, she had not been able to mind-skim any of his thoughts or feelings. She had never experienced this with any man before him. Even the wine and double strength incense had not helped.

Selicia contacted her a couple of days earlier and told her to expect Brad and Farric. She told her that, the head of their order, Katzin wanted to know everything about Brad and what had brought these two unlikely companions together and more importantly why they had travelled to Krendyra. Nyree had never received a message like this before and realised that it was important. She was not told why they wanted the information and would never take it on herself to ask.

Nyree planned for the arrival of her guests with meticulous detail and left nothing to chance. She placed her most skilled mind-skimmer with Farric and she would spend time herself with Bradley White. As the head of the House of Secrets in Krendyra, Nyree spent less time entertaining the sexual needs of her guests, reserving herself for those that were more important and those that she was physically attracted to. She couldn't wait to read this man, to find out all about him, to find out what Selicia and Katzin wanted to know.

But she couldn't, he was a closed book to her and she failed in her task, in her duty to the House of Secrets. The only thing that she had discovered was that, unlike other men, he couldn't be mind-skimmed. On an instinctive level, she sensed that there was something different about this man and she was certain that he wasn't from any of the Five Lands but she had no idea where he came from.

There was something else. For the briefest of moments, during the height of their lovemaking, when her mind-skimming powers were at their strongest, Nyree thought she sensed magic in him. It was illusive, like gossamer floating on a summer morning's breeze. One moment it was there, or at least she thought it was there, and the next it disappeared without trace, and try as she might she couldn't find it again. She had slept with many men who possessed innate magical ability and on each and every occasion, she had sensed their magic strongly and in many cases before their bodies had even touched. With Bradley White, it was different and she couldn't honestly say if he had magic or not. If he did, it was unlike anything she had come across before. If it wasn't for the fact that she had been told to report every detail, no matter how seemingly unimportant, she would have let the matter drop and would not have included it in her report. But she knew that it might be important and that Selicia would want to know about it. Maybe she could make some sense of it.

Nyree did not sleep that evening; despite her best effort, her mind was too active. Normally, she would retire to her room after her client was satisfied and bathe before going to bed. This time she decided to stay. She lay facing Bradley White's back and attempted the mind-skim once again. There was no preparation required and no chanting, all she had to do was relax her mind and listen. She listened, but again there was nothing. She wasn't altogether surprised, because mind skimming an unconscious person was at best hit or miss, but she was nonetheless disappointed that this second attempt had also failed.

It was early in the morning, but Nyree could wait no longer. White was still asleep, but she knew exactly how to wake him. Pulling the satin sheet down slowly, his naked torso was revealed. He was in pretty good shape and the sight pleased her. Better still, he must have been having a good dream because he appeared to be semi-erect.

Perfect! she thought. *This should be easy.* She slid down the bed and gently rolled him onto his side. As he started to wake, she took him into her mouth and used all her skills to ensure that he would be thinking of nothing else.

"Good morning, Nyree!" he said, now fully awake. Nyree intensified her efforts. She knew from experience that men took longer to climax shortly after waking. This was perfect because it would allow her more time to mind-skim. She continued her work and cleared her mind. Nothing. She tried repeatedly, but each time the result was the same; she just couldn't read him at all. White's quickening breathing told her that she had little time left to find out what she wanted and she never did. She understood now why Selicia and Katzin were so interested in this man; a man that cannot be read is a dangerous man.

Nyree didn't leave Bradley White's bedroom for another hour and felt weak and had to steady herself as a wave of vertigo threatened to claim her. It didn't last long but the feeling remained for long moments after. She went to the personal room of Enaryu, the girl she had assigned to Farric Clearwater. Enaryu was asleep when Nyree knocked on her door but soon woke up and let her in.

"Selicia, can you hear me?" Nyree sat in her office with the door locked. She had the Zindaw Stone in her hands and called the image of Selicia to her mind, seeing every feature in her mind's eye, from her lustrous ebony hair to her flawless pale skin and perfectly formed features.

"Yes Nyree, I can. What did you find out from your guests?"

"I couldn't read Bradley White at all, it was like there was nothing there to read. I tried repeatedly and used the double strength incense as you suggested, but nothing worked. I stayed with him whilst he slept and made sure that his mind was focused as soon as I woke him in the morning, but still nothing."

"It certainly sounds like you were thorough!" Selicia said with a slight mocking tone to her voice.

"Well, I can't say that it was altogether unpleasant!" Nyree said picking up on Selicia's meaning. "You've slept with this man too and I seem to remember a certain fondness in your tone when you talked about him!" Mercifully, the Zindaw Stone didn't provide a visual link as for the briefest of moments Selicia's face was not its characteristic pale colour.

"I did find out something that may be useful." Nyree continued, "I felt magic in him, or at least I think I did."

"How do you mean?" Selicia asked, her tone suddenly serious.

"It's difficult to describe, but for the briefest of moments I was convinced that I felt magic inside him and then it disappeared, without a trace. I didn't feel it again. Maybe I imagined it."

"I doubt it," Selicia replied. "This is important, and Katzin will want to know this. Can you think of anything else Nyree, no matter how trivial?"

"I don't know, but there may be something else, Selicia."

"What's that?"

Nyree went on to tell Selicia about the weakness and vertigo she had experienced a little earlier.

"The same thing happened to me, Nyree," was all that Selicia said in reply after a longer than normal pause.

"Who is this man Selicia, is he dangerous?"

"I don't know. He seems pleasant enough, quite charming even, but appearances can be deceptive. We know next to nothing about him except that he doesn't keep good company and he cannot be mind-skimmed. That makes him dangerous; you need to be very careful."

"I will be," Nyree replied.

Selicia paused for a moment before she continued. "What did Enaryu find out from Farric Clearwater?"

"She found out the name of the person that they came here to meet. It's a man called Draxan Longseer."

"Good. Did she find out why they are meeting him?"

"All that she could read from Farric Clearwater was that they are to collect something from him, but he didn't know what it was and he was pretty certain that Bradley White didn't know either. Enaryu also believes that White didn't undertake this journey completely of his own free-will."

"Do you know what she meant by that?" Selicia asked.

"Because I couldn't read White it's impossible to tell for certain, but Enaryu believes that he is being forced to do this, to meet this Draxan Longseer and collect whatever it is he has to collect from him."

"She got this from mind-skimming Farric Clearwater?"

"Yes."

"Does she think that Clearwater is forcing him to do this?"

"No, she is convinced that it isn't him," Nyree replied.

"Does Clearwater know who is?"

"He knows that a man called Garan Smithson is involved because this is the man who paid him. They have known each other for some years. But Clearwater suspects that Smithson is not behind this. He thinks that someone else is involved."

"And who is this person?" Selicia was getting impatient.

"He believes it is Zoryn Dakor."

"But how can that be?" Selicia exclaimed. "Zoryn Dakor has not been seen in weeks?"

"That's just it, none of this makes any sense."

"Do you know where and when they will meet this Draxan Longseer?" Selicia asked.

"No, and neither do they. Farric Clearwater had been told to ask for him in a tavern on the quay and that Draxan Longseer would make contact."

"I see," said Selicia.

"They went to the tavern last night and it seems that they were followed back here by someone." Nyree said.

"Do we know anything about the person that followed them?"

"No, Selicia. One of our guards saw that they were being followed when they returned and he sent one of his men out to find out more. It turns out that whoever was following them didn't want to be followed himself and quickly lost our man."

"It is of little importance. From what you have said, I am sure that you will be receiving more visitors soon. Double your guard Nyree. I will speak with Katzin.

Contact me immediately if anything happens or if you find out anything more. You have done well, she will be pleased."

"Thank you, Selicia." Nyree sensed that Selicia had broken the link before she had finished her last sentence.

Chapter 50
Draxan Longseer

Brad took his time getting out of bed after Nyree left. He had nothing to do and for the time being at least, nowhere else to go. Servants brought in hot water to fill the sunken bath that seemed to be a common feature in the House of Secrets and he was invited to take a bath when it was full. They left him after they laid out luxuriously soft towels of the purest white in easy reach of the bath. He suspected that something had been added to the bath water to increase its soporific effect, but he didn't mind as he gave himself up to this moment of tranquillity. A loud knock on the door ended Brad's reverie and Farric didn't wait for a reply as he bowled into his room. "Get your lazy ass out of that tub Brad; we have a meeting to go to!" he declared.

"So, this Draxan character has made contact then?"

"Yes, one of Nyree's guards woke me just now saying that there was a man at the front door with a message for me," Farric replied. "He wouldn't say anything more to the guard and insisted on delivering his message in person."

"What did he say?"

"Nothing at first. He said that he wasn't going to say anything within earshot of this place, so I went outside with him."

"Why didn't you get me first, weren't you taking a risk?" Brad asked.

"Not really, if this whole thing was about killing me, why go to the trouble to drag us all the way to Krendyra and pay me so much money. A hired mercenary would have been a whole lot cheaper and much less bother. Not that there are any I know of that would be good enough to get the job done!"

"So, what did he say?"

"He gave me directions to a disused boat-builders shed down at the quay and said to be there at midday which to my reckoning is in about an hour or so."

"Did he say anything else?"

"No. Now get dressed I'll meet you downstairs."

As Farric turned away, Brad saw that he had a short sword strapped to his back in a well-worn brown leather scabbard.

"Are we expecting trouble, Farric?" Brad asked.

"I always expect trouble Brad, that's what keeps me alive."

It took them an hour or so to find the boat builder's shed that Draxan's messenger had told them would be the meeting place. It stood apart from other buildings, in what was clearly the poorer end of the quay. The other buildings in the vicinity were, by contrast, alive with the hustle and bustle of a busy seafaring dock. Farric spotted the boatshed when they were a hundred feet or so away and led them towards it by a circuitous route so that he could survey the building from all angles, wary of a potential ambush or trap.

This part of the quay was where the fishing boats brought their catches ashore and was busy as the first of the days boats had already started to return. It was a noisy and smelly place and the people that worked here were dirty and rough-looking. Brad doubted whether anyone here would bother to look twice if someone was murdered in front of them. Farric was right to be suspicious and he was feeling uneasy as they made their way toward the boatshed.

The shed was made from timbers that were old and gnarled and that in all likelihood came from boats that had served their time and had been de-commissioned. It was painted with a bituminous like substance and looked like it had stood for a hundred or more years and could easily last another.

Farric knocked three times loudly on a small wooden door that was set into a much larger door that ran the entire length of the front of the building. He waited a moment then knocked again, this time it was four knocks and then he withdrew, walking backwards slowly to a distance of about fifteen feet or so from the building.

Brad stood a few feet to Farric's side allowing him plenty of room to move if he had need of his sword. The detached feeling that Brad had experienced, during periods of danger and stress, returned once again. It was a good feeling. He stood relaxed, calm but very alert to everything around him and he was ready. His senses were heightened and he could feel the cold hard steel of the blade Farric had given him pressing against his body under his jacket. He loosened the ties on his jacket to allow easy access to the blade if it was required as he waited with Farric.

They didn't have long to wait. A woman of about thirty opened the door and walked towards Farric, stopping a few feet in front of him. She was easily six feet tall and was dressed in utilitarian clothing. Her arms were exposed revealing toned muscles that only became like that after years of training. It was clear from her demeanour that she had the confidence that came from years of combat training probably through military service. Brad suspected that she was a mercenary like Farric. His suspicions were reinforced by the weapons that were strapped to her. A short sword hung loosely from a thick leather belt that was fastened about her midriff with an oversized ornately decorated buckle. A wicked looking thin bladed dagger was strapped to her leg, its razor-sharp edges dazzling in the midday sunlight. Brad was mesmerised by the reflected light that held just a hint of blue.

There was a raw beauty to her features and she stood barring their way, her hard stare locking with Farric's as she stood there defiant. For a few tense moments, there was a standoff, neither looked away from the other or spoke. The air between them was crackling with tension and a serious confrontation seemed inevitable. Brad knew that Farric could handle himself, but there was something very dangerous about this women and he feared that this would not end well for anyone. He reached inside his jacket and felt reassured when his hand made contact with the handle of the knife.

"Yusana, won't you bid our guests welcome?" A disembodied voice called out from inside the building.

"I don't trust this one," she replied without turning away from Farric.

"These men have come a long way to see us, now please show them inside." The owner of the voice detached himself from the shadows and stood in the doorway of the boatshed.

"Well," said Farric addressing Yusana directly, "aren't you going to do what your master commands?" His words were mocking but there was no humour in his voice or in the fixed smile on his face.

"He is not my master," she spat in disgust, "I answer to no man."

"I don't really give a fuck who he is to you, or who you answer to. I've been paid good money to introduce him to my companion, now are you going to do what he has told you to do, or is this going to get interesting?"

For the briefest of moments, Brad was convinced that Yusana was going to attack Farric.

"I hope you fuck as hard as you talk," she said as she laughed and turned towards the man and bade Farric and Brad to join her.

"Good luck with that one," Brad muttered under his breath just loud enough for Farric to hear.

"Gentlemen, do come in," said the man as he welcomed them inside. He led them into the centre of the boatshed that was empty except for a large wooden table and two plain but sturdily constructed wooden chairs.

"I am Draxan Longseer and I am very pleased to meet you at last." His tone was welcoming and his smile seemed genuine.

Draxan Longseer was six-foot-tall and exuded presence. There was something about him that hinted at danger despite his seemingly charismatic personality. It was difficult to age him but if pressed, Brad would say that he was probably in his fifties, but his slim body and finely sculptured muscles would be the envy of a man half his age.

"Please forgive Yusana. She appointed herself as my bodyguard several years ago, despite my protestations and she takes her work very seriously," Draxan said. "I should have said no from the start but I have a weakness for attractive women."

"Pah!" spat Yusana. "If it wasn't for me, you would have been killed a thousand times over."

"You must be Farric Clearwater." Draxan said ignoring her and addressing Farric directly. "Thank you for bringing your companion to me." Farric nodded but did not reply.

"And you must be Bradley White," Draxan said as he walked over to Brad. "You are not at all what I expected," he said, his gaze unwavering as he surveyed the man in front of him.

"And what exactly were you expecting?" Brad sneered instinctively in response.

"I don't know, but I meant no offence."

"None taken," replied Brad.

"Good." Draxan turned his attention to Yusana. "Please take Mr Clearwater to our private quarters, my business is with Mr White and we are not to be disturbed. I will send for you when our business has been concluded."

"Come," said Yusana as she beckoned Farric to follow her. She led him to a side door which closed with a loud click as she shut it behind them.

"Please Mr White, sit down." Brad did as he was bidden. "So Zoryn has chosen you," Draxan said, his features suddenly hard and serious.

"If that's what you like to call it," Brad replied.

"I take it you are not a willing party to this?"

"Why the fuck would I tell you." Brad could feel his anger rising.

Draxan stared at him without speaking. Gone were all traces of the friendly image that he had presented just moments earlier.

"If Zoryn has sent me here to be killed by you." Brad continued, "Then get the fuck on with it. I'm sick and tired of these fucking games." As he spat the words, the anger left him and was replaced with the detached calm feeling which Brad knew was his body's newfound way of preparing for action.

"It seems to me that Lord Zoryn may have made a mistake," Draxan hissed. "Maybe I should kill you," he said as he attempted to stand up. But before he could, sensing an attack, Brad was instantly on his feet. With astonishing speed, Brad kicked the table into Draxan. Already half out of his chair, Draxan couldn't steady himself as his chair toppled backwards taking him with it crashing to the floor. Brad vaulted the table and landed on top of Draxan, pinning him to the floor with his knees, the weight of his body preventing any escape. He had drawn the knife from within his jacket without conscious thought and the tip was pressed against Draxan's throat.

"Try killing me now, you fucking cunt."

"I am beginning to see why you were chosen after all." Draxan laughed as he made a small gesture with his seemingly trapped right hand. Instantly, the blade in Brad's hands became red hot and he dropped it to the floor. Where it landed, small tendrils of smoke snaked upwards. Draxan rolled to one side with such strength and speed that Brad was thrown off him. He landed hard and was winded; black spots were fighting for dominance over his vision. Draxan was already on his feet and righting his chair offered it to Brad, as he lurched his way off the floor.

"Please Mr White, sit down. I had to be certain that you were the one your companion claims you to be. I now believe that you are."

"And if I hadn't been this person?" Brad asked as he dusted himself off and took the chair he had been offered.

"Then you would already be dead."

***

"So, you are Farric Clearwater, the famous mercenary I have heard so much about?" Yusana said mockingly, as she ushered him into Draxan's private quarters.

"Don't believe everything you've heard," Farric replied.

"Maybe I should. I reckon that there must be a price on your head that's worth collecting, and I could do with the money."

"But it's not the money that you want, is it Yusana?" His own tone now mocking. Yusana swore at him and slapped him hard across his face. Farric hated being slapped, worse still, he hated the fact that she hit him so fast he didn't have time to block the attack. Instinctively, he responded by hitting her with the back of his hand across her face knocking her back a few steps.

Yusana wiped a bead of blood from her mouth. "Now wouldn't it be a whole lot more interesting if we put our energies into fucking instead?" she said, as she unbuckled her belt and threw her arms around him, taking him to the floor with the skill of a wrestler. This time Farric did not fight back.

***

"Do you know why Zoryn Dakor made you come here?" Draxan asked.

"No, he doesn't really confide very much in me," Brad replied sarcastically.

"But you do know what you have to do for him, don't you?"

"Yes, he made that part very clear. Is that why I'm here, is this where it will happen?"

"No, you're here to collect an item that you'll need to complete your task."

"And what do you know about my task?"

"Probably less than you, but that conversation is for a different time and place. I do know however, that you will need this," he said as he placed an object on the table in front of Brad that looked like a pile of rags.

"Unwrap it," Draxan demanded.

Brad lifted the object and peeled away the rags to reveal what was at first sight a plain looking dagger. Only it wasn't plain at all. It was a small knife, no longer than the length of the palm of his hand and it was made entirely of a black metallic-like substance. It appeared to be at once both real and insubstantial, a paradox, a contradiction, a meeting of what was and could never be. He stared at the blade in wonder. Where it lay on the cloth, it was almost without form. The utter blackness of its surface absorbing so much light that its edges were indistinct and blurred. But there was something more Brad could sense power radiating from the object. No, it wasn't radiating power, it was absorbing power. But where was it absorbing power from? He suspected that Draxan might be its source. Brad had seen this substance before. It was made of the same strange Black Metal that the bands were made of that the chemist had put on his wrists back home.

"Pick it up," Draxan demanded.

Brad did and the instant that he made contact with the knife he felt its presence. It was warm to his touch as if it was alive and it felt familiar as if it belonged to him, as if it was a part of him. He was so captivated by the object that he barely registered Draxan's voice.

"Your wrists, what is happening to your wrists?"

Brad tore his eyes away from the dagger and saw that both his wrists were glowing an intense crimson colour. The blade responded and started to glow the same impossibly intense colour. Then without warning, the crimson glow intensified and became a massive conflagration that burned with the intensity of a supernova for the briefest of moments before vanishing, leaving phosphenes that obscured both men's vision for several long moments.

"I have never seen it do that before," Draxan said, more to himself than Brad. He looked visibly stunned and for just a moment Brad saw a weariness in his eyes and he knew in that moment that the blade had taken some power away from him and that this was the cause of his apparently weakened state. Regaining his composure, Draxan continued. "The blade contains a powerful magic that renders it invisible to conventional magic which should enable you to get close to your target without detection by Sanjin's magicians as they will just see it as an ordinary knife," Draxan said. There was a small tremor from the weakness in his voice. "But you must not rely on this and the blade must be kept hidden at all times, no one must know that you possess it. If it falls into the wrong hands, Zoryn will kill you."

Brad said nothing, as he wrapped the black dagger in the rags and put it inside his jacket.

**

Yusana left Draxan alone shortly after his guests had departed. She was a free spirit and he never asked her where she was going or what she was doing, no matter how long she was away. It wasn't that he didn't care for her or was so sure of their relationship that he knew she would come back, it was just the way that things had always been between them. There was no love in their relationship, but there was a mutual respect and that was enough. Draxan retrieved the small green ball from his belt pouch and threw it against the wall in front of him. It hit the wall noiselessly and a wicked green glow sped from the point of impact, rapidly covering the wall which pulsated in time to a silent rhythm. For a moment, nothing else happened and then shapes and colours started to coalesce and quickly became clear.

"Lord Zoryn." Draxan was the first to speak as he addressed the image of Zoryn Dakor.

"Has my servant taken possession of that he was tasked to collect from you?" The puissance of the power of the Black Metal that was infused into Zoryn's being was palpable even in his image.

"Yes, he took the knife and has left with the mercenary that Smithson appointed to protect him."

"Then all is good. Are your forces positioned as agreed?"

"Yes," replied Draxan, "they are camped in the wastelands to the east of the Krendyran Mountains, awaiting their orders."

"Good, should my plan fail and my accursed brother does not fall, you are to march on Gaardsholme and destroy what remains of the Elite Guard and any of Sanjin's army that are fool enough to stay loyal to him."

"I have some concerns about this outlander, Bradley White."

"And what are they?" Zoryn's image glared into Draxan's very being as he spoke.

"Something unforeseen happened when he touched the knife. The bands of Black Metal you have placed within him flared to life and discharged magic into the air without any apparent thought, or action on the Outlander's part. I have not seen a reaction like this before, it's almost as if…" Draxan Longseer broke off mid-sentence.

"What are you saying, Longseer?"

"If I didn't know any better, I would say that there was another magic at play, but if there is, it's one that is alien to me."

"There is no magic in the world I have plucked White from," Zoryn declared, "and he does not possess any magic himself, you are mistaken." The image of Zoryn flickered once and vanished, leaving Draxan alone once more.

"I am not as sure of that as you are." Draxan muttered to the silence.

Chapter 51
Secrets

It was late afternoon by the time that Brad and Farric arrived back at the House of Secrets. Neither man said much during their walk back, but once their destination was in sight Farric spoke. "So, was it worth the journey?" he asked.

"I really don't know," Brad said in all honesty.

"I was told not to question you about your meeting with Draxan and as I agreed to the terms of the agreement with Garan, I will keep my word."

"Thanks, Farric. The less you know the better for both our sakes."

"Well, we have one more night here Brad, so let's make the most of it. If you don't hear from me before the morning, please don't go looking for me!"

"Are you staying here tonight?" Brad asked.

"To freshen up and get something to eat yes, but afterwards I have some of my own business to see to."

"That wouldn't involve a certain Yusana by any chance, would it?"

"It just might, but then we all have our secrets, don't we?"

Farric left the House of Secrets later than he had planned. Nyree knew that the only way she was going to be about to find out more about her guests was through Farric. She arranged for two of her prettiest girls to be waiting for him when he went back to his room. They were engaged in a sexual act together as he walked into the room and it was a little over three hours later that he left.

***

"Selicia."

"Yes, Nyree." The reply came almost instantly. Nyree never lost her awe for the power of the Zindaw Stone and this time was no exception.

"Our guests will be leaving in the morning,"

"Have you found out any more?" Selicia asked.

"A little. It would appear that they met with this Draxan Longseer."

"What happened at the meeting?"

"That part is unclear. Longseer had company, a bodyguard called Yusana who took a shine to Farric Clearwater."

"I see," said Selicia.

"Yes, it was clearly all set-up. Farric was led away from Longseer and Bradley White and did not see what happened between them."

"Did White tell him about the meeting afterwards?" probed Selicia.

"No, it turns out that Clearwater is a man of honour and was made to swear to Garan Smithson that he wouldn't ask any questions and he kept to his word," said Nyree. "But there is a chance that we may be able to find out more from this Yusana."

"How do you propose to do that?" Selicia was intrigued.

"It turns out that Nia, one of the girls I had waiting for Clearwater's return, knows this woman."

"So Longseer's bodyguard is a woman?" Nyree could sense the raising of Cilicia's eyebrows in the tone of her reply.

"Yes, and she is known to enjoy the company of pretty girls," Nyree affirmed.

"I see where this is heading!"

"Yes. I wanted to be certain that Clearwater was distracted as soon as they came back so that we could get a good mindskim and so I arranged for Nia and one of our prettiest young girls to provide that distraction. Neither had been with a man for a few days and I knew that they would probably start before he arrived. Nia is very inventive in that way and didn't need any encouragement!"

"We may have got lucky there."

"Yes, I believe that we did. Nia took the lead and tricked Clearwater into telling them that he had been with a mercenary woman earlier that day. When Nia suggested that he bring her back to play later, Clearwater seemed only too eager to comply!"

"I doubt that many men would be able to resist such a request!" Laughed Selicia.

"Farric assured our girls that he would not return alone that evening!"

"Good. I want to know everything that happens."

***

Brad was shown to his room and for once was pleased to be alone. He locked the door and sat on an ornately carved wooden chair next to a small table that had some light refreshments laid out on it. He poured himself a glass of wine from a cut-glass decanter and pushed everything else to one side. Reaching into his jacket, he laid the bundle of rags on the table before him. He felt excitement as he slowly unwrapped the knife, peeling back the dirty rags carefully until it was revealed to his eager gaze. For the second time that day, he was completely captivated by the blade, its utter blackness and ethereal presence was spellbinding. The way that its surface captured light, not releasing it from its midnight grasp made it almost seem as though it wasn't there at all. It could easily have been dismissed as a black stain on the already filthy rags that had covered it.

He picked the blade up and could feel its presence both through his skin and with his senses. This time, the blade did not flare to life neither did the bands that were a part of him.

Something was troubling Brad, and it took him a moment longer to realise what it was. When he had first touched the blade at the boatshed, Draxan Longseer appeared visibly shocked by the reaction and clearly hadn't expected anything like that to happen. Although Draxan quickly regained his composure, Brad knew that something significant had happened. But what it meant was unclear. Maybe if Draxan hadn't expected that reaction, then Zoryn wouldn't have either. Maybe this was significant.

***

Mind-skimming was both a useful tool and a potent weapon. A useful tool because the skimmer could learn about the thoughts and feelings of the person being skimmed. A potent weapon because the skimmer could use those thoughts and feelings to manipulate and control. So it was with Nia. Although young and relatively inexperienced, her talent to manipulate was stronger than any Nyree had had working for her before. Nia came to the House of Secrets to escape the many wives whose husbands she had taken for fools and had used and discarded. Her innocent appearance and coquettish charm were a powerful enough combination, but with her ability to mind-skim and manipulate, Nia was by far and away Nyree's best asset. This also made her Nyree's best-paid girl. It was hoped that by rewarding her well she would remain loyal to the House of Secrets. There was little doubt in Katzin's mind, the head of the order, that Nia would one day run her own house.

Nia's manipulation of Farric worked even better than expected. Farric mentioned the invite to Yusana during their lovemaking that evening. Yusana, it would seem, was as eager as Farric and when he whispered the suggestion to her, she promptly flipped him onto his back and rode him fiercely, climaxing several times before she finally dismounted. This was to be the start of the best evening's sex that Farric could have ever dreamt was possible. Nia personally ensured that it was.

***

In the early hours of the following morning, an exhausted Nia made her way to Nyree's chambers and knocked on the door. Nyree answered quickly and Nia suspected that she had not been to sleep either that evening.

"I have some information that Katzin will want to hear Nyree."

"Come in, Nia, I don't want anyone else to hear what you have to say," Nyree replied. Nia nodded mutely.

"I didn't find out much from Clearwater but Yusana, well she was quite another matter. Her master is Draxan Longseer, a Mage who I understand teaches magical fighting at Gaardsholme."

"Yes," replied Nyree. "I know of this man."

"Well, it would appear that Longseer is working for Zoryn Dakor."

"You have done well Nia, I will speak highly of you in my report to Selicia," said Nyree.

"I live to serve my mistress!" Nia said in her familiar teasing way.

Ignoring the comment, Nyree added. "You must not discuss this with anyone."

Chapter 52
Yusana

Brad and Farric left the House of Secrets early the next morning. It was a bright sunny day and both men were more rested and visibly cleaner than when they had arrived a few short days ago. Nyree paid Brad a visit later the night before. She had given up all hope of reading him and saw him as much for her own pleasure as for her duty to the House.

Farric spent a good deal of the morning procuring a pair of horses and other provisions that they needed for their return trip. Brad had mixed feelings about returning to Garan Smithson's house. Although he had spent practically no time with Hania, they had both felt a connection and he ached to be with her. He was, however, pretty certain that if Smithson had anything to do with it, he wouldn't be able to see her. But going back also meant that he was moving closer to the fate that Zoryn Dakor had planned for him. He wasn't ready and had no idea how he would carry out Zoryn's demands, or defeat Zoryn. The small amount of hope he had felt previously evaporated as he was gripped by despair. How could he possibly stand up to the might of Zoryn and free his wife and son from his wicked grasp? It all seemed impossible to him as he mutely followed Farric.

"So, what happens now?" Brad demanded, as they finished packing their horses and prepared to mount.

"Now I take you back to Garan Smithson and collect the rest of my fee," Farric replied.

"I already guessed that bit," Brad replied dryly, "I meant after that."

"When I take you back, I will have done what I was paid to do and that's pretty well that as far as I'm concerned."

"Aren't you in the least bit curious as to what this has all been about?" Brad asked incredulously.

Farric turned to face him. "The reason that I am paid so well is that I get the job done and don't ask questions."

"But what if what you are doing is helping evil people do terrible things? How do you fucking sleep at night?"

Farric paused for a while, holding Brad's fierce gaze before he replied, turning away as he did. "It's because I don't ask questions that I can sleep at night."

They left Krendyra in silence. Brad was inwardly seething. It wasn't that he expected Farric to be his best friend after the time that they had spent together, but his callous disregard for what would happen to him pissed him off. He was so caught up in his own thoughts that he failed to see the danger until it was upon them. It was mid-day when they drew level with a small copse, and they were set upon by a group of six armed men.

Farric's first thought was that they were opportunists looking for easy prey leaving the city, but they were too well organised and well-armed to be simple bandits. Three men stood in front of them forcing them to bring their horses to a stop and as they did so, more men quickly emerged from their concealment and surrounded them. Each man had the same-style close-quarters sword in their hand and from the way they stood they were clearly well-trained. Farric knew who these men were; in fact, he had trained with men like this back in his military days. These were members of Sanjin Dakor's Elite Guard, a force feared throughout the Five Lands. But something was wrong and it took Farric a moment to realise that these men were in fact renegades, or deserters. They were unshaven and dirty and weren't wearing the tabards of the Elite Guard or any insignia. Sanjin Dakor demanded high standards from his Elite Guard and these men fell a long way short of those standards. By the look of the men, they hadn't eaten much for days.

"Gentlemen," Farric said in a low tone. "How may we be of assistance to you this fine day?" There was a smile on his face but no humour in his voice.

"You will dismount and surrender yourselves and all your property without trouble." Came the reply from a man who detached himself from the three standing in front of their horses blocking the way. His burnished skin did little to hide the criss-crossed battle scars on his thick powerful arms. As he spoke, he levelled his sword at Farric and Brad.

"On whose fucking orders?" Farric hissed.

"On my fucking orders,"

"And if we don't?" Farric's response was little more than a snarl between his clenched teeth. All pretence of a smile now gone from his handsome face.

"I told you once to dismount; I will not tell you a second time."

Farric turned in his saddle just enough to make eye contact with Brad. He didn't say anything, he didn't need to. Brad knew that Farric was going to attack these men and without warning, Farric leapt from his saddle and cut the first man down before he had time to raise his sword in defence.

Two of the men rushed Farric at the same time, their blades tracing wild arcs in the clear morning sunlight. Brad jabbed the flanks of his horse with his heels spurring it on in an attempt to charge down one of the men. His horse, however, had different plans and reared up trampling one of the men with its mighty hoofs before Brad lost his hold on the animal and fell to the ground hard. Stars danced in front of his eyes as he fought the blackness that was fighting to claim him.

The blade that was crashing down towards his head was wielded by the man who had led the group and should by rights have killed him but just as it made contact with his scalp there was an explosion of crimson light and the blade shattered into a thousand pieces. Unable to stop himself, the man's forward momentum propelled him into Brad's elbow, shattering his jawbone in the process. Rolling quickly to his right Brad kicked the nearest man just below the knee. The man stumbled and lost his balance giving Brad enough time to get to his feet and kick him hard in the groin. The man did not have time to defend himself and fell unconscious into his own vomit.

Brad scanned the area and saw that there were three men remaining. Farric was still on his feet but had taken a vicious sword cut to his arm and was bleeding heavily. His attackers, sensing victory, focused their attention on him. The remaining man kept Brad at bay with a series of feint attacks to prevent him from helping Farric. Despite his injury and loss of blood, Farric managed to cut another attacker down before he too fell to his knees.

Brad couldn't get to Farric and was certain that he would die at the hands of these men. Just then, a sharp movement caught his eye. Shrieking a fierce battle cry, Yusana appeared from nowhere. The forward momentum of her attack knocking one of the men down. The last thing he saw was her blade as it came crashing down smashing his ribs as it cut through him.

Her speed and aggression rivalled Farric's as she engaged Farric's last attacker. They stood a few feet apart, both swinging their swords, striking and parrying in their deadly dance. Neither wanting to give ground. They seemed evenly matched and then Yusana seemed to be weakening as she gave first a few inches and then a few feet of ground, seemingly beaten back by the guard's attack. The guard sensing victory pressed his advantage and realised too late that that he had played into Yusana's hands and fallen for her ploy. Rushing forward to finish her, his unguarded attack left him open to her sword thrust and he died before he fell to the ground, still clutching his sword.

While Yusana was battling to save Farric, the last guard attacked Brad. He was well trained and quick. Brad could barely raise his own sword in time to deflect the blows that were raining down on him in rapid succession. He didn't have any sword fighting skills himself and knew that he wouldn't last much longer. Nobody was coming to his rescue. The guard sensing his opportunity redoubled his efforts and with a massive swing of his sword shattered Brad's sword. The guard shoulder barged him hard to make room for the killing blow. Brad felt the black knife that Draxan had given him pressing against his body, and reached inside his jacket and pulled it out. The rags fell to the ground as he freed the blade. Thrusting with his sword the guard attacked Brad with everything he had. Brad did not have time to move back and would have almost certainly been run through by his attacker's blade if he had. He somehow managed to twist his body to one side deflecting the guard's sword thrust with the blade, just enough to avoid being run through. At the moment of impact, the black blade came to life and flared its terrible crimson fire in a detonation that engulfed both men. Brad was untouched by the flames, but the guard was not so lucky and he screamed in agony as the fire ripped through his body. He was dead before he hit the ground.

"So, you are the one," Yusana said as Brad stared in disbelief at the knife that was still glowing a wicked crimson in his hands. She stood a few feet away from him with Farric lying unconscious on the hard ground beside her.

"Is Farric going to be okay?" Brad asked.

"No," she said. "He has lost a lot of blood and will die if he isn't treated soon."

"How can we help him, Yusana? Where do we get the sort of help he needs?" Brad hadn't seen any signs of emergency services in this strange place. There must be doctors, or some form of medical care in these lands but he didn't have a clue where to go about finding such help.

Yusana didn't answer and instead asked him to help carry Farric's unconscious body into the small amount of shelter afforded by the copse. They laid him down on a patch of soft grass that had grown thick and lush under the shade of the trees.

"Leave the knife over there; it must not be anywhere near him." Brad obeyed without question, wrapping the blade in the dirty rags and laying it down a few feet away.

Farric's breathing was shallow, and his face was drained of colour. It was not looking good for him. If Farric died, how would Brad find his way back to Garan Smithson? It wasn't that he wanted to see the old man, but if he didn't return he had no doubt that Zoryn would exact his revenge on Gina and David just as he threatened he would. And besides, where else was there for him to go?

Distracted by his thoughts, it took him a moment or two to realise that something was wrong. There was a pervasive silence and a stillness in the air around him which had a strange familiarity to it. And then he remembered when he had experienced this before, it was when Velhanna stopped time.

Yusana was kneeling beside Farric gently chanting. Her eyes were closed and Brad could not make out the words but as he approached, he felt a static charge in the air which made his skin itch and feel like he was covered in thousands of biting insects. If that hadn't been strange enough, it felt to Brad that the imaginary insects were all moving in the same direction, towards his hands. Yusana stopped chanting and opened her eyes and looked at Farric, her expression concerned. Brad's itching stopped instantly.

"I have suspended time for Farric to give me more time to heal his body, but his injuries are severe. I should be able to do it, but something's wrong, I don't have enough strength to do it. This has never happened to me before; it feels as if my strength is being drawn away from me."

"Does this mean that he will die?" Brad asked.

Yusana responded without looking up. "Yes, he will. I can keep him this way for a while longer but without more magic I can't do any more."

"I don't believe that I have magic Yusana, but twice now there has been a reaction when I have touched or used this knife. Is there something that I can do to help Farric?"

Yusana tore her eyes away from Farric and looked up at Brad. "Your wrists!" she exclaimed pointing. "They are glowing the same colour that the blade did when you used it against the guard. You must have Black Metal inside you, move away from here now, quickly." Brad moved away and as he did so, he noticed that the glow from his wrists started to fade and disappeared entirely when he was about fifteen or so feet away.

Yusana turned her attention back to Farric and started to chant again. This time Brad could not feel the static charge but instead noticed that a faint greenish glow covered Farric's body. The glow intensified as Yusana's chanting become louder and higher pitched until Brad had to look away. Yusana screamed and the light went out. It took a while for the phosphenes to clear from Brad's vision, but when he could see clearly, he saw that Yusana was slumped over Farric's unconscious form.

"Yusana," Brad called. There was no answer. "Yusana." He repeated louder and more urgent but heeding her instruction, he didn't draw any closer. Yusana raised her head.

"What just happened?" Brad demanded.

"I've done all that I can for him. The bleeding has stopped, and I've repaired some of his internal injuries, but he has lost a lot of blood and is very weak. I cannot suspend time for him any longer; his life now hangs in the balance. The rest is up to his own body, I can do no more."

Not all of their attackers were dead and those that remained alive would awaken soon. They posed little threat in their weakened state; however, there was no point in taking unnecessary chances. Farric was now conscious but desperately weak. Yusana gently helped him to his feet and with a surprising display of strength, lifted him onto his horse. He perched precariously on his mount as Yusana took the reins.

"Mount your horse Bradley White; I will lead Farric's horse. We must leave now."

Brad nodded mutely in agreement and did as she bade but was surprised to see that Yusana started to walk in the direction they were headed before they were attacked.

"Aren't we going back to get help for Farric in Krendyra?" he asked incredulously.

"No, it's not safe to return." Yusana continued walking and did not turn to face him as she replied.

"What do you mean?" He asked.

"Those men you killed weren't ordinary bandits, they were deserters from the Elite Guard. That means that they are wanted men and are being hunted. Sanjin Dakor's spies will be looking for them and it won't take a genius to work out that Farric's injuries and these dead men may be connected. It is a risk we cannot take."

"But we haven't done anything wrong, have we?" Brad protested. "All that we did was defend ourselves."

"Yes, that much is true but Sanjin's men, even renegades such as these, are highly trained and he would take more than a passing interest in how so many of them could be overcome so easily." Yusana replied, still leading Farric's horse with Brad reluctantly following. "Besides, we can't risk you being captured."

"And why would that be so bad? Maybe if I met with this Sanjin Dakor and told him about his brother's plot, we could put an end to this madness," Brad protested.

"Maybe you are right Outlander, or maybe that was Zoryn's plan all along."

"You called me Outlander; somebody else called me that on the way to Krendyra. So that was how you were able to suspend time earlier."

Yusana stopped and turned to face him. "Yes, I did, but on my own my magic is only strong enough to suspend time for a short period. In Farric's case, just long enough to stop him from losing any more blood and to repair the worst of his injuries as best I could."

"You said that I have Black Metal inside me, what does that mean?"

"To be truthful I don't know. We have known about the existence of Black Metal since the time of Jal Chindo, but he used it as a talisman of dread power, he didn't have it within his body. It would appear that Zoryn has found a way to fuse Black Metal with its user, making it a part of them. This is why my magic was weakened earlier; the Black Metal inside your body was drawing my magic away."

"Is this where the magic, that people say I have, is coming from?" Brad asked.

"Perhaps, but I think there is more to it than that."

"How do you mean?"

"I suspect that Zoryn infused some Black Metal into you to help transport you to our world and to protect you to keep you alive long enough to carry out his plan. It would have had other effects on your body too, and would have made you stronger. But I sense another magic in you. I detected it when we first met."

"None of this makes any sense, Yusana. You yourself called me Outlander and know that I am not from this world. Where I come from magic doesn't exist."

"Maybe, or maybe your people have forgotten how to use it, Outlander."

Part IV
Destiny

Chapter 53
Ambush

During the fray, one of their horses had taken fright and run off, so they were left with just two horses between the three of them. Yusana lead Farric's horse in silence. There was no need for further conversation and they shared a common determination to put as much distance as possible between themselves and the tattered remnant of the renegade Elite Guard. Not that they believed they would attempt a further attack, they were more concerned about an encounter with the renegade's pursuers.

***

"Captain Jhardha," said the leader of the group of twelve armed guards who encircled the three survivors of the clash with the travellers from Krendyra. "From what I can make out it would appear that you may have run into a spot of bother. Tell me captain," he said, spitting the title as if it was poison in his mouth, "do you not bother to bury your dead these days." The guards had passed Jhardha's fallen comrades a short time earlier, still laying where they fell.

"Fuck you, Droken."

"Well, it's good to see that you haven't lost any of your charm." Droken's tone was flat and his gaze hard as he studied the man in front of him. "You sicken me, I would cut you down where you stand you piece of shit, but our King has requested your company. I am to take you back with me to Gaardsholme where you will answer to the Council of Lords for your crimes."

"You will have to get me there first," Jhardha shouted in reply as he pulled a knife from the waistband of his trousers and ran at Droken Arrowsmith.

Droken moved with the speed of a man half his age and had dismounted before Jhardha reached him. Feinting an attack, Jhardha quickly moved to Droken's side and slashed with the knife targeting an area where he knew the other's armour was most vulnerable. Droken Arrowsmith was battle hardened and saw the feint for what it was. Moving at the last moment, to ensure that Jhardha believed he had fallen for it and was fully committed to the attack, Droken moved to the side just enough so that the knife scraped across his armour but didn't penetrate it. Jhardha couldn't defend himself in time as Droken drove his own short sword with surprising strength right through the centre of his toughened leather breastplate which did nothing to stop the blade from piercing his heart. Jhardha was dead before his lifeless body hit the ground.

"I enjoyed that!" Droken roared at the two remaining renegades who stood there stunned that their leader, feared for his fighting skills, had been dispatched so easily. "Now are you fuckers going to lay down your arms or would you rather play as well?" There was a clatter as both men dropped their weapons instantly and knelt in the dirt with their hands behind their heads. It took all their restraint for Droken's men not to

217

laugh aloud at the comic spectacle, but knowing their Captain well, they thought better of it. There was however little doubt that the story would be repeated many times in the barracks at Gaardsholme.

***

The travellers stopped briefly later in the afternoon for a meal of dried meat and fruit which they washed down with a bitter tasting ale. Yusana helped Farric back onto the saddle of his horse. He had spent most of the day dozing and Brad found it fascinating how he managed to stay on the horse, in what at times appeared to be a gravity defying position.

They left the relative lushness of the region close to Krendyra and travelled through the desert like terrain that Brad remembered only too well from his earlier journey. It was a barren and desolate place. The pale blue rays of this alien sun beat down on them mercilessly as they made their way toward the Krendyran Mountains which now appeared as a smudge on the horizon.

The day wore into evening with the rapid transition that Brad had now become accustomed to. He expected Yusana to stop and make camp but she did not.

"Are you planning on stopping at all tonight, Yusana?" He asked with more than a little annoyance in his tone. It had been a long day and he was tired and testy.

"We've left tracks that a blind man could follow, Outlander. Our only chance of concealment is to reach the Krendyran Mountains before daybreak."

"But I thought that the mountains were dangerous?"

"Yes they are, which is why our pursuers will not follow us into them."

"How can you be certain that we are being followed?" He asked.

"I left a magical ward in the area where we met our 'friends' outside of Krendyra. It can't be detected by any but the most skilled magic-user; it was designed to alert me if it was tripped."

"And was it tripped?" asked Brad with some scepticism in his voice.

"Yes it was, Outlander," Yusana replied flatly.

"But how do you know it was Sanjin's men?"

"I can't know for certain, but I can tell the direction the people headed after tripping the ward because I set a further one a mile after the first."

"I take it by that that you mean they are headed this way?"

"Will we make the mountains before they catch up with us?" Brad asked.

"I fear we may not, but we have no option other than to try. Farric is in no condition to fight but the stupid bastard will try anyway. These are trained men who will be on their guard after seeing their comrades beaten the way they were."

"Do you know how many are following us?" Brad asked the question but was not sure that he really wanted to hear the answer.

"I cannot say for certain, no ward is that precise, but judging by the strength of the response I felt I would estimate that at least ten went through it in a fairly tightly knit group."

"Oh fuck," said Brad. "That's all we fucking well need."

"Indeed, Outlander!"

It was a perfectly clear evening which meant that they had the most of the meagre light that the starry sky had to offer. However, without clouds to retain the warmth of the day, it was also bitterly cold. Brad drew his leather jacket about himself as tightly as he could to conserve what little heat his body generated.

"Do you have seasons in this land?" he asked.

218

"I don't understand what you mean by that word?" Yusana was walking slightly ahead, leading Farric's horse as he slept perched precariously in the saddle. They only had two horses between them which meant that Brad and Yusana had taken turns leading Farric's horse. This time it was Yusana's turn to walk. Her strength seemed almost super-human to Brad and she insisted on walking for longer periods when it was her turn. The pace she set was almost a canter, much to the chagrin of Brad's recalcitrant mount.

"In my land, we have four seasons a year where the weather alternatives between hot and cold with a transition period, or season, in between each cycle where the weather is a little of both." To his own ears, his description of the four seasons sounded clumsy, but hopefully, Yusana would understand what he meant.

"Your land is indeed a strange place, Outlander. We do not have these *seasons* you refer to. Here we have regions that are hot and regions that are cold. If you have a desire for either, then you have only to travel to that part of the land. I guess you could say that we have transition areas too where the temperature and climate is more moderate. We call these places the borderlands." Brad was no physicist, but it sounded like this planet was in some kind of *geo-stationary* type orbit around its blue sun.

Oh well, he thought, *at least I appear to have been transported to a warm part of this land.* Brad hated the cold with a vengeance.

The *smudge* Brad had seen earlier in the day developed into an ever-increasing area of darkness that stretched out in front of them. He assumed that they were now close to the Krendyran Mountains, but it was so dark that it was impossible to tell with any certainty. Although he couldn't see the mountains, he felt their towering presence and his mind wandered back to his encounter with the Blackreach Wolves. He didn't want to face them again, and with Farric in his weakened state, he didn't feel confident that they would survive any attempt to cross the mountains at night.

Yusana stopped and turned to him. She held her hand over her mouth signalling to keep quiet and gestured for him to dismount which he did so as quietly as he could. Sanjin Dakor's men must be close now he thought. With Brad's assistance, Yusana managed to free the comatose Farric from his saddle and take him off his horse. As they did so, he let out a small groan but did not wake. Farric had been asleep for most of the day and Brad noticed beads of sweat on his forehead, a clear sign that fever was beginning to set in. Without medicine, he feared that Farric would die if they did not find help soon.

Cradling Farric like a baby, Yusana whispered to Brad to take their provisions off the horses. He did as she instructed and soon had a very heavy saddlebag slung over each of his shoulders. Yusana brought both horses together and standing in front of them whispered something under her breath. The horses nickered softly as if understanding what she said to them and headed away on a path that led away from them along the face of the Krendyrans.

"Hopefully, this will buy us a little time," Yusana whispered as she started to walk directly towards the darkness that was the Krendyran Mountains.

It was another half an hour or so before they reached the foothills of the mountains. Yusana carried Farric and showed no signs of slowing her pace as she led them through a series of barely visible game trails. They were gaining height as they continued their trek through the mountains. Brad's legs felt heavy and were slow to respond as tiredness and the cold seeped deeper into his core. In another life, before he had had the misfortune to become Zoryn Dakor's puppet, he would have reached the point of exhaustion hours ago. Still, much fitter or not, he was close to that point now and marvelled at Yusana's super-human stamina.

"We will stop for a rest soon, Outlander. Sanjin's men will not follow us into the mountains at night, but we still need to put as much distance between them and us as we can," Yusana called softly over her shoulder to Brad, as if she could read his thoughts. He was too tired to reply and nodded mutely in response.

Brad soon realised that Yusana had no concept of the word *soon*. It was easily two hours later when she eventually stopped and laid Farric down on a patch of lush grass that contrasted sharply with the sparse vegetation they had seen since entering the mountains. They had been following a game trail for the last hour or so that was almost impossible to make out but Yusana was sure of her way and never once hesitated. The trail led to a small open area with the face of a mountain on one side providing some cover. There was a ledge just above head height that jutted out from the almost sheer face of the rock.

"Come Outlander, there is a basin in this ledge that is always full of water. It will revive you."

Brad didn't need to be told twice. He climbed the rock face surprisingly easily, finding hand and footholds in just the right places. It struck him that it was a little too convenient but the holds and crevices from which he found purchase for his hands and feet looked natural enough.

As he drew level with the top of the ledge he was startled by what he saw, nearly losing his foothold. From underneath, the ledge looked like a natural rocky protrusion that tapered a little but was unremarkable. However, from Brad's vantage point he could see a perfectly still pool, of the blackest water, that looked as if it had been carved into the very rock. Stranger still was that there was no obvious source for the water as the ledge itself was sheltered by an outcropping of more gorse bushes seemingly growing out of the face of the mountain a little further up. He doubted that any rainwater could reach this place.

He was very thirsty and bracing his feet in a small crevice to keep his balance, he cupped his hands and filled them with the water from this natural basin. But as soon as he touched the water, he could tell that there was something different about it. It was icy cold and still looked black in his hands, so black he couldn't see through it to the palms of his hands. He was convinced that it wasn't just the fact that it was night and everywhere was dark, the water itself was absorbing what little light there was.

"Are you sure that this water is safe to drink, Yusana?" he asked sceptically, calling down to her.

"Yes Outlander, in fact this water will do more than simply quench your thirst, it will revive you in all ways possible."

If it doesn't kill me first, he thought, viewing the water suspiciously.

Sensing his trepidation Yusana continued. "It comes from a spring deep within the mountains. The same source as that which feeds the Lake of visions. It is imbued with magic. Drink deeply, Outlander."

Despite his misgivings, his body craved refreshment and so he lifted his hands to his lips and drank deeply. The last thing he remembered was an icy-cold burning sensation as the water entered his body.

Chapter 54
Hope

Without warning, Brad found himself back in the Forest. Gina stood in front of him, her ethereal beauty spellbinding in the preternatural gloom. Although it had the appearance of a forest and looked real enough, there was nothing natural about it. The Forest was intensely silent, like it was waiting, a massive entity holding its breath in anticipation that something dreadful was about to happen. Brad had no doubt that sooner or later that was precisely what would happen.

This wasn't the first time he had met Gina here, and he found himself wondering where exactly it was? He was certain that it wasn't on Earth. However, the very notion of considering himself away from Earth seemed totally ridiculous to his rational mind even now when he had been away from Earth for some months.

So, if the forest wasn't on Earth, where was it? Surely it had to be in the Five Lands, but where? He knew nothing about the geography of this place, but there had to be maps of this world he reasoned, even though he hadn't seen any.

He was certain, beyond any reasonable doubt, that it wasn't actually Gina who stood in front of him now. Gina's physical body was still in the hospital bed in a coma, which meant that the apparition in front of him was a representation of Gina, a shade. In some ways real, but in other ways as insubstantial as the tendrils of mist that gave way to the rays of the morning sun.

Brad was convinced that the apparition of Gina was endowed with her consciousness and that when they spoke, it really was Gina that he was talking with. He was similarly convinced that he was not actually in the forest either and that he must appear as insubstantial and wraith-like to Gina as she did to him.

He could see, touch and smell all that was around him and his senses told him that the forest was real. His reasoning mind however, knew that it was not real, or at least not real in any conventional way. So maybe the Forest didn't actually exist anywhere? Maybe it was a virtual place that only he and Gina could enter. He quickly dismissed the thought when he remembered Gina telling him that Zoryn was here the first time she came to this place. But for now, he didn't care about any of this. All that mattered was that this was the only place he could be with his wife, even if only for brief moments at a time. He needed to know that Gina and his son David were still alive if he was to keep going and see this through to the end. "If I survive that long" He thought wryly to himself.

The lines of concern etched into Gina's face brought Brad back from his thoughts and he realised that long moments must have passed whilst he was deep in thought.

"Brad, is everything all right?" Gina was anxious.

"Sorry, Gina. I'm still trying to make sense of all this, but yes I am alright at least I think so!" he replied. "How did I get here?"

"I don't know," she replied. "But this time I didn't hear you call out to me and I hadn't called out to you either. I was pulled here forcibly and I tried to resist because it

felt different, but the pull was too strong and there was nothing that I could do to stop it."

Brad's 'summoning' to the forest was also different this time. Every other time, except when he had walked into the lake of Visions, he had been asleep, but this time he was wide awake when it happened. His last memory was of drinking the black water from the basin in the Krendyran Mountains and then he was here in the forest. He couldn't remember making the short climb down from the basin to the ground and realised that he must have been transported to the forest whilst he was still clinging to the rock-face. He may have been only a few feet up, but he was in for a hard landing nonetheless when he returned and didn't relish the thought much.

"Do you remember when I told you about the vision I had about a strange black knife?"

"Yes, I remember."

"Well, the vision has come true, as bizarre as that must sound. In the vision, I met a man who I now know is called Draxan Longseer. I actually met him, a few days ago, in a place called Krendyra and he gave me the knife. It was as strange as it had appeared in the vision. But as soon as I touched it, something unexpected happened."

"Unexpected?" Gina interjected

"There was an explosion of sorts that Draxan Longseer wasn't expecting and for a moment I saw a look of shock in his eyes. And then, there was this morning…"

"This morning?" Gina echoed his words.

"I used the knife to defend myself when we were attacked. It was the only weapon I had. I killed a man with it Gina, without meaning to. But I didn't stab him or cut him. It was like the knife exploded and the man was killed by the explosion."

"Were you hurt?"

"I was in the middle of it but I felt nothing. I was unharmed. The knife was glowing and looked like it was practically molten but I felt no heat at all."

"It must have been magic that caused the explosion." Gina declared.

"It has to be," Brad replied.

"So you must have found a way to use the magic?" Gina's assertion was more of a question than a statement.

"Maybe, but if I did Gina it wasn't a conscious act, it just happened when my life was in danger. It seems like I have some inbuilt mechanism that protects me from harm as odd as that fucking sounds! Something very similar happened at a small town called Dumas on the way to Krendyros."

Brad told Gina about the fight he had had with the man in the tavern and how he believed that magic had saved his life.

Gina listened intently than said. "But you still haven't told me how this Black Metal came to be inside you."

"I think that it happened at the beginning of all this a few weeks before I was transported to this place." Brad relayed the story of his chance meeting with the Chemist. As he told her, he realised that it was no chance meeting and that the Chemist, who later turned out to be Zoryn Dakor, must have planned it all along. But that begged the question, why him? It just didn't make sense.

He told Gina everything that had happened from his first meeting with the Chemist to being transported to the other world, except for details of his sexual encounters with Lauren and Sarah, who turned out to be Zoryn's partner. In part to preserve his marriage, should he ever return and in part because it added little of value to the story.

After listening intently, Gina agreed that it was highly likely that the bands that Zoryn had placed around his wrists contained Black Metal. It was this that had changed Brad, making him physically stronger and apparently better able to deal with the rigours that beset him in this land. They also concluded that the Black Metal was protecting him from danger and speeding his recovery time.

They talked for a long time, quite possibly hours. It was impossible to track time in the Forest, as it seemed to exist in a state of suspended animation where time had no meaning. Whatever power had brought them both to the Forest was stronger than before and kept them here much longer this time. Brad suspected that it was a reaction between the Black Metal within him and the strange black water. Whatever brought them together was starting to weaken and Gina's ethereal body was becoming even less substantial as she smiled sadly and faded altogether.

Chapter 55
Brad and Yusana

Without warning, Brad was back on the mountain wall. His foot was still braced in the crevice and his hands were wet with the cold black water. Black wings of vertigo assailed his vision and overcame him. With uncanny speed, Yusana caught him before he hit the hard ground, breaking his fall, but she wasn't able to catch him quickly enough to prevent his ankle being twisted badly as the crevice refused to let go of his foot until it was too late.

The break was bad, and it was clear to Yusana that he had broken at least one bone in his ankle and would not be able to walk unaided, if at all, through the mountains.

"Fuck." She spat the word out as if it was poison in her mouth. "That's all we fucking well need." Brad came to on the ground, next to Farric who was muttering something unintelligible in his delirium. He didn't need to look at his ankle to know that he was in trouble, that they were all in trouble, the pain from his injury told him this in no uncertain terms. If they had stood any chance of escaping Sanjin Dakor's men before, they certainly didn't now.

"The best I can do is to make a splint and set your bones and give you something for the pain. But I can't use magic to treat your injury like I did to Farric, I just can't take the risk."

"What risk?" The pain making Brad's voice sound a little harsher then he intended.

"The Black Metal inside your body will draw the magic away as soon as I attempt to use it on you, which means that at best the healing won't work," she replied.

"And at worst?"

"At worst, it may draw all my power. Jal Chindo used this quality of the Black Metal to increase his power. He would draw the innate magic from others, mostly from his defeated enemies but also from his slaves or anyone that crossed his path."

"He sounds a right bastard. Did any of his victims recover their powers, Yusana?" Brad asked.

"No, they died. The magic was an intrinsic part of their being. The shock of losing all their magic in such a way was always fatal."

"But I don't know how to use this Black Metal, let alone use it against anyone as a weapon."

"I understand that," Yusana replied. "But it would appear that it doesn't require your summons to be effective. If I attempt to use magic on you, I am certain that it will see it as an attack against you and will defend you by drawing the magic into itself. But it won't stop until all my magic has been taken."

"Does this mean that I have some kind of inbuilt defence to protect me against an attack with magic?" Brad forgot all about his pain, as he realised that he may finally have something that he could use against Zoryn Dakor.

"To an extent, it does I guess. You would almost certainly survive a direct magical attack and if the person attacking you was in close contact with you, they would perish in the attempt. But it wouldn't help much if you were attacked indirectly."

"How do you mean?" Brad asked.

"If the magic wielder used their power to hurl a boulder at you, you had better duck quickly!"

"Ah, I see what you mean. But if that person was close to me?"

"Now you are beginning to understand," Yusana said. "The Black Metal would draw some of their power away and they would be diminished and probably not able to hurl the boulder in the first place."

"Would they be able to detect that I have Black Metal inside me?" Brad asked.

"No, they wouldn't. I couldn't detect it until my magic was being drained when I was healing Farric and my people are amongst the few in the Five Lands that have any understanding of Black Metal. If you were attacked in such a way, your opponent would be unlikely to realise what was happening until it was too late and even then, they would have no defence against its power."

If Brad could use the Black Metal to drain Zoryn's power, then there really was a chance that he could defeat him. Surely, it couldn't be that difficult to get Zoryn to attack him and then the Black Metal could draw his power, killing him in the process.

"What if my attacker also had Black Metal?" he asked.

"You mean what if you were to come up against Zoryn Dakor? Then that would be interesting, Black Metal versus Black Metal!"

"Does Black Metal change a person?"

"That Outlander, has been a source of debate within my people for centuries and no one knows for certain."

"What do you think?" asked Brad.

"I believe that it does. But you will know the answer to that question better than I. Has it changed you?"

"I have changed Yusana, that's for certain, but whether it's because of this Black Metal I don't know," Brad answered truthfully.

"Tell me what changes you have noticed?"

"Well for a start, I seem to recover quicker from injuries. My ankle still hurts a lot but already the pain is a little less than when I fell, and how long ago was that? Another change which started in my world is a detached feeling when I should be afraid."

"Like you are a spectator rather than a combatant?" Yusana interjected.

"Yes, that's precisely how it feels."

"That is almost certainly an effect of the Black Metal. I have thought for a long time that the substance changes or corrupts whoever wields it. Jal Chindo was not the nicest of people before he discovered it, but he became a tyrant when he mastered its power. Zoryn Dakor was a cruel and spiteful child and as he became older, his disdain for others and hatred for his brother just got worse. I shudder to think of the monster that he has become now that he has Black Metal."

"I've met him Yusana, and monster doesn't even come close to describing him."

"You, however, Outsider are an enigma to me. The Black Metal has clearly affected you, made you stronger, detached from fear and it would appear that it protects you, but you do not seem to be corrupted by it."

"Maybe it's just early days, Yusana," Brad said.

"Maybe indeed, or maybe you are different in some way and the Black Metal has a different effect on you."

Yusana sat with her back braced against the rock of the mountain to give her some rest after helping Brad position himself in a similar fashion. He was still in too much pain to sleep, despite being past the point of exhaustion. It was several hours later and not long before dawn, that the first Blackreach Wolf struck their makeshift camp.

Chapter 56
Battle for Control

Yusana reacted first. Leaping to her feet, she slammed into the first Blackreach Wolf before it could reach the still unconscious form of Farric Clearwater. The force of the impact momentarily stunned the great beast, which gave Yusana just long enough to free a long thin knife from its worn leather sheath. As the wolf launched itself at her, she thrust the blade between its eyes, the forward momentum of the wolf's attack sealed its fate. The wolf howled one last time before it died; a mixture of anger and despair. It wasn't alone and quickly a second and then a third animal appeared.

They were easily the largest and most ferocious looking beasts that Brad had ever seen and were made of the very stuff of nightmares. His last encounter with Blackreach Wolves did not last very long and ended badly for him, and he was determined not to let that happen again. He didn't feel fear, even though he knew that he should, and put it down to the detached feeling that was almost certainly an effect of the Black Metal. "Don't let them bite you," Yusana shouted somewhere to his right, "their bite is venomous and you won't survive it."

Brad didn't respond, in part because he didn't want to distract her, and because the wolf stalking him looked ready to pounce. He took the black knife out from inside his leather jacket and held it in front of himself protectively. The wolf circled around him, wary perhaps after seeing his pack member killed by Yusana. Its snarling twisted mouth revealed row upon row of razor sharp teeth, flecked with venomous foam.

Brad had felt the power of the jaws of a Blackreach Wolf and experienced the searing pain as the fang-like teeth embedded themselves into his arm on his last encounter with them and did not want to repeat the experience. But because of the damage to his ankle, he could not get off the ground and onto his feet. If he remained on the ground, he was literally a sitting target, a fact that the wolf seemed to be aware of. He should, by all rights, have been terrified, but he wasn't. The now, very familiar sense of detachment flooded his body with its unique ability to increase his confidence and allow him to think with clarity under the most extreme situations. Brad knew that he had to kill this beast and that nobody was coming to his rescue.

With a tremendous effort of will, he hauled himself to his feet, quicker than he would have thought was possible, but with as much pain as he knew was inevitable. The wolf held its ground, neither taking more ground nor conceding any of its own. The two combatants stood facing each, their eyes locked, both slightly crouched and ready to attack. If it was possible for a wolf to look surprised, then the slight change to the wolf's visage was the only such sign. For the briefest of moments, it seemed to Brad that the beast was not so sure of itself. Its eyes with their dilated pupils edged by the zig-zagged, orangey-red coronas were locked with his own eyes which must have appeared the same to the wolf. Brad realised that the animal might have recognised this and maybe this was why it hesitated. Maybe it thought that he was from another pack, another albeit strange, wolf. It didn't matter, all that Brad needed was an advantage, a distraction no matter how small so that he could turn the tables and launch his own attack.

Brad leapt at the wolf planning to stab it as he did so. Despite its previous hesitation, the wolf was an animal of great strength and primal instinct and moved to the side just in time to avoid being stabbed. It didn't however, move quickly enough to avoid being struck by the hilt of the black knife as Brad pulled it back from his missed thrust, smashing it into the side of the wolf's head with crushing force. Crimson fire exploded from inside Brad's body and erupted from the hilt of the blade where it made contact with the beast. The wolf didn't stand a chance as wicked tendrils of crimson fire wound their way around its writhing body, biting into the animal and constricting the life out of until it lay dead on the ground. Two other wolves, seemingly unaware of the fate of their brother, appeared out of nowhere and launched themselves at Brad, despite the fact that he was still wreathed in crimson fire. The flames instantly burned brighter and both wolves burst into flames before they could reach him.

Gone now was the detached feeling and in its place Brad felt euphoric, powerful, unbeatable, more than a match for the wolves or any other foe. The pain in his ankle had gone, the bones already mended. He was stronger than he could ever have imagined possible. Charging at the last wolf, that Yusana was just about keeping at bay with her sword, he thrust the black knife towards the beast. He was still several feet away and not yet close enough to strike the animal, but without warning, a bolt of crimson fire shot from the tip of the blade finding its mark on the wolf's body, instantly incinerating the beast where it stood.

"Come on you fuckers, is that all you've got?" Brad howled, his snarling face twisted in rage and bloodlust, his body still burning with crimson fire.

"We must get away from here now." Yusana's voice barely reaching him through the wall of crimson fire that surrounded his body. "Sanjin Dakor's men must have heard what just happened; they will be on us soon."

"Let them come, what can they do to us?" Brad snarled in reply.

"That's just it Outlander, if they come here now you will kill them all. I can't let that happen."

"Why should I care? If they come here in pursuit of us, then they deserve to die."

"Outlander, this is not you. Can't you see what's happening? What's becoming of you? You are turning into the very person you despise the most. The Black Metal is changing you; you are becoming the same as Zoryn Dakor. You have to fight it."

"Why would I want to fight this power that I have? With it, I am more than a match for Dakor and I will kill him. Isn't that what you and your people want?"

"No Outlander, at least not this way. If you don't gain control over yourself and make the power of the Black Metal your servant, rather than being its servant, then all is lost and that includes your beloved wife and son and maybe even your home world."

Some part of Brad knew that Yusana was right, he knew that his words and actions were not his own. He fought to control the conflicting feelings and emotions that were raging war inside his body. The power of the Black Metal was seductive, making him stronger, more powerful, capable of anything. But inside, there was a quiet voice, the old Bradley White that was warning him that it was an illusion. Telling him that it wasn't right, that he would lose everyone he loved if he didn't gain control of himself.

"Give me the knife Outlander, let go of it, you must do it now," Yusana pleaded.

Brad could see Gina and David in his mind. His wife and son, the only family he had, the only people he ever cared about. He couldn't lose them, couldn't live with himself if he let that happen, or worse still caused it to happen. An image of Hania came to his mind, her pale skin and emerald green eyes melting his heart. He remembered the connection he had felt when they touched. They were connected in a way that he didn't understand. With a supreme act of will, he slowly managed to unclench the knotted muscles in his hand and let the knife fall to the ground. It landed silently, and the crimson fire was extinguished, leaving them in near total darkness with iridescent phosphenes in its wake.

Yusana threw a cloth over the knife and managed to catch Brad in her strong arms before he fell towards the ground unconscious.

She laid his body gently on the ground next to Farric. His breathing was shallow and his body was spent from wielding the mighty power of the Black Metal. The effort caused black spots to fight for her vision in a bid to claim her and take her consciousness away.

During her fight with the wolves, Yusana had been bitten by a wolf and the fast-acting venom was working its foul way through her body. She knew that her own magic should save her, but it was reduced by the proximity of the Outlander and the black knife, each containing the magic draining Black Metal. Sitting with her back braced against the hard bones of the mountain, as far away from Brad and the black knife as she could, she hoped that Sanjin Dakor's men would not have risked entering the mountains at night. It was their only chance of escape.

Chapter 57
The Dyroshin

Yusana's people, the Dyroshin, were caught up in a dangerous game. It was one that destiny had set for them and they were like the pieces in a child's game, having to play by the rules, but these rules were not of their making. They had known for some time that they would be involved in a series of events that would decide the future of the Five Lands and that their future was inextricably linked to it. What wasn't clear was if their involvement would be for good or ill. This was despite the fact that they believed that they fought on the side of good, and that they were acting in defence of the Five Lands. The prophecies however showed a divergence; two futures, and in one of these the Dyroshin's involvement led to destruction.

As self-appointed guardians of the Lake of Visions, the prophecies had been put together over many generations as successive Dyroshin who bathed in the lake, added their glimpses of the future to those of others. But the Lake was capricious and gave away such glimpses erratically and sometimes not at all. Those that were lucky enough to experience a vision received only fragments, and much of what they saw was random and meaningless. It was the work of the Clerics who pieced these fragments together. Each piece was painstakingly woven into what would later become known as the Prophecies.

The Dyroshin were frequently divided in their interpretation of the prophecies, and debates amongst the Elders were often heated as one group sought to impose their views on the other. This came as no real surprise, as a common theme to the visions was one of contradiction. One vision would hint at bumper harvests and plenty, and the next would depict the same scene but this time it was ravaged by pestilence and war.

The prophecies predicted that the Destroyer of Worlds would find the long lost Black Metal and that he would wield its cruel power for his personal gain, crushing all who stood in his way. The more he used it, the more the tremendous power would corrupt him. But it would also create in him a hunger that could only be satisfied by continued use of the magic. This hunger would lay waste to the Five Lands and beyond. The prophecies also revealed glimpses of strange other worlds that would also fall to the Destroyer of Worlds. If he was not opposed, his power would grow after every conquest until none could oppose him.

Although its existence had been questioned over the years, it was widely agreed within the Dyroshin, that Black Metal was a corruption of the naturally occurring White Metal. Piecing together stories from the days of Jal Chindo, it was clear that the Black Metal drew on the innate magical abilities of its user.

Jal Chindo had never been a good man. He was a savage and cruel warrior and his personal life bore much resemblance to the horrors he inflicted on others in battle. He started off as a soldier of no rank, but his complete lack of regard for his and later anyone's safety, gave him a fearsome reputation and he quickly found himself in charge of a cohort in the King's army. The men that formed the group were handpicked by Chindo and either attempted to emulate his battle skills or died in the process. It was rumoured that some of those who died, did so at his own hands. Whether the rumour was true or not no one had the temerity to accuse him, and even the King feared the monster that he had helped to create.

The story of how Jal Chindo acquired the Black Metal was not clear. It was suspected that he had stolen it during one of his men's many raids against factions opposing the crown. The cohort had become his private army and swore their allegiance to him. It was only a matter of time before he would march against the King and the other Generals and once he had acquired the Black Metal, this is exactly what he did. The battle didn't last long. Fleeing for their lives, the King and his court fled the Five Lands leaving only the Generals and the men they commanded to oppose Jal Chindo's force. Many of the crown's soldiers quickly surrendered and joined forces with Chindo, those that did not, including all the Generals, were not spared. Within days of defeating the fallen army of the crown, Jal Chindo was proclaimed King. Any that still opposed him were hunted down and killed.

Jal Chindo's rise to the throne had been at the expense of many lives and his brutality and cruelty became still worse during the period of his reign. This, the Dyroshin believed, was a direct effect of wielding the Black Metal. It was a corruption of nature, and it stood to reason that it would equally corrupt the wielder.

For their part, the fate of the Dyroshin was inextricably linked to Black Metal, but the irony was that they would never wield its might themselves. They saw from the visions that if they were to use it, they would be corrupted by it and the fate of the Five Lands would be sealed, as they would become the weapon of the Destroyer of Worlds.

So they had to await the arrival of one from another place whose world was not subject to the same rules as theirs, who could wield the power of Black Metal without being consumed by it and corrupted. Their role was to guide and help the one that they referred to as the *Outlander,* oppose the Destroyer of Worlds without succumbing to the siren song of Black Metal.

It took many generations for the fragments that comprised the prophecies to be pieced together and completed. They were deemed completed because the visions had been repeated over and over for the last five years with no new glimpses of the future.

Many began to doubt the prophecies, and as time wore on the threat, which was once so palpable, seemed to diminish. Velhanna, however, never doubted the warning she saw in the prophecies and took it on herself to make sure that her people were prepared. It was the love of her people and her belief that the Dyroshin were central to the survival of the Five Lands, that was to see her become their leader. Velhanna ruled her people with kindness and wisdom but ensured that the prophecies were kept alive in people's minds. Still there were those that continued to have their doubts, that is, until the cataclysm that was later to be known as Dakor's Darkness.

It was at this point that the Dyroshin realised that Zoryn Dakor was the Destroyer of Worlds and that the time of the prophecies was upon them. The identity of the Outlander remained a mystery to them until recently.

The Dyroshin were sensitive to the use of magic and could sense the ripples it created in the fabric of the land from many miles away. When Zoryn acquired Black Metal and used it for the first time, it sent out a shockwave many times more powerful than anything they had experienced before, even during the time of the great magical war over a hundred years ago. The Dyroshin instantly recognised it for what it was.

***

Draxan Longseer had always been an ambitious and ruthless man. During his time as Velhanna's life-mate he had publicly supported her, but privately he coveted her power as leader of the Dyroshin and he despised her lack of ambition, believing her to be weak. Why he chose to follow the dark path, as it later became known, was not clear. He managed to convince many of their people that they had simply misinterpreted the prophecies and that the age of Zoryn Dakor would be a time of growth and renewal for the Five Lands. So many believed him that almost half their number, nearly five thousand in all, left to follow their new leader, Draxan Longseer.

Those that joined him were mostly Warrior Mages, magicians adept in the use of destructive magic in the theatre of war. They had formerly been in the service of the crown but there had been little trouble in the Five Lands in recent years and their skills were rarely called upon, except in the training of the Elite Guard. Draxan's ideology and strong leadership appealed to the Archmages, who as Military Generals, saw it as a chance to prove themselves once more in battle. They believed that Draxan Longseer would lead them to glory. Draxan, however, cared little for the fate of others. He had pledged his and his force's allegiance to Zoryn Dakor in exchange for great wealth and a position of power in the new order that would emerge when Zoryn was triumphant.

Draxan led the Warrior Mages away from their settlement and was careful to keep their whereabouts a secret. It was largely assumed that they had formed a camp somewhere in the arid lands that lay to the west of Krendyra. Velhanna believed otherwise and was convinced that Draxan had dispersed his force into smaller groups scattered amongst the Five Lands, waiting for their *call to arms*. Now that Bradley White was in the land, both Velhanna and Yusana believed that Draxan would once again unite his breakaway group and together with mercenaries and other disillusioned soldiers, would march on Gaardsholme with Zoryn Dakor leading them into battle against his brother.

During her time with him, Draxan had revealed nothing of his plans to Yusana. She had been sent by Velhanna to get close to him and to find out anything that could help the remaining Dyroshin thwart his ambitions. Posing as a disenchanted follower of Velhanna was a high-risk strategy because she was known to him. But Velhanna was no fool, she knew that Draxan was attracted to Yusana and that his vanity and lust would be his undoing. Yusana played her part well and used her empathic skills to read him and to keep him interested. They became lovers and although he was physically unattractive to her, Yusana kept her feelings under close control so that she could remain professionally detached. Despite her skills, it was impossible to know for certain whether he trusted her or was using her in the same way that she was using him. Their courtship was more of a tactical exercise played out between two seasoned generals, than a conventional romance.

When Draxan met with the Outlander, it had been arranged that Yusana would make sure that they were not interrupted. She knew that the meeting was important, but she couldn't risk making her interest too obvious or Draxan would have been suspicious, so she had to play along with his plan. As it turned out, she found that spending time with Farric Clearwater was most enjoyable and she nearly forgot her whole reason for being there.

What gave Draxan away was his demeanour after the meeting with Bradley White. He was normally very much in control of his thoughts and emotions and barely gave any outward impression of what he was thinking of feeling. But that day he was visibly unsettled by the encounter, shaken even.

Velhanna was convinced that the Outlander was the one that the prophecies pointed to. Yusana wasn't convinced of this until the meeting between Bradley White and Draxan Longseer where she sensed the use of Black Metal. It was in that moment that she knew Bradley White, Outlander, was the one the prophecies said would be the tool of the Destroyer of Worlds.

***

Bradley White, Outlander, had been drawn unwillingly into Zoryn Dakor's game to wrest control of the Five Lands from its rightful ruler, Sanjin Dakor. The prophecies, known only to Velhanna's people and the break-away group led by Draxan Longseer, told of these things. But the prophecies were unclear and two paths could be seen emerging from this point in time. One which would lead to a period of calm and bounty, the other that would destroy much of what was good, laying waste to the Five Lands and other lands and worlds beyond, and causing the deaths of thousands of innocents.

When the Outlander entered the Five Lands, the shockwave was strongly sensed by the Dyroshin and they knew that some major event had happened. They had no way of knowing that it had been caused by Zoryn using Black Metal to pluck Bradley White from his world and that he would be the one the prophecies had foretold would be there at the time when the fate of the Five Kingdoms would be decided.

Finding Bradley White had been relatively easy. Smaller disturbances were felt and these were easy to locate. Velhanna had discovered the Outlander by tracking these disturbances.

It was clear that Bradley White would play a key role in the battle for control between Zoryn and Sanjin and had to be allowed to play his part, for good or ill, even if that meant that he fulfilled the ambitions of Zoryn. That much the Dyroshin knew for certain. The prophecies showed that there was no other path, that the fate of the Five Lands would be decided by the outcome.

Chapter 58
Pursuit

"Yusana, wake up," Farric said as he shook her, his voice was hoarse and he was weak from the fever. "We have to get out of here now."

She groaned as she hauled herself to her feet and cursed herself for falling asleep and leaving their makeshift camp unguarded. How could she have been so careless? She knew that the Blackreach Wolf's venom would be hard to fight, because she had used up so much magic in her efforts to heal Farric, but she didn't count on losing consciousness. Her proximity to Black Metal had clearly weakened her. It seemed ironic to Yusana that her destiny was to ensure that Black Metal was in the hands of the Outlander when he confronted the Destroyer of Worlds. "If I live that long," she grumbled under her breath.

But she was alive and had survived the bite, despite her weakened state. She felt shaky as she stood up, but seeing Farric at least partly recovered, gave her hope. She had been sent by her people to make sure that the Outlander met with Draxan Longseer to take possession of the black knife, which she had done. The next part, she feared would be the hardest and that was to ensure that the Outlander made it to Gaardsholme to fulfil his destiny.

Yusana was chosen by her people because her skills as a fighter and her innate healing magic were strong and her reliability and professionalism were beyond question. But despite that, she hadn't bargained for how she would feel about Farric Clearwater. He was known to her people, both by reputation and by glimpses in visions that hinted of his involvement in what would happen. She knew of his many romantic conquests but was too grounded to be taken in by such a man and yet despite her best intentions, she knew that she was falling for him. She saw something in Farric Clearwater, a loneliness that maybe others didn't, and she knew from that moment that destiny had brought him into her life for a reason. Besides, he was without doubt the sexiest man that she had ever met!

"How long have I been asleep?" Yusana asked, her mind foggy with sleep.

"I have no idea. The last thing I remember is fighting those renegade bastards, and judging by the fact that it's dark now, that must have been some time ago. What happened?

"We don't have time for that now. You're right we have to get away from this place. Have you tried waking your friend?"

"If you mean Brad, no I haven't, I wanted to make sure that you were okay first."

"How sweet of you!" She said mockingly.

Farric ignored her remark and continued, "I think that we may have some uninvited visitors soon. I heard voices over in that direction a few moments ago," He said, pointing back down the trail. "From what I can make out, I think our would-be visitors may have encountered the wolves that me and Brad bumped into on our way through here last time. It's gone quiet again which either means they are dead or the wolves are dead, either way we have to go."

"I'll wake the Outlander; you pick up that bundle of rags over there."

"Looks like a pile of crap to me and besides, why can't you do it yourself?" Farric replied dismissively.

"What's inside those rags is why you travelled to Krendyra in the first place and it may well be the only thing that will get us out of this. You have to trust me on this Farric, I can't touch what's inside those rags."

Although he barely knew her, Farric trusted Yusana and that was a new feeling for him, having never trusted anyone before. If she believed it was that important, he wouldn't argue the point. Besides, the wolves wouldn't hold their pursuers off forever and they were wasting valuable time.

Brad was already stirring and Yusana quickly helped him to his feet.

"Farric," He said in greeting, pleased to see that he was finally awake. "I thought you were going to die."

"Thanks for the vote of confidence," Farric growled in mock annoyance. "But how could I die when I still have the other half of my bounty to collect from Garan Smithson? You don't honestly think I would let you go back there alone to collect it now, did you?"

Brad laughed. "It's good to have you back Farric; at least I think it is!"

"Enough of this, we've got to go and now."

Farric although visibly weak, led the three of them deeper into the mountains. At times, their course took them away from the worn trail that Brad remembered from earlier, onto barely visible game trails that only a hunter would be able to follow. But Farric never slowed or showed any hesitation as he continued to lead the way.

***

During his time in the army of the Five Lands, Farric served much of it as a scout. The work suited him as he wasn't a team player and he could disappear for days on end without raising suspicion. He was also very good at his job. His ability to track came from within, as he had never been formally trained to track an animal or a man. In even the most unforgiving terrain, he found his prey.

After he left the army, Farric put his skills to use as a bounty hunter and supplemented his income with some well-paid mercenary work when it became available, and it always did. His fearsome reputation as a fighter, and his uncanny ability to track even the most elusive of targets, kept him gainfully employed.

Farric Clearwater also had a reputation for being a womaniser. The latter eventually leading to his dismissal from the army for sleeping with the wrong woman, on this occasion, it was the wife of his commanding officer. Farric never really stood a chance after that and was dishonourably discharged on trumped-up charges, he didn't bother defending himself against. The truth was that he had grown tired of submitting to military discipline and answering to the bullshit demands of those of higher rank.

Garan Smithson had also been dishonourably discharged around the same time as Farric. Smithson was distrustful of everyone, particular since he became the guardian of his niece Hania. Farric, however, was one of the few people that Garan had any time for, perhaps he saw a little of his younger self in the man. But even though he liked him, he never left him alone with his beloved Hania. He didn't trust anyone that much.

When Garan chose Farric for the job of ensuring that Bradley White did as Zoryn Dakor had demanded he knew that he was the only person for the task. Garan was a formidable fighter despite his age and could easily protect Bradley White and ensure that he got to Krendyra and back. But if White managed to escape during the journey, his chances of finding him again were not good. Zoryn Dakor was not a man that accepted failure and it was for this reason that Smithson had hired the best tracker, who also happened to be one of the finest fighters in the Five Lands.

***

Farric Clearwater didn't know for certain how many men were pursuing them, but he suspected that they were significantly outnumbered. Their pursuers were also likely to be in much better physical shape too. He was still weak from the fight with the renegades, Yusana was recovering from a Blackreach Wolf bite and Brad was still an enigma to him. Farric had seen him fight. He was stronger than most, and his skills as a fighter, although unorthodox and clearly untrained, were good but not exceptional. In the short time that Farric had known White, they had been involved in several confrontations. On two of these occasions, White should have been killed and only escaped death by the intervention of magic. A magic that he claimed he didn't have and yet just when he needed it, it had come to his rescue. Farric couldn't figure it out, he had never seen or heard of this type of magic before.

The sounds of pursuit were now much louder and it was clear that the men tracking them had dropped all pretence of stealth and were gaining on them. Farric didn't fancy their chances if they stopped and waited for the fight to come to them. Besides, they were in an area that was open on too many sides and was impossible to defend with just the three of them. If he remembered correctly, there was a pass not too far ahead that was very narrow and would only permit their attackers entry one man at a time. Even Brad, with his limited sword skills, could hold off an attack for hours. This was their best, if not their only, hope.

Chapter 59
Velhanna

"Yusana, the time is almost upon us," said a soft-spoken woman in her early fifties who appeared in front of Yusana like a wraith in the night. She was dressed in simple homespun clothing of non-descript browns which served only to highlight her prematurely grey hair, contrasted by its striking jet-black locks at her temples. Her piercing blue eyes held Yusana captive in their unwavering, but friendly gaze.

"Well met, Velhanna. We could use your help right now."

Brad and Farric stood motionless, seemingly oblivious to the presence of Velhanna. The sounds of pursuit had also been replaced by a preternatural silence.

"That's why I've come, but I cannot offer you the help you want," Velhanna replied. "I can't suspend time long enough to help you even if that was the right thing to do, which it is not. The presence of Black Metal in the Outlander and the knife that the traitor Draxan Longseer has given to him, are draining my magic. We don't have long."

"So why are you here? Can't you see that we need your help?" Despite her affection and respect for the leader of her people, Yusana's bluntness revealed her frustration.

"You have to trust me, Yusana. You of all people know that the Outlander has to meet the Destroyer of Worlds. Well, that time is much closer than we had first thought and the Outlander must be in Gaardsholme soon."

"How soon?"

"That we don't know for certain, but the quickest way to get him there is to let yourselves be captured by Sanjin Dakor's men," replied Velhanna.

"What makes you think they won't kill us anyway, whether we submit to them or not?"

"Sanjin Dakor is not an unreasonable man. He is aware of the Outlander and probably sees him as a threat. His men will be under strict orders to bring the three of you back to Gaardsholme alive."

"And if we make a stand and fight them…"

"They are soldiers Yusana, they will fight back and you will lose and may even be killed. We can't take that risk. There are too many of them for even you and Farric to fight off."

"But if you were to help us?"

"I cannot without risking all that our people have been working towards for generations. The risk that our meddling will settle matters in favour of the Destroyer of Worlds is just too great. Even at the risk of the loss of my most beloved of friends." Velhanna looked down as she spoke, unwilling now to engage with Yusana and show the pain that she was feeling.

"But what of the Outlander? Surely, his powers are more than a match for them?"

Velhanna looked up, a steely determination in her eyes. "Yes, they are Yusana. This is a critical moment in the future of the Five Lands, right here, right now. If the Outlander uses his powers now, all is lost. That is why you have to betray him."

Chapter 60
Betrayal

The three travellers didn't reach the pass. Somehow, their pursuers had managed to get in front of them. They must have either split their force and circled around them, or joined up with a separate group that were laying in ambush. Farric thought that this was the more likely possibility which could only mean that their capture had been planned some time ago. Whatever they wanted, someone had gone to a lot of trouble to make sure that they got it.

So now, a phalanx of heavily armed Elite Guard stood barring their way, barely a dozen feet in front of them. They looked like deadly wraiths in the feint light emanating from the rock, but these were no ghosts. Farric instinctively dropped into a fighter's crouch, his short sword in his hand as soon as he saw the men. Yusana had her back to him, a deadly looking throwing knife in each hand. Brad lacked Farric's and Yusana's military training and had been caught unawares by this sudden turn of events, but to his credit he had drawn the short sword that Farric had given him. Despite the seriousness of the situation Farric couldn't help but smile when he looked at him. Brad looked awkward with the blade and obviously lacked any training, but in the short time Farric had not known him, he had not avoided trouble and from the look of steely determination on his face, he wasn't going to start now. Not that he, or any of them, stood a chance of walking away from this.

A voice called out from behind them in the direction that Yusana was facing and a man of similar age to Farric detached himself from the shadows, behind him stood more armed guards. "Farric Clearwater." The man's gravelly voice cut through the night like a hot blade through butter. "It's been a long time." Farric didn't turn to face the man.

"Not long enough, Droken Arrowsmith," He responded, his back still to the other. "But I don't have time for a reunion right now." Then turning to face Droken Arrowsmith, with speed that belied his weakened condition, he continued. "So, if you'd like to order your men to move aside we'll be on our way and you just might survive to brag about this day with the poxed up whores you are so fond of."

"Oh fuck." Brad cursed to himself a little louder than he meant to as his hand tightened on the hilt of his short sword. He didn't know Farric well enough to tell if he was bluffing, but having seen the tremendous fighting skills of the man, he doubted that he was. Either way, this was not going to end well and he didn't fancy their chances against so many soldiers.

"Ha!" Droken laughed. "I see you've lost none of that famous whit Farric! But no, I don't think my men will do that. You see, as good as you might think you are, you are no match for my men and each one of them wants to be the man that beats the shit out of the *legendary Farric Clearwater*. You can't defeat all of them Farric, although it may be a pleasant diversion to watch you try!"

"That's as maybe, but you will be the first to die." Farric took a step forward menacingly.

Droken ignored Farric as he replied. "So how about you and your friends lay down your weapons and come with us, nobody needs to die in these shit-awful mountains."

"And why would we want to do that?" Farric's grip on his short sword tightened.

"Your King has requested your company at Gaardsholme."

"Requested you say? And why would he request my company?"

"The King does not confide in the likes of me." Droken laughed. "But I'm fairly certain that his majesty doesn't give a royal shit about you, no offence intended. No, I think that he may be more interested in the company that you've been keeping recently," he said, nodding towards Brad. Farric turned slightly to look at Brad, curious as to why Sanjin Dakor would be interested in this man. At the same instant, his vision exploded as if a firecracker had gone off inside his head.

"I'm sorry Farric," were the last words he heard before darkness consumed him. Yusana stood over him the hilt of her sword covered in blood from the vicious blow to the side of her lover's head.

"Quickly, tie the Outlander up!" she shouted to Droken. "I can't hold him much longer." Brad stood motionless, seemingly oblivious to all that was going on around him as if he were frozen in time. And that was precisely where Yusana had trapped him. He could see and hear everything that was happening around him but he couldn't move, couldn't act and couldn't stop Droken Arrowsmith's men from binding him tightly in thick coils of rough rope. The strain of using magic against one imbued with Black Metal, was draining Yusana, killing her. She held out until Brad was securely tied and then fell to the ground motionless.

***

Tracking Farric Clearwater and his companions had been easy for the leader of Sanjin Dakor's task force of Elite Guard, Droken Arrowsmith. He was well-trained and knew this part of the mountains better than anyone. He had led many missions into the mountains to seek out and in most cases, eliminate potential threats to the stability of the Five Lands. This, however, had been no ordinary mission. His orders had come from Sanjin Dakor in person and he had been allowed to hand pick his own team from the very best amongst the Elite Guard. This was a rare honour and Droken knew that this mission was important. His orders were to seek out and bring Bradley White and Farric Clearwater back to Gaardsholme for questioning. If there were others with them, they were to be brought in as well. The use of extreme force had been authorised, but Sanjin Dakor wanted the two men kept alive unless there was no alternative.

Droken knew Farric Clearwater but had never heard of the strange sounding *Bradley White*. In former times, Droken and Farric were like brothers, their sense of adventure and total lack of fear for their own safety, and in Farric's case also the safety of others, was the bond that had brought them together. But, it was difficult to be Farric's friend because his total lack of respect for the military hierarchy grated against Droken's total acceptance of it. Farric's dishonourable discharge from the army was the final straw and it was on that day that their friendship ended. It was a fight over nothing of any importance and had been brewing for some time. Much to his frustration, Droken was no match for Farric and the fight ended with Droken so badly beaten that he had to spend two weeks in the infirmary. He swore to himself that he would make Farric pay for this humiliation the next time they met.

And so, they were reunited, only this time it was Farric that was unconscious at Droken's feet. Droken resisted the urge to kick him in the face. Ordinarily, he wouldn't have hesitated. His men would never betray him, but Sanjin Dakor wanted Farric kept alive and he knew that if he kicked him, he wouldn't stop until he was dead. Despite the pleasure he would get from this, it wasn't worth a court martial.

As soon as Yusana fell, Brad regained full use of his limbs, but it was too late, he was bound so tight that he couldn't move.

"You fucking bitch." He spat at the motionless body of Yusana. "I hope that you are dead." Brad couldn't believe it, it just didn't make any sense. Without Yusana's help the day before, he and Farric would have almost certainly died at the hands of the deserters. And now she betrays them. It just didn't make any sense.

Brad didn't know what would have been in store for him if he had gone back to Smithson's place with Farric, but it was part of Zoryn Dakor's plan which meant that his family would have been safe, at least for the moment. Yusana had taken that possibility away from him. What fucking chance did he and his family now stand?

Droken Arrowsmith also couldn't understand why the warrior sorceress betrayed her companions? With her skills, the small band at least stood a chance. Not of defeating his guards, there were too many of them for that, but maybe of escape. Unfortunately, by the look of her motionless body on the hard ground he may never find out. Droken knew little of magic but it was clear even to him that she had exerted so much magic to hold Bradley White that if she wasn't dead, she would be soon. He called one of his men over to check her lifeless body

"She's dead, Captain," the man said.

"Make sure that our remaining guests are securely bound and let's get the fuck out of these bloody mountains."

"Yes sir, but what about the female?"

"Leave her for the wolves, maybe they will leave us alone if we leave them something to play with."

The guards pulled Farric to his feet and dragged him along between two of them until he came around enough to walk unaided. Brad didn't put up any resistance and walked behind Farric, flanked by a large guard on either side. The rope was so tightly coiled around his body that he couldn't move his arms at all. Yusana was left where she lay as the Elite Guard under the command of Droken Arrowsmith headed back to Gaardsholme with their captives.

***

"Yusana, my dear, dear friend, I'm so sorry that this had to happen." Velhanna sobbed as she knelt over the body of her fallen friend. "If there could have been another way I…" Velhanna stopped abruptly. To all appearances Yusana was dead but for just a moment Velhanna felt something. She checked Yusana's neck for a pulse but it wasn't there, looked for the slightest rise and fall of her chest, but there was no movement. But something was nagging at her senses and she refused to believe that her friend was dead.

Maybe Yusana had managed to suspend time? But the tell-tale signs of the magic were not there. Velhanna cleared her mind and concentrated with all her might, desperate to find any signs that she had missed, desperate to believe that her friend was still alive.

She concentrated for minutes, or hours, as she lost track of her own time. Just when she was about to give up and resign herself to her friend's fate, she felt a light magic brush her senses with the caress of gossamer. It was hard to latch onto but it was there, right at the edge of her senses. But it was different, not what she had expected, the magic had been changed somehow. Maybe it had been the proximity of Black Metal when Yusana had used her magic? Velhanna didn't know and didn't really care right now. All that mattered to her was that her friend was alive.

Concentrating on Yusana, Velhanna brought the magic up from deep inside herself, feeling its warm embrace as it spread from her core and radiated throughout her body. It was a seductive feeling and the temptation to give herself over to it utterly was as strong as ever. But Velhanna had been using magic for as far back as she could remember and knew that the embrace of magic could be deadly, taking as it gave, until there was nothing left to take and the magic wielder died. Even the strongest and most experienced could never let their guard down. Velhanna gently lifted her friend's head off the ground and held her as a mother would when comforting a child. The warmth of her magic breaking the barrier between them and flowing into Yusana. Time stopped for Velhanna as she joined her friend between moments.

Chapter 61
The Elite Guard

For the first two days of the long trek to Gaardsholme, Farric said nothing and Brad respected his silence. Despite being with Farric almost constantly for the best part of two months, he didn't really know the man at all. Brad suspected that their betrayal at the hands of Yusana had affected this battled hardened mercenary deeper than he would have thought was possible. Farric was not the sort to trust anyone and had said as much to Brad during their journey to Krendyra. But he had let his guard down with Yusana and let her get close to him, and now he was paying the price for his misplaced trust.

Why the fuck had Yusana betrayed them? It didn't make any sense to Brad. She didn't seem to have any connection with Droken Arrowsmith and Droken himself showed no concern for her leaving her for dead where she fell. And if she was going to betray them anyway, why did she bother to heal Farric's injuries and why did she try to lead them to safety? Droken made it clear that Sanjin Dakor sent the guard to capture him and the way he said it, implied that Sanjin had little interest in Farric. So, wouldn't it have been easier if Yusana had let Farric die and turned on him then? She was a formidable fighter, maybe even as good as Farric. If she had turned on him, he wouldn't have stood a chance. Maybe it was the Black Metal inside him that had made her wary of going up against him? But nothing in her actions up to the point that they had become trapped by Droken's Elite Guard gave him any reason to suspect her. Even now looking back, there were no hints, no clues, no reason to suspect her. Brad's mood was almost as dark as Farric's as he tried to make sense of recent events.

During the day, the Elite Guard marched with their captives at a quick pace. It was fascinating to Brad to begin with but became tiresome as the days wore on. The soldiers marched at a relaxed but fast pace for a certain number of steps, Brad lost count at three hundred, and then they would break into a jog which would last for a similar number of steps. Their march would alternate between these states constantly. None of the men complained and very few words were spoken. Twice a day, at seemingly random times, two groups of two men would detach themselves from the main group and scout ahead. Sometimes, they would return the same evening and sometimes they would disappear for a day or two. But always, when they returned, they reported back to Droken Arrowsmith who received their reports away from the main body of his company.

Brad was beginning to understand why the Elite Guard were so respected. They were well disciplined men who clearly worked well together as a team, with everyone knowing what part they had to play and playing that part without the need for instruction. The renegades that he, Farric and Yusana had encountered the previous day were skilled fighters and clearly dangerous, but they had acted independently of each other and this ultimately contributed towards their defeat. Brad shuddered at the thought of how things would have turned out had Droken Arrowsmith's orders been to attack rather than capture them.

The stamina of the soldiers was impressive; they marched from less than an hour after first light, until the strange blue sun set in the evening. They didn't stop once during this time. If a soldier needed a toilet break, he would break ranks and catch up a little further on. The Elite Guard even ate as they marched, passing heavily sweetened seeded biscuits up and down the column until each man had his quota.

That evening Farric eat his meagre meal of soldiers rations in silence and turned to Brad, with an unconvincing smile and said, "Looks like I misjudged you Bradley White, you must have done something pretty bad to warrant this number of guards being sent to take you to our beloved King. Sanjin Dakor must really want to talk with you!"

Farric had a number of cuts and bruises to his face and his left eye was almost entirely closed from a swelling that reached half-way down his face. As if sensing his thoughts, Farric looked at Brad and said, "I let my guard down back there Brad, I'm sorry."

"How could you have known? How could either us have known that we had a traitor in our midst?"

***

They were treated no differently to the other men and were expected to match their pace and were passed food and water as they marched. They were marching across open ground and Brad didn't see any advantage in trying to escape, and even if he could somehow get away from these men, where would he go? If he was being taken to this place called Gaardsholme, then it was likely that he would meet Sanjin Dakor and maybe this insane game of Zoryn's would finally end, one way or another. Marching back with the guards would certainly get him there much quicker than if he had returned with Yusana and Farric and if they were attacked on the way, they had the Five Lands finest to defend them.

That's it Brad thought as the clarion bell of realisation rang through his mind. *Yusana didn't betray us, she just found a way to get us to Gaardsholme faster.* He was so wrapped up in his thoughts that he missed the silent beat of the march and tripped and fell and was nearly trampled by the soldiers behind him.

The soldiers stopped their march and two of them broke ranks and hauled him to his feet as Droken Arrowsmith looked on. Smiling as he did so, one of the guards head-butted Brad before he could react and avoid the attack. The blow was not intended to cause any real injury. It was a warning, intended to dispel any thought of escape and to demonstrate the mastery of his captors. But it was still hard enough to momentarily make him dizzy, causing him to lose his balance and fall to the ground a second time.

"Get up and get back into line with the others, you piece of shit," barked Brad's assailant as he stood over him menacingly. Brad was more pissed off than injured by the attack and felt his temper rising. But he didn't have the luxury of time to fight with this man. All he wanted to do was to get the fuck to Gaardsholme and end this. For a brief moment, he wrestled for control over himself and forgot all about the cause of his anger which was the guard who was standing above him.

It was then that he noticed it. Something was stirring deep inside him, something that came from deep within him but didn't feel like it was a part of him. The feeling reminded him of every time that the Black Metal had come to his aid unbidden and saved his life. But his life wasn't at risk now, so what did this mean? Was the magic of the Black Metal acting independently of him again? Was he just a conduit for it, or had he somehow summoned it himself? Whatever the reason, he could feel the magic of the Black Metal coiling inside him, the tension building with every rapid beat of his heart. Its eagerness to attack was palpable to his senses and was seductive. Brad felt invincible like he had done back in the mountains when he unleashed the power of the Black Metal against the Blackreach Wolves. No one and nothing could stand in his way.

"You heard me, get in line," the guard shouted as Brad came to his feet, head bowed as he struggled for control. He said nothing as he slowly lifted his head up to meet the other's gaze. The guard went to grab Brad, to force him back in the direction of the others, who by now were some way ahead of them. But he stopped as soon as saw Brad's eyes. The zig-zagged, orangey-red corona's surrounding his pupils of darkest black, blazed with an intensity that screamed of power and malevolence. For the first time in his adult life, this battle-hardened soldier of the Elite Guard felt fear.

Chapter 62
Return to Zandyros

Zoryn's plans were proceeding exactly as planned. He had implanted just enough Black Metal inside Bradley White to enable him to transport him to the Five Lands of Zandyros without having to accompany him. For his plan to succeed, he needed to keep his own presence undetected until the last moment. His brother would still be looking for him of course, but neither Sanjin, nor any of his advisers could possibly find him in this world.

Zoryn had chosen well in Bradley White, a witless pawn who would help him to bring about the destruction of his brother. White had survived the harsh training of Garan Smithson, no doubt due to the effects of the Black Metal, which was essential to help keep him alive long enough to fulfil the destiny that Zoryn had created for him.

He needed White to attract the attention of Sanjin. White looked ordinary but stood out on closer inspection. It was difficult to pinpoint exactly why, but he did have an *other worldliness* about him. Smithson's training would also mark him apart from the bandits that hunted those parts. Sanjin's spies were everywhere and he would be sure to hear about this strange man.

White collected the Black Metal knife from Draxan Longseer and had caught the attention of Sanjin as Zoryn predicted he would. At this very moment, White was being escorted to Gaardsholme by a detachment of the Elite Guard. *The fool,* Zoryn thought to himself. *My brother is bringing the very weapon of his destruction to himself.*

***

With his attention on this strange outlander, Sanjin Dakor's focus wasn't on the guerrilla war that was waging in the Western Peninsula as much as it should have been. His general, the very capable Zanshin, was keeping him briefed. Sanjin sent reinforcements to the west and a separate task force had been dispatched to cover any attack to the east. But what Sanjin Dakor didn't know, had no way of knowing, was that the whole thing had been set-up by Zoryn.

There had been unrest in the west for many years, but until now, it hadn't really caused much of a problem to the Five Lands. That was until Zoryn held secret meetings with the leaders of the guerrillas and formed an alliance. He promised them lands that they could call their own in the rich farming belt of the Western Peninsula in return for their co-operation in an exercise to convince Sanjin that he faced a much bigger and more immediate threat on at least two fronts. This, coupled with the outlander Bradley White's appearance, would provide all the distraction that Zoryn needed. Of course, he had no intention of honouring this 'so-called agreement'. Zoryn planned to rid himself of his ally and his forces shortly after they conveniently presented themselves to him in one place that they thought would be their new home.

Zoryn had no interest in the Western Peninsula, what he wanted was the White Metal stockpile in the Mine of Renshaw hidden deep within the Zindaw Mountains. It was his insurance against his plan to overthrow his brother failing. He was confident that his plans would succeed, but if they did not he would own enough White Metal to equip an army that would be the equal to anything the Five Lands could throw against him. Zoryn didn't fear open warfare with his brother, but if he could take the throne by succession, without losing half of what would then become his army by annexation, he would conquer and crush any that stood in his way and his kingdom would grow.

***

Few knew of the location of the Mine of Renshaw and it was heavily protected by Elite Guard. To control the distribution of White Metal, a massive store of the magical substance had been hidden away by Sanjin Dakor deep within the stronghold of the mine. With massive amounts of White Metal at his disposal and the Black Metal that only he possessed, Zoryn knew that none could possibly stand against him. His plans were audacious and would herald the start of his reign as a conquering warlord King, the King the Five Lands deserved rather than the weak caretaker king it currently had as its monarch. It was now only a matter of time before his plans would lead to the overthrow of his brother's regime.

****

"Kaiya, it is time," Zoryn declared.

"Yes, my love. I grow bored of this place too."

"We will return. There is much here that I would have as ours. But first we must tend to matter's in our own land. The time is drawing near and my presence is required. When we return to this place, it will be at the head of an army the like of which these weaklings have never beheld. I will conquer and crush them until they submit to my will."

"This land is so alien to our own Zoryn, what do you see here that makes it so important to you?"

"They have machines where we have magic. They can travel much faster than we can between places and they have weapons that can be used vast distances from their targets. By combining the magic from our world with the machines from this world, we can go on to conquer other worlds. None will stand against us; we will have dominium over entire worlds, Kaiya."

Chapter 63
Control

Brad clenched his teeth and somehow managed to control the magic that was fighting to break free. The other guard was oblivious to what had happened to his fellow soldier as he shoved Brad forward in the direction of the main body of the Elite Guard. The instant his hand made contact with Brad's shoulder, the magic escaped Brad's control for just a moment and crimson fire erupted at the point of contact. But that was all that it took. In that instant, the guard's hand was badly burnt and he screamed in agony and shock. Brad turned and pushed him away in an effort to save him from further damage. As he did so, the first guard had regained his composure and believing that this fellow soldier was under attack, lunged at Brad with his short sword; all thought of taking his prisoner back alive had gone.

Brad turned to face the man. He didn't have time to defend himself and watched as the blade arced towards his head. The familiar detached feeling returned. Brad knew that he couldn't evade the blow but he could feel the might of the Black Metal building inside himself and knew that he would survive the attack.

As the blade descended, it seemed to slow down and then impossibly, it stopped, suspended in mid-air. The guard's face was contorted in rage but this too looked as if it had been frozen in time.

"Outlander, step back from the guard. You must not let his sword strike you." The voice came from behind him. Brad whirled around to confront the speaker, his fist was tightly clenched but tendrils of crimson fire escaped between his fingers. The orangey-red, zig-zagged coronas around his pupils blazed with power.

Yusana stood a few feet in front of him with Velhanna at her side.

"You," He snarled at Yusana. "You dare to tell me what to do after you betrayed us to these men?" His rage fuelled by Black Metal was rapidly reaching its flashpoint.

"You mustn't do this," Velhanna replied before Yusana could respond. "The safety of your family and the fate of the Five Lands depends on your next action. I sense that your control over the Black Metal is slipping and if that soldier strikes you it will unleash power that will kill all around you. If you destroy these men Outlander, all is lost."

Somewhere deep inside, Brad knew that Velhanna was right. Even though he had only met her once before, he trusted her more than any other he had met in this strange place. But the Black Metal was screaming to him to release its power and lay waste to those that stood in his way and he was finding it hard to resist its siren call. After all, what did he care for any of them? They had captured him and taken him prisoner. He hadn't asked for any of this. Surely they deserved what they got?

"You have to go to Gaardsholme with these men, Outlander. It is there that you will face Zoryn Dakor and it is there that the outcome will be decided," she continued.

"And what if I don't want to face Zoryn Dakor?" He demanded. "What if I don't give a fuck about what you want, this place or anything else?"

248

"Nobody can blame you for feeling that way, Outlander. You have been thrown into the very heart of the troubles that beset this land and you owe us no allegiance. But can you turn away so easily from your family? You know that Zoryn will kill them if you do not do his bidding."

"What's happening to me, Velhanna?"

"I don't know for certain, but the Black Metal is changing you and you must resist it. It draws on the magic of others and attracts this power unto itself and I believe that it is melding with you, becoming a part of you and eventually you will become indistinguishable from each other. I fear that if that happens, you will become lost to us and will be every bit as dangerous to the Five Lands as Zoryn Dakor. You have to resist it."

"If that's meant to make me feel better Velhanna, it isn't working." His control over his anger was returning. "But I just don't get it. I'm not from your world so why would Zoryn go to all the bother of travelling to my world and force me to come back here to kill his brother when he could have paid some assassin from this world to do it for him? None of this adds up."

"Zoryn discovered your world by accident when he unwittingly created that which is known as Dakor's Darkness."

"What is this fucking Dakor's Darkness?" Brad asked incredulously. "I've seen it but surely no man could have made such a thing, could they?"

"It is a portal, a doorway between two realities that was created by Zoryn by accident. It was forged by an uncontrolled massive release of the Black Metal's magic. Such a thing should not be possible and yet it exists."

"Could this *portal* be the way back to my world?"

"I am certain of it. Doubtless it was the way that Zoryn travelled to your world."

"But it still doesn't make any sense that he would choose me?"

"Do you have magic in your world?" Velhanna asked.

"No, we don't. Our world is similar to yours in many ways, but we have technology, man-made devices that do many things for us that magic does for you here, but we don't have magic."

"Then that's why he chose from your world. He needed his assassin to be protected by the power of Black Metal but he couldn't run the risk of using someone from this world because many people here have magical abilities. A person with magic could learn how to use the Black Metal and eventually master it and that would make them a dangerous threat to Zoryn. There is no way that he would take such a risk."

"But that still doesn't answer the question, why did he choose me?" Brad continued.

"I don't think that he particularly chose you, it may be that you just happened to be in the wrong place at the wrong time, not just for you Outlander, but maybe also for him."

"What do you mean?"

"Because Zoryn couldn't detect magic in your world, I believe that he assumed it didn't exist there, and if that was the case he would assume that no one there would possess any innate magical abilities. But he was wrong because you do have some natural ability. I wasn't sure at first, because the nature of your magic was so alien to my senses that I didn't recognise it for what it was and didn't believe that you had any. I dismissed it then, but now your magic has grown stronger, and although still alien and indistinct, I am certain of its existence."

"I can't possibly have any magical abilities," Brad scoffed. "Magic doesn't exist in my world, so how could I?"

"But magic does exist here, Outlander. I don't know if your magical abilities are surfacing now because you are here in a world full of magic, or if this is another effect of Black Metal. I suspect that it may be a combination of both of these factors. It may even be that there is magic in your world and that it is dormant. But the fact remains that you do have magic."

"This is all very hard to believe, Velhanna."

"Yes, I suppose it must be, but if you are to stand any chance of defeating Zoryn you have to believe in yourself."

"That's easy for you to say," Brad retorted. "You are saying that I have to stand up against a man who single handedly ripped a hole in the fabric of the Universe and without trying created a portal between two realities! You may not be surprised to hear that I am lacking somewhat in the self-confidence needed to do this!" Brad laughed humourlessly at the absurdity of Velhanna's assertion.

"One thing's for certain," Velhanna responded. "Zoryn cannot suspect that you are gaining some control over the Black Metal and can consciously call on its magic."

"And how do you work that out?"

"If he realised you could Outlander, you would already be dead. There's no way that he would risk leaving you alive if there was even the slightest chance that you could use the magic against him. It's crucial that he doesn't find out either."

"Well that's at least one thing that we do agree about!" Brad said. "So what happens now?"

"Now Outlander, you must submit to these men and go with them to Gaardsholme."

"And just how do I do that, this guard..." Brad said nodding in the direction of the guard who was frozen in time in mid-strike. "...seems pretty intent on killing me. How do I stop the Black Metal killing him in my defence?"

"You need to move away from him now. The blow will miss you but judging by the force he is attacking you with, he will over-balance and this should give you a moment or two to throw your hands up and show that you are not going to fight back."

"I hope you're right about this!"

"One more thing, Outlander," Velhanna said. "Be careful what you say when you meet Sanjin Dakor. He is a just king, but distrusts magic and those that use it."

"I'll try to remember that!" Brad replied flatly.

"Now move, Outlander."

Brad barely moved out of the way in time as his assailant's short sword slashed through the air where his head had been only a fraction of a second earlier. As Velhanna predicted, the guard had put so much force into the attack that his momentum caused him to stumble and nearly fall. Brad stood a few feet to the man's side with arms raised, clearly showing that he was unarmed. But inside, he could feel the eagerness of the Black Metal and he fought for control once more. The guard was furious that his prey had escaped so easily and advanced on Brad for a second time, raising his sword. But before he was close enough to strike, his eyes rolled back into his head as Droken Arrowsmith's fist connected with the side of the guard's head in a blow that was hard enough to shatter bones.

"You," Arrowsmith snarled to Brad. "Get back into line." Brad could feel his anger rising even higher as he stared into the eyes of the other, his control over the magic slipping once more and threatening to engulf him utterly. But he remembered Velhanna's words and mustered what remained of his strength to tear his eyes away from this man and rejoin the ranks of the guards. As he walked over, Brad looked over in the direction of where Velhanna and Yusana had stood and wasn't surprised that they had disappeared as quickly as they had arrived.

Droken left the fallen guard where he lay and gave the order to resume the march to Gaardsholme. The Elite Guard were well trained and didn't once look back. Droken joined the rear of the column and only a slight tremor in his otherwise strong gait gave away any sign of the weakness that he felt in his legs. Had any of the men turned around they would have seen the relief in the face of their leader, relief that he had somehow faced this Bradley White down without further bloodshed. He had seen the man's eyes, the zig-zagged, orangey-red coronas that flashed with malice was something that he had seen only once before and that had been in the eyes of Zoryn Dakor.

Chapter 64
The Journey to Gaardsholme

It was the end of another gruelling day's march at the indefatigable pace of the Elite Guard. In his previous life, he would have probably died from exhaustion during the first week. But the effects of the Black Metal had endowed Bradley White with far greater strength and resilience than he would have thought was possible.

"So, it looks like you've caught the attention of our illustrious leader the great Sanjin Dakor, King of the Five Lands!" Farric announced wryly breaking Brad's musing. Farric had been withdrawn and uncommunicative for the first week or so of their forced march to Gaardsholme. Brad suspected it was due to the apparent treachery of Yusana and on several occasions had tried to talk with him about it. But Farric was having none of it and turned away from Brad every time he made the attempt. Maybe today he would listen.

"I've already met one Dakor, Farric, and that was more than enough for me! I'm really not looking forward to this meeting any more than you are," Brad replied truthfully.

"But the fact remains that he seems pretty keen to make your acquaintance. It's not everyone that has an escort of Elite Guard to come and collect them."

"Well, he could hardly have sent a taxi I suppose," Brad quipped.

"What the fuck is a taxi?"

"Don't worry about it Farric, it would take too long to explain, and I doubt whether you would find it that interesting."

"Probably not," Farric agreed. "You never did explain what your connection was with Zoryn Dakor?"

"You never asked," Brad replied flatly.

"Fair comment. In my line of work, sometimes knowing less is safer, but I suspect in your case…" Farric left the sentence hanging.

"In my case Farric, I'm not so sure that it would have made any difference what you knew. If Yusana's people are correct, it would appear that we were both fated to take this path together whether we chose to or not."

"Yusana's people?" Anger at the mention of the betrayer flashed dangerously in Farric's eyes. "What the fuck do you know about her people?"

Finally, thought Brad. *Now at last, I can tell him the truth about Yusana.*

"You might as well sit down Farric, I've got a lot to tell you."

Farric listened to Brad without interruption and let him explain how he had concluded that Yusana had not betrayed them. Brad told him that it had been confirmed when Velhanna appeared the previous day. Farric's eyes widened as Brad described how Velhanna had frozen time and by doing so, had saved the life of the Elite Guard who had attacked him. Brad didn't tell him about his near loss of control of the magic of the Black Metal. Although he respected Farric, Brad was not prepared to reveal too much about himself, or his increasing powers. There was just too much at stake.

"You do indeed mix in esteemed circles," Farric said, breaking his silence long moments after Brad had finished talking. "First you have some fucking encounter with Zoryn Dakor, then the leader of Yusana's people and now Sanjin Dakor wants to meet you. I had no idea I kept company with such an illustrious and sought-after character. You will forgive me if don't fucking curtsy your highness?" Farric said with a flourish as he genuflected.

"Knock it off Farric; I don't like this any more than you do." Replied Brad. "Your King has made his invitation a little hard to refuse."

"Hmmph."

Despite his piss-taking, Farric appeared to have accepted Brad's version of events and Brad was surprised that he hadn't scoffed at the notion that Velhanna could freeze time. Maybe it was well known in the Five Lands that Velhanna's people could do such a thing, he wondered.

"It all happened quickly, Farric," Brad replied. "And I'm pretty sure that it takes a lot of their magic to stop time. They only appeared because they had to. Well that's if all this destiny shit they talk about is true. If it's any consolation, it was Velhanna who did all the talking."

"Well, that makes me feel so much better. So, do you really believe this fucking bullshit you've been telling me?" Farric pinned Brad with his icy stare. Maybe he hadn't accepted his story after all.

"I have no idea what you mean?" Brad replied flatly.

"You don't trust me much, do you?" Farric's question an accusation. "There's a lot more to all this, a lot more that you aren't telling me."

"It's hard to trust anyone in this land Farric, but no I don't trust you. You know that I've been forced to do things I haven't wanted to from the day I fucking arrived in this accursed place. And to be blunt, I suspect that you were paid to make sure that meeting with Draxan Longseer went ahead whether I agreed to it or not. What would you have done Farric, knock me out and strap me to the fucking cart if I had refused to go along willingly?" Brad could feel his anger rising.

"Was my plan that obvious?" Farric replied but sensing the tension that was emanating off Brad in waves he added, "Yes I would have done that and more."

"So, you will understand why I don't trust you?"

"You're right not to trust me. I was hired by Garan Smithson because I'm the best there is, and he knows that I always see a job through whatever it takes."

"Well, at least you've been consistent about that." Brad had respect for Farric and despite his better judgement, he liked the man.

"The rules of engagement have changed. Being hauled against my will to the court of Sanjin Dakor was never part of what I signed up for. But I'm beginning to wonder if that was the plan all along. I've been lied to and manipulated by Smithson, the one man I believed to be honest, at least with me. Smithson wouldn't betray me this way, unless there was a lot at stake. This changes everything."

Hania. That was it. Zoryn Dakor did have a hold over the old bastard and it was his beloved niece, Hania. At the very thought of her, Brad could see her in his mind, her brilliant piercing emerald eyes, her strawberry blonde hair that smelled of summer meadows. That bastard Zoryn hadn't taken any chances.

"So how exactly does this change things?" Brad asked.

"Well, one thing's for certain, if I survive this, then me and Garan Smithson will be having words. But first, we need to figure out a way to get through this alive?"

"We?"

"If you want to get through this, you will stand a better chance with my help. Now tell me what's really going on."

And so, against his better judgement, Brad told Farric about his life on his home world and how everything changed following a chance encounter with the Chemist who later turned out to be Zoryn Dakor. They spoke in hushed voices away from the body of the Elite Guard, but Brad was certain that Droken had posted men under cover nearby to monitor everything that was said between the two men.

Brad told Farric that Zoryn was holding his family hostage to ensure that he did his bidding. But when pressed by Farric as to what exactly Zoryn's bidding was, Brad refused to answer. Farric glanced around them and nodded, silently acknowledging that revealing too much here would be dangerous for them both.

"Well whatever Zoryn's plans may be, it would appear that Sanjin Dakor sees you as a threat. He clearly doesn't know you at all, does he?" Farric laughed.

"Clearly," Brad replied dryly.

"So, what happens when you are brought before our King?

"I have no idea, but if you are right and he does see me as a threat, then I guess things aren't going to end well for me?"

"True enough, but if he questions you and releases you, which I must say is most unlikely, then what?"

"Then I guess I still have Zoryn Dakor to deal with," Brad replied.

"Hmmph, it's not looking good for you, is it?"

"It hasn't, from the day I met Zoryn Dakor."

Chapter 65
Choices

"Gina, come to me." Brad was in the Forest, the preternatural gloom an impenetrable cloak suffocating the life out of everything it touched. Even though he was alone, he could sense Gina's presence. It was barely there, like gossamer but definitely there nonetheless. As he called out to his wife, across the unfathomable distance that lay between them, her image came to his mind in crystal clarity and he felt her presence around him becoming stronger.

Within moments, Gina appeared in front of him, a wraith emerging from the gloom. His heart ached when he saw her, aching for his previous life, aching to be with her and to be reunited with his son. Brad had been brought up by parents who never revealed their emotions and perhaps because of this conditioning he generally supressed his own. But standing in front of his wife in this moment, he felt overwhelmed with love for her and realised that this would be the last time he would ever see her.

"I've missed you, Brad." Gina said, as if reading his thoughts as she caught him in a fierce embrace. The softness of her image belying the strength that lay within. He didn't say anything, couldn't say anything, not trusting his voice to remain calm as he held her in his arms. He could feel the warmth of her body as she pressed herself against him, closing the gap until there was no space between them. They held each other for a second, a minute, an hour, time seemed to mean nothing in this place and its passage was impossible to follow.

Gina pulled back just enough for her to lay on the soft leaf litter of the forest floor. Pulling at his clothes, Brad quickly joined her and then undressed her tenderly. They made love, each knowing that this would be their last moment of intimacy. Afterwards, they lay naked in each other's arms and fell asleep.

Gina was the first to awaken. She didn't move, didn't want to wake her husband, not wanting to end this moment. She had no idea how long she had slept, and she was surprised to have woken-up in this place, expecting to have been transported back to her own world as she slept.

It wasn't long before Brad stirred and opened his eyes. He smiled and pulled Gina close. They lay in each other's arms for a while, neither wanting to end the embrace as if fearing that once broken it could never be restored. "This is the last time that we will be with each other Brad, isn't it?" Gina broke the silence.

"Honestly Gina, I don't know." Brad replied. "All I do know is that I'm getting closer to this place called Gaardsholme and this is where everything's going to happen. At least according to the visions of Velhanna and her people."

"What are you going to do when you get there?"

"I have to find a way of getting you and David away from Zoryn. If I somehow find a way to kill his brother, Zoryn isn't going to simply send me back to you and leave us alone. For a start his brother, Sanjin Dakor is the King of these lands and is bound to be well protected. Even if I did kill him, I would never escape his palace alive and one thing's for certain, Zoryn won't come to my rescue. In fact, I'm convinced that that was his plan all along, no loose ends. It also means that he can deny any involvement with the murder of his brother, as there will be nobody to testify against him. And if I am killed, what will become of you and David? No, I have to find a way of breaking his hold over you."

"Have you thought of a way of using this Black Metal you mentioned before, to break the link between our worlds?" Gina asked.

"There's a phenomenon here called Dakor's Darkness which was created during a freak accident and Velhanna believes that it is a portal between our worlds," Brad replied.

"And this Dakor's Darkness was made by Zoryn Dakor?"

"Yes, it was. Apparently, it was created by an uncontrolled massive release of the Black Metal's magic. And if Black Metal made it…"

"Black Metal can destroy it!" Gina said, completing his sentence.

"Precisely. Or at least that's what I hope. I just don't know how to do it and that's assuming that it is even possible to destroy it in the first place. But if I can destroy this Dakor's Darkness and close the portal, then you and David will be safe."

"But you will be on the other side of the portal, won't you Brad?"

"There is no other way, Gina. I'm not a brave man, if there was a better way of doing this that didn't leave me stranded here, or worse, believe me I would attempt it."

"This is the last time that I will see you, Brad."

"However this turns out, I can't see a future where I will ever be able to return to our world. If I do manage to close the portal, our link to each other through this place, would almost certainly end because I'm certain now that 'this' he gestured around them, "must surely be a construct, or at least an effect of the portal."

"And if you close the portal…"

This time Brad finished her sentence. "Yes Gina, there would be no way back to you and David and the life I have left behind."

"I know,"

"If I do find a way of breaking Zoryn's hold on you, promise me that you will take David and move to another town where we aren't known and where Zoryn could never find you if he was ever to return?"

"Yes, I promise, Brad." Gina's voice was thick with emotion.

"David must know by now that I killed your attacker and it will look like I've run away to escape justice. I love our son Gina and it would break my heart if he hated me because of this." Brad's eyes burnt with unwept tears as he spoke.

"David will understand that you did what you had to do Brad, he loves you too and has always looked up to you. He will find it hard to accept that you won't be coming home and that he didn't get a chance to say goodbye to his Father."

"I'm not afraid to face Zoryn now, Gina. I was before, but that cunt has to pay for what he has put my family through."

"I wish I was a better person and could persuade you not to Brad, but I can't. If you get the chance to kill him, don't hesitate, kill the bastard."

"I love you, Gina."

"I love you too, Brad." Gina replied as her form melted for the last time back into the mist.

Chapter 66
Escort

The remainder of their journey to Gaardsholme with Droken Arrowsmith and his detachment of Elite Guard passed without any major incident. When they were a week from Gaardsholme, they were unwittingly attacked by a group of bandits who mistook their camp for one of a band of travelling merchants. The Elite Guard dispatched the attackers with ruthless efficiency and none of them survived the encounter. This was the way of the Elite Guard and their fearsome reputation was built on their savagery.

Gaardsholme was a garrison city that grew-up around a port that later adopted its name. The port was of huge strategic significance. Its deep waters and access via a narrow strait bordered by the treacherous rocky shoreline of the uninhabited Isle of Shadows made it easy to defend. In times long past, attempts had been made to take Gaardsholme from the sea, and each attempt failed with the deaths of those who tried.

As Droken's band approached the city limits, they were met by a similar sized detachment of mounted armed guards. Unlike Droken's men these men wore magnificent tabards of the deepest blue with Sanjin Dakor's insignia of a brown hawk swooping in for the kill with its mighty talons extended, emblazoned across their chests and on their shields. Despite his growing unease, Brad couldn't help but be impressed with this show of the obvious power and authority of the King of the Five Lands. Their horses were huge battled hardened beasts and reminded Brad of the shire horses of his own world. Each horse wore the striking blue livery of their King and light chain mail type armour about their flanks.

"Well met, Droken Arrowsmith," said the leader of the group, as he detached himself from the main body of his men and stopped his horse in front of Arrowsmith who had stepped in front of his men to greet their escort.

"Denshin Farrower," Droken replied. "How kind of you to join us!" Denshin Farrower was a giant of a man and was the most feared of the Elite Guard. His reputation for fierceness and his prowess in fighting both on horseback and hand to hand, was legendary. As he dismounted from his horse and stood in front of Droken, he towered above the other who was easily six foot tall himself. The two men said nothing as they faced each other. Without warning, Denshin threw his head back and howled with laughter. "It's good to see you again, my friend," he announced as he slapped Droken on the back. Although it was a friendly slap, it would have felled a smaller man.

"You too, you ugly tosser!" Droken replied, as he extended his arm to his childhood friend.

The two men stood apart from both groups of Elite Guard and continued their conversation in hushed tones.

"So, you managed to capture the legendary Farric Clearwater and this stranger our King is so interested in?" Denshin said.

"Yes, and it was easier than I expected," he replied without the slightest hint of humility.

"Though you say so yourself?"

"Actually, we received help from a woman that was travelling with them. A warrior who was almost certainly Dyroshin." Droken recanted the story of the betrayal of Bradley White and Farric Clearwater by Yusana.

"Didn't you question her?" Denshin asked.

"No, she rather inconveniently died, must have used up all her magic I guess. I doubt that Sanjin Dakor will be best pleased, but there wasn't anything I could do."

"And where is her body?" Denshin asked. "Don't tell me Droken, let me guess…you left her there?"

"Seemed like the only sensible thing to do," Arrowsmith replied flatly.

"You never were one to be sentimental my friend, were you?"

"So, what happens now?" Droken asked, ignoring the other's question.

"Well, me and my men are to escort your detachment and the prisoners to the Royal Keep where you will hand the prisoner over to the head jailer. Our King is away from court until tomorrow and will deal with them then."

"Do we know what they have done?" Droken asked.

"No Droken," Denshin replied. "Security on this has been tighter than anything I've seen in years. All I know is that only the heads of the Council of Lords will attend court under a sealed session. Oh, and your men will be on guard duty outside the court."

"Outside the court?" Droken repeated his friend's words. "So, I guess that means that you and your men will be inside the court as the King's personal bodyguard?"

"Yes it does seem a little much but our beloved king is clearly not taking any chances."

Droken didn't reply but instead cast an eye over his shoulder to where Brad and Farric stood amongst his men.

"I hope he knows what he's doing." Droken murmured more to himself as he turned to face Denshin Farrower.

"He's the King and pretty useful in a fight himself, besides he will have General Zanshin with him. I doubt that there's many that could stand up to the four of us."

"Was that a compliment?" Droken said smiling at his friend and fellow captain of the Elite Guard."

"Piss off, Droken," he replied flatly.

"I'll take that as a yes then!"

"You can take it up the ass for all I care!" Denshin couldn't help but laugh. "Come on, let's get your ragtag group and these prisoners into the city. They've got a sweet new dark-haired girl at the House of Secrets and a room with my name on it tonight. I sure as fuck don't won't to waste my time with you when I could be fucking her now, do I?" Denshin was still roaring with laughter, as he mounted his horse and led the way to the city of Gaardsholme.

***

The terrain at the outskirts of Gaardsholme was marked by a serious of steep hills and lush valleys that were fed by numerous springs that gave rise to small rivulets on the slopes. The hills were covered in a sea of rich grass and the occasional stand of evergreen trees. This made it ideal land for the grazing of animals that belonged to the numerous farms that were dotted to either side of the road that led to the city. It was a beautiful, peaceful place and Brad's mind wandered as he kept pace with the inexorable march of the now swollen ranks of the Elite Guard. In much of the lower ground, grazing land gave way to arable farming and they passed many fields of corn and other crops which were less familiar to Brad. He surmised that Gaardsholme must be a pretty big city if it needed this amount of farmland to support it.

Something that had struck Brad since he entered this land was that animals, trees and plants seemed to be almost identical, if not identical, to those back home. It wasn't at all like some of the science fiction books that he had read as a teenager where everything was alien. He could hardly even refer to the people of this land as alien either. Their society, or at least as much of it as he had seen, was not too dissimilar to that of his home world, except that it seemed to be stuck in a time warp at a time just before the industrial revolution. Maybe that was it. The industrial revolution hadn't happened here because it didn't need to. This place had magic, and from what he could make out, magic could do all the things that science and technology could and more besides. So mechanisation wasn't needed and the society had probably stayed the same for centuries.

Brad was so caught up in his thoughts that at first he didn't notice the sight before him. They had just reached the peak of one of the larger hills and from this vantage point, he saw for the first time, the splendour of the City of Gaardsholme as it lay before them. He couldn't help but take a sharp intake of breath as he surveyed the magnificence of the garrison city which hugged the coast line for what must have easily been five miles or more in each direction. They were still several miles away, but even from this distance, the impressive stonewall that surrounded the city was plainly visible. Gaardsholme was a heavily fortified and formidable city. It appeared impregnable and drew its beauty from its austerity. Suddenly, the impossible enormity of the task that the destiny of the Dyroshin and the dark machinations of Zoryn, had set for him weighed impossibly on his shoulders.

"I can't do this." He mumbled more to himself than to anyone else. "I can't fucking do this." Fear and anger flared within him as this time he yelled the words. For the first time since Brad and Farric had been captured by the impassive Elite guard, they stopped as one and turned towards him. What they saw in him caused each soldier to step back a pace and draw their short swords, forming a ring of steel around him.

"Let me talk with him," Farric implored Droken. Both men were standing outside of the ring of Elite Guard. "If your orders are to bring him to your King alive, it's not looking too good right now. I've seen what he can do, and I think that you know what I'm talking about. There's gonna be a bloodbath if your men attack him."

Droken looked at Farric and then turned towards his men as he barked the order.

"Let Clearwater through."

The ring opened closest to Farric just enough to let him squeeze inside. Then without a further order from Droken, the ring closed again like a steel trap that had just been sprung. Farric could see the anger rising in Brad and knew that he was about to lose control.

"Don't do this, Brad. Remember what Velhanna told you. If we stand any chance of getting out of this, we have to see this thing through."

Brad wheeled to face him and for the first time Farric saw for himself the change in Brad's eyes which seemed to blaze and even from a few feet away Farric could see the iridescent zig-zagged, orangey-red coronas that surrounded the man's pupils. Farric felt a sensation that he had never felt before; his pulse quickened, his hands became clammy and he could hear his heart bounding. In that instant, he felt confusion and an inner conflict with the urge to flee competing with the urge to fight. For the first time in his life, Farric Clearwater felt fear. Although, it was an emotion that he had never experienced himself, he was no stranger to fear, having seen it in the eyes of his opponents hundreds of times during his life. He didn't care much for the sensation and fell back on his military training and his determination to stand firm. "If you attack these men Brad, all will be lost and you will never return to wherever the fuck you came from."

Farric's voice was the only sound and cut through the silence. Brad turned away from him as he looked into the faces of the men that surrounded him.

"I'm not going to attack anyone Farric, I'm tired, pissed off and fucking hungry and the last thing I want to do is fight," he said.

"I'm fucking hungry too. The rations that these twats eat is dog shit." Farric replied, as he sneered at the faces of the guards closest to him. "But I can tell you from experience that the food in the dungeons at Gaardsholme is much better than these twats eat."

"Then what are we waiting for?" Brad replied. "Let's get on with it!" The ring of Elite Guard broke up and the men quickly formed back into the same formation they had before Brad's outburst. The only difference this time was that they made a space so that Farric and Brad would finish the journey side by side, rather than being separated as they had been before. The Elite Guard resumed their familiar march with their escort of mounted guards and it was a half an hour or so before Farric broke the silence.

"I told you I liked that word," he said in a self-satisfied tone.

"What word?" Brad replied intrigued.

"Twat," replied Farric. "Did I use it the correct way?"

Chapter 67
Gaardsholme

They reached the great city of Gaardsholme at some time after midday. It was difficult to judge time in this place and as nobody seemed to care about it, it had little or no meaning here. Brad was tired and hungry. They had been marching at the accelerated pace of the Elite Guard for about three weeks by Brad's reckoning and he longed for the comfort of hot food and somewhere softer than the ground on which to sleep. A bath would have been nice too. He doubted that the prison in Gaardsholme would provide the luxuries he craved, but even a prison cell had to be an improvement on what he had endured on his journey to this place. He still found it ridiculous that he was to be locked-up like a criminal when he had done nothing, but in reality, he had been a prisoner from the day he first met Zoryn Dakor.

The city was surrounded by the sea on one side and a wall of some hard-grey rock that was easily twenty feet high on the other side and along its flanks. A pair of massive steel bound wooden gates stood open at the only visible entrance to the city. The gates ran to half the height of the wall and were easily two feet thick but no wider than ten feet across. If an attacking army ever breached the gates, the narrow entrance would slow the ingress of soldiers and would be easy to defend. The crenulations running along the top of the wall gave it the appearance of the maw of a savage beast that would consume any stupid enough to attack it.

Gaardsholme was the ancestral seat of power for the Five Lands. It was heavily fortified and was built to withstand a siege, which it had done on many occasions during its long history. Access from the sea was all but impossible too. The coastline behind the city was protected by a natural cliff, and where it gave way to lower ground, huge boulders and masonry fortifications, dotted with heavily fortified look-out towers, provided a formidable defence. The port itself was accessed by a narrow shallow channel of water a half mile long that was heavily defended and littered with razor sharp rocks. An attacking armada of ships would never make it through the channel without suffering crippling losses.

The gates of the garrison city were open but heavily guarded. As the group approached, they came to a stop twenty feet from the gate. Denshin Farrower dismounted and walked up to the guards with Droken Arrowsmith at his side. Brad couldn't hear what was said but after a short while, Denshin turned towards his men and nodded. At the unspoken command, his detachment of Elite Guard also dismounted and split into two smaller groups, one in front and the other to the rear of Droken's men and they all marched at a relaxed but purposeful pace into the city.

The city of Gaardsholme looked similar to Krendyra except that where Krendyra was opulent, Gaardsholme was utilitarian and bordered on the austere. The military presence was obvious; everything was ordered and organised. It was clear to Brad that the strategic importance of this place had dominated its history and growth.

The walk to the palace where Farric had told Brad they would be staying, as guests of the King, didn't take long once they had entered the city. They turned a sharp corner, following a line of more opulent but still somewhat austere houses, which clearly demarked an invisible boundary between the better off and worse off parts of the city. And then, in a clearing where there were no houses, the palace loomed in front of the group, seemingly growing in height as they approached. Brad assumed that no houses were allowed to be built too close to the palace so that lookouts and archers, stationed within its walls, would make this a killing ground if an enemy had managed to breach the outer defences of the city.

The palace itself looked more like a castle than the stately home Brad had expected would be the residence of the King of the Five Lands. The entrance to the palace was through an even narrower entrance, than that of the city gates, constructed of towering granite blocks with angular arrow-slits cut into the rough rock. An invading army would be cut to ribbons by archers if they attempted entry and the narrow entrance would soon become blocked by their dead. It was a formidable sight especially with the spiked portcullis currently down, blocking their entrance.

Five fully armoured men, with massive broadswords already drawn, stood a few feet inside the entrance. Brad's company came to a halt a dozen feet from the portcullis.

"Captain of the King's Guard," Denshin bellowed in the direction of the guards. "I am Denshin Farrower, and my companion is Droken Arrowsmith. We are both captains of the King's own Elite Guard. We bring prisoners as ordered by our King Sanjin Dakor. Will you stand down and allow entry?"

There was a moment of silence and then a sixth man appeared. Although wearing only light armour and carrying nothing more than a pair of throwing daggers strapped to his legs, there was something about this man that put Brad instantly on his guard.

"I know who you are," The other said in a voice that, although quieter, cut through the silence. "Our King is indeed looking forward to making the acquaintance of his *guests* and bids them *welcome*." He emphasised the words in a way that left Brad in little doubt that they were to be locked-up as prisoners. "Yes, we will permit entry but only to you and your prisoners, your men are to remain outside."

At a glance from Denshin, his men dismounted and joined ranks with Droken's Elite Guard. Drawing their weapons, they formed a circle of steel around Brad and Farric that was open in the direction of the palace. The men advanced slowly towards the portcullis forcing Brad and Farric to move in front of them.

"When they open the portcullis walk inside in single file, I will lead and Denshin will be behind you," Droken snarled at Farric and Brad. "The city is under heightened security and the captain of the King's Guard has the authority to cut you down where you stand if you make any attempt to escape, or if you do not co-operate. The man you see before you would take great pleasure in the act and he will react to the slightest provocation. I personally don't give a fuck what you do because in about two minutes you will be his problem, but try to live at least that long."

"Your concern is most touching, Droken!" Farric said without humour, as he mock curtsied. Droken head-butted him without warning, breaking his nose which erupted in a fountain of blood, but Farric stood his ground and did not move.

"What's this?" Droken asked looking to his men as he addressed Farric. "The Farric Clearwater I have heard of would never have been so easily struck. Maybe the stories aren't true and he really is the miserable, worthless piece of shit you see before you?" His men laughed.

"Maybe, Droken," Farric hissed. "I just wanted to see what you had for when we meet again, and as I suspected its fuck all."

Before Droken could respond, the portcullis started to rise silently and he turned towards it and walked through with Farric and Brad trailing him and Denshin bringing up the rear. As soon as they were inside, the portcullis dropped back into place soundlessly.

Chapter 68
Prisoner

Brad and Farric were taken straight to their cells which were at the bottom of an interminable descent of stone stairs. Although the weather had been comfortably warm outside, it was noticeably colder within the granite walls. They were put in separate cells. Brad had no idea how far apart the cells were as he was placed in the first cell and the door was locked behind him. However, he could hear footsteps continue for several long moments after and suspected that Farric's *accommodation* was too far away from his to allow them to speak with each other.

Farric Clearwater was not a man who enjoyed being indoors unless he had a beer in front of him and a women beside him. Even then, he rarely stayed inside longer than he had too. So being forced to walk through this subterranean passage to a prison cell did not put him in the best of humours. His guards walked him past many cells, some occupied and some not, and then to his surprise he looked at one of the cells and could see the face of Garan Smithson glaring out at him. "You and I have some business to settle, when I get out of this shithole," Farric snarled at the old man who looked like he had been badly beaten.

"Fuck off," was all he heard in reply as the guards forced him on to his own cell at the end of the corridor.

Brad's cell looked like it had been carved out of the very rock itself, which he considered likely as the cells must be a considerable depth below ground and there were no visible lines to suggest that bricks or stones had been used in its construction. The door was made of a dark, almost black, hardwood. It had a clear glass window about a foot square at head height which the guards could use to see into the cell without opening it. The glass was thicker than any he had seen before and had a faint translucency about it. There was no visible lighting, no candles, no lanterns of any description and yet there was light which led Brad to the conclusion that magic must have been employed in the construction of this place and that maybe the luminescence came from the rock of the cell itself. Any chance of escape appeared impossible. Not that he planned to, but his enforced incarceration was making him feel claustrophobic.

The only items in the cell were a hard bed, with the thinnest of blankets that felt rough to his touch, and a bucket. It was cold, bloody cold, and Brad pulled the blanket off the bed and wrapped it around himself in an effort to warm-up, not that it made much difference. With nothing else to do, he lay on the bed and thoughts of the impossibility of his plight washed over him, threatening to drown him.

How could Zoryn possibly believe that he could kill the King of a place as well defended as Gaardsholme? Did he really just expect him to walk up the man and kill him? And why the fuck, if he hated his brother that much, didn't he just do it himself? Unless Zoryn was completely insane, there had to be more to this. But what the fuck was really going on? And apart from anything else, Brad didn't even have the weapon that he was supposed to use to kill Sanjin Dakor. It had been taken off him when he had been captured by Droken and his men. Droken was hardly going to hand the knife back to him. And even if he had it and somehow against all the odds killed Sanjin Dakor, what then? Zoryn was never going to let him walk away from this.

Brad overheard Droken and Denshin talking as they approached the city earlier. From what they were saying, it would appear that his meeting with Sanjin Dakor would happen the following day. Did that mean that Zoryn would be expecting Brad to kill his brother then? As unlikely as it seemed, Brad was certain that Zoryn knew that he was a prisoner of the king, and that Sanjin Dakor would be back tomorrow. Brad's plan, such as it was, was that he would attempt to find a way to kill Zoryn, but that depended on Zoryn also being present. But what if he wasn't? What was he to do then?

Whatever happened tomorrow, Brad was certain that he wouldn't walk away from it alive. How could he? If he attempted to kill Sanjin Dakor, or even if he succeeded, he would almost certainly be cut down by his guards and that was assuming that he even got close enough to the man in the first place. After all, he was a prisoner and even if, by some fluke chance, he did get close enough, how was he going to kill him? He didn't have the weapon that Zoryn had made him travel halfway across this fucking country to get. From the little he knew about Sanjin Dakor, he gathered that he was a warrior King and he stood no chance against such a man.

Maybe the Black Metal would come to his aid and imbue him with the power it had before? Surely, that would be enough? Brad knew that the magic of the Black Metal was powerful enough to kill a man. In fact, with its assistance, he had already killed. But, with the exception of Raymond Oliver, that had been in self-defence. Could he call on its power to kill a man, who he had never even met, in cold blood? He was certain that the answer to that question was no.

If, somehow, he did manage to kill Sanjin Dakor, the magic of the Black Metal would probably come to his aid if the guards attacked him. But just how powerful was it? Brad doubted that any magic would be strong enough to protect him the sheer number of guards that a King would have at his disposal.

One thing, however, was certain. And that was that if he killed Sanjin, Zoryn was not going to come to his rescue and get him out of there before the guards killed him. Brad's death had to be a part of Zoryn's plan from the beginning. With Brad dead, a loose end was very neatly tied-up. And who could possibly prove that there was a link between Brad and Zoryn, particularly with him dead? The only people who knew were Farric, Garan Smithson and possibly Hania. Brad was certain that Farric would meet the same fate as he would himself; after all, he was another *loose end*. Although he could hardly describe Farric as a friend, he was the closest thing to a friend Brad had in this place and Farric would probably be stupid enough to try to help him if he was attacked.

Garan Smithson was a surly bastard and more than capable, despite his age, of standing up to any man. Brad doubted that Smithson cared enough about himself to be afraid of anyone and would probably relish the thought of pitting his skills against the might of Zoryn Dakor. But something was holding him back, Zoryn had some sort of hold over the man. It didn't take a genius to work out what that hold was. It was his beloved niece, Hania. Just the thought of her brought a vivid memory of her delicate form to his mind. Garan Smithson was also a link to Zoryn and another *loose end* that he would almost certainly eliminate.

Brad had no idea what time of day it was in his windowless cell. It was somewhere around midday when they arrived at Gaardsholme, but it felt a lot later now. He knew that he should get some sleep, that this would help to keep his wits sharp for tomorrow, but he doubted that sleep would come easily, if at all, this evening,

His thoughts turned to the possibility that Zoryn Dakor might actually be there tomorrow. After all, if he hated his brother that much, he would want to be there when he was killed? And if Zoryn was there, Brad had almost exactly the same set of impossible obstacles to overcome, except if anything it may be even worse. Brad had no idea if Sanjin had the use of magic. He suspected that even if he didn't, he would be surrounded by those that could protect him from a magical attack. He didn't, however, have Black Metal but Zoryn did.

Brad still had a slight advantage. Zoryn had implanted Black Metal into him. As magic didn't exist on Brad's world, Zoryn had no fear that Brad could possibly gain any control over its power and use it against him. And yet, as impossible as it seemed, Brad did appear to have some kind of innate magic and was able to call on the power of the Black Metal. He certainly didn't have control over it, but at least he could access at least some of its power. But would that be enough to defeat Zoryn Dakor?

At some time that evening, Brad must have finally fallen asleep because the next thing he knew was being awakened by the heavy footsteps of the armed guards who opened the door to his cell. The light from their burning torches was almost blinding after the dim light of the cell and phosphenes danced across his vision as he tried to focus. Three massive guards entered Brad's cell and he could hear more outside.

"Hold your arms out in front of you," a harsh voice commanded. "Do as I say or I will kill you where you stand."

Judging by the look on the man's face, Brad believed that he meant every word and did as he was commanded. As the heavy manacles were applied to his wrists, Brad felt the full weight of the impossible situation that he found himself in bear down on him, suffocating him in its completeness. The room started to spin and darkness gathered at the edges of his vision as despair came for him like a deadly assassin, and in that moment all hope was gone.

Chapter 69
Deception

Sanjin Dakor was not in the best of humours when he returned to Gaardsholme later that evening. He had spent the last week with his closest advisor, the redoubtable General Zanshin, inspecting his forces. Suspecting that the increase in skirmishes in the West may be a diversionary tactic by their foe, Sanjin had split his force in two to protect against an attack on his less well defended eastern flank. But other than some minor disturbances, the feared attack had not happened and Sanjin Dakor was beginning to doubt that it would. For months, they had been playing a *cat and mouse* game with their enemy and despite the strength of his forces and the brilliance of Zanshin and his other generals, Sanjin had not made any headway in ridding his kingdom of those that opposed him. Worse still, he had been fooled by his opponent, out-witted and he was furious.

Sanjin Dakor had sent reinforcements of cavalry and foot soldiers to his training garrison in the Zindaw Mountains. The garrison had been built centuries earlier to protect the White Metal mines and to keep the extraction of the rare and precious magical ore under the control of the crown. Stationed a day's ride from the western front, with the foot soldiers close behind, the plan was to deploy this rapid response unit if it was needed.

Within a matter of weeks the enemy launched its biggest attack on the least guarded section of Sanjin's western defences and punched through in great numbers, laying waste to all that stood before it. Villages were plundered and burned to the ground and crops were destroyed. Nothing survived the passing of this army. Zanshin executed his carefully laid plans and the forces stationed at the garrison in the Zindaw Mountains were deployed, and within three days the crown's forces had regained control of the area and killed most of the attackers.

The sheer ferocity of the enemy's attack had forced Sanjin to commit not just the extra cavalry and foot soldiers that were temporarily based at the garrison, but also nearly all the guards that were stationed there permanently, such was the threat. But Sanjin and his military advisers had been deceived, even though they were expecting a diversionary tactic from their enemy.

Sanjin believed that an attack from the West would draw his forces to it leaving the eastern flank of his kingdom dangerously exposed. Despite the military intelligence available to him, Sanjin didn't know the full size of the forces that opposed him. He couldn't take the risk that they may close in on his own forces on both flanks, preventing retreat and forming a killing field in between.

That decision turned out to be the biggest mistake in his otherwise flawless military career. The enemy had indeed planned a decoy attack just as predicted, but its goal had never been the routing of the Crown's armies and a military coup, it had been to launch a massive raid against the store of White Metal that had been stockpiled in the Zindaw mines. With only a skeleton guard remaining, the enemy fell on them, slaughtering everyone and making off with the entire stockpile of White Metal. Sanjin Dakor had unwittingly played right into the hands of his enemy and made them immeasurably more powerful in the process.

He lay awake in his bed in the royal palace. His mistress and head of the House of Secrets, Katzin, lay asleep at his side. Sleep did not come to him that evening. He had fucked-up massively and didn't deserve its soothing embrace. Because of his mistake, the Five Lands were in great peril. He swore to himself that he would atone for it by recapturing the stolen White Metal and make those that took it pay with their lives, even if it cost him his own in the process. He would use all the resources available to him to track the perpetrators down. With his network of spies, not least of which included Katzin and her House of Secrets, he was confident that he would eventually find those that were responsible.

But that was the problem, eventually. It needed to be resolved now, immediately, not later. He had to sort this out quickly before the White Metal could be sold or distributed, or whatever else his enemy had planned to do with it. If the whole thing had been a ruse and was just an elaborate robbery that was bad enough. But if his enemy planned to use the powerful magic of the White Metal against his forces, he doubted they could withstand such an attack. The only thing that gave him some degree of comfort was that he doubted that there were enough renegade magic users in the Five Lands with military experience around to wield it. But even if that was true, more could be trained and unlike him, they had time on their side. His best hope was that it had indeed been a well-planned robbery and that the Five Lands may well be at risk but would survive because the White Metal would be sold off and distributed far and wide. But, he had a nagging suspicion that somehow his brother was behind all this. There was nothing to implicate Zoryn, just Sanjin's feeling. He was also suspicious of the strange disappearance of both Zoryn and Kaiya.

And then, there was the matter of this stranger, the one called Bradley White. What drew him to Sanjin Dakor's attention was a first-hand account from one of Katzin's most trusted agents who saw him use a powerful magic without any visible White Metal. And if that wasn't unusual enough, no agent of the House of Secrets had been able to mind-skim him, despite their best efforts. Sanjin knew of no instance where that had happened before.

No one knew where this man came from and despite their best endeavours, Sanjin's scribes could find no record of his existence, either in the Five Lands or any of their allies This would have been enough to bring him in for questioning, but it was his association with the mercenary Farric Clearwater and his employment by Garan Smithson that intrigued Sanjin the most.

The agents of the House of Secrets had been able to mind-skim Farric Clearwater with ease, and early on they found out that he was to accompanying Bradley White to a rendezvous in Krendyra. Clearwater had been paid to make sure that White got to Krendyra for the meeting to take place. It was clear from the agent's mind-skims that Farric had been instructed to use whatever force was necessary to get him there. Although Katzin's agents were unable to mind-skim White, they were pretty certain that he had been coerced into making the journey.

Clearwater's services had been engaged by Garan Smithson who was well known to Sanjin. In fact, Sanjin's skill as a fighter was largely due to Smithson's savage but effective training style. But it didn't make sense, why would Smithson be behind such a scheme and what could possibly be in it for him? He would soon find out because his guards had brought a somewhat reluctant Garan Smithson into the palace, and right now he was locked up in the cells below, along with Bradley White and Farric Clearwater.

Sanjin couldn't help but smile when he heard the report of Smithson's arrest. He doubted that the man would come willingly so he sent a dozen of his regular soldiers to make the arrest. There had been a fight, as he had expected, but eventually the sheer force of numbers had overwhelmed even the talents of the legendary Garan Smithson and they managed to subdue him. It wasn't, however, without cost as now fully six of his soldiers were in the infirmary and at least one of these men was so badly injured that it was unlikely he would walk again without the aid of a stick.

What Sanjin Dakor was struggling to understand was why, with his apparent magical abilities, did White go with Clearwater to Krendyra? It just didn't make any sense. Sanjin realised from the first report that this matter merited his personal attention. However, he decided to let it play out to see where it was going rather than arrest both men at the earliest opportunity. He suspected that his brother's hand may be involved with whatever was going on despite his absence.

Following the capture of White and Clearwater, a report reached Sanjin that a strange black knife had been confiscated from the men by his Elite Guard. Droken Arrowsmith, captain of the detachment, described the blade as a relatively small knife, about the length of the palm of his hand made entirely of a black metallic looking substance that was blacker than anything he had seen before. Could this blade be made of the mythical Black Metal? Sanjin must have asked himself this question a thousand times since he had read the report. He had not had chance to view the object himself and would deal with the matter tomorrow.

If White and Clearwater had got themselves into a scheme where Black Metal was involved, his brother Zoryn must be behind it. But, even that didn't make sense because surely Zoryn would never let a substance as rare and powerful as Black Metal, if it even existed, out of his sight? None of this made any sense and Sanjin's normally clear head swam with possibilities.

"My liege." A voice as smooth as silk and as ripe with promise as the finest red wine interrupted his ruminations. Katzin was awake. Sanjin had no idea what time it was but as the skies beyond the windows of his room were just beginning to lighten it was approaching dawn. He had been awake all night and not for the first time, he had hardly slept in the last week since the raid.

"Your cares lay heavy on you, my King. You didn't sleep at all last night. Come join me and get some rest. I'm sure that whatever is troubling you can wait just a little while. You have more pressing matters that require your personal attention!"

Katzin was the only person in his court that would presume to speak to him in such a manner. Sanjin glanced over to where she lay next to him in bed. Somehow, the crisp white sheet that should have preserved her modesty barely covered her feline-like grace, revealing a very long and perfectly formed golden brown leg. She smiled seductively at her lover and moved her leg slightly causing the sheet to fall away to reveal her naked beauty. All thoughts of magic-wielding strangers and Black Metal left the King of the Five Lands mind as he fell into his mistress's embrace. She welcomed him utterly, wrapping herself around him, offering all that she had to give to her lover and he accepted.

She teased and tormented him. None from the House of Secrets was more skilled in the art of love than Katzin. She prolonged their lovemaking until he could take no more and threw her on her back taking her hard and fast. His climax a battle cry, but one in which both were victorious. Utterly spent, he rolled over and fell instantly to sleep which had been Katzin's plan all along. "Maybe now, my beloved Sanjin, you will get a little rest," she whispered quietly, as she kissed his handsome face and curled around his massive frame.

Several hours later, breakfast was brought in by the palace servants. Katzin had already risen and bathed and dismissing the servants, she gently woke her lover. Sanjin sat bolt upright instantly. "What time is it? How long have I been asleep?" he demanded.

"Still early my liege and not nearly long enough, but I guess it will have to do," she replied, "have some food, my King," she said offering a plate of cold meat and cheese to him. "Even Kings must eat!"

Chapter 70
The Palace

Bradley White paid little attention to the details around him during his forced march through the labyrinth of tunnels beneath the palace of the ruler of the Five Lands. He was a prisoner, and the heavy manacles that shackled his wrists bore testament to the futility of any resistance. Not that he would resist, even if he could. He had come this far, he might as well see it through, besides what choice did he have? There was no fight left inside him. Before he thought that he might have stood a chance, albeit slim, but now he was here and the reality of the situation was staring him in the face, he knew that he didn't. He was up against insurmountable odds, and people and powers that were beyond his feeble abilities. He never stood a chance and was a fool to have thought otherwise. After all, he was a drug's rep not a warrior. His enemies were born to this life in a land where magic existed. And, he was a long way from home. An incalculably long way from home, a world where magic didn't exist.

He was led through a series of seemingly endless corridors, and apart from the guards that formed his escort, he didn't see another person. Not that he cared. Right now, he didn't care about anything. But as they ascended towards the ground floor of the palace, there was more activity. When they passed through a heavily guarded doorway that led out of the subterranean passages that housed the cells, there were people everywhere. Or so it appeared to Brad. After having been locked away for what he assumed must have been less than twenty-four hours, where all he could hear was the sound of his own breathing, the sight of all these people seemed unreal to him. It was as if he had been transported to yet another strange land. He stood motionless just inside what he assumed must be the palace's main reception room. Still more utilitarian than ornate, the room was breathtaking in size and its high vaulted ceiling only added to the effect. He was certain that he had not passed through this room the previous day when he had been taken to his cell.

"This way, move or I'll fucking run you through where you stand." A gruff voice said as he was roughly pushed from behind. The magic of the Black Metal instantly flared inside him, burning away all fear and despair. Brad wheeled on the guard with such force and speed that the man didn't have time to reach for his short sword which hung limply at his side still in its sheath. The other guards looked on dumbly, too slow to react.

"Keep your fucking hands off me." Brad snapped at the guard. The power of the Black Metal coursing through his veins, urging him on, intoxicating him in its desire for release. The guard reached for the pommel of his sword but as he did so, he looked into the eyes of his prisoner and halted in his tracks. He was paralysed with fear as he saw the zig-zagged, orangey-red coronas in the eyes of the man who stood before him.

Brad fought desperately for control over his emotions, over his body, over the power of the Black Metal that was threatening to consume him. With a supreme act of self-control, he turned around and started to walk slowly in the direction he had been shoved only moments earlier.

The guards resumed their silent march, bemused by what had just happened and surprised that their sergeant hadn't struck the prisoner for such a display of defiance. They knew better than to take matters into their own hands and strike the prisoner themselves, that was a privilege that belonged to their sergeant. He had a reputation for dealing with any subordinate who over-stepped the mark, in the old-fashioned way which generally ended up with them having an extended stay in the infirmary. There would be plenty to talk about in the barracks later.

Up to this point, Brad and his armed escort had been all but unnoticed by those going about their way in the great palace of Gaardsholme. But now, every eye was on the stranger. It was then that he saw her. Amongst the sea of faces before him, Brad's eyes met with those of Hania. She smiled a thin worried smile at him and in that moment time stood still as he held her gaze. The fire he had felt from the flames of the Black Metal were as nothing compared to the flame that burned within him for Hania. Although his heart yearned for her, he didn't stop, he couldn't take the risk that the guards might be stupid enough to strike him again. He couldn't risk that the Black Metal could take him over and lay waste to all around him which could include his beloved Hania.

Hania didn't seem surprised to see him here, or if she was surprised, she hid it remarkably well. He wondered why she was here, maybe Garan Smithson had been arrested too. If he was then Sanjin Dakor must have found out that Farric had been hired by Garan. Brad doubted that Farric would discuss his business with anyone, and he was certain that Garan wouldn't either. And if Sanjin had made that connection, then did he also know that his brother Zoryn was behind everything? Brad suspected that Sanjin knew some, but not all of the detail which was why they had been arrested. It crossed Brad's mind that Sanjin's guards might resort to torture to find out more, but so far he had been treated relatively well, a little harsh perhaps, but these were a hard people so that didn't surprise him much.

The throng of people went silent as the guards stopped a few feet in front of a large wooden door that was every bit as sturdy as the entrance gate to the palace, but much shorter in height and wider to facilitate the ingress and egress of people into the room that lay beyond. But unlike everything he had seen so far in the palace, which was utilitarian in design and function, this door was highly polished, had the appearance of the finest quality rosewood and was exquisitely carved. Tableaus were etched into the grain of the wood with scenes that Brad assumed depicted major battles and events in the history of this place.

Six guards stood outside the door, two in front of the door itself and these were flanked by a further two on each side. Each wore a tabard of royal blue with an insignia across their chests of a fierce brown hawk with its talons extended swooping in for the kill. Patches of highly polished chain mail protected their shoulders and below they wore dark brown, loose-fitting trousers of a heavy looking material. Brad assumed that this was the ceremonial dress of the Elite Guard, but as with everything he had seen in Gaardsholme, their clothing was utilitarian and would not hinder them in battle. He recognised the men as being those belonging to Droken Arrowsmith's command but only half seemed to be present.

"Who approaches the great Chamber?" Both guards that were standing outside the door took a step forward in unison as one of them issued the challenge.

"The palace guard requests access to bring the prisoner Bradley White to the King's Court."

Two of the ceremonially dressed Elite Guard walked towards Brad and took the places of the palace guards. The Elite Guard who had spoken first, pulled his short sword from its leather scabbard in a stylised way that reminded Brad of movies he had seen were a samurai warrior drew his sword. He made eye contact with Brad, issuing a further challenge that this time did not need words to convey its meaning. Holding his gaze for several long moments, the guard wheeled about and approached the door once again, and raising his sword, struck the door hard with its hilt.

In the silence of the vast chamber, the blow sounded like a thunderbolt. Several moments passed, and then without warning a white light appeared at the middle of the top of the door and quickly ran down its length as the door opened into two symmetrical halves from the centre. The men who had been guarding the door moved to either side of the now open entrance and Brad was led through the doorway by the guards flanking him. As soon as they were inside, the door slammed shut behind them and once again, it was solid and seamless.

Chapter 71
The King of the Five Lands

Soldiers from the Elite Guard stood on either side of the ornate door inside the chamber and Brad recognised them as being from Denshin Farrower's command. He was taken to the centre of the room where he was made to stand next to Farric Clearwater who gave him a crooked smile as he took his place. They were separated by a guard and a heavily bruised Garan Smithson stood by Farric's other side again separated by a guard. The guards wore the same ceremonial dress as those that stood outside the chamber and those that guarded the inside, but these men were from Droken Arrowsmith's command.

The chamber itself reminded Brad of the main lecture theatre at the university that he attended after leaving school. There were rows of seats on five levels in a sweeping semi-circle with the area that the company occupied being at its epicentre. In the middle of the seated area, at the highest level, was a single seat that gave it a commanding view of proceedings. It was currently unoccupied but Brad had little doubt that this seat belonged to Sanjin Dakor.

Brad didn't know what to expect but was somewhat surprised by the relatively small number of people in the chamber. There were no more than ten seated and perhaps another dozen guards who stood around the entrance. Of those seated two-thirds were men and all appeared to be relatively old, with one striking exception. A dark-skinned woman in her mid-thirties, with piercing green eyes and exquisite features, eyed him with the precision and calculated look of a hawk that was about to strike. She smiled as he met her gaze and in that moment, Brad felt as if she could see inside him and could sense his innermost thoughts. He assumed that these people must be Sanjin Dakor's most trusted advisers, and judging by their small number it would appear that the King intended to keep matters private. The chamber was in silence and all were observing the three captives. Some quizzically, and others barely containing their contempt. *This isn't going to be a pleasant experience,* he thought, *however it turns out.*

In the silence Brad observed those that were studying him and made eye contact with several. He didn't know how, but he was certain that he could sense magic emanating from some of Sanjin's advisers. It stood to reason that in a kingdom where magic was commonplace, at least some of the King's advisers would be magic users themselves. It was also likely that these were to be amongst the highest skilled in the Five Lands. The confidence that the flush of power that the Black Metal had given him only scant minutes earlier drained away at the overwhelming enormity of what lay before him. But that wasn't all that was troubling him, something wasn't right. One of the faces staring down at him seemed familiar, which surely couldn't be possible? He had never been to this place and there was no way that he could have seen any of these people before. And yet he felt certain that he knew this man from somewhere, but he just couldn't place where.

"All stand, His Royal Highness the King of the Five Lands enters the chamber." A disembodied voice bellowed, shattering the silence and Brad's ruminations. Glancing over his shoulder, he saw that the voice belonged to Droken Arrowsmith who was standing next to his friend and comrade in arms Denshin Farrower.

Everyone stood as Sanjin Dakor entered the room and took his seat. Brad was immediately struck by how similar Sanjin Dakor was to his brother. Both looked like they were in their late thirties, maybe even early forties and they shared the same jet-black hair and dark skin. Sanjin was easily over six feet tall and looked every inch the military leader. In this land, it would appear, Kings fought alongside their men in battle which was something that hadn't happened for centuries back in Brad's world. Sanjin wore a chest plate of what appeared to be an impossibly white substance that had the appearance of metal, but Brad had never seen metal like it before.

This is what White Metal must look like, he thought. He had not seen it before and it was stunning to behold.

Where Sanjin was notably different to his brother was in the way he looked at those around him. Before he sat down, which was the signal for the others to do likewise, he made eye contact with several of those assembled. Sanjin's gaze was welcoming and accepting. However, by his overall demeanour and the deference afforded to him, there was no doubt who was in charge, as the King of the Five Lands took his seat.

This was the first time that Sanjin Dakor had seen Bradley White. White appeared pretty much as Katzin had described him based on the reports she had received from her spies at The House of Secrets. Nobody other than Katzin and Sanjin knew of the existence of this network of spies, and how well it had served the crown over the years.

There was nothing remarkable about White's appearance and he could easily be lost in a crowd. And yet, something about the man wasn't right, was out of place. It was like he just didn't belong here. And not just here, in the King's Court, but in the very land itself. But whatever it was about the man that made Sanjin think this, it wasn't obvious. It was a feeling, but Sanjin Dakor trusted his feelings, after all, they had saved his life on more than one occasion in the past.

Sanjin glanced over to where his mistress Katzin sat and with an almost imperceptible nod of her head, she signalled that she couldn't detect any signs of magic from their prisoner. Katzin was a natural empath and was Sanjin's most skilled adviser when it came to sensing the presence of magic in others. Sanjin noticed that she had a frown on her face, as she studied this man and suspected that she too sensed the strangeness that he had.

The three prisoners stood in silence looking up at the great leader. Glancing to either side Brad could see that Farric seemed relaxed and as confident as ever.

Does nothing unsettle this man? He thought. Whereas Garan, despite his obvious injuries, glared at the King and looked like a coiled spring that was straining for release and was bent on destruction. What a strange bunch they must seem to this man who had brought them here.

"Where are my Captains?" Sanjin Dakor demanded.

"Here, Sire." Both said in unison as they stepped around the prisoners to face their King.

"And which one of you has the blade?"

"I do," said Droken Arrowsmith, as he took one step forward holding the black knife across his open palms offering it up so that his King could see it clearly. Sanjin looked at the blade without leaving his seat. If he was as mesmerised by the impossible blackness of the blade as Brad was, he gave no hint of it in his demeanour.

Turning his gaze to Brad, he looked at him clinically as if measuring him up. His gaze was hard and direct but when Brad momentarily locked eyes with him he didn't detect any malice from the other. "You." Sanjin Dakor said at last. "Who are you, where do you come from and why are you here?"

Oddly, the simplicity and directness of the King's questions caught Brad completely by surprise. He didn't know what to expect but suspected that he may have been accused of something, or maybe even tortured. He knew that he must have broken laws in this land, particularly as he and Farric had killed some of those that had attacked them, even though they had acted in self-defence. Brad felt certain that the justice in this land was almost certainly metered out by the King and would be swift and harsh. These were a hard people and he would be surprised if their legal system was anything like it was back home.

How could he answer the King truthfully? Surely, talk of coming from another world would brand him as a mad man, and every word he uttered afterwards would be dismissed accordingly? And then, there was the reason he had been brought to this land by Zoryn Dakor, the King's brother. Brad was heavily manacled, surrounded by Elite Guards and without the weapon that Zoryn had sent him on such a long and now pointless journey to collect, how could he possibly attack and kill Sanjin Dakor? Even if somehow, he managed to free himself and launch an attack, the King was formidable and must have had years of military training and would easily over-power him. And if Brad, by some lucky break, did kill Sanjin Dakor and achieve Zoryn's desired goal, what then? For certain, he would be killed by the Elite Guard and would never know if his beloved wife and son were free from the clutches of Zoryn.

"I am not from these parts and I am not acquainted with your customs. If I have broken some law or caused offence in any way, it was not intended and I offer my apologies." The salesman in him took over, playing for time so he could find space to think and maybe even survive this encounter.

"Why do you think I have summoned you here with your friends?" Sanjin asked flatly.

"They are not my friends. Farric is known only to me because he acted as my guide through these lands on a recent trip I had to make."

"And Garan Smithson? How exactly is he known to you?" And there it was, the killer punch. Brad knew that his next answer was critical.

"He knows me because I kicked his fucking ass. That's how he knows me." Garan Smithson growled before Brad could respond. In actual fact, what he said was technically correct, Smithson had kicked his ass on many occasions during Brad's enforced stay with him.

"And why would you want to kick this man's ass?" Sanjin continued his direct line of questions.

"He had his eye on my niece. The filthy piece of shit. What does a man his age want with a girl like her? We don't need the likes of him sniffing around our farm, so I suggested that he left us alone." Smithson replied glaring at Brad.

"And is this true, Bradley White?"

"Yes, I do have feelings for his niece, not that it's any of his business, and yes we ended up in a fight."

"It takes two to fight, you fucking scum, and you never got the chance to lift your fists, next time I will kill you." Smithson declared keeping in character with his story.

"You don't change, do you Garan?" The King asked rhetorically. "Threatening another in the King's Court isn't the smartest thing you've ever done, but by no means the dumbest."

"I will kill him."

"Silence," Sanjin shouted, his voice like thunder but his expression composed, "if you open your mouth once more without my permission, I will hold you in contempt and have you flogged in public until you learn your lesson, which in your case I suspect will take a very long time."

"Farric Clearwater, how do you know Bradley White? And before you answer, don't feed me the same pack of lies that Garan Smithson has." Sanjin turned his attention to Farric.

"I was hired to act as his guide and protector for a journey to Krendyra." Farric replied. Both Farric and Brad had not technically lied so far and there was an element of truth in what Garan had said, even though Sanjin didn't believe him. Yusana had warned Brad that Sanjin would have advisers whose magical abilities would include being able to detect if a prisoner was telling the truth or lying. Brad's reasoning was that the closer he kept his story to the truth the more likely it was to be believed, at least to some degree anyway.

"Who hired you, Clearwater?"

"In my line of work, it is unwise to reveal the name of those you do business for." Farric replied and then collapsed to his knees as the guard closest to him punched him in the ribs with his chainmail covered fist. Ignoring this, Sanjin Dakor turned his attention back to Brad.

"So why did you *need to go* to Krendyra? If you are not from these lands, then you must have had a pretty good reason to travel first here and then on to Krendyra. So, what was your business there?"

"I'm a salesman, a merchant of sorts, and I'm looking to expand my trade into these lands." Brad was a salesman, so in part his reply contained some truth.

"And what do you sell? I'm sure that my own merchants would be most interested, so please indulge me and tell me more."

"I sell…" Brad was struggling to keep this pretence going. "I sell medicines."

"And what exactly is medicine?" It hadn't occurred to Brad that Sanjin Dakor wouldn't know what medicine was. After all people must fall ill in this place and require treatment?

"Medicines are preparations made from herbs and other plants and minerals that are given to sick people to help them get better."

"In the Five Lands, we do not make our sick eat weeds like a pig. Do you not have healers where you come from?" Sanjin replied incredulously. "I've never heard of such a place. So I ask you again Bradley White, who are you, where do you come from and why are you here? This time I caution you to tell me the truth. Whilst I have found our discourse amusing, it begins to tire me and I will have the truth. But before I do, let me tell you what I think."

This was the moment that Brad had been afraid of. Their story was at best weak and Sanjin Dakor clearly saw right through it. At some unseen command, the Elite Guard that stood by the entrance took a step forward and each man withdrew his short sword. Whilst their uniforms may have appeared ceremonial, their swords looked anything but.

"We believe that you are not from these lands, that much is self-evident." Sanjin looked at Brad as he spoke. "Farric Clearwater is well known to the crown and will sell this sword to the highest bidder, which on this occasion was Garan Smithson. He was hired to make sure you made it to Krendyra, whether you wanted to go there or not. The crown is of the opinion that you went against your will, but you did not appear to have tried to escape. And you," he said, addressing Garan Smithson directly. "Are a

277

poor liar. I have no doubt that you were protecting your niece, but I don't believe that the threat was coming from this man.

Bradley White, you have brought back an object from Krendyra that, if it is what it appears to be, has incalculable value and would corrupt the most honest of men. Someone has a hold over you or is threatening someone, or something, that in your eyes has an even higher value. So, who is behind this and what are they planning to do?"

While Sanjin was talking, Denshin Farrower held the black knife up for all in the chamber to see.

Beads of perspiration formed on Brad's brow as he struggled to find answers that would de-escalate the situation that was growing in tension by the second. This was it. This was the moment that had been inevitable from the instant that he had been torn away from his family and his previous life and thrown into this accursed land. The detached feeling that had accompanied previous confrontations seemed to elude him now. Maybe it only kicked-in when his life was in danger? He was certainly in danger now and the threat was real, but it wasn't a physical threat at least not yet.

That's it, Brad thought. *The magic of the Black Metal isn't sentient and can't detect an implied threat. It can only respond to a physical attack.*

Realising this didn't make Brad feel any better, but it did help to explain things. The salt from his sweat blurred his vision as beads of perspiration ran into his eyes. He looked up at the King and blinked to clear his sight. The heavy manacles and the presence of the guard beside him prevented him from raising his hands to wipe his eyes. The old man he had noticed earlier, who seemed familiar, sat in the closest seat to that of the King.

"Well?" The growing impatience of the King was clear in his voice. But Brad was distracted. The man beside Sanjin Dakor was staring intently at him, waiting for him to respond to the King. If anything, his gaze was even more intense than Sanjin Dakor's, as if Brad's reply was even more important to him. For those looking on Brad seemed to be lost for words, momentarily stunned, like a wild animal caught in the headlights of a car. And then Brad's eyes locked with those of the old man and he saw nothing but malice and hatred in his manic stare, and in that instant he knew for certain that it was Zoryn Dakor.

"Your highness." Brad shouted to warn the King. "You are in grave and immediate danger." But his warning was too late.

Suddenly, everything seemed to happen at once. Denshin Farrower drew his sword, seemingly in defence of his King but instead of rushing to his side, he charged at his friend Droken Arrowsmith and ran him through before his own sword was out of its scabbard. Droken was dead before he hit the floor. The other men from Denshin's command took this as a signal and attacked the Elite Guard that were loyal to Droken. Droken's men didn't stand a chance. They were outnumbered and were not expecting an attack from their own. They fought with the ferocity of their Elite Guard training and killed several of Denshin's men and inflicted grievous injuries on others before they were all killed.

Brad and his fellow prisoners were in the centre of this killing frenzy but were manacled and unable to do anything but observe the maelstrom around them. Sanjin's advisers were desperately trying to get out of the chamber but were cut down and slaughtered by Denshin's men before they could get to the great door. Brad couldn't see the dark-skinned woman that had been amongst them and wondered if she had managed to escape. He was powerless, the Black Metal within him still not responding.

As Brad had expected Sanjin Dakor was a warrior and with his own sword drawn, he launched himself at Denshin Farrower. Before he could reach him, Farrower threw the black knife at the old man. Farrower was arguably the most fearsome warrior in the Elite Guard and he stood his ground after the initial clashing of swords with his King. But Sanjin Dakor was a powerful, highly skilled and relentless warrior and quickly wore Denshin down. Reacting to a feint attack, Denshin misjudged the king's true intent and let him through his guard. Sanjin Dakor ran his sword through the man. Remarkably, Denshin found the strength in his dying breath to plunge a blade that had appeared in his hands, as if from nowhere, into the King's chest. As the blade made contact, it exploded into shards without leaving so much as a mark on Sanjin's Dakor's White Metal chest plate.

As this was happening, Brad saw the old man catch the black knife with impossible speed. In the instant that he caught the blade, the air shimmered around him, like heat rising from a parched desert landscape, and in the place of the old man stood Zoryn Dakor. Brad had only seen the man once in his natural form but knew beyond any doubt that it was him.

"Brother," Zoryn Dakor shouted, "your reign has come to an end."

"Zoryn," Sanjin howled in anger as he ran to face his brother, "you are a traitor to the crown and to our people." The clash of swords sent a ripple like a seismic wave throughout the chamber. Zoryn had drawn his own short sword and the black knife was nowhere to be seen. They were evenly matched and it was impossible to tell who would emerge triumphant. If anything, Sanjin seemed to have the edge, but Zoryn was relentless in his attacks, paying scant regard to defence as he launched attack after attack. Surely, he would tire soon, Brad thought, no one could sustain this for long. But he didn't tire. The magic of the Black Metal that was inside him, sustained him. The King, however, was beginning to tire and his defences were slower and more laboured as Zoryn's attacks continued unabated. And then without warning, Zoryn's blade shattered during a fearsome overhead attack. Sanjin should have finished him then but for some reason he faltered. Maybe it was some misplaced love for his younger brother. But whatever the reason, it turned out to be a fatal mistake. The black knife appeared in Zoryn's hands and he drove it through Sanjin's White Metal chest plate. Like a hot knife through butter the White Metal yielded to the midnight blade as it cut straight through into the heart of the King. In an explosion of crimson fire, the Black Metal knife absorbed the magic of the White Metal in an instant, turning it to ashes as it absorbed its magical power.

Zoryn withdrew the blade and let it fall to the floor of the chamber. Holding the dying king to him Zoryn said, "You were never meant to rule, my brother." And then he released his body, letting it fall to the floor in a last display of the contempt in which he held his sibling.

The fighting in the chamber had stopped and the only people left standing were Brad and Garan Smithson, half a dozen of Denshin Farrower's men and Zoryn. Farric lay unmoving on the floor with a wicked looking cut to his head.

"Long live the King," shouted one of the guards as they all sank to one knee in supplication to their new ruler. "Long Live Zoryn Dakor, King of the Five Lands."

Chapter 72
Black Metal

"Did you really think that you could stand against me and hope to get away with your life?" Zoryn snarled at Brad. "I will kill you where you stand. But before I do, aren't you forgetting something?"

"Like what?" Brad hissed, barely controlling his rage.

"Do you forget your wife and son so easily?"

"They are safe, Zoryn." Brad spat the other's name as if it was poison in his mouth. "They are beyond your reach, somewhere you will never find them."

"Fool, no one is safe from me. I reached into your world and made you my slave and I can do it again. What makes you think I can't reach back there and end their lives now?"

"Because for all your so-called power, this is one thing you cannot do. Maybe it is you Zoryn, who is the fool after all."

"We shall see about that." Zoryn snarled as he closed his eyes.

Brad could hear the low, barely audible, sound of his chanting and could feel the static charge of Zoryn's magic building in the very air of the room around him. His skin started to itch as if it was covered in thousands of angry stinging ants.

He can summon the magic without having the Black Metal in his hands, Brad thought to himself, doubt creeping into his mind. *He must have it inside himself too, maybe I have underestimated him.* But it was too late for second thoughts now.

Zoryn's chanting increased in tempo and pitch as the static charge around him grew and grew in intensity. The air crackled as if in anticipation of a massive discharge of pent-up energy. The itching Brad felt just moments earlier increased in intensity tenfold until it felt like the flesh was being flayed from his bones.

And then a faint image appeared on a wall about ten feet behind Zoryn. Except that this wasn't an ordinary image, it was Brad's world that he saw increasing in clarity as it coalesced before him. Zoryn had reached into the portal of Dakor's Darkness and created a bridge between the two worlds with his magic.

All Brad had to do was to enter the image and he would be back home. For the first time in all the months he had been held captive in this land, he saw his chance to go home. It was agonisingly close and tore at his heart, but he knew that he couldn't go back now and that he would probably never get another chance.

He knew without any doubt that if he fled back to his world, Zoryn would follow him and kill Gina, David and himself. Brad didn't care much about his own fate right now, but he couldn't bring the vengeance of Zoryn down onto his family. In that moment, he knew what he had to do and was prepared to pay any price to keep them safe, even if that meant he would never see them again, even if it meant his own death. Brad was not by nature a brave man, but mercifully one of the effects of the Black Metal that had fused with his body was the detachment that he felt now.

As the image coalesced Brad recognised the scene, it was the hospital where Gina and David were being treated. The image came into sharp focus and he could see his beloved wife laying in her hospital bed. Her face was as beautiful as the day they first met but she looked so small and vulnerable as she slept. Glancing down for a moment, Brad saw the black knife that lay a few feet in front of him was starting to glow red at the edges. It was absorbing some of Zoryn's magic, just like Velhanna said it would. But would it absorb enough of his magic to sever Zoryn's link to Brad's home world and free Gina and David? And would Zoryn sense what was happening? Brad fought to control his thoughts in case Zoryn could read his mind and work out what he was planning to do.

"Do you see your wife, Bradley White?" Zoryn stopped chanting as the image cleared. "I would have killed you of course, but I would have let your wife and son live had you done my bidding. Their lives mean nothing to me and I wouldn't have wasted my time going back to your world to kill them. But by your own words, you have sentenced them to death. Before I kill you, I want you to see them suffer and die knowing that you caused this to happen and that you were powerless to help them."

"You really are a brave man, aren't you *Lord Zoryn?*" Brad spat the words in disgust. The calmness of mind wrought by the Black Metal helping him to keep his rage under control so that he didn't reveal his hand to his enemy. "Killing a woman in a coma in her hospital bed and a boy that has been crippled by one of your people. Maybe your people will immortalise this day in song you fucking cunt, Zoryn the brave who kills women and cripples."

Zoryn nodded at one of his guards who punched Brad in the stomach with his chain mailed fist. Brad would have fallen to his knees with the force of the blow but the guards on either side of him held him firm. As he looked up, Brad's vision erupted into a thousand shooting stars as his attacker hit him with a vicious back handed slap clean across his face. Blood poured from Brad's nose.

"Your death will be a slow and torturous one and will be one that I will enjoy above all others." Zoryn's words dripped with malice.

Zoryn took a step toward the image and it was clear to Brad that Zoryn was going to walk into the vision to enter his home world and kill his wife and son, just like he had threatened to do. Brad had to stop him, and he had to do it now.

Velhanna had told him that the black knife could absorb magical power and the strange reddish glow around its edges seemed to testify to this. But she also said that it had never been used against anyone as powerful as Zoryn. It was his family's only chance of escape from the clutches of Zoryn and even then, the odds of it working were slim if not none at all.

Brad knew that if there was any way to stop Zoryn, he would need the power of the black knife. He wasn't sure that he could harness the magic within him sufficiently without it. But how was he going to get it with the guards and Zoryn watching his every movement? If he was to attempt to grab the knife, he would have to do so quickly and even then, it was unlikely that he would be able to reach it in time.

But then without warning, assistance came to him from the most unlikely place.

Garan Smithson had been silent throughout the slaughter in the King's Court, dodging the occasional sword thrust that had gotten a little too close, but other than that, he had not moved. He was still closely guarded, as were Brad and Farric, but he caught the guards completely by surprise. Garan dived to the ground and with his hands still manacled, somehow managed to grab the black knife. As he got to his knees, one of the guards ran his short sword through Garan Smithson's chest, an attack that he would normally have easily evaded. But Garan had ignored the inevitability of the attack, giving his own life in the process, as he gained just enough time to throw the blade to Brad. "Save my niece." Were the last words of Garan Smithson as he locked eyes with Brad and then fell the short distance to the floor.

The guard that had killed Garan wheeled on Brad, swinging his sword as he did so at Brad's head. It was his last act. Brad caught the knife and with his hands still manacled, instinctively raised the knife in an effort to stop the guard's sword making contact. The moment the guard's blade made contact with the black knife the power of the Black Metal flared into life engulfing the soldier where he stood in a fury of crimson fire. He died too quickly to shout out in shock or pain. Brad turned the blade in his hand and like a hot knife through butter, he cut through his shackles.

Zoryn halted in mid-step as his guards raised the alarm. Summoning his magic, he hurled a bolt of power as black as midnight at Brad. The force of the attack should have killed Brad instantly, but he had the knife in his hands and the detached feeling that had come to his aid countless times already, allowed him space to raise the blade in front of him and it absorbed the magic of Zoryn's attack. Zoryn raised his fist a second time unleashing another magical bolt that he hammered towards Brad, and again the blow was absorbed by the knife. This time Zoryn saw the object in Brad's hands clearly and could see the flaming red edges of the knife that was as black as his own heart. "I have been betrayed," he howled, as he unleashed another and then another bolt of magic, reigning strike after strike at Brad.

As the bolts struck, Brad was rocked by the convulsive power of each detonation, but he managed to hold the blade before him as it absorbed more and more of Zoryn's power

"It ends here Zoryn," Brad howled with rage as he ran towards the image of the hospital. He gave up his struggle to control the power of the Black Metal as it surged through his body and embraced it utterly, giving himself up to its savage might. The zig-zagged, orangey-red coronas surrounding his pupils burned with the magic of the Black Metal.

"How can this be?" Zoryn screamed with rage as he threw another midnight bolt of magic at Brad. "You don't have magic, you cannot use Black Metal, I will kill you."

Brad was now standing less than five feet from Zoryn. Each blast that Zoryn threw at him made Brad stronger and Zoryn weaker. Brad wanted to strike back, wanted to pitch his might against Zoryn in a battle to the death, but he couldn't take the chance, even though his very being was screaming at him to strike back.

Brad threw the glowing blade at the ground by Zoryn's feet, directly in front of the vision. The blade exploded into a million shards of crimson power and each shard detonated with cataclysmic force. Brad was close to the conflagration and was hurled by the might of the explosion into a stone pillar ten feet or more behind him. Black spots were crowding his vision as he felt his consciousness ebb away. Through the darkness that was threatening to engulf him, he saw Gina open her eyes in shock and then the vision shattered like glass, breaking forever Zoryn's link with Brad's world.

The room had been all but destroyed by the blast and the pillar that Brad had been hurled against was now only a pile of rubble. Brad couldn't see Zoryn's body but he had to be dead, nobody could have survived being that close to the explosion. "Fuck you, Zoryn." Brad's body was broken by the impact and his voice was thick with blood and barely a whisper as the world where he had been held prisoner went black.

Epilogue

Gina White woke up in her hospital bed. The starchy white sheets reluctantly giving way as she stiffly hauled herself into an upright position. A nurse was adding her observations to Gina's notes and was so engrossed in her work that she failed to notice that her patient was awake until she looked up and saw her sitting there. The nurse was so shocked that she dropped the notes and they clattered as the metal clipboard struck the polished linoleum of the hospital floor. "Mrs White, you're awake." Was all she could say as she rushed to Gina's side and quickly placed some pillows behind her back for support.

"My son," Gina's voice was hoarse from not being used for so long and sounded alien to her. "I want to see my son."

***

Some time later, after David had left his Mother's side, Gina's consultant entered the room.

"How are you feeling, Mrs White?" Gina had lost her voice completely after talking with David and could only nod her response that she was okay.

"We still don't know why the coma lasted so long, your injuries were not bad enough on their own to have caused it. And we also don't know why you suddenly came out of it, but you have and all the signs are that you have made a remarkable recovery. You will need a few weeks of physiotherapy to improve your strength as you were in the coma for a long time and have lost a lot of muscle, but you will make that back and your voice will recover soon. I do, however, have another concern. We gave you a pregnancy test shortly after you were admitted and another two weeks later and a third one month after. This is standard procedure in sexual assault cases. All three tests came back negative. What concerns me is that during a routine blood test two days ago, your sample showed signs of a pregnancy hormone. We repeated the test today and the results are conclusive, you are pregnant. This means that you would appear to have become pregnant whilst in the coma. I am so sorry Mrs White, but we suspect that you may have been raped during your stay here. We have reported the matter to the police and I can assure you that we take this matter very seriously and will fully co-operate with the police to track down whoever did this to you."

***

Later that evening, Gina rested her hand on her stomach. She knew that she was pregnant before the doctor had told her and that she was having a daughter. Gina thought about the last time that she had been with her husband in the forest of her dreams. Except that it hadn't been a dream, it had been real. She was pregnant and could sense the life inside her. As strange as it seemed to her, she could also sense strength, vitality, power even, in her child as it grew inside her womb. She knew instinctively that she wasn't imagining it, her daughter was imbued with her Father's magic.

***

"Will he survive?" asked the dark-skinned woman. She sat next to the leader of the Dyroshin people who was accompanied by a female warrior of her race, atop a simple merchant's horse drawn carriage that wound its way out of the city of Gaardsholme.

"In truth, I do not know, Katzin. The visions did not show a future for Bradley White beyond the events of this day, only vague images. I was convinced that he wouldn't survive his confrontation with Zoryn Dakor. He is alive, but only just and we must find shelter and treat him soon, otherwise he will join your lover in death. Katzin had witnessed the killing of her King and lover at the merciless hands of his younger brother. She had been rescued from the killing frenzy inside the Kings Court by her two travelling companions. She would grieve for Sanjin Dakor later when she was alone.

"Why did you save me?"

"We cannot interfere directly with events and could not save Sanjin Dakor. I sensed something in you and have seen glimpses of you in visions. Destiny holds more in store for you, I believe that you were meant to survive this."

"And Zoryn, what of him?" Katzin asked.

"I fear that he may also live," Velhanna replied.

"But how can this be?"

"Again, I do not know, but after the Outlander Bradley White destroyed that which was Dakor's Darkness, I could sense Zoryn Dakor's presence, even though there was no sign of his body. But in a different way than before."

"Different? In what way?"

"It's hard to describe, but it's like he is here and not here, that there is a veil between us, dulling my senses. I have never experienced this before."

***

"Are you alright buddy?" A concerned voice called through the pain of his injuries.

"Where am I?" The other's voice, a guttural rasp.

"You look terrible man, have you been attacked? Do you want me to call you a medic?"

His pain receded as the injured man stood up and shook his head to clear his vision. "I asked you where am I?" he said, as he grabbed the man by the throat and lifted him off his feet. "Don't make me fucking ask you again." The zig-zagged, orangey-red coronas of his eyes blazing with might, as he dropped the terrified man to the ground.